The Exile Book of
CANADIAN
SPORTS
STORIES

The Exile Book of

CANADIAN SPORTS STORIES

edited by

Priscila Uppal

Exile Editions

Publishers of singular
Fiction, Poetry, Translation, Nonfiction, Drama, and Graphic Books
2009

Library and Archives Canada Cataloguing in Publication

The Exile book of Canadian Sports Stories / edited by Priscila Uppal.

ISBN 978-1-55096-125-6

1. Sports stories, Canadian (English). 2. Short stories, Canadian (English). 3. Canadian fiction (English). I. Uppal, Priscila II. Title: Canadian sports stories.

PS8323.S6E95 2009   C813'.0108357   C2009-905678-X

Design and Composition by Active Design Haus
Typeset in Garamond and Gill Sans at the Moons of Jupiter Studios
Cover painting, Tour de Force 86, by Charles Pachter
Printed in Canada by Gauvin Imprimerie

The publisher would like to acknowledge the financial assistance of the Canada Council for the Arts and the Ontario Arts Council, which is an agency of the Government of Ontario.

Published in Canada by Exile Editions Ltd.
144483 Southgate Road 14
General Delivery
Holstein, Ontario, N0G 2A0
info@exileeditions.com
www.ExileEditions.com

Canadian Sales Distribution:
McArthur & Company
c/o Harper Collins
1995 Markham Road
Toronto, ON M1B 5M8
toll free: 1 800 387 0117

U.S. Sales Distribution:
Independent Publishers Group
814 North Franklin Street
Chicago, IL 60610
www.ipgbook.com
toll free: 1 800 888 4741

for Emmitt Avtar Uppal
ready, set, go

CONTENTS

INTRODUCTION

For the Love of Sport Art

Dear Reader,

Did you know that art competitions used to be part of the modern Olympic Games from 1912 to 1948? Medals were awarded for works of art inspired by sport, divided into five categories: architecture, literature, music, painting, and sculpture. Two people have actually won Olympic medals in both the sports and arts competitions: American Walter Winans, marksman and sculptor, and Hungarian Alfréd Hajós, swimmer and architect. Art competitions were dropped in 1954 because it was argued artists were professionals, while Olympic athletes were required to be amateurs.[1] Now that NHL and NBA professional players, among others, are permitted to compete in the Olympics, I wonder whether or not this old judgement on professional artists should be revisited. Many contemporary writers, composers, and visual artists would welcome the opportunity to vie in fierce competition for a medal, especially since most of us are not getting any younger, faster, or healthier.

If the arts competition had persisted to the present day, perhaps more people wouldn't bat an eye when presented with the words "sport" and "art" side by side; artists and athletes have more in common than our stereotypical image of jocks on one side of the gymnasium, and the intellectuals nowhere near them (perhaps reading books in the stands). However, both pursue excellence through discipline and rigour, both sacrifice other pleasures in this pursuit, and both are actively engaged in what

---

[1] For more information on this, see Richard Stanton's *The Forgotten Olympic Art Competitions.*

I would call "pain management" (the ability to turn pain into a creative, dynamic force). Moreover, truly great practitioners in both arenas are possessed with the curious ability to actively change the rules the games are played by, consummate originals rather than followers. There are many other ways that sport and art are complementary, and we could learn a vast amount from each other if the two worlds met more frequently. From this desire arises this one-of-a-kind literary anthology bringing together 26 Canadian sports stories – stories about sport from some of this country's greatest storytellers and most compelling imaginations. It seems absolutely preposterous that this book is the first of its kind in Canada; but it is.[2] So, medal or no medal, let's celebrate this first together.

Although I have already mentioned that sport and art rarely find themselves on the same playing fields, it is not surprising that the sport world provides the keen writerly imagination with ample subject matter, drama, and a myriad of emotions with which to produce exciting, moving, and provocative fiction. Some of the greatest novels of all time – novels not considered to be "sport novels" – have made highly effective use of sport in their plots, though this is rarely acknowledged. The 17th century Spanish masterpiece *Don Quixote*, considered by

---

[2] Other Canadian sports stories anthologies do exist. However, all the ones I've been able to find are either devoted exclusively to sports journalism; combine some sports fiction with sports journalism; or combine fictional short stories with excerpts from longer fictional works such as novels or plays. In addition, the majority of these anthologies are devoted to representation of a single sport activity only (baseball or hockey, for instance), rather than a variety of sports. Furthermore, almost none of these anthologies feature female writers or stories about women playing sports. Therefore, I believe that this is the first anthology to represent Canadian literary short stories about nearly two dozen sports, penned by men and women writers, and exploring the sports experiences of men, women, and children.

many to be the greatest novel of all time, introduces us to a hero bent on proving himself in combat – one of his goals is to test his mettle at the Zaragoza jousting competitions and win praise and fame for his deeds. One of the most important scenes in Tolstoy's Russian classic *Anna Karenina* occurs during a riveting steeplechase race. Ernest Hemingway's bullfighting scenes are famous, but he also wrote about fishing, hunting, boxing, skiing, bobsledding, and more. Water imagery abounds in Virginia Woolf's work, and therefore references to rowing, swimming, and boating. Academic Caroline Spurgeon has identified a total of 240 sports and games images in Shakespeare's plays. And sport theorist Ronald J. Meyers claims that the classical Greek poet Homer, in describing the funeral games in *The Iliad* XXIII undertaken to give recognition to the hero (most of which are still played today), was "the world's first sports writer." And so, our Canadian authors are in good company for taking on this worthy subject. Now, the question is, what have they done with it?

The first story in this collection, Clarke Blaise's "The Sociology of Love" does not at first even seem to be a sport story per se. A blonde university student interviews a successful South-Asian immigrant for a sociology project. The two seem to have little in common and cultural misconceptions and tensions arise; however, they are soon bound by tennis: memories of tennis, South-Asian and western tennis stars, tennis players in their lives. And sports is one of the ways that the man's children assimilate into North American culture; his son playing tennis, skiing and surfing, the daughter a figure skater: "To pay for tennis and ice-skating lessons takes up all our cash," we are told. While most of the stories included herein present us with narratives we would clearly and immediately identify as sports fiction, "The Sociology of Love" and a handful of others present to us further possibilities for the use of sport in narrative. Sport is real but it is also metaphor, paradigm, a way to experience some of the harsher realities of the world, a place to escape to, an arena from which endless lessons can be learned, passed on, learned again.

People are surprised when I tell them how many sports stories I've managed to find in Canadian literature.[3] We tend to associate certain sports with national character – U.S. with baseball, Canada with hockey, Brazil with soccer, Kenya with long-distance running – and so the makeup of our literature should tell us something about ourselves. What I discovered is that baseball is king in terms of the number of sport fictions produced by our writers (the unquestionable leader in American fiction as well), with hockey a very close second (but I bet hockey will overtake baseball in time, as more of our younger writers seem interested in writing about it). Our stories, however, also focus on all manner of athletic activities from basketball to surfing, skiing to diving. Like the makeup of our vast country, our sports stories are diverse in subject, tone, and perspective, and present us with unique as well as universal experiences. Nevertheless, W.P. Kinsella's claim that baseball, due to its silences and stoppages of play, is "the most literary of sports," is intriguing. I've chosen three baseball stories: George Bowering's witty and suspenseful "October 1, 1961," Linda Griffiths' lust- and longing-driven "A Game of Inches," and W.P. Kinsella's loving and elegiac "Die-hard." These three narratives constitute the most fantasy-oriented stories in the book: the first a time-travelling story that will change the history of baseball, the second a girl-meets-boy, girl-falls-for-boy-and-therefore-must-fall-for-baseball tale complete with seduction sequences involving pro ballplay-

---

3 And the stories collected here are certainly not exhaustive of what is available. There is more to enjoy; fine stories by other Canadian writers not featured in this book: Dave Bidini, Anne Carson, Lynn Coady, Bill Gaston, Steven Hayward, Paul Quarrington, David Adams Richards, to name only a few, who were not included due to space limitations and other considerations.

ers, the last a road-trip concerning the afterlife of an old baseball
player. We love hockey stories and write them with panache and
with an authenticity that speaks to every Canadian who has ever
anticipated ice-covered landscapes with delight, or has ever fid-
dled with rabbit ears on the television on a Saturday night. Roch
Carrier's French-Canadian classic, "The Hockey Sweater," is practically a Canadian anthem – our most famous short story, period,
a tragicomic parable of Anglophone and Francophone relations
so quintessential to our national character that lines from it are
printed on our five-dollar bill. But also included are stories running the gamut from poets turned into hockey stars to how sport
can create both fond memories and rifts in marriages to secret
information collected from participating on the inside; Brian
Fawcett's farcical "My Career with the Leafs," Diane Schoemperlen's moving coming-of-age story "Hockey Night in Canada,"
Mark Jarman's compelling dramatic monologue "The Scout's
Lament," and Rudy Thauberger's much-anthologized "Goalie."
We also write about basketball (Barry Callaghan's lyrical descrip-
tions of the feather touch needed for perfect arcs in "The Cohen
in Cowan," and Craig Davidson's cringe-worthy scenes in "The
Rifleman"), football (Dionne Brand intersects war with sports
in "I Used to Like the Dallas Cowboys"), boxing (Morley Callaghan's minimalist classic "The Chiseler," Steven Heighton's
erotically playful "A Right Like Yours," Guy Vanderhaeghe's absolutely cinematic "The Master of Disaster"), skiing (we welcome
getting stuck on a gondola in Katherine Govier's "Eternal
Snow"), running (Matt Cohen's "Vogel" gives us a glimpse of the
infidelity that can occur when one marriage partner decides to
get active and buff and the other doesn't, and Barry Milliken's
"Run," which shows us how people sometimes literally run for
their lives), swimming (Lisa Moore's sensual "The Stylist"), diving (Priscila Uppal's depiction of an athlete under research in
"Vertigo"), extreme marathoners (Marguerite Pigeon's fascinating

portrayal of those who take the body to its very limits in "Endurance"), softball (Mordecai Richler's laugh-out-loud funny look at film men and ex-wives who jeer them in "Playing Ball on Hampstead Heath"), surfing (Jordan Wheeler's tragicomic midlife-crisis story "The Seventh Wave"), and more. I've also included some sports stories from the 19th and early 20th centuries, on fishing (Stephen Leacock's charming "The Old, Old, Story of How Five Men Went Fishing"), hunting (the queen of 19th century CanLit, Susanna Moodie's "Brian, The Still Hunter") and rowing (L.M. Montgomery's story of averted tragedy "Natty of Blue Point").

In a country as large as Canada, we write about these sports with our differing landscapes (our small towns and our cities, our mountain tops, prairies, and coasts) and our complex social and cultural histories (including shared fears and jokes and misunderstandings) in mind. The narrator of Dionne Brand's "I Used to Like the Dallas Cowboys," confesses her past preference for American football over Canadian football; a fiery office worker looking for love and for a fight spars with a reluctant male target in "A Right Like Yours"; a woman's memories of her childhood vacations to Banff and Lake Louise are dimmed by her return with a lover in "Eternal Snow"; in "Hockey Night in Canada," a lingerie seller whose husband and baby have died finds passion in being a hockey fan "who shrieked and howled and paced around the living room... begging them to score"; in Stephen Leacock's story five men sabotage their own fishing expedition, and this "has happened and is happening to all the other fishing parties" in Canada and the U.S.; an Aboriginal university student goes along with his young girlfriend's friends to surf the west coast in "The Seventh Wave," even though "in Canada the best known surfing spot is the West Edmonton Mall." These stories contain several more stories within them, and point to hundreds more beyond these pages.

Sports experiences can cross boundaries of gender and help overcome stereotypes. Critic Michael Oriad even suggests that "participation by girls and women in sports will probably do more to change male *and* female attitudes about gender roles than any other factor." Whose admiration for female athletes wouldn't grow when presented with the boxer in "A Right Like Yours," who throws herself in the ring even though "breast shots really kill," or the mental strength demonstrated by the narrator in "Endurance" to continue racing after hallucinations and other gruelling physical punishments have afflicted her body?

Sports also appeal to a respect for measurement, mathematics, going from nothing to something (zero is the worst number in the world), rules, order, our need for judgment criteria (the diver in "Vertigo" states: "An athlete lives by numbers. And by belief in change. For better or worse, we're all a series of calculations"). Here is where sport differs from art, where judgments are considered subjective, and the only statistics that matter are book sales, not usually an indication of the quality of the artist. Perhaps this is also a reason why certain artists are drawn to sport. Artists and athletes both love the competitive arena, but with sport, you can't fake it. You can either score that basket, run faster than your competitor, land that triple axle, or you can't. You are awarded by merit and demonstrated ability. You compete. There are clear victors and clear losers. You attain greatness, or you are humbled by the greatness of others. What writer wouldn't want the bragging rights of being the current gold medallist of the novel? The physicality of the body must be trained to perform the correct actions effectively and efficiently, but the mind and spirit must also be strong – as many athletes tell you, the mind game can be far more important than the physical game. And how athletes think and feel, rationalize and experience – an arena that few fans or spectators of sport can enter – can be imagined and represented by artists, which is why sport art can do so much, not just to counter gender stereotypes, but to counter stereotypes of all kinds (nationality, religion, race, class, and more) with understanding and empathy, and to highlight how important sport experience is beyond the body.

However, the body still counts for a great deal. Sports are sexy – the physical beauty, perfection of the human form – Dionne Brand waxes poetically on the male form of football players, while the narrator of "The Stylist" dreams about kissing her coach, "A kiss so ripe and desperate, nothing ever comes close," and the pining protagonist of "A Game of Inches" has her first satisfying sexual experience with baseball player George Bell, who touches her with "the sweetest part of his bat." And vulgar – the distortions of the body, the brutality – such as the frostbitten toes of Alaskan racers in "Endurance" or the viscerally described beatings dished out in "The Master of Disaster." Steroids and other drugs are realities in the sports world, as our insider informs us in "The Scout's Lament," because "Not everyone's a star or a rocket scientist. Not everyone has a million choices." Threat of injury is ubiquitous: the narrator of "Vertigo" will never dive again, the boy's glove hand in "Goalie" is always swollen. Sports can cost: physically, mentally, emotionally, financially. But like the little boy in "The Hockey Sweater," we too know there is regular life of school, home, and church (or insert your own noun here), and then there is "real life," the life of the rink. Or in the case of Susanna Moodie's obsessed hunter, the bush, or Barry Callaghan's Jewish businessman, the court. And we create our own narratives when we play sports – how many of us put ourselves into sport types and roles (which is where much of the humour comes from in "My Career With the Leafs" when the poet turned hockey player is told post-interview, "You're supposed to pretend you're really dumb"; or the sad helplessness in "Eternal Snow": "If I jumped and succeeded, I would be a heroine. If I jumped and failed, a fool.")

Sport appeals to our need for strength, stability, vitality (the boy in "Run" claims "It is a power that makes me know that when I run I am strong, and there is nobody who is better"), but also to our knowledge of frailty, vulnerability, weakness. Sports are filled with danger: of overexertion (the father in "The Rifleman" tortures his son to practice in the winter in the middle of night with the threat "Every minute you're not practicing is a minute some other kid is"); the whims of mother nature (and the state of the art equipment needed to fend her off evident in "Endurance"); and public intimidation (George Bowering's story begins, "Do you remember those death threats Roger Maris was getting in August and September of 1961?"). Sometimes sports are connected to our livelihoods, not just for professional athletes but for others like the PEI lobstermen in "Natty of Blue Point," or the film industry professionals in "Playing Ball on Hampstead Heath," whose actions on the baseball diamond have direct consequences on workplace politics.

And then there are all the great sport aphorisms, adages, sayings, terminology, what writer Don DeLillo has called "elegant gibberish." Who can resist the language of slam dunks, foul balls, right hooks, sow cows, butterfly strokes, $3^{1}/_{2}$ somersaults in the pike position? The language of sport is a shared narrative among those initiated, welcomed into the world of the game, who think and live and even die by these truisms. I know I can't help smiling, and tearing up a bit, every time I read in W.P. Kinsella's "Diehard": "You know, Hec, if there's anything after this life, the first words I want to hear when I wake up are 'Play Ball!'"

Sports intersect into all areas of our lives, whether we want them to or not. But, I think, they also give back to us many parts of selves we wouldn't otherwise acknowledge. And sport also reinforces the mystery, the precariousness, the randomness of existence. The athlete and the sports fan are always anxious: the outcome of a match, race, or game, no matter what the odds, how conscientious the training and planning, is always un-known, just like the paths of our lives.

The experience of sport is, arguably, universal. All of us have memories of sport – some good, some bad, some foundational and fundamental, some less than inspiring, perhaps even haunt-ing and humiliating – and sport, one of the most ubiquitous of human activities, frequently impacts the most important aspects of our lives: our friendships, love affairs, family dynam-ics, workplace dynamics, vacation plans, leisure time, commu-nity involvement, and more. Playing sports throughout school – basketball, volleyball, hockey, softball, track – was a way for me to escape my troubled family home, to spend time with my brother, to build friendships and meet people from other cities and countries, to test my body's limits and experience its sen-suality, to express my energy and anger and creativity, and to compete against others for praise and fame. It was also, as a spectator – and I would watch just about anything – a way to enjoy an afternoon or evening, to cheer on excellence, and to be part of someone's biggest dreams. In the last several years, I have taken instructional classes in diving, swimming stroke mechan-ics, fencing, and figure skating, a way to keep learning in an arena where, unlike my artistic and professional pursuits, I have no pressure to be the best, only to keep improving. Each sport continues to teach me something new about myself, and about the world. And like me, many of the writers in this book have also played sports (Barry Callaghan was a high school basketball and baseball star, Matt Cohen played competitive tennis. Steven Heighton boxes and runs, Katherine Govier not only skis, but has martial arts weapons-training belts, many play hockey, soft-ball, and more). And sometimes, I must admit, that like Joseph

Epstein who writes in his article "Obsessed with Sport" that he has "heard more hours of talk from the announcer Curt Gowdy than from my own father, not a reticent man," I have spent more hours watching hockey with my father and brother than I have asking them about their lives. And I've cared more about the outcome of an Olympic swim race than I have about the results of certain important literary competitions. I wrote about sport when I was in high school, but then I think I was unconsciously convinced that it was not considered a "literary" topic. How silly. I'm glad I've come through on the other side and am able to collect together for the first time, for the enjoyment of many, great literature about an activity I have loved since childhood, and which continues to sustain me. Sport, like art, is about potential and possibility. And therefore sport is the perfect subject for those of us interested in the pursuit of excellence, fame, dignity, and joy. As David L. Vanderwerken and Spencer K. Wertz, in *Sport Inside Out*, posit: "Sport is better than life. Perhaps this is so because the spirit of play is triumphant in such scenes." I must agree.

In these stories there are dreamers, visionaries, rebels, mad geniuses, benevolent greats. We encounter current players and past players, pros and amateurs, coaches, scouts, parents of athletes, friends of athletes, trainers, researchers, sports writers; the months and years of training, and the moments of competition, some deciding fate in weeks or days, sometimes in mere hours or split seconds. There are, I must admit, a few more tragic stories than there are victorious ones. But this, of course, testifies to the fact that glory in sport is as elusive as our dreams, and why sport draws our attentive fascination to its peculiar machinations of fate over and over and over again. And failure can be funny in sports. We can laugh about weakness, limitations, and pain through sports stories in a way we usually can't otherwise. So, dear Reader, there is tragedy and comedy in what is to follow.

What is most inspiring and devastating in both the athletic and artistic realms, is that the majority must lose.

Lucky for us, these stories represent some of the best writing in Canada, from coast to coast, across genders and across ages, from our past to our present. In sports and in art you must have the courage to put yourself out there. Spectators and readers, qualified or not, criticize your performance, skills, or lack thereof, openly, publicly. Nothing is more frightening or more exciting. Talent and ability only take you so far. One must risk, and dream. And we do so regardless of medals. We do so for love. Dear Reader, allow the stories before you to inspire, fascinate, and amaze.

Priscila Uppal
Toronto 2009

ACKNOWLEDGEMENTS

Thank you to all the authors and publishers for permissions and for your enthusiasm for this project. Thank you to Barry Callaghan and Michael Callaghan, Richard Teleky, the Exile Editorial Board, Marilyn DiFlorio, Matt Shaw, Leigh Nash, and others who worked on this book or offered story suggestions, including Len Early and Claire Dé. Thank you to graduate assistants William Lind, Laura Scoufaris, and especially Jennifer Hann, Anthony Hicks and Kathryn Roberts. Thank you to Charlie Pachter for the fabulous cover, I have coveted "Tour de Force 86" for years. Thank you to my female sports heroes, Ann Peel, Suzanne Zelazo, and Jane Roos at Canadian Athletes Now Fund, who join me in my passions for sport and art. Thank you to Jit Uppal, Jen Hacking, Dean Penny, Justin Connidis, Julia MacArthur, Leon Berdichevsky, Marc Zahradnic, and my other sports fan friends, the time I spend laughing and cheering with you is some of the best time of the year. Thanks to all the cool coaches I've had in my life, both athletic and artistic. Thank you to Mats Sundin and number 13. Go Canada Go.

And thank you to Christopher Doda, my number one goalie, for saving me time and time again.

CLARKE BLAISE

THE SOCIOLOGY OF LOVE

A monstrously tall girl from Stanford with bright yellow hair comes to the door and asks if I am willing to answer questions for her sociology class. She knows my name, "Dr. Vivek Walde-kar?" and even folds her hands in a creditable namaste. She has researched me, she knows my job title and that I am an American citizen. She's wearing shorts and a midriff-baring T-shirt with a boastful logo. It reads, "All This and Brains, Too." She reminds me of an American movie star whose name I don't recall, or the California Girl from an old song, as I had imagined her. I invite her in. I've never felt so much the South Asian man: fine-boned, almost dainty, and timid. My wife, Krithika, stares silently for several long moments, then puts tea water on.

Her name is Anya. She was born in Russia, she says. She has Russian features, as I understand them, a slight tilt to her cheeks but with light blue eyes and corn-yellow hair. When I walk behind her, I notice the top of an elaborate tattoo reaching up from underneath. She is a walking billboard of availability. She says she wants my advice, or my answers, as a successful South Asian immigrant, on problems of adjustment and assimilation. She says that questions of accommodation to the U.S., especially to California, speak to her. And specifically South Asians, her honours project, since we lack the demographic residential densities of other Asians, or of Hispanics. We are sociological anomalies.

It is important to establish control early. It is true, I say, we do not swarm like bees in a hive, "Why do you criticize us for living like Americans?" I ask, and she apologizes for the tone of her question. I press on. "What is it we lack? Why do you people think there is something wrong with the way we live?"

She says, "I never suggested anything was wrong—" She drops her eyes and reads from her notes.

"—That there's something defective in our lives?"

"Please, I'm so sorry."

I have no handkerchief to offer.

Perhaps we have memories of overcrowded India, when everyone knew your business. I know where her question is headed: middle-class Indian immigrants do not build little Chinatowns or barrios because we are too arrogant, too materialist, and our caste and regional and religious and linguistic rivalries pull us in too many directions. She hangs her head even before asking the next question.

No, I say, there are no other South Asian families on my street. My next-door neighbours are European, by which I mean non-specifically white. I correct myself. "European" is an old word from my father's India, where even Americans could be European. Across the street are Chinese, behind us a Korean.

That's why I'm involved in sociology, she says, it's so exciting. Sociology alone can answer the big questions, like where are we headed and what is to become of us? I offer a counter-argument; perhaps computer science, or molecular biology, or astronomy, I say, might answer even larger questions. "In the here and now," she insists, "there is only sociology." She is too large to argue with. She apologizes for having taken my name from the internal directory of the software company I work for. She'd been an intern last summer in our San Francisco office.

I say I am flattered to be asked big questions, since most days I am steeped in micro-minutiae. Literally: nano-technology. I can feel Krithika's eyes burning through me.

The following are my answers to her early questions: We have been in San Jose nearly eight years. I am an American citizen, which is the reason I feel safe answering questions that could be interpreted by more recent immigrants as intrusive. We have been married 20 years, with two children. Our daughter Pramila was born in Stanford University Hospital. Our son Jay was born in JJ Hospital 17 years ago. When he was born I was already in California, finishing my degree and then finding a job and a house. My parents have passed away; I have an older brother, and several cousins in India, as well as Canada and the U.S. My graduate work took four years, during which time I did not see Krithika or my son. Jay and Krithika are still Indian citizens, although my wife holds the green card and works as a special assistant in the Stanford Medical School Library. She will keep her Indian citizenship in the event of inheritance issues in India.

Do I feel my life is satisfactory, are the goals I set long ago being met? Anya is very persistent, and I have never been questioned by such a blue-eyed person. It is a form of hypnosis, I fear. I am satisfied with my life, most definitely. I can say with pride and perhaps a touch of vanity that we have preserved the best of India in our family. I have seen what this country can do, and I have fought it with every fibre of my being. I have not always been successful. The years are brief, and the forces of dissolution are strong.

Jay in particular is thriving. He has won two junior tennis championships and maintains decent grades in a very demanding high school filled with the sons and daughters of computer engineers and Stanford professors. As a boy in Dadar, part of Bombay – sorry, Mumbai – I was much like him, except that my father could not offer access to top-flight tennis coaching. I lost a match to Sanjay Prabhakar, who went on to the Davis Cup. "How will I be worthy?" I had asked my father before going in. "You will never be worthy of Sanjay Prabhakar," he said. It is your fate. You are good, but he is better and he will always be better. It is not a question of worth. I sold my racquet that day and have never played another set of tennis, though even now I know I could rise to the top of my club ranks. I might even be able to beat my son, but I worry what that might do to him. I was forced to concentrate on academic accomplishment. In addition, public courts and available equipment left much to be desired.

Do I have many American friends? Of course. My closest friend is Al Wong, a Stanford classmate, now working in Cupertino. We socialize with Al and Mitzie at least twice a month. She means white Americans. Like yourself? I ask, and she answers "not quite." She means two-three-generation white Americans. Such people exist on our street, of course, and in our office, and I am on friendly terms with all of them. I tell her I have never felt myself the victim of any racial incident, and she says, I didn't mean that. I mean instances of friendship, enduring bonds, non-professional alliances… you know, friendship. You mean hobbies? I ask. The Americans seem to have many hobbies I cannot fully appreciate. They follow the sports teams, they go fishing and sailing and skiing.

In perfect frankness, I do not always enjoy the company of white Americans. They mean well, but we do not communicate on the same level. I do not see their movies or listen to their music, and I have never voted. Jay skis, and surfs. Jay is very athletic, as I have mentioned; we go to Stanford tennis matches. I cannot say that I have been in many American houses, nor they in mine, although Jay's friends seem almost exclusively white. Jay is totally of this world. When I mention Stanford or Harvard, he says Santa Cruz, pops. He's not interested in a tennis scholarship. He says he won the state championship because the dude from

Torrance kept double-faulting. Pramila's friends are very quiet and studious, mostly Chinese and Indian. She is fourteen and concentrates only on her studies and ice-skating. I am not always comfortable in her presence. I do not always understand her, or feel that she respects us.

We will not encourage Pramila to date. In fact, we will not permit it until she is finished with college. Then we will select a suitable boy. It will be a drawn-out process, I fear, but we are progressive people in regard to caste and regional origins. A boy from a good family with a solid education is all we ask. If Pramila were not a genius, I would think her retarded. When she's not on the ice, she lurches and stumbles. Jay does not have a particular girlfriend. He says don't even think of arranging a marriage for me. Five thousand years of caste-submission will end here, on the shores of the Pacific Ocean.

"So, you and your son watch Mike Mahulkar?"

"Mike?" I must have blinked. "It is Mukesh," I say. "My son models his tennis game on Mukesh Mahulkar. Some day Mukesh will be a very great tennis player."

Neither my son nor I would ever be able to score a point off Mukesh Mahulkar.

My father has been dead nearly 20 years. I think he died from the strain of arranging my marriage. Krithika's parents never reconciled to my father's modest income. In my strongest memory of him, he was coming from his bath. It was the morning of my marriage. His hair was dark and wet. We will never be worthy, he said. A year later, I was sharing a house with Al Wong and two Indian guys. Jay was born that same year, but I was not able to go back for the birth, or for my father's funeral services. Fortunately, I have an older brother. My father was head clerk in Maharashtra State Public Works Department. In his position, he received and passed on, or rejected, plans for large-scale building and reclamation projects. Anywhere in Asia, certainly anywhere in India in the past 20 years, such a position would generate mountains of black money. Men just like my father posed behind the façade of humble civil servant, living within modest salaries, dressed in kurta and pyjama of rough khadi, with Bata sandals on their dusty feet. They would spend half an hour for lunch, sipping tea under a scruffy peepal. But in the cool hours of morning or evening, there would be meetings with shady figures and the exchange of pillow-thick bundles of stapled 100-rupee notes. They would be pondering immense investments in apartment blocks and outlying farmhouses and purchasing baskets of gold to adorn their wives and daughters.

But Baba was one of the little folk of the great city, an honest man mired in universal graft. He went to office in white kurta. At lunch, he sat on a wall and ate street-food from push-cart vendors and read his Marathi paper. He came home to a bath and prayer, dinner and bed. Projects he rejected got built anyway, with his superiors' approval. He was seen as an obstruction to progress, a dried-up cow wandering a city fly-over. So we never got the car-and-driver, the club memberships and air conditioning. He retired on even less than his gazetted salary, before the Arab money and Bombay boom.

I suddenly remember Qasim, the Muslim man whose lunch cart provided tea and cigarettes and fried foods to the MSPWD office-wallahs. My father and Qasim enjoyed a thirty-year friendship without ever learning the names of one another's children, or visiting each other's houses, or even neighbourhoods. Dadar and Mahim are different worlds. We never learned Qasim's last name. But whenever I dropped in on my father on lunch or tea breaks, I would hear him and Qasim engaged in furious discussions over politics, Pakistan, and fatherhood. Qasim had four wives and a dozen children, many of them the same age, all of them dressed in white, carrying trays of water and tea. Qasim and Baba were friends. To me, they are the very model of friendship. You might find it alien. You might not call it friendship at all. If, as rarely happened, Qasim did not appear on a given day, my father would ask a Muslim in the office to inquire after his health. Once or twice in a year, when my father took leave to attend a wedding, a strange boy would appear at our door, asking after Waldekar-sahib. I'm certain my father expressed more of a heartfelt nature to Qasim than he ever did to his wife, or to me. In that, I am my father's son.

"My father, too," says the blue-eyed girl in the T-shirt. All This and Brains, Too. Suddenly, I understand its meaning, and I must have uttered a muted "ahhh!" and blushed. Breasts, not height and blondeness. I feel a deep shame for her. Krithika reads the same words, but shows no comprehension. I have a bumper sticker: My Son Is Palos High School Student of the Month. When I put it on, my wife said I was inviting the evil eye. For that reason, we have not permitted newspaper access to Pramila. We are simple people. Our children consume everything. To pay for tennis and ice-skating lessons takes up all our cash. I could have bought a Stradivarius violin with what I've spent. When she was ten years old, after a summer spent in Stanford's Intensive Mathematics Workshop with the cream of the nation's high school seniors, Pramila wrote a paper on the Topology of Imaginary Binaries. I do not mention it, ever.

"My father says that if he'd stayed in Russia and never left his government job, he would be sitting on a mountain of bribes. Over here, he started a Russian deli on Geary Boulevard."

"You have made a very successful transition to this country," I say. All this. "I personally have great respect for the entrepreneurial model."

She takes the compliment with a shy smile. "Appearances can lie, Dr. Waldekar," she says.

Krithika brings out water and a plate of savouries.

I am of the Stanford generation that built the Internet out of their garages. I knew those boys. They invited me to join, but I was a young husband and father, although my family was still in India waiting to come over, and I had a good, beginning-level job with PacBell. I would be ashamed to beg start-up money from banks or strangers. My friends said, well, we raised five million today, we're on our way! And I'd think you're twenty-five years old and five million dollars in debt? You're on your way to jail! I have not been in debt a single day of my life, including the house mortgage. It all goes back to my father in frayed khadi, and three-rupee lunches under the dusty peepals.

"I notice an interesting response to my question," she says. "When I asked if you've fulfilled your goals, you mentioned only that your son is very successful. What about you, Dr. Waldekar?"

Krithika breaks in finally, "We also have a daughter."

"I was coming to that," I say.

"She is enrolled in a graduate-level mathematics course," says Krithika.

"That's amazing!"

"She is the youngest person ever enrolled for credit in the history of Stanford. She is also a champion figure skater. My husband forgot to mention her, so I thought you might perhaps note that, if you have space."

"I believe I mentioned she is very studious," I say.

Anya breaks off a bit of halwa.

I rise to turn off the central AC. The girl is undressed for air conditioning, and I am disturbed by what I see happening with her breasts, under the boastful logo. They are standing out in points. Krithika returns to the kitchen.

"I am content, of course." What else is there on this earth, I want to ask, than safeguarding the success of one's children? What of her father, the Russian deli owner? Is he happy? What is happiness for an immigrant but the accumulation of visible successes? He cannot be happy, seeing what has happened to his daughter. Does the Russian have friends? Does he barge into American houses? Do Americans swarm around his? Who are his heroes? Barry Bonds, Terrell Owens, Tiger Woods, Jerry Rice? We share time on the same planet; that is all. We will see how much the Americans love their sports heroes if any of them tries to buy a house on their street. Mukesh Mahulkar is big and strong and handsome and he is good in his studies and I'm sure his parents are proud of him and don't fear the evil eye. He'll play professional tennis and make a fortune and he won't spend it all on cars and mansions. He will invest wisely and he will be welcomed on any street in this country.

"My father works too hard. He's already had two heart attacks. He smokes like a fish. He dumps sour cream on everything. Everything in his mouth is salty, fatty meat, and more meat, and cream, and cheese and vodka. Forgive the outburst."

"We are vegetarian. We do not drink strong spirits."

"So's Mike. Veggie, I mean. He's teaching me."

"You mean Mukesh, the tennis player?"

"His name is Mike. He's my boyfriend, Dr. Waldekar."

The ache I feel at the mention of a boyfriend is like the phantom pain from a lost limb. If I could even imagine a proper companion for this Russian girl, he would be as white and smooth as a Greek sculpture, built on a scale of Michelangelo's David. The thought that it is a Mumbai boy who runs his hands over her body, under those flimsy clothes, makes my fingers run cold.

"I might as well come out with it, Dr. Waldekar," she says. "We've broken up. His parents hate my guts."

Good for them, I think. Maybe you should dress like a proper young lady. I knew a Mahulkar boy in Dadar. I knew others in ITT, but no Mahulkars of my generation in the Bay

Area. So many have come. Given my early advantage, the opportunities I turned down, I am a comparative failure.

"This is my honours project, but... it's personal, too. I love India and Indians. I love the discipline of Indians. No group of immigrants has achieved so much, in so little time, with such ease and harmony. I love their pride and dignity. I even love it that they hate me. I can respect it." She is smiling, but I don't know if I should smile with her and nod in agreement, or raise an objection. She might be a good sociologist, but there is much she is missing in the realm of psychology. So she goes on, and I don't interrupt.

"But what I don't love is that Mike won't stand up to them, for me. You know what his father said? He said American girls are good for practice, until we find you a proper bride. When Mike told me that, we laughed about it. I'm friendly with his sister and I said to her, your game's a little rusty. Think you need some practice? And we laughed and laughed. Mike said he'd show me Mumbai, and I said I'd take him to Moscow. He's twenty-two years old, but the minute his father said to stop seeing me, he stopped. One day we're playing tennis, or at the beach or he's cooking Indian vegetarian and I'm learning, and then, nothing. Nothing." She lets herself go, drops her head into the basin of her hands, and sobs. It is a posture I, too, am familiar with. Krithika rushes in from the kitchen, stops, frowns, then goes back inside. I will be questioned later: what did I do, say, what didn't I do, didn't say? She will suspect some misbehaviour.

So, I think, Mahulkar has found a bride for his son. This is very good news. Who could it be? Why hadn't I heard that the famous Mukesh Mahulkar was getting married? It means there is hope for every Indian father with a son like mine.

"Please, take water," I say. I would be tempted to hold her, or pat her back, but my arms might not reach. It would be awkward, and perhaps misinterpreted. Now that she has pitched forward, I see deep into her bosom; she has a butterfly tattoo on one breast, well below the separation-line. A girl this big, and crying, in my living room, wearing such a T-shirt, has brought chaos from the street into our life.

"I'm so sorry," she says. "That was inexcusable. You must think I came under false pretences. Mike's getting married in Mumbai in three weeks. It's very hard, to be told, without warning, without explanation, that you're just... unworthy."

She has a beautiful smile. It's as though she had not been crying at all, or knew no sadness, or had a Russian childhood and a father with a mouthful of meat and vodka. I will ask around and discover the bride's name.

I stand. "I must ask you quietly to leave. I must pick up my daughter from practice. My son will be home soon." I do not want her defiling my house, spreading her contagion into our sterile environment. She has no interest in successful immigrants, or in me. "I have no special Bombay advice to offer." When I open the door, my fingers brush the white flesh of her back, just above the tattoo. I don't think she even feels it. She says only, "You have been very kind and hospitable. Please forgive me."

I could not go home for my father's funeral. I did not see my son until he was four years old and had already bonded with my wife's family. I think he still treats me like an intruder. So does my wife. It has pained me all these years that I permitted my studies and other activities to take precedence over family obligations. I have been trying to atone for my indiscretions all these years.

In three of the four years I shared a house with Al Wong and the Mehta boy who went back and a Parsi boy who married an American girl and stayed, I remained steadfast to my research. I got a job at PacBell, where they immediately placed me in charge of a small research cell with people like myself, debt-free, security-minded team players. Suddenly, I had money. I bought a car and a small bungalow in Palo Alto, suitable for wife and child. No one in the group knew I was already married, and a father. We were all just in our twenties, starting out in the best place, in the best of times.

In my small group there was an American girl, a Berkeley graduate. Her name was Paula, called Polly. Pretty Polly, the boys liked to joke, which embarrassed her. On Fridays, our group would join with others for some sort of party. I would allow myself a beer or two, since carbonation lessened the taint of alcohol. Those sorts of restaurants made vegetarianism very difficult; I was admired for my discipline. Polly was naturally less restrained than I, especially after sharing a few pitches of beer, a true California girl from someplace down south. Watching closely, I could gauge the moment when a quiet, studious girl, very reliable and hard-working, would ask for a cigarette, then go to the bathroom, come back to the table, and sit next to someone new. She sat next to me. One night she said, "You're a very handsome man, Dr. Waldekar." No one had ever told me that, and to look fondly at one's reflection in a mirror is to invite the evil eye. "Take me home," she said. "I don't know where you live," I answered. She punched me on the arm. "Ha, ha," she said, "funny, too."

It's that transformation, not the flattery that got to me. All week in the office, she was a flattened presence. She totally ignored me, and I, her. I imagined she was one of the good girls, living with her parents.

The passion that arises from workplace familiarity is hotter than hell. It is hell, because one must hide certain feelings, erase recurrent images, must put clothes back on a girl you've been with through the night. Above all, it must be secret. On Friday nights, she must not sit next to me. "May I call you Vivek, Dr. Waldekar? she would ask. After the first time, I told myself it was the beer, but I knew it wasn't. The sexual acts that had resulted in the birth of my son back in India, a boy whose pictures I now had to hide, had seemed, in comparison to Polly, a continuation of tennis practice, slamming a ball against a wall and endlessly returning it. She took drugs, expensive drugs, and I was helpless to stop her, or complain. "Go to her, if that will make you happy," says Krithika. "I know your secrets."

"What foolishness."

"You were staring at her. You shamed me. You behaved disgustingly."

"If you were interested in the facts you would know I threw her out."

"Remember," she mumbles, "I get half."

I reach out for her, but she pulls away. This is the woman, the situation, I left Polly for. Eventually, I left PacBell because of her, which has worked out well for me. Polly left California because of me. Al Wong is the only person I confessed it to; I think he's mentioned it to Mitzie because of the ways she sometimes scrutinizes me. What do you think of her, Vivek? she'll ask me, as though I have a special interest in attractive women, instead of Al. Maybe she's mentioned it to Krithika. The promiscuous exchange of intimacies, which passes for friendship in America, is a dangerous thing. It is the sad nature of the terms of a marriage contract that the strongest evidence of commitment is also the admission of flagrant unfaithfulness.

One night 14 years ago, I went up to SFO to meet Krithika and Jay who were arriving in my life after a thirty-hour flight from Bombay. I got there early and pressed myself close to the gate, but Sikhs from the Central Valley, rough fellows with large families and huge signboards, pushed me aside and called me names. It was a time of deep tensions between Hindus and Sikhs. If I had stood my ground, they threatened to stamp me into the floor. The Indian passengers poured through, fanning out in every direction, pushing carts stacked high with crates and boxes. Waiting families ducked under the barriers to join them, and I waited and waited, but no wife, no child. The terminal is always crowded, but the number of Indians diminished, to be replaced by Mexicans and Koreans. Perhaps she was having visa problems, I thought, or the bags had been lost.

After two hours, just as I'd decided to go back to my empty house, I heard my name on the public announcement. Please pick up the courtesy phone, Vivek Waldekar. Your wife wants you to know that since you were not here to meet them, she and her child have gone to a safe address provided by a fellow passenger, and she will contact you in the morning.

Two days later, I got that call. Perhaps you forgot you have a wife and son, she said. Perhaps you no longer remember me. She has remained on friendlier terms with that generous family who took her home on her first night in America than she ever has with me.

At four a.m. when the streets are dark and only the dogs are awake, the rattling of food carts begins. Barefoot men and boys dressed in white khadi push their carts heavy with oil, propane, and dozens of spiced tufts of chickpea batter ready for frying, all prepared during the night by wives and daughters. Each cart is lit by a naphtha lamp; each man fans out to his corner of the city near big office buildings, under his own laburnum, ashoka or peepal tree. Qasim died one morning as he pushed his cart through the streets of Mahim. His son Walid appeared the next day, with his father's picture and a page of Urdu pasted to the cart's plastic shield. Even Hindus knew what it meant. My father took his retirement a month later – his superiors were truly sorry to see him go, since he was the obstruction that enriched everyone around him. He arranged my marriage, I received my Stanford scholarship and went to America, leaving a pregnant wife behind. After three years of bad health, Baba

died. And I didn't attend the services because I was involved
with an American girl named Polly who thought burning one's
father's body in public was too gross to contemplate.

GEORGE BOWERING

OCTOBER 1, 1961

Do you remember those death threats Roger Maris was getting in August and September of 1961? There he was, wearing the Babe's pinstripes, and he wasnt even Mickey Mantle. At least Mickey Mantle was a Yankee from the word go. Maris was a Cleveland Indian first, of all things, and he was never going to hit .300. Mantle was chasing Maris all summer, and one thing was for certain: as a couple they were going to knock off Ruth and Gehrig.

But Mantle didnt get any death threats.

Even I got some death threats. One of them is coming true right here on this foldaway couch.

Do you remember those death threats Roger Maris was getting? Did you think they were all from fans of the Babe? Old timers who didnt want anyone to get 61 home runs, even with the schedule expanded to 162 games?

For those who dont know what I am talking about, here are the bare details, though why I should bother, I dont know. Babe Ruth's record of sixty home runs in 1927 was the favourite myth in baseball. Ty Cobb's lifetime batting average of .367 was harder to do. Joe DiMaggio's 56-game hitting streak is not likely to be topped, as they say. But Babe Ruth's sixty dingers gave the biggest galoots in the game a yearly target to assault. A few guys had got into the fifties. Trivialists like to point out that the second-best total was Ruth's 59 in 1921.

Then along came 1961. It was as if the last two digits called for some kind of disrespect toward the Bambino. Two things happened in 1961 to break a lot of hearts, or at least to leave the sour taste of ambiguity in baseball fans' mouths.

In 1961 the American League of baseball added two teams. Until then each team played 154 games a season, 22 against each of the other seven teams. In 1961 they would have to play 162 games, 18 against each of their nine opponents.

In 1961, Roger Maris and Mickey Mantle staged a home run race that had every newspaper in the western hemisphere providing a graph on the front page every playing day. By mid-August it was clear that Roger Maris at least was going to hit more than sixty home runs. The commissioner of baseball said that if Maris didnt have 61 by the 154th game, the Babe's record was still there. After 154 games Maris had 59 homers. In the last eight games he got two more. They put an asterisk after the number wherever it was reprinted.

But those 61 homers were still there. And as the years went by the asterisk disappeared, along with other records by the Babe, such as his 714 lifetime homers. Sixty-one years after Maris' meretricious heroics the asterisk was not even remembered. And for sixty-one years no other big leaguer was ever able to hit more than sixty homers, no matter how many games there were to a season. I know. I was born in 1961, and I was in the stadium in Toronto on the October day when Coral Godard hit his sixty-first homer.

That was seven games from the end of the season. In those seven games big hairy Godard marched to the plate thirty-three times. He struck out twenty times. He was walked once. He was hit with a pitch once, a wonderful piece of ironic bravery by a rookie left-hander who had gone to Godard's high school ten years after the hairy person more or less graduated. Once he got the ball on the fat part of the bat, but this was to centre field in the plastic Miami ball park, and it was pulled down on the Cubaturf warning track.

In his last time at bat in the last game, when the divisional results had been settled for three days, the large first baseman hit a foul ball that passed the pole at mid-height and probably reached the Gulf Stream. On the following pitch he swung his lamino-club so hard that idlers in both dugouts involuntarily flinched. But he caught only the top third of the ball. The Miami infield dawdled and posed and lobbed a man out. The season was over, and so was the pursuit.

Coral Godard had sixty-one poppers, just like Roger Maris. He had no asterisk. The Toronto sportswriters started what they supposed would be a traditional journalistic remark, noting that Godard had achieved the highest total in the 21st century.

The total would do a lot for Godard's already inflated salary. But the pelf was offset by the remarks he would hear all winter and well into the following season. People felt that they had to comment upon that last week, with those thirty-three trips to the platter. At least Roger got two long balls in his last week, they would point out, and he had nothing but an old-fashioned bat made from a mountain tree.

A typical bad day would be May second in Cleveland. Standing three metres off the bag at first, Godard had acquired the skill of singling out sentences and near-sentences from the thin roar of the usual light assemblage of Indians fans. If you were there and had his ability, this is some of what you might have heard:

"You couldnt carry Roger Maris' jockstrap, ya bum!"

"He cant carry his own jockstrap!"

"Yer a choke artist, ya big hairy creepoid!"

"Roger woulda hit a hundred homers if he was alive now!"

"He woulda hit seventy-five when he was seventy-five, ya jerkoff!"

"Belle montre et peu de rapport!"

"Shaddup, Frenchie!"

"Hey, Coral, yer sister..." [etc.]

You will have noted that abuse from the grandstand did not evolve much as major league baseball stepped across the century line for the second time.

Godard, and even most of the sportswriters in the American League thought the razzing and threats would begin to fade away as the season proceeded into the hot months, especially if he had, say, twenty homers in June. But on June twentieth in Baltimore someone left a dead cat with a pinstriped baseball uniform at the door of his hotel room. There was a number three on the back of the little uniform. In Detroit later that week Morgana IV the kissing bandit ran out to first base in the home half and kicked the great hairy firstbaseman in the slats.

In August Coral had seven home runs and twenty-five runs batted in. The Jays' psychologist advised Grand Cayman Island, where the team's spring training facility could be set up for rest and recuperation. Coral was opposed to the idea. Then in Kansas City someone took a shot at him. He left for the Caribbean the next morning. The paper sent me down with him. I thought I would stay for a few days, file a couple stories about how the big fellow was filling his days, and coincidentally pick up a few rays. I had not imagined how hot it gets on Grand Cayman in August. I decided to leave after three days. So did Coral.

As we were on the same plane, I thought I would play my hunch, and go wherever he was going. He took a connector flight from Atlanta to St. Louis. St. Louis hasn't been in the American League since 1953. This was getting pretty interesting, especially because it was obvious that I was going to follow him everywhere I could. First he tried to shake me, but when he found me sitting on his lap in a taxi, he just laughed, and then sighed and then said:

"The season cant get any worse than this," and away we went.

To see a voodoo queen. To see a Washington University physics professor. Maybe not quite a professor. Sort of a graduate assistant. She was gorgeous, a St. Louis honey-blonde, but you dont want to hear about that. It certainly didnt seem to matter to Coral Godard, not at first.

Now I am not a science reporter, and I dont expect that 21st century physics is going to make much sense to a fuddy-duddy reader in the 20th century (remember, I used to live there), so I will not spend a hundred pages on the plans and specs of the Deutero-Tempus machine, patent pending. In fact, I still cant believe that's what that lady graduate assistant called it. I think she was razzing me with a Midwest sense of humour. Who knows? She said she was from *East* St. Louis, and you might know what they are like over there.

How did Coral know about Lorraine Knight? Hey, how did your favourite NFL lineman know about Dr. Needle? If there is something illegal but helpful, your professional athlete will hear about it. If there is a new gadget on any university campus on the continent, there will be two people wanting to know what it is capable of: the contract lawyer from the Pentagon, and a veteran ballplayer who needs an edge.

I think Lorraine had a liking for a man with curly black hair on his back. Either that or she had a romantic notion about the relationship between science and the human heart. She thought the Pentagon and most of the Scientific Community was a little short in the heart. Whatever the case, she said that the Deutero-Tempus could put a human being back into any year in the last hundred and ten. She was working on longer range stuff, while there were hardly any professors at Washington University who would even believe a decade. Most of those physics professors didn't even have straight hair on the tops of their heads.

I stuck with Coral as much as I could, but there were times over the following week when I lost track of him *and* Lorraine Knight. She was apparently a lot nicer to him than the fans in either Cleveland or Toronto. She told me later that she faced a tough conflict when Godard volunteered to be her first sixty-two-year voyager.

You see, she had to explain to her ballplayer that time travel is so far a one-way trip.

I say this despite the strange logic of narrating this tale in the past tense about events that will not happen until another fifty-nine years have transpired.

Be that as it may.

In the old movies people like Danny Kaye were always zipping back to more scenic times, and then zooming back home in the present. But put your head to this: if you are going to send me back to Chicago in 1882, for instance, you just have to send me back over the tracks the world has made since then. But how are you going to send me into the future? There arent any tracks.

That is not the real scientific explanation, but it is close as you can get in a journalist's language.

"She says she wants me to take a short trip first," Coral told me in the bar at the Mark Twain Hilton.

We sportswriters are often cast in the role of straight men. That might explain why so many of us evolve smartass writing styles.

"What does that mean?" I asked.

"She says I should go back one year. Then I could look her up and we could get together and have some fun for a year before I head out."

"Head out?" I asked.

"That's the technical language for going back through space in the Duteous Tempo," he said. A lot of ball players couldnt have got that far without saying "you know" at least once.

"One," I said. "That is not quite the right name for the gizmo. Two. There isnt any technical language for all that yet. Cripes!"

That's what I said. Cripes. In the 21st century.

"Be that as it may. I told her I thought she was a very nice person as well as a great scientist, but."

"But?" I asked.

"But I have to get back to 1961. Before the end of the season."

"What are you going to do that for?" I asked. "You cant come back, you know."

"I know. I think I can handle living in the 1960s. As long as I stay away from my family. I think I could even manage to handle living in Toronto in the seventies and eighties. But…"

"But," I said.

"But the main reason is I have to do Something about Roger Maris."

"Tell me about Something."

"I think I might let him get sixty. Maybe fifty-nine."

Have you ever read any novels about time travel? They always bring up this basic problem: what if the time traveller does something to mess up history? What if the gink from the future sees the lamp beside the cow and takes it away, and there's no great Chicago fire? I wrote a story about that a long time ago when I was still wondering what kind of writer I was going to be. I had a historian from Northwestern University go back and torch Mrs. O'Malley's barn after all. He felt terrible about all the suffering he caused, but there are certain higher principles, which means greater dangers. He went back to his job a hundred years later at Northwestern. I didnt know real time travel would have to be one-way.

To tell you the truth, there were times I wished I were inventing this story instead of covering it.

One morning I went over to Frankenstein Knight's condo and they werent there. So I went to the laboratory and he wasnt there. But she was. There was a scent of eucalyptus in the air, used to be my favourite smell.

"Gone?" I enquired.

"Gone," she said. Her demeanour was ambiguous as you can get. She was deprived of Coral but she had sent Godard along the tracks.

"How do you know he didnt go to 1927?" I asked.

"Check the encyclopedia," she said.

I went back to Toronto and tried to re-enter normal life, if talking to naked men in a dressing room after they've been getting all sweaty playing a boy's game in front of thousands of people eating junk food can be called normal life. I guess you might call me and my colleagues the historians of popular life. I shared a desktop at the *Toronto Star* instead of Northwestern University.

Yes, you know what I was thinking. But I needed some time to think *about* it. I figured I had all season anyway. I could even cover the Jays if they made it into the late-Fall Classic. Coral Godard might be following Roger Maris around the league in 1961, but if I was going to go back I could go whenever I wanted to. Time was something we didnt know everything about, but I knew that much. If you are going to travel to Minneapolis, you can get there from Vancouver or Miami or Keokuk. If you are going to September 1961, you can get there from today or next Tuesday or a year from now.

Yep, I had time pretty well figured out. Then I woke up one night on a littered floor, surrounded by lockers, and I couldnt remember how I got there. A doctor who usually looked at the bare bodies of much younger men told me something I hadnt thought of regarding how much time I had.

"If you're one of those newspaper guys who have a novel in the desk drawer, get busy on it," he said.

I like a guy with that kind of an attitude. Reminds me of the guy I thought I would make of myself.

So you know why I went back to St. Louis.

"Why haven't you sprung your success on the world?" I asked.

There was still a part of me that thought she had Coral hidden away in her bedroom closet, or in a shallow grave on the banks of the Mississippi. I thought maybe Coral had decided to live somewhere up a river in Paraguay, with some refugee Nembutal dealers.

And I know this much about science: whenever there is a landmark invention or discovery, there are usually hundreds of people involved. Whenever the Nobel prizes in physics or medicine are announced, they name several guys in white coats at Berkeley and Manchester. Whenever it is a single maverick you have to be a little suspicious.

On the other hand, she told me, there were those two men who did nuclear fusion in a pot of heavy water at room temperature.

"I still don't know whether he is there in 1961," she said. "The message he was going to send hasnt arrived. He might have been spread out and sent all over the time map, for all I know."

I, of course, transferred that notion to myself. I could not imagine my molecules sprayed all over the last half of the 20th century.

"What was the sign?"

"He was going to jump out on the field and greet Roger Maris when he hit his sixtieth whatchamacallit," she said.

That's what he told *her*, but I thought I knew a little better.

"Send me to spring training, 1961," I said. "I'll send you a sign. I've been thinking about this: if I arrive safely in 1961, I'll talk to somebody in the printing trade who needs a few dollars. That's the year Allen Ginsberg's *Kaddish and other poems* came out. Lot of people still think it's his best book."

"I know less about old poetry than I know about baseball," she said, with a little patronizing impatience.

"Take my word for it. If I make it, you can have a look at page 38 of the first edition of *Kaddish*. If the second line still says "or will we find Zoroastrian temples flowering on Neptune?" I didnt make it. If it says 'be' instead of 'we,' that will be the misprint I paid for."

"Why did it have to be something about ancient poetry?"

"I didnt think I could influence Khrushchev about the Berlin Wall."

"Why would you want to go back there when you cant return?"

"A guy in expensive shoes told me I'm not going to see the 2023 season, anyway. So I figured I would like to watch Mantle and Maris slug it out. And I want to get reacquainted with baseball on natural grass."

Here is something we should all know about scientists. They deal with objects and forces and energies they tell us are objectively observable, though one of their own tribe told us a century ago that that was a myth. But in the middle of all this impersonalism they are as vain as opera singers and novelists. You can get them in their vanity.

So I played that card. I loaded myself down with little valuable things I could trade for the local currency, and miss Svengali Knight turned the dial.

Later, or should I say earlier? Anyway, on the day that Maris hit number 33 off Bill Monbouquette in Yankee Stadium, I had this thought: if I could talk her into sending me after the large hairy one, somebody else could talk her into sending him after me. The hit man always looks over his shoulder for *his* hit man.

Of course you people would never know the full ramification of these pursuits. If a contract killing occurs you see it as a newspaper crime with an unknown motive. Then you are stuck with the new history. As far as you are concerned, if I failed in my quest Roger Maris never did hit his sixty-first.

If that is the case, I just had to leave this letter, to let you know that at one time he did. Maybe it never got into your *Official Encyclopedia of Baseball*, A.S. Barnes & Co., 1970, but it could have if I had succeeded. (Is this foreshadowing or backshadowing?)

Of course you will be justified in disbelieving all this. Roger Maris got an asterisk for *tying* Ruth, you can say.

Unless you are reading this in 2022, and thinking this confirms where I went when I disappeared.

A blast from the past, I suppose you might say. A present meant for the future. ·

September 27, 1961 in New York City. Who would want to be anywhere else, any other time? It was certainly a baseball writer's dream to be there. I guess I was the only person in town for whom the dream was edged with a bone-scraping nightmare. I dont know whether Roger Maris got any sleep last night, and I dont know where Coral Godard spent the night, but I can report to you that I sat up all night smoking cigarettes because

in September of 1961 you could not get in New York City what
I was accustomed to employ to get through a bad night.

The night before, Baltimore's young Johnny Fisher had
offered Maris a fastball at the knees, and Maris had shown his
appreciation with a high drive that curled around the right field
foul pole for his sixtieth homer. I saw this from a seat I had
bought the rights to from a gent in the parking lot. It felt rather
nice to be in the paying seats instead of the press box. But I
could not sit back and relax, glug beer, joke with my neighbours, the special grace of the baseball park. I was scanning the
crowd for Godard. I didnt see him till the home run. Ruthian
clout, I caught myself saying in my head.

Most of the crowd of sixty-two-thousand people yelled
their heads off, delirious that they were here to see this historic
dinger. A few thousand of the older fans booed or remained
seated, getting out their asterisks during the ten minutes it
took to get the game started again. I stood up, mainly so that
I could see. As Maris circled the bases, the Yankees in their
milky white pinstripes rushed out to greet him. Some of them
did. It would be interesting to look back at whatever photographs there are, to see which Yankees were still in the dugout.
John Blanchard was out there first because he had been the
on-deck hitter. Yogi Berra was there. Hector Lopez was there
with his enormous toothy smile. He jumped on Maris and
demanded to be carried to the dugout, but he was pulled off
by Whitey Ford.

Coral Godard was there. Or almost there. All at once we
thousands could see a new dark blue blazer among the pinstripes. Then we could see a number of New York's Finest in
leather jackets, converging on the suit and leaving the field for
the ball players. I dont know exactly what Coral had planned
for that moment, but I was grateful for the foresight of the people who run the House that Ruth Built.

In all the noise and turmoil I was out of my seat and headed for the exit. I figured I wouldnt run into much traffic headed that way, and I banked on the cops' deciding they just had to get that hairy and over-excited fan outside the stadium rather than cuffing him and hauling him to the slams. Yes. I found Coral outside section 12, trying to rub a mark off the toe of a brand-new loafer.

"Was that just the signal, or did you have more in mind?" I asked.

"If I'da had a gun they wouldnt have just left me here, would they?"

"Dont play dumb, Godard. You could kill a gorilla with your bare but furry hands. If they still have gorillas in 1961."

He looked at me hard, under the shadow of his single head-wide eyebrow. He emanated protein. He was strength personified, or maybe beastified. I wasnt afraid of him. But I was getting confused about history.

"I gotta stop him," he said at last, having reached as complex a conclusion as we were likely to see.

"Okay," I said. "Let me ride with you again."

"You try and stop me, and you'll wind up in the same basement," he advised.

I had to start thinking on my feet, and while sitting in the cab. I had to think about how to stop this creep from killing Roger Maris, and I had to think about the ramifications regarding time and space, which simple people in the 20th century thought were aspects of each other. In the world of physics Albert Einstein had been the Bambino, but someone was going to come along and hit sixty-one in that league, too. I was thinking as fast as I could, and I was not about to take the time to think about how Coral Godard managed to get the address of Roger Maris' apartment. I will only say that a guy who can find Houdini Knight's laboratory in St. Louis should be able to find an outfielder's abode.

I thought and I thought. Coral didn't interrupt me: he was trying to think too, I guess. When we got out of the cab on that darkened corner in Greenville, Coral was going to kill the home run leader of the American League. But by the time he was banging on the front door with his fist or his head – I forget which – we had a deal. This is the sentence with which I ended my persuasive argument:

"There's more than one kind of time travel."

Which meant this: there were three letters in a green metal box in the office of an editor of the *New York News* – or was it the *New York Times?* – written by your humble servant, who had the advantage of knowing which New York newspapers would still exist in 2021. One letter instructed a sequence of editors on what to do with the other two letters. The other two letters were addressed to the president of Washington University in St. Louis and to the commissioner of baseball. Those letters are there right now. They are part of the reason for my writing this story.

In other words I got it through Coral's well-armoured cranium that his great venture would come to nothing if it was proven that he had been alone in breaking Ruth's record only due to an act of homicide. He would, I said, receive the asterisk that would have gone to Maris.

You can see the problems in tense created by the combination of narrative, speech, and time travel.

Roger did not look like a front-page athlete. He did not even look like the Roger who had slapped homers all through spring training. He had lost a lot of hair, and his skin had gone grey. There was some kind of colourful disorder spreading on the skin of his lower arms. He stooped. He seemed unable to lift the long revolver he was carrying when he came to the door of his green-sided bungalow. It was three in the morning. Roger Maris was not going to sign an autograph.

Coral reacted to the armament by rushing his predecessor, driving him against all the furniture in the living room. Luckily there was no one else in the house, or if there had been they had departed by the back door or window at the first sign of athleticism.

Coral banged Roger several times. He socked him once on the nose and once on each eye.

"Why the deuce are you doing this, man?" might be a paraphrase of the only question Roger could get out. But his words did stop the knuckle man from the future.

"He doesnt want you to hit sixty-one home runs," I said.

"He's got company," said Maris, between energetic gasps. "That's why I'm living in this nowhere dump."

He opened the door a little wider and spit some blood mixed with sputum outside.

Then he agreed to the deal. This deal, like all realistic pacts, would disappoint all three of us a bit, but make the times we were living in habitable.

The hard part was going to be persuading the New York Yankees. The second hardest part was going to be fooling or placating the home plate umpires. The surprisingly easy part was going to be making Coral Godard look like Roger Maris. He wasn't that much bigger, maybe a little more muscular around the chest and shoulders. A lot of the difference faded when we shaved a kilogram of hair off his arms and the middle of his long eyebrow.

Anyway, it worked, more or less, or you wouldnt need this story now. You might remember that there were suspicious stories at the time, but they were chalked up to the circus atmosphere of the homer hunt. The ball player the reporters saw after the game was Roger Maris, a man with two black eyes. The out-

fielder the Bronx beer swillers saw in the wide green was Roger
Maris, an oddly bent figure in pinstripes. Yogi Berra and Mickey
Mantle and Bobby Richardson ducked interviews all that week.
Coral Godard was a 20th century major league purloined letter.

He went to the plate at Yankee Stadium twenty-three times
over the next four and a half games. Although it was illegal
according to the rules of baseball, he was wearing the same
number on his back as that on the back of his teammate in the
dark tunnel behind the dugout. Have a look at pictures of Bill
"Moose" Skowron during those tense nights: his facial expression can not be attributed to the pennant race. There wasnt any
pennant race. Bill really thought he could solve Maris' dilemma
by socking the interloper in the front of the head. Organized
baseball, or at least a local contingent of it, kept the wrappers on
him. It's only for five nights at the most, Bill, they said.

Coral struck out and grounded out and lined to the firstbaseman. He could not reach the Orioles pitchers and then he
could not handle the Red Sox pitchers. Once he got within fifteen feet of the warning track in centre field, no mean feat at
Yankee Stadium. Roger Maris stood in the dark tunnel, smoking Chesterfield cigarettes and wishing he were in the game
offensively. On the plus side you might say that it was a good
thing that Coral didnt reach base very often. There was no guar-
antee that a Boston infielder might not spill the baked beans.

But thank goodness, as millions of unknowing fans said, for
Tracy Stallard, a name that will live forever in the annals of the
game. On October 1, 1961, the last day of the season, Tracy
finally dealt Coral Maris a knee-high fastball, and the shorn one
lifted it magisterially into the upper deck of the next borough.
Babe Ruth had hit his sixtieth on the last day of the 1927 season, off Washington's left-hander Tom Zachary, right here at
Yankee Stadium. Coral rounded the bases, got jumped on by
twenty-eight people in Yankee uniforms, including one with the

duplicate number on his back, as you can ascertain by looking at a photograph in *Sport Pictorial*, and then left big-league baseball for forty-five years.

He was not, as he told me in athletese, completely satisfied. He would be condemned, through some portion of the 21st century, to sharing the major league home run record, but at least he will have been the only person ever to have hit a sixty-first home run.

"Who knows? Maybe you would have hit sixty-*three* home runs if you had stayed around for the 2023 season," I said. I admit that I was sporting a grin that showed just the tips of my teeth.

He stared at me with the rudimentary beginnings of emotion on his face. He hadnt thought of that.

After he left that game, I was hoping that Maris would pop number sixty-two in his last at-bat. But he grounded to second on a pitch he should have taken for ball four. Ain't that always the way?

The Yankees won the World Series easily, in five games over the Cincinnati Reds. Maris hit a homer in the third game. I watched it on a rudimentary black and white television. I dont think Coral was interested. Then, as always happens when the World Series is over, a winter loomed, and the reality of the workplace reasserted itself. As I did not have a workplace I had to find myself some fake I.D. and hit the concrete. It didnt take as long as I had feared. I landed a sports page job in White Plains, mainly horseraces and track meets. I didnt tell them about the little visitor inside my middle regions. But it's a couple of years later now, and they are going to learn. I haven't been able to get out of this foldaway couch for seven days.

So here I am completing the last part of the deal, the part Roger wasnt told about. Coral wanted me to tell the whole story. I am supposed to consign it to a time capsule at the *News*. Coral got the idea from me, of course. His idea was that the time capsule is to be opened the day after he disappears from the Blue Jays in 2022. Well, it appears that I was able to get the story down, but I dont know about the time capsule. Maybe the person who finds this will seal it and deliver it to the *News*.

Coral said to tell every detail and make it realistic. He said that way history would eventually get it right. People would know that Roger Maris never hit a sixty-first homer. All I had to do was tell the story and not leave any loose ends.

DIONNE BRAND

I Used to Like
the Dallas Cowboys

I used to like the Dallas Cowboys. Steel grey helmets, good luck grey, bad luck blue, skin tight, muscle-definitioned thighs. I'd prepare for Sunday's game, beer and my pillows at the ready. Rushing to the kitchen between commercials, burning the chicken or the boiled potatoes, depending on whether there was money, or making split pea soup, scraping up the last grain of garlic and the onions growing stems in the dark corners of the cupboard below the sink. I'd neglect the dishes from the night before or the week before, depending on the week, set up a phone line with Tony or Jo as the case may be, put the bottles of beer in the freezer, if I had beer, and wait for the game, sit through the pre-game or the highlights, have a 15-minute nap, time permitting. This was after I'd just risen from an eight-hour sleep, most of which was devoted to regenerating the body after dancing and drinking till four in the morning. Whatever liquor wasn't danced out had to be slept out. Naturally, sometimes even sleep would not produce the miracle of waking up without a vicious headache and feeling water-logged, but I had prepared for this by putting the television near to my arm.

Seems a while now, but back then, I used to really love the Dallas Cowboys. It's funny what things occur to you lying in a corridor at 3:00 a.m. in the morning in the middle of a war. Which is where I am now. The sky is lit bright from flares and there's a groaning F16 circling the sky like a corbeau. The flares give off the light of a red smoky dawn, except for their starkness which makes you feel naked. The air, seeping through the wood latticework, smells chemical. A few minutes ago, before the flares went up, the cat, who lives in the house whose corridor I'm huddled in, ran screaming and scratching over my back. She had heard the incoming planes long before they hit the island again, on this second day... night of the war. Having no sixth sense like hers, the rest of us dove for the corridor only when the flares went up and we'd heard the crack of the F16s through the sound of speed. I wasn't asleep. Just waiting. Amazing how your mind can just latch on to something, just to save you from thinking about how frightened you are. It reaches for the farthest thing away... That's how come I remember that I used to love the Dallas Cowboys.

The Cowboys shone, the Dallas sun glancing off their helmets. They weren't like other football teams. They were sleek where the others were rough; they were swift where the others were plodding; they were scientific where the others were ploughboys; they were precise where the others were clumsy mudwaders; they were slim, slender where the others were hulking, brutish. Even their linebackers had finesse. Not for them the crunch and bashing of the Steelers, the mud and squat of the Raiders: they were quick, clean, decisive. Punters trembled before the upraised arm of Harvey Martin, linebackers dreaded his embrace. Too Tall Jones had too much oil, too much quickness for a defensive lineman, too long a right arm. It was ecstasy when Hollywood Henderson intercepted a pass or caught a running back for a loss. But most of all it was Drew Pearson, Tony Dorsett, and Butch Johnson who gave you a look at perfection of the human, male, form.

Mind you there were a few from other teams, like Lynn Swann, who was with Pittsburgh. He was as graceful as the rest of his teammates were piggish. Sometimes, I think he flew. He was so lithe, I think everyone on the field stopped to watch him, this bird of beauty among them, so tied to their squat bodies and the heavy ground. He should have been with the Cowboys, really.

The Cowboys were fine. They had a move which befuddled their opponents while it raised something in me that... It was when they were waiting for the quarterback's call. Hunched over, they would rise in unison for the quickest of moments and then settle in for the count again. The look of all those sinewy backs rising and falling was like a dance. A threatening dance. It reminded me of "the breakdown" which we used to do every Thursday, Friday, and Saturday night at the Coq D'Or.

Rufus Thomas started it with his song, "Do the Breakdown," and we just got better and better, perfecting the bend from the waist and the shudders to the left and right. Some added variations in the middle or with the hips and the motions of the crooked arm as the weeks went by, till the next new dance; but everything about Black dance was there in the breakdown. So when the Dallas Cowboys did the breakdown, it really sent me. I was their fan, the moment I saw it.

Seems like I made a circle with my life. Then, I was in Toronto. Now, I'm back here on the island, not the one I came from in the beginning, but close by. Speaking of circles, there is... was a revolution here and I came to join. Correction, revolutions are actually not circles but upheavals, transformations, new beginnings for life. I'm greying by the minute in this corridor. I feel feverish. That is a circle, ending where you began. The war outside is ending the revolution. We have nothing to listen to since the radio went off at 9:00 a.m. on the first day of the war, only the crack of the F16s over the house.

Rufus Thomas... tata ta tata tata pada ta pada pada boom... do the breakdown... That was in 1970 or '71. Seems a long time ago now, considering. That's when I first went to Toronto. I was sixteen. I went to school. I partied. I learned to like football. Not Canadian football, American football. Actually it was Sundays. Sundays. I had never liked Sundays. Back home everything stopped on a Sunday. The shop was closed; people didn't walk on the street, except in quiet penitence and their Sunday best; and worse, the radio no longer blared calypso and soul music but Oral Roberts' "The Hour of Decision."

Canadian football was too slow, the downs were too few, and the ball seemed to be perpetually changing hands from one incompetent lot to the other, blundering up and down the field. American football, on the other hand, now... Well, come to think of it, it was all the build-up, the pre-game assessment of the players, who was injured and who wasn't. You would swear that this was the most important event to take place in history – the tension, the coach's job on the line, and the raw roar of winning. When my team lost, I cannot explain the deep loss, the complete letdown which would last until Monday morning. My sister and I would remark to each other every so often, in the middle of doing the washing or in the middle of a walk, "Cheups! Dallas could disappoint people, eh?" This would be followed by a pregnant silence and another "Cheups." The next Sunday, up until game time we'd be saying, "I can't watch that game, I just can't." But the call of the steel grey and the American star on the helmet was too much and Dallas! Dallas was good! You have to admit.

To be honest, if I really look back, it was the clandestine *True Confessions* magazines from America which I read at thirteen that led to my love for the Dallas Cowboys. There was always a guy named Bif or Ted or Lance who was on the college football team and every girl wanted to wear his sweater. Never mind we didn't have sweaters or need them in the tropics, this only made them romantic items. We didn't have cars either in whose steamy back seats a girl became "that kinda girl," or a wife.

So anyway, because it was so boring in Canada on Sundays and because it was winter, morning, noon and night, I learned to like football.

And basketball. Mind, I always liked netball which was what they made girls play at Rima High School in San Fernando. And tennis, dying, dy…ing for Arthur Ashe to whip Jimmy Connors which he finally did at Wimbledon, which all North American sportscasters call *wimpleton*, which really gets me, like every broadcaster in North America says *nukular* instead of *nuclear* and they're supposed to be so advanced. Me and my sister could not bear to watch it, the tennis game that is, because we had already said too often,

"This Arthur Ashe can disappoint people, boy!"

Nevertheless we gave in. We were walking along Dufferin, that was when we used to live on Dupont, we were walking along Dufferin at Wallace and we suddenly made a run for Dupont after several long "cheups" and pauses and after hearing an Italian boy say something about the match to another Italian boy. We couldn't let Arthur go through that match alone. It was a battle of the races. Some people would be looking and cheering for Jimmy Connors. As we ran home it became more and more important that we watch the match to give Arthur moral support. Somehow if we sat and watched the match, it would help Arthur to win. And if we didn't and he lost, it would have been our fault. So we sat in pain, watching and urging Arthur on, on the television. It was tense but Arthur played like a dream, like a thinker. Connors was gallerying, throwing tantrums like a white boy; but Arthur was cool. Connors would use his powerful forehand trying to drive Arthur to the base line, Arthur would send him back a soft drop shot that he couldn't make. Connors would send hard, trying to get Arthur to return hard, but Arthur would just come in soft. Arthur beat his ass ba…ad. I swear to God if we didn't sit and watch that match we would not have forgiven

ourselves. This was like the second Joe Louis and Max Schmel-
ing fight. Nineteen thirty-six all over again.

And boxing, I liked that too, and track. Never liked hockey,
except when the Soviets came to play. And golf, would you believe. That's to tell you how far I'd go to escape the dreariness of
Sundays in the winter. I'd even watch an old, lazy, white man's
sport.

Last Sunday, here, was a little sad... and tense. Only, on
Sunday, the war hadn't started yet. There was a visit to Mr. Mor-
ris from which you can see, as from most places on this island,
the sea. Talk, a little hopeful but bewildered, that surrounded by
water like this, one could never be prepared for war even if one
could see it coming over the long view of the horizon.

The war was inside the house now. The light from the flares
ignores the lushness of this island turning it into an endless
desert.

I used to love the Dallas Cowboys like you wouldn't believe.
How I come to love the Dallas Cowboys – well I've explained,
but I left something out. See, I wasn't your cheerleader type; I
wasn't no Dallas Cowgirl. I knew the game, knew all their
moves and Dallas had some moves that no other football club
would do. They would do an end around, which most other
teams would think belonged in a high school or college game.
So it would shock them that here was Dallas, America's team,
doing a high school move.

I learned about American high school and college lore
watching American football. In my own high school, where
football was soccer, we didn't play it because I went to a girls'
school. We played whatever we did play rough mind you, but it
wasn't soccer. Football was played by Pres' College and St. Benedict's. Boys' high schools. Benedict's always won but Pres' was
the star boys. This was mainly because they were high-yellow
boys. Red skin, fair skin, and from good families. Every high

school girl was after them, god knows to do what with, because there was no place to do it that I could find. Benedict's was black boys, dark-skinned and tough, tall and lanky or short and thick like a wall. Convent girls and Rima girls vied for Pres' boys, Benedict's was a second choice. Benedict's boys were a little aloof though; they were the first ones to be turned on by the Black Power movement. They stopped wearing their uniform right, they were the first to grow afros and get suspended or expelled from school for it. They were the first to have a student strike and a protest march around the school. Then they became popular, or clandestine anyway. Pres' star boys looked pale against them and everybody now started to look for the darkest Pres' boy to walk with, because the boys in Pres' who weren't red skin began to join Black Power too. My friend Sylvia was the first to go afro in my school, and it was as if she had committed a crime, or as if she was a "bad" girl or something.

That year, the Black Power year, I didn't get to go to see Pres' and Benedict's play in Guaracara Park. But I heard it turned into a Black Power demonstration. Well truthfully, I never got to go but once that I could remember, my family being so strict; and anyway, I was always at a loss to know what to do with a boy after, which was supposed to be the highlight of the evening and anyway, I never had a boyfriend really. The other thing was, I really couldn't get into jumping around in the stands as a girl, not looking at the game and yelling when everybody else yelled "Goal!" All of us who would leave without a boy would walk behind our next best friend who had one, looking at her boyfriend and snickering. The girls who had boyfriends on the teams that played were way above us.

But this was soccer, which we called football, so I didn't know American football.

I really didn't like soccer until television came in, in Trinidad, and not until years after that when we got a TV and we could watch Tottenham Hot Spurs at Trent and you could really see the game and the moves. And we watched the World Cup and found Brazil was who we could cheer for, because Brazil was Black; and then there was Eusebio of Portugal who was Black, too. Now that's when the game got good. Pele and Eusebio made us cheer for both teams at the same time if they were playing each other because Black people had to shine anyhow they come. Never mind the Spurs, we wanted England to lose because they didn't have any Black players. That was an insult.

"What happen? They don't like Black people or what? They don't give Black people any chance at all?"

If the game was between two white teams, we'd root for the team with the darkest hair. So Italy and Mexico were our teams. If it was British teams, the most rough-and-tumble-looking would be our favourites. So when TV came in, then is when I got into soccer.

Soccer didn't have any cheerleaders, but American football did. I was embarrassed when I saw them. They looked ridiculous and vulnerable at the same time. I suppose they were supposed to look vulnerable; but it looked like weak shit to me. Since I was a kid I had a disdain for that kind of girl or woman. I never liked not knowing exactly about a thing and I had always felt uncomfortable wearing a mini skirt or can can, when they were in fashion.

So I learned about American football. This standing around like a fool while men talked about football was not for me. Sometimes after Saturday night, and usually during the playoffs, someone, maybe Joe, would have a brunch and part of the programme was that we'd watch the game. That usually meant that the men would watch the game and the women would rap with each other (nothing wrong with that mind you), walk around, hassle, or humour the men about watching the game, or observe the new "chick" belonging to whichever reigning cock on the walk. Well see, I never came with nobody except that one time that I was almost married. But that's another story, thank God. I'd get a place at the TV and not without feeling that I was ingratiating myself and that I wasn't quite welcome. Well, I'd make some comments about what call the referee made on such and such a play and nobody would take me on. Then I'd get a rise out of them if I said that their backs moved before the snap of the ball. Well, at first they humoured me. Mind you the worst of them left the room, objecting to watching football with a woman present. Then they realized that I know my game, you see. I'd bet them money too, just to prove how serious I was. I out-machoed the machoest. I yelled and pointed and called them suckers, and then I'd laugh and tease them. Well, most of them were Trinidadian, so they rose to the bait. You could always catch a Trinidadian man in an argument defending the most unlikely prospect and the most ridiculous outcome.

Before you knew it, every time I lost a game, to be sure that phone would ring and one of the guys would be taunting me saying, "You see how to play football? Dallas is dead, bet you 10 bucks." I'd take the bet because the Dallas Cowboys were magicians. They could take 60 seconds left in a game and turn it into two touchdowns and a field goal. Robert Newhouse, before he got injured, could plough through a Steelers defense like an ant through a hibiscus hedge. See, I wasn't no cheerleader. I knew my game. Roger liked the Steelers cause they had Franco Harris; but to me Franco was kind of clumsy. I know he ran so many yards and everything, but when he started to get old I figure he should have left, because he started to look bad to me. Other people wouldn't say that, but I didn't like the look of him. He looked too much like a white boy to me, which is why I hated quarterbacks. They were always white, except for James Harris who was with L.A. and then what's-his-name with the Bears. Roger Staubach I had to tolerate and anyway, he was clean. I mean he could throw a pass. He could go up the field in 30 seconds. Of course, one of *us*, Drew or Butch, had to be there to catch it. But Roger was clean. Never mind he was born-again and probably a member of the Klan, after all we're talking about Texas, where they still fly the Confederate flag and all.

Another thing about the Cowboys, all my football buddies used to say that they were the most fascist team. Well I agreed, you know, because football, or most any American sport, has that quality to it. I said that was exactly why I liked Dallas because in this gladiatorial game called football they were the most scientific, the most emotionless, and therefore exactly what this game was about. I called my buddies a bunch of wimps. "How you could like football and then get squeamish? You got to figure out what it is you like, see!" Anybody can watch a game and say, "Oh I hate that. It's so violent." But they still live with it and in it. That person's just an intellectual. When I finally got to see the Dallas Cowboys in person, no set of intellectuals could have explained it, and neither could anybody who didn't understand the game.

To cut a long story short, because I probably don't have time for a long story, even though I loved the Dallas Cowboys, I had to leave the country. So I had to wean myself off of football because where I was going there was no American football. There may be cricket but certainly no football. It wasn't easy. You get used to a way of life, even though you don't know it. And you take everything it has in it, even if you think you can sift out the good from the bad. You get cynical and hard-arsed about the bad, in truth. So you find a way to look at it. So cynical and hard-arsed that when you see good, it embarrasses you.

The jets breaking the sound barrier keep rushing over the house. I've never ever heard a noise like that. Oh, my God! It's a wonder I can remember anything. Remembering keeps the panic down. Remember your name, remember last week...

There's a feeling somewhere in my body that's so tender that I'm melting away, disintegrating with it. I'm actually going to die!

Someone in the corridor with me says, "It's the ones you don't hear…" Yesterday, we thought we heard MIGs overhead… wishing… we know that no one will come to help us. No one can.

I was going on to another kind of place, much quieter. A cricket match now and then, maybe… One Sunday, in March this year, I went to one. It was a quiet Sunday, the way Sundays are quiet in the Caribbean, and I slept through half of the match. It was West Indies versus the Leeward Islands. Cricket is the only game that you can sleep through and it wouldn't matter. They say it started in the Caribbean as a slavemasters' game. Of course, they had all the time in the world. Matches can last up to five days. They break for tea and long lunches and they wear white, to show that it's not a dirty, common game. Even the spectators wear white.

You can tell that it was a slavemasters' game if you notice where most cricket pitches are placed. You just look and you'll find them all laid out, green and close-cropped grass, at some remote end of what use to be a plantation, or still might be for that matter. Remote enough so that the players would have some peace from the hurly-burly of slave life, but close enough in case of an emergency whipping or carnage. If you pass by a cricket pitch in the Caribbean, not the modern stadiums they built but the ones that have been there forever, there's a hush over them, a kind of green silence, an imperious quiet. You will notice that children never play on them. They play somewhere on the beach or in the bush. See, there's no place to hide on them, which is why slave owners liked them, I suppose. While they had their dalliances there, they could be sure to see a coming riot.

Which, oddly enough, is why I left, here first, then there. I could no more help leaving Toronto than I could help going there in the first place or coming here eventually. I came to join the revolution; to stop going in circles, to add my puny little woman self to an upheaval. You get tired of being a slave; you get tired of being sold here and there; you assault the cricket pitch, even if it is broad daylight and the slave owner can see you coming; you scuttle pell-mell into death; you only have to be lucky once; get him behind the neck; and if it doesn't succeed... well, you're one of millions and millions. Though lying in a corridor in the end, or for those lying dead, it doesn't feel that way, you're trembling, you lose sight.

So no Cowboys, no apartment buildings, no TV to talk about, not so much time to kill on a Sunday. Today, if it turns into day, it's not Sunday. What day is it? The red smoke dawn of the flares has given way to a daybreak as merciless as last night. Each day lengthens into a year. Another afternoon, God fled a blinding shine sky; wasps, helicopter gun ships, stung the beach, seconds from the harbour. Four days ago the island was invaded by America. The Americans don't like cricket. But deep inside of those of us hiding from them in this little corridor, and those in the hills and cemeteries, we know they've come to play ball. Dead-eye ship, helicopter gun ships, bombers, M16s, troops. I've seen my share of TV war – *Hogan's Heroes*, the green berets, and *Bridge on the River Kwai*. Well none of that ever prepares you.

Because when they're not playing, the Cowboys can be deadly.

I've had four days to think about this. War is murder. When you're actually the one about to get killed, not just your physical self but what you wanted badly, well then it's close. I find myself having to attend to small things that I didn't notice before. First of all my hands and my body feel like they don't belong to me. I think that they're only extra baggage because there's nowhere to put them or to hide them. The truth is I begin to hate my own physical body, because I believe it has betrayed me by merely existing. It's like not having a shelf to put it on or a cupboard to lock it in; it's useless to me and it strikes me how inefficient it is. Because the ideal form in which to pass a war is as a spirit, a jumbie. My body is history, fossil, passé.

And my thoughts. I begin to think, why didn't I think of this? or that? I think, why isn't it yesterday? or last year? or year after next? Even a depressing day, any other day, a day when my menses pained me, occurs to me like a hot desire. I try to evolve to a higher form. I want to think out of this place where I'm crouched with four other people; but my thoughts are totally useless and I know it, because I think that too.

And the noise of the war. That horrible, horrible noise like the earth cracked open by a huge metallic butchering instrument. That noise rankles, bursts in my ear, and after a while it drones in my ear and that droning says that I'm not dead yet. I don't know when I'll get hit; the whole house could be blown away and this corridor which I chose, if I really think about it, and all the safety which I imbued it with. I would stand in the middle of the street and wave to the bombers in the sky to come and finish me off.

If I don't die today, the one thing that will probably dog me for the rest of my life is that I'm not dead. Why am I not dead now... now... now...

I began well. I tried to make it decent, to die clean and dignified; but I don't want to die and my greed to live is embarrassing. I feel like a glutton about how much my body wants to hang on and at the same time it does not want to be here, in this corridor, in this world where I'm about to die. And so, in the middle of the noise, through the gun fire, the bombs and the anti-aircraft guns, I'm falling asleep. Can you imagine! I'm falling asleep. Each time I hear the bombers approaching, I yawn and my body begins to fall asleep.

Like now. Someone else in the corridor is watching me trying to sleep in the middle of disaster. If we survive, she will remember that I tried to sleep. I will remember that she watched
me, tears in her eyes, leaving her. We hum and flinch to each
crackkk, each bomb… We're dancing the breakdown. But if I
fall asleep, I know that I won't wake up, or I'll wake up mad.

For four days now, a war in the middle of October, on this
small unlikely island. Four days. I crouch in a corridor; I drink
bottles of rum and never get drunk. I stay awake, in case. I listen for the noise of the war because it is my signal, like the snap
of the ball, that I'm not dead.

*But the signal is not from my team. I'm playing the Dallas
Cowboys.*

The day I finally creep to the door, the day I look outside
to see who is trying to kill me, to tell them that I surrender, I
see the Dallas Cowboys coming down my hot tropical street,
among the bougainvillea and the mimosa, crouching, pointing
their M16 weapons, laden with grenade-launchers. The hibiscus
and I dangle high and red in defeat; everything is silent and
gone. Better dead. Their faces are painted and there's that smell,
like fresh blood and human grease, on them. And I hate them.

BARRY CALLAGHAN

THE COHEN IN COWAN

Cowan's my name and in case you don't know Cowan's cut down from Cohen 'cause Cohen meant you were a king but I'm a Cowan, which lets you know right away where I stand, which is on my own two feet, and where else, 'cause I used to be Jewish but now I'm very successful, otherwise would I have a black car like a regular mayor or a mortician if I wasn't successful? But mostly I know I'm okay 'cause I get no secret sweats in the night though I got a lot on my mind and sometimes the pressure is a cooker like you wouldn't believe, but I don't owe no one in this whole world for what I got, which is to say my company from day one was a money-maker I thought up in the shower room at the Y and where the idea came from is one night I'm watching the Oscar awards and this song *You Light Up My Life*, which I always thought was a Flick-Your-Bic commercial, wins 'cause it turns out it's a song about God but what I'm looking for's got nothing to do with God but only this company I put together as a dodge for tax purposes, out near the old cemetery and it has got to look legit. So in the shower after playing basketball I think to myself I'll get into the T-shirt business with T-shirts from Taiwan, to which if you send me a photo I'll put your face dead centre between your tits for all the world to see, which is better than all these Day-Glo slogans 'cause it's you yourself, which is when I get the company name when I hear myself saying U-yourself, and that's where we all live 'cause nothing counts like old Number One, which doesn't mean I don't have a Number Two, namely my wife who loves me a lot, but the fact is, I'm at my best alone in the Y and so standing next day in the shower room I think, why not lampshades with your face on your own lampshade, which my wife says is a little weird for a Jew but I say forget the Jewish problem and let the light that lights up your room light up your face. That's what we all want, to look good in a good light, and pretty soon there's so many orders I know I'm on to a lucky streak, and sure enough one afternoon I'm out walking past one of these religious stores with prayer books and those beads and I stop dead in my tracks. I can feel for sure somebody's got their eye on me and pretty soon I figure it out, it's this 3-D holy picture with the big heart bleeding and my wife she says she's worried about lampshades being in bad taste, and there I am looking at this dripping heart with a red light bulb in it, which to me is really sick, but bleeding hearts are not my business except the world's full of bleeding hearts, but these big mooning eyes no matter where I move, they follow me 'cause of the way they're printed in this pebbly plastic and bam like a light it hits me. Put U-yourself In The Picture With A Frame Of Simulated Walnut. I tell you this is terrific like you can't believe 'cause there's nothing people like better than the look of themselves on the wall keeping an eye on everything and you think T-shirts are big, I'm getting photographs from the end of the earth and I'm making big bucks, which suits me fine except suddenly I'm a businessman tied to an accountant instead of a tax dodge, and I don't want to be a businessman like that 'cause actually though I'm very respectable you see I'm a bookie.

But even more than being a bookie I like playing basketball, but mostly by myself 'cause it's not that I can't keep up with the boys, being only thirty-six and I got what my wife calls a little pleasure-pillow paunch, but I don't like to complicate my life with too many other people who only make demands and one demand leads to another. So I like being alone bouncing a ball on Sunday mornings at the Y when there's nobody on the floor and usually there's only one old guy out that early jogging around the upstairs track like he's chasing his own shadow. He don't pay attention to me and I don't pay attention to him but we quit around the same time 'cause other guys are now on the floor and B-ball is really only terrific when you're by yourself 'cause when you're alone you can get this feather touch in the fingers, your whole body light like weightless, and you take off and float with the ball, looping it up off the backboard and bam it goes swish. That's as close to perfect perfection as you're gonna get, knowing you're totally in tune between yourself and the ball, and before you even take a look you see it happen before it happens, which my wife she tells me is almost mystical or musical, I forget the way she says I talk about it, but it's true. The only time I felt close to totally happy is the one or two times I got that feather touch in my fingers, like the little flutter I feel sometimes from my wife except my wife and me, who everybody says we were made for each other in heaven, one week we nearly come apart at the seams and for Christsake can you believe it, all over a lousy Christmas tree.

Which was not because I'm Jewish but the way I remember being Jewish, which in some ways is worse than being Jewish because it's always in the back of your mind and by and large what you remember is what you are which is why I figure that what a person wants to forget should take care of itself, except there are some things you can't do nothing about and for me it's the smells I smell, and comes Christmas time and I see Christmas trees what I think of is *shiksas*, and what I thought about *shiksas* when I was a boy was pork, and when I think of pork I get queasy 'cause unclean's unclean, which don't make much sense 'cause actually I like eating great big *goyish* hams with pineapple rings. But what can I do about what I smell in my head whether it smells that way or not, so when my wife says she wants a Christmas tree so my two little daughters can open up their presents like regular kids, and I say they're not regular kids, she says why not, and I say 'cause they're nothing the way everyone else is something, and she says that don't make no sense 'cause nobody's anything these days so what's the difference and what do I care, and I tell her I care and she says not about them and then I'm suddenly screaming pork and she looks at me for the first time in our lives like I'm crazy, which I suddenly feel I am, standing there in the kitchen going pork pork, but there's no way I'm gonna be the first person who's Jewish or not in my family who has a Christmas tree in his house. For all I know what she wants is a star up on top like I'm supposed to be one of the three wise men wishing I knew which way to turn, which is the trouble with wise guys who got all the answers for everybody but themselves, 'cause they got stars in their eyes which I don't.

Nonetheless now I'm in the dark with my wife who is a looker and she's cut me off with absolutely no nookie no way and let's face it, I'm a very sexy person who doesn't like lying awake in the dark, so I'm sitting up downstairs half the night trying to figure out what's going on, staring at the turned-off TV tube staring back at me like I'm nuts, and there's my own face on the lampshade over the piano all lit up and so I turn on the matching lamp on the mantelpiece and there's my wife all dolled up like Snow White staring at me smiling in the lampshade and between us on the wall my little girls are hanging in their plastic pictures looking at me no matter where I move like the world's coming to an end over this lousy tree. I can't stand it 'cause my wife says why should people who're nothing sit around with nothing to do, especially when we don't care what's what with anyone, except I know we care 'cause we're screaming at each other the whole time, and I tell her we're making something outa nothing 'cause already I'm sleeping on the sofa and what's even worse everything's out of whack with me being a bookie 'cause now I'm losing.

And I want you to know bookies don't lose unless something is really wrong 'cause betting is the way I see things hanging together in a framework, and when I used to bet myself I was always looking for the sign when I couldn't do nothing wrong no matter how I played it, like the hand of God was with me, and lots of times I got the sign, but even when you believe you're so right you win big, you know you always got to end up losing, like no matter how successful we are we know we all got to die, so one day I can see the only winner is whoever's collecting the bets 'cause the world's full of losers, so I got into being a bookie and right away I'm on the side of the angels and getting rich. Except now I'm sleeping on the sofa and every *putz* in town is picking winners so I'm going broke, and I figure it's all 'cause of that tree, so I'm driving home in a snowstorm the day before Christmas and there's this lot full of scruffy trees for 15 bucks each, which is outrageous, but I buy one anyway 'cause I'm suddenly so excited like I haven't been for a long time. I can't wait to see my wife's face light up like I flicked her Bic when she sees this tree.

So what I see as soon as I say hello is my wife standing with her arms crossed in the living room in front of a great big tree. It's all dripping with tinsel and tiny lights and there's a lopsided star up on top and my kids are sitting cross-legged in the corner looking scared but she's staring at my tree and I'm staring at her tree and all of a sudden we both start laughing ourselves to death, thank God, 'cause maybe I would've killed her for doing that to me if I hadn't done it to myself. So after we stop laughing she says I can't just throw my tree away so maybe I should call the cathedral but I say what do I know about cathedrals, and she says that's exactly their business, looking after poor people who need a tree, but now I think I'm losing my mind when I call the cathedral and this priest is talking very softly to me saying yes, and what a blessing and don't I know there's plenty of families who not only don't have trees but they don't have turkeys either, and like I'm going crazy I whisper back to him, how about I buy them a nice big ham. But he laughs real quiet like we're sharing some secret and says a turkey'll do just fine and he's very touched, and I tell him no I'm the one that's touched, right in the head, and he gives me this little chuckle again saying the Lord really does work in wondrous ways.

The only way I feel is like I'm bleeding to death when two guys from the church show up all smiles, and when I give them the cheque for the turkey the guy with the peak cap says it's a fine tree you have for yourself there Mr. Cowan and a fine Christian thing you do, and I'm smiling like my face is falling apart at the seams. Suddenly I want to yell Cohen you creep, I'm Cohen, but my wife's giving me her little flutter touch on the small of my back and I get this loose feeling like everything's okay and pretty soon me and my wife are standing in the doorway like a couple of loonies saying Merry Christmas to these two guys carrying the tree to their pickup truck. Later we lie around with the kids gone to bed listening for reindeer on the roof and I say maybe I should come down the chimney and my wife says chimneys are a very bad joke for a Jew but I tell her for Christsake cut it out 'cause I'm already feeling a little lost like it is, lying there looking out the window at the really shining stars I never really saw like that before.

In the morning I can't believe it 'cause I'm lying there in this terrific sleep when the phone rings beside the bed, and I hear giggling downstairs that makes me think of summer and the water sprinkler on the lawn, but this voice is saying in my ear he wants to thank me especially Mr. Cowan for my kindness, and I don't know who hell he is so I say he's very welcome but then I realize he's talking about how tickled he is by my tree and my turkey. He says he took a chance looking up my name in the book because there's got to be only one Adrian H. Cowan, which I tell him is true, and he says he can believe it and sounds so warm and pleased I'm suddenly sitting up smiling and puffing the pillows, asking him how it all looks and he's talking terrific, until he says so why not drop over Mr. Cowan and take a look 'cause it'd be a real pleasure to meet a man like me, which I say likewise I'm sure and I will and I hang up and think oh my God, I'm gonna hang myself, 'cause I can't believe how I've done this to myself, telling this poor guy I'm gonna come around and stand in his kitchen and stare at his turkey and tree, which is really my tree, and so I go downstairs and this I can't believe either. The whole room is littered up with paper and my little girls are laughing and yelling Daddy Daddy, giving me gifts, and I can't stand it 'cause for them I got no gifts, but my wife says the whole day's this wonderful gift from me and what a wonderful man I am, and like she's at last telling me the biggest secret of her life she says she's already made a plum pudding.

Which is what happens when you give a little you get a lot and I'm gone all the way from pork to plum pudding, so all of a sudden I feel like I'm sitting in a corner with my thumb in someone else's life and I really pulled out a plum, except this is no plum, this is painful, 'cause she says she's got Irish coffees and plum pudding at eleven o'clock in the morning for neighbours who don't care about Jewish, and why, I want to know, is this happening to me in my own house, that everybody is so happy when all I want is nothing except a little piece of the action and no talking to smooth-talking priests. So I say thank you very much, I don't want to be a spoilsport, but I'm going to the Y while it's still early and play a little B-ball by myself. My wife, she taps me on the cheek like it's my *tuchis* and says she understands, smiling, when I know she don't understand at all, and I tell her for the last time that this is the way I am, which is nothing, and kiss her hard 'cause I'm holding her so hard I feel I'm gonna cry, and even when I'm in my big black car I feel I'm gonna cry, driving like I got nothing but time through the streets that are so empty.

And all I can think of is going to see this guy with my tree, which is his fault 'cause I didn't call him, he called me, and actually he lives down close to where my father lived, which is not such a bad place except I haven't been there for years, and when I'm driving down the street I feel a little weird, like I'm moving back into my father's life which is my life, and suddenly I wish I had a son looking for himself in me the way I could look for me in my father if I wanted to, even though my father's dead 20 years, but still I got his old gabardine coat somewhere in a box with his long underwear that he died in when he fell down in the slush in the street and some cop said to me like I was someone else's son, the old *sheeny's* dead, which made me want to kill him when I was a little boy but instead I grew up and got smart and changed my name to Cowan so my kids don't get that kinda crap in case I die in the street. Then before I know it I'm getting out of my car facing this number 48 like the guy on the phone said, and I mean this house is so bad it's nothing like my father ever knew, 'cause the verandah's slipping left while the house is leaning right, and I'm standing there in the street in my own very terrific suede coat with the fox-fur collar and bam, it hits me like I can see this guy's face go out like a light. No matter how much he says he wants to thank me personally there's no way he'd like me looking down at his family beaming up at me and all of a sudden I feel this terrific sadness like I just lost my whole childhood, 'cause I hear myself humming I'm the king of the castle and you're the dirty rascal, and I know if I go in there, then there's no way I can come out clean, so I feel kinda left out like I'm trapped between what I done and what I can't do so that almost without thinking I lifted my hand like I was saying goodbye, and it was only when I was back driving alone in the car that I saw my hand in the air like it was a blessing the way my father used to bless me.

And I want you to know it's not a question of counting blessings, but I can't remember blessing anybody, not even my own kids, which makes me feel even a little more sad but when I'm in the locker room putting on my running shoes I know I'm all wound up and alive inside like I can't wait to get on the floor and then I find the gym is totally empty with not even the old guy running around the track, like he knew this morning I needed to be alone absolutely, and everything I do with the ball feels loose and I'm doing lay-ups real easy and I get this weird feeling that whatever I want is right there at my finger tips. I start dropping in shots from 15 feet and I suddenly start doing backhanders and scoops and crossovers and double pumps. I can't miss like I'm unconscious I'm so good, and then I drop this long looping hook shot like a rainbow from almost centre court, which I know before I even let it go it's perfect, and for a minute I want to cry again and I want the guy with my tree to be there sitting maybe in a folding chair with his turkey in his arms seeing this, 'cause suddenly I got the conviction that we're connected though I never seen him and he's never seen me, but somehow I know I got the touch like it was given to me maybe in the street when I had my hand in the air, which is what my father always used to do when he'd just put his hand in the air over my head and say nothing like he was real peaceful, and so I'm thinking about this guy like he's there all peaceful with his face lit up, and suddenly I'm standing at centre court doing something I could never do before, which is get the ball spinning on my fingertip like it is the whole world and I feel this terrific astonishment which I can't explain, I'm so surprised at being alive let alone I should have this special touch, which for once in my life I really know I got, 'cause for once I did what I didn't intend to do, which was leave the guy alone with whatever happiness he got from what I gave him, and my only regret was he couldn't call me by my real name which is Cohen 'cause now my name is Cowan, which lets you know right away where I stand except standing there at centre court I didn't feel that I was me at all 'cause I don't exactly know who I am but now I know I'm not nothing.

MORLEY CALLAGHAN

THE CHISELER

Old Poppa Tabb was never really cut out to be a manager for a fighter. He seemed too short and too fat, although he'd only got soft around the waist during the last year as Billy got a lot of work in the small clubs, fighting at the flyweight limit. If it had not been for his old man, Billy would have been a chesty little bum standing at night on street corners spitting after cops when they passed. The old man and Billy were both the same size – 5'2" in their bare feet – only the old man weighed 135 pounds and Billy 112.

Poppa Tabb had always wanted his son to amount to something and didn't like the stories he heard about his son being chased by policemen. It hurt him when Billy was sent down for three months for tripping a cop and putting the boots to him. So he thought his son might want to be a fighter and he made an arrangement with a man named Smooth Cassidy, who was very experienced with young fighters, to act as Billy's trainer and handler, and he himself held the contract as the manager. After Billy started fighting in the small clubs, Poppa Tabb bought two white sweaters with "Billy Tabb" on the back in black letters, one for himself and one for Smooth Cassidy. It was at this time that Poppa Tabb began to get a little fat around the waist. He used to sit over in the sunlight by the door of the fire hall and tell the firemen about Billy. He used to sit there and talk about "me and Billy," and have a warm glowing feeling down deep inside.

Late at night he used to wait for Billy to come home from drinking parties with fast white women. He waited, walking up and down the narrow hall of their flat, and he shook his head and imagined that Billy had gotten into an accident. When Billy came in and started to take off his shoes, Poppa Tabb, sitting opposite him, was so worried he said: "I don't want you strolling your stuff so late, Billy."

Billy looked at him. Standing up and coming closer, he said to his old man: "You tryin' to get on me?"

"No, only I know what's good for you, son."

"Yeah. Maybe I know what's good for me. Maybe I know you ain't so good for me."

"There some things you got to do, Billy."

Billy raised his fist. "You want something? Some of this?"

"You don't go hitting me, Billy."

"Say you want some and I smack you. Or get off me."

After that, when Billy came in late Poppa Tabb just looked at his bright sharp eyes and smelled the cologne on his clothes and couldn't say anything to him. He only wished that Billy would tell him everything. He wanted to share the exciting times of his life and have the same feeling, talking to him, that he got when he held up the water pail and handed the sponge to Smooth Cassidy when he was ringside.

Billy did so well in the small clubs that bigger promoters offered him work. But they always talked business with Smooth Cassidy, and Poppa Tabb felt they were trying to leave him out. Just before Billy fought Frankie Genaro, the flyweight champion, who was willing to fight almost anyone in town because the purses for flyweights were so small, Poppa Tabb heard stories that Dick Hallam, who liked owning pieces of fighters, was getting interested in Billy and taking him out to parties. At nights now Billy hardly ever talked to his old man, but still expected him to wait on him like a servant.

Old Poppa Tabb was thinking about it the afternoon of the Genaro fight and he was so worried he went downtown looking for Billy, asking the newsboys at the corner, old friends of Billy's, if they had seen him. In the afternoon, Billy usually passed by the newsstand and talked with the boys till smaller kids came along and whispered, staring at him. Poppa Tabb found Billy in a diner looking to see if his name had gotten into the papers, thrusting big forkfuls of chocolate cake into his wide mouth. The old man looked at him and wanted to rebuke him for eating the chocolate cake but was afraid, so he said: "What's happening Billy?"

"Uh," Billy said.

The old man said carefully: "I don't like this here talk about you stepping around too much with that Hallam guy."

"You don't?" Billy said, pushing his fine brown felt hat back on his narrow brow and wrinkling his forehead. "What you going to do 'bout it?"

"Well, nothing, I guess, Billy."

"You damn right," Billy said flatly. Without looking up again he went on eating cake and reading the papers intently as if his old man hadn't spoken to him at all.

The Genaro fight was an extraordinary success for Billy. Of course, he didn't win. Genaro, who was in his late thirties, went into a kind of short waltz and then clutched and held on when he was tired, and when he was fresh and strong he used a swift pecking left hand that cut the eyes. But Billy liked a man to come in close and hold on, for he put his head on Genaro's chest and flailed with both hands, and no one could hold his arms. Once he got in close, his arms worked with a beautiful tireless precision, and the crowd, liking a great body-puncher, began to roar, and Poppa Tabb put his head down and jumped around, and then he looked up at Billy, whose eye was cut and whose lips were thick and swollen. It didn't matter whether he won the flyweight title, for soon he would be a bantamweight, and then a featherweight, the way he was growing.

Everybody was shouting when Billy left the ring, holding his bandaged hands up high over his head, and he rushed up the aisle to the dressing room, the crowd still roaring as he passed through the seats and the people who tried to touch him with their hands. His gown had fallen off his shoulders. His seconds were running on ahead shouting: "Out of the way! Out of the way!" And Billy, his faced puffed, his brown body glistening under the lights, followed, looking straight ahead, his wild eyes bulging. The crowd closed in behind him at the door of the dressing room.

Poppa Tabb had a hard time getting through the crowd for he couldn't go up the aisle as fast as Billy and the seconds. He was holding his cap tightly in his hands. He had put on a coat over his white "Billy Tabb" sweater. His thin hair was wet as he lurched forward. The neckband of his shirt stuck up from under the sweater and a yellow collar-button shone in the lamplight. "Let me in, let me in," he kept saying, almost hysterical with excitement. "It's my kid, that's my kid." The policeman at the door, who recognized him, said: "Come on in, Pop."

Billy Tabb was stretched out on the rubbing-table and his handlers were gently working over him. The room smelled of liniment. Everybody was talking. Smooth Cassidy was sitting at the end of the table, whispering with Dick Hallam, a tall thin man wearing well-pressed trousers. Old Poppa Tabb stood there blinking and then moved closer to Billy. He did not like Hallam's gold rings and his pearl-grey felt hat and his sharp nose. Old Poppa Tabb was afraid of Hallam and stood fingering the yellow collar-button.

"What's happening, Pop?" Hallam said, smiling expansively.

"Nothing," Pop said, hunching his shoulders and wishing Billy would look at him. They were working on Billy's back muscles and his face was flat against the board. His back rose and fell as he breathed deeply.

"Have a cigar, Pop!" Hallam said.

"No thanks."

"No? My man, I got some good news for you," he said, flicking the end of his nose with his forefinger.

"You got no good news for me," Poppa Tabb said, still wishing Billy would look up at him.

"Sure I do. Billy gonna be big in a few months and I'm gonna take his contract over – most of it, anyway – and have Cassidy look after him. So he won't be needing you no more."

"What you say?" Old Poppa Tabb said to Cassidy.

"It's entirely up to you, Poppa Tabb," Cassidy said, looking down at the floor.

"Yes sir, Billy made good tonight and I'm going to take a piece of him," Hallam said, glancing down at the shiny toes of his shoes. "The boy'll get on when I start looking after him. I'll get stuff for him you couldn't touch. He needs my influence. A guy like you can't expect to go on taking a big cut on Billy."

"So you going to butt in?" Poppa Tabb said.

"Me butt in? That's ripe, seeing you never did nothing but butt in on Billy."

"I'm sticking with Billy," Poppa Tabb said. "You ain't taking no piece of him."

"Shut your face," Billy said, looking up suddenly.

"Shut your face is right," Hallam said. "You're through buttin' in."

"You don't fool me none, Hallam. You just after a cut on Billy."

"You just another old guy trying to chisel on his son," Hallam said scornfully.

Billy was sitting up listening, his hands held loosely in his lap. The room was hot and smelled of sweat. Old Poppa Tabb, turning, went to put his hand on Billy's shoulder. "Tell him to beat it, Billy," he said.

"Keep your hands off. You know you been butting in all my life."

"Sure I have, Billy. I been there 'cause I'm your pop, Billy. You know how it's always been with me. I don't take nothing from you. I don't take a red cent. I just stick with you, Billy. See? We been big together."

"You never went so big with me," Billy said.

"Ain't nothing bigger with me than you, Billy. Tell this hustler to run." Again, he reached to touch Billy's shoulder.

"You insult my friend, you got no call," Billy said. He swung a short right to his father's chin. Poppa Tabb sat down on the floor. He was ready to cry but kept on looking at Billy, who was glaring at him.

"Goddamn, he your old man," Hallam said.

"He can get out. I done with him."

"Sure you are. He'll get out."

They watched Smooth Cassidy help Poppa Tabb get up. "What you going to do about this?" Smooth Cassidy was muttering to him. "You ought to be able to do something, Poppa."

Old Poppa Tabb shook his head awkwardly. "No, there's nothing, Smooth."

"But he your boy, and it's up to you."

"Nothing's up to me."

"It's all right with you, Poppa, then it all right with me," Cassidy said, stepping back.

Old Poppa Tabb, standing there, seemed to be waiting for something. His jaw fell open. He did not move.

"Well, that be that," Hallam said. He took a cigar out of his pocket, looked at it and suddenly thrust it into Poppa Tabb's open mouth. "Have a cigar," he said.

Poppa Tabb's teeth closed down on the cigar. It was sticking straight out of his mouth as he went out, without looking back. The crowd had gone and the big building was empty. It was dark down by the ring. He didn't look at anything. The unlighted cigar stuck out of his mouth as he went out the big door to the street.

ROCH CARRIER

The Hockey Sweater

The winters of my childhood were long, long seasons. We lived in three places – the school, the church and the skating-rink – but our real life was on the skating-rink. Real battles were won on the skating-rink. Real strength appeared on the skating-rink. The real leaders showed themselves on the skating-rink. School was a sort of punishment. Parents always want to punish children and school is their most natural way of punishing us. However, school was also a quiet place where we could prepare for the next hockey game, lay out our next strategies. As for church, we found there the tranquility of God: there we forgot school and dreamed about the next hockey game. Through our daydreams it might happen that we would recite a prayer: we would ask God to help us play as well as Maurice Richard.

We all wore the same uniform as he, the red white and blue uniform of the Montreal Canadiens, the best hockey team in the world; we all combed our hair in the same style as Maurice Richard, and to keep it in place we used a sort of glue – a great deal of glue. We laced our skates like Maurice Richard, we taped our sticks like Maurice Richard. We cut all his pictures out of the papers. Truly, we knew everything about him.

On the ice, when the referee blew his whistle the two teams would rush at the puck; we were five Maurice Richards taking it away from five other Maurice Richards; we were 10 players, all of us wearing with the same blazing enthusiasm the uniform of the Montreal Canadiens. On our backs, we all wore the famous number 9.

One day, my Montreal Canadiens sweater had become too small; then it got torn and had holes in it. My mother said: "If you wear that old sweater people are going to think we're poor!" Then she did what she did whenever we needed new clothes. She started to leaf through the catalogue the Eaton company sent us in the mail every year. My mother was proud. She didn't want to buy our clothes at the general store; the only things that were good enough for us were the latest styles from Eaton's catalogue. My mother didn't like the order forms included with the catalogue; they were written in English and she didn't understand a word of it. To order my hockey sweater, she did as she usually did; she took out her writing paper and wrote in her gentle schoolteacher's hand: "Cher Monsieur Eaton, Would you be kind enough to send me a Canadiens' sweater for my son who is ten years old and a little too tall for his age and Docteur Robitaille thinks he's a little too thin? I'm sending you three dollars and please send me what's left if there's anything left. I hope your wrapping will be better than last time."

Monsieur Eaton was quick to answer my mother's letter. Two weeks later we received the sweater. That day I had one of the greatest disappointments of my life! I would even say that on that day I experienced a very great sorrow. Instead of the red, white and blue Montreal Canadiens sweater, Monsieur Eaton had sent us a blue and white sweater with a maple leaf on the front – the sweater of the Toronto Maple Leafs. I'd always worn the red, white and blue Montreal Canadiens sweater; all my friends wore the red, white and blue sweater; never had anyone in my village ever worn the Toronto sweater, never had we even seen a Toronto Maple Leafs sweater. Besides, the Toronto team was regularly trounced by the triumphant Canadiens. With tears in my eyes I found the strength to say:

"I'll never wear that uniform."

"My boy, first you're going to try it on! If you make up your mind about things before you try, my boy, you won't go very far in this life."

My mother had pulled the blue and white Toronto Maple Leafs sweater over my shoulders and already my arms were inside the sleeves. She pulled the sweater down and carefully smoothed all the creases in the abominable maple leaf on which, right in the middle of my chest, were written the words "Toronto Maple Leafs." I wept.

"I'll never wear it."

"Why not! This sweater fits you... like a glove."

"Maurice Richard would never put it on his back."

"You aren't Maurice Richard. Anyway, it isn't what's on your back that counts, it's what you've got inside your head."

"You'll never put it in my head to wear a Toronto Maple Leafs sweater."

My mother sighed in despair and explained to me:

"If you don't keep this sweater which fits you perfectly I'll have to write to Monsieur Eaton and explain that you don't want to wear the Toronto sweater. Monsieur Eaton's an *Anglais*; he'll be insulted because he likes the Maple Leafs. And if he's insulted do you think he'll be in a hurry to answer us? Spring will be here and you won't have played a single game, just because you didn't want to wear that perfectly nice blue sweater."

So I was obliged to wear the Maple Leafs sweater. When I arrived on the rink, all the Maurice Richards in red, white and blue came up, one by one, to take a look. When the referee blew his whistle I went to take my usual position. The captain came and warned me I'd be better to stay on the forward line. A few minutes later the second line was called; I jumped onto the ice. The Maple Leafs sweater weighed on my shoulders like a mountain. The captain came and told me to wait; he'd need me later, on defence. By the third period I still hadn't played; one of the defencemen was hit in the nose with a stick and it was bleeding. I jumped on the ice: my moment had come! The referee blew his whistle; he gave me a penalty. He claimed I'd jumped on the ice when there were already five players. That was too much! It was unfair! It was persecution! It was because of my blue sweater! I struck my stick against the ice so hard it broke. Relieved, I bent down to pick up the debris. As I straightened up I saw the young vicar, on skates, before me.

"My child," he said, "just because you're wearing a new Toronto Maple Leafs sweater unlike the others, it doesn't mean you're going to make the laws around here. A proper young man doesn't lose his temper. Now take off your skates and go to the church and ask God to forgive you."

Wearing my Maple Leafs sweater I went to the church, where I prayed to God; I asked him to send, as quickly as possible, moths that would eat up my Toronto Maple Leafs sweater.

MATT COHEN

VOGEL

Sam Vogel carried, between his social- and medical-insurance cards, a picture of his high school graduation class. He had chanced upon it the night before he got married, and being sentimental he put it in his wallet and promised never to throw it out. In this memento he was standing in the middle of the third row, with black hair coming low on his forehead, a square almost fleshy face, round eyes. Compared to the others, he was short and unformed. Compared to himself 25 years later, he was almost unrecognizable. The two Sam Vogels had left in common only their dark hair, and their round child's eyes.

Because the picture was in his wallet and he had preserved it through his whole adult life, it was his first image of himself. The second, more recent, existed solely in his mind and was not something that could be seen. It was a sensation. The feel of his own body in flight, running: one foot on the ground, taking his whole weight and springing it back, while the other kicked out front, confidently reaching. And it was in the middle of such a stride, confident and exact, when his back was straight and his muscular legs were pumping, that he felt a fast and sudden gripping in his chest, and before anyone could reach him he was curled up like a baby on the special composition surface of the track.

He had been going to the health club for almost five years, starting the day Henry Weinstock took a deep breath, tapped his fingers like an accountant, and said, "Sam, your body's on a one-way trip. What are you going to do about it?"

"Get old," Sam said. "Do you want me to eat royal jelly?"

"No jelly," said his doctor. Henry Weinstock, that is, because he had started off being Henry, a friend and classmate who had stood in the back row, tall and thin, looking down sceptically on the others as if anticipating the future.

"You can start by losing weight. Every year, you come in here five pounds heavier. It's not doing you any good."

Not only did Sam go on a diet, but he also joined the Men's Health Club and learned how to jog. It took him a whole year to get under 200 pounds, and on the same day he ran his first full mile without stopping. In that 10 minutes he crossed the magic watershed; when it was over he wanted to be thin and athletic more than he wanted to put food in his mouth.

"Growing old," he said to his wife, Alison. "It's not so bad." They were lying in bed, the house uncharacteristically silent. Henry, their eldest child and the doctor's namesake, had moved out a few months before, and Marilyn, their teenage daughter, was going through a phase of domestic bliss, sitting in her room and reading, going to sleep early.

He reached under the sheet, slid his hand to his wife's belly and squeezed it.

"Don't," Alison said.

"What's wrong?"

"I feel fat."

In the old days when she demurred, he used to rest his hand on her stomach, conjure the currents of her being, try to imagine her sexual need of him into existence. Now he took his hand away.

"You should exercise," he said. "It's great."

"I tried running. I feel like I'm falling out of my shorts."

"You could swim."

"When?"

"In the morning. Or the afternoon. Or at night. Can't you spare an hour a day?"

But his voice had already become sarcastic and she had switched off the light and rolled over to her side of the bed.

"Come on," Sam said. "We can discuss things." He waited in the silence, then felt for her shoulder.

"You discuss things. You come into bed and poke me like I was some goddamn sack of flour and then you give me your interrogation. I can't look twenty again." She turned her light back on and flung aside the blankets. She was starting to cry, tears running in the shadows around her eyes. In the old days, when he was in love with her and yearned for nothing sweeter than the knowledge that she would be his to share and protect, the changing lights of her eyes mesmerized him, a continuing proof that no one could be more real, more beautiful, more blessed by fate. "Look, for Christ's sake." Her breasts, which had once been full in his hands, now were narrow and slack, drained by the sucking of children. Her stomach rippled with folds and one side was gathered by the scar of the Caesarean that had freed Marilyn.

"So," Sam Vogel said to his wife, "you're human. You could still go swimming. You don't have to be a movie actress to put on a bathing suit."

That moment, Sam remembered: himself leaning on one elbow, other arm extended in a gesture of utmost reasonableness, voice low and calm – for once he knew that justice was on his side. And yet, when Alison again rolled away from him, he did not object. Only thought about a magazine article that described the recommencement of the cold war, and tried to convince himself that he could overcome his craving for a cigarette.

The moment of justice lay fallow. It became a place that he returned to, an expanse of his own that he roamed and examined. Then, in a surprise manoeuvre, he cashed it in one afternoon on the office carpet, where he made love hastily to a girl who helped at his store, Vogel's Haberdashery. She was a third-year psychology major who was working mornings in order, she claimed, to broaden herself and gain life experience. It was the only time in 22 years of marriage that Sam Vogel had been unfaithful, and even during the act he regretted it, compared the joys of this smooth but unaccustomed body unfavourably with the deeper and more voluptuous motions of his wife. And catching himself with both in his mind was disgusted.

"What's wrong?" asked the girl. Her name was Emily Gathers.

"I haven't done that for a long time."

"Me neither," Emily said. But when she smiled, he felt like a newly discovered virgin.

At home, every movement of Alison's, every inflection, grated on his nerves. She seemed fat, baggy, careless of herself. He suggested drinking wine with the meal.

"What's wrong?" she asked. "Are you sick?"

"I just feel like a glass of wine. Since when are we prudes around here?"

After his third glass he looked across the table to his daughter and realized she was hardly younger than Emily, that concealed by her carelessly worn sweaters and pants was skin as sweet and desirable as Emily's, that in fact she might be offering it up to anyone, not only the boyfriends she so considerately kept away from the house, but to older men, fools like himself who were tired of their wives. And so what's wrong with that? he thought. If she wants to let herself go, why should I pay? And when dinner was finished, exhausted and unpleasantly drunk, he went to take a bath.

While he was lying in the tub, his track-hardened feet wrapped around the hot-water tap, his head resting on a towel so he could doze, Alison came in.

"Look at you," she said.

"What?"

"I can hardly recognize you."

"It's just me," Sam said.

"You look cute," Alison giggled. "You want me to soap you?"

"It's okay," Sam said. "I already did."

"Really," Alison said. In her hand she carried a glass of the red wine and it tipped with her every motion. "I wouldn't mind."

"I was just tired," Sam said. "Maybe I had too much to drink."

"It's amazing what you've done. Look at you."

"Anyone can eat less."

"Don't kid yourself. Eat less. Look at you. You've got muscles all over. Practically a boy again."

"All right," Sam said. "Don't get bitchy."

"No one's getting bitchy. I'm trying to compliment you. Can't a wife tell her husband how handsome he is? Maybe I should send you some flowers to get you into bed."

"You get me in bed every night," Sam said. "What are you talking about?"

But it was three whole days before Emily came into his office again, and shut the door behind her.

"Mr. Vogel," she said.

"Don't call me Mr. Vogel."

"Sam."

"Yes, Emily. I've been wondering where you were hiding."

"I was sick, Mr. Vogel. Nothing personal. I must have caught a flu from the rug."

"I should get it cleaned," he said. "I don't mean it to be a hazard."

Emily laughed. "Mr. Vogel, don't worry about the rug. Maybe it would be better if you got a couch."

"Don't call me Mr. Vogel."

That afternoon, she called him on the telephone and invited him to dinner. After his running, which seemed to go more smoothly than ever, he stood in the shower washing himself with special care, almost able to believe that beneath the white foamed lather lay skin deep and shining, as supple and sensuous to her touch as hers had been to his. This despite the fact he had decided to tell her that their relationship would be returning to normal, and that he would promise always to be her friend and counsellor, in fact like a father, which he already was, to say nothing of a husband who had a wife so suspicious she had not spoken to him for three days except to call him Adonis and comment on his new red underwear.

Showered and resolved, he followed Emily's directions to a narrow Victorian house. It was on the edge of the university area, just a mile from his store. Walking the street and climbing the stairs to her attic room, he was conscious of only one thing, his fear that his son would see him or, worse, be visiting a friend at this very house and witness his own father puffing nervously toward the third floor, a bouquet of yellow roses furtively tucked under his arm.

"Look!" Emily exclaimed. "Yellow for friendship. How sweet!" She put the flowers in an empty tomato juice jar, in the centre of a small table.

"Just relax," she said. "You just be still and I'll cook." The hotplate was jammed with steaming pots. Sam was so thirsty from running, he quickly drank two glasses from the bottle of wine she had set in front of him.

"I was going to tell you," Sam said. "I have a son at the university. Henry Vogel. Do you know him?"

"You told me that," Emily said. "The day you hired me. And twice a week for the first six months."

"I'm sorry."

"I myself have a father. His name is Ralph Gathers and he works for the Winters accounting firm."

"He must be proud of you," Sam said.

"He's an asshole, Mr. Vogel. That's why I moved out."

When he stood up to help her set the table, Emily, laughing, pushed him onto the bed and jumped on top of him. "Your dignity, Mr. Vogel. I love you for your dignity."

It was only on his way home that he realized he had been celebrating his birthday, his forty-fourth. When he came in the door of his house it was midnight. Alison was reading a book; the table was set with white linen, a bottle of champagne in the center, and a vase of red roses.

"I'm sorry. I should have phoned."

"You should have done something." Alison seemed composed, her face still and decided.

"Where's Marilyn?"

"She went out tonight. Staying at a friend's." Alison lit a cigarette, automatically offered him the pack, then retracted it. "So," she said. "What's new?"

"Nothing much."

"Maybe you were having a fire sale at the store. I know how busy it gets there."

"It does get busy," Sam said.

"Tonight you sleep in Henry's old room. Tomorrow you hear from my lawyer."

"Alison."

"Good night, Sam. Happy birthday."

She walked up the stairs. Sam walked out the door, to his car, and drove back to Emily's place. All night he lay in her bed: curled up, awake, while she enclosed his back like a warm shell, her fingers entwined in the hair on his chest, her warm breath on his neck.

In the morning, while they were drinking coffee, they sat at her small table and Sam watched the yellow light searching its way through the roses. "I can't leave my wife," he said.

By now he was so open to her that the sound of her voice penetrated to his heart, her every word and breath excited him, fluttered through his blood, making him feel born again. But in his mind he knew better; and as he drove back to his store, the city streets seemed passive and complacent beneath his car, waiting for the inevitable.

He made his peace with Alison and fired Emily Gathers. They threw out their double bed and bought new, fashionable twins, each with its own bedside table and its own clock radio and alarm. He kept running around the track, four days a week after work, but it was different. His stride slowed and stiffened, and the image of himself running became almost abstract: a moment frozen out of a grainy black-and-white movie: he was the old pro now, the veteran, the man who kept running without feeling his own body, without consciousness of anything but the track jolting beneath him, his bones keeping and carrying the rhythm. And though his pace slowed, the distance he ran correspondingly increased. So by the time he was forty-six he was doing five miles, indoors in the winter and outdoors in the summer, and he felt himself running through the middle of his own life, running into darkness.

One night, late at work, he went across the street to eat supper at a delicatessen. Sitting at the next table was Emily Gathers. It took him a few seconds to recognize her. She was now polished and sophisticated. Her blonde hair was long and curled onto the shoulders of an expensive suede coat. She looked entirely grown and inaccessible, but it was she who waved and smiled at him.

"Mr. Vogel," she said. "What are you doing here?"

"I have a store across the street."

"This is my friend, Janet. Janet, this is Mr. Vogel, my old boss. He has a store across the street and I used to work there until he fired me for getting the carpet dirty."

Sam blushed. And wondered if it showed on his face that it was exactly that long, two years, since he had last made love.

"Call me Sam."

"Vogel's Haberdashery," said Janet. "I used to buy my father ties there, when he was still alive."

"I'm sorry to hear that," Sam said. "We're an old store."

That night, he took Emily Gathers home. She was living in a high-rise, and once inside her apartment he had no fear of being discovered by his children. After two glasses of brandy they somehow ended up on her carpet, which was broadloom and not oriental.

"Did you miss me, Mr. Vogel?"

"Sometimes."

"I missed you, too." She sat on top of him, her legs straddling his waist, knees digging into his ribs, squeezing him as if he were a horse. Which in a way was what he felt like with her, a horse, an animal being driven to its limits. Her hands were open, palms stroking his cheeks, stroking them at first and then gently caressing them, caressing them and then slowly slapping back and forth, palms back and forth so in a lazy way he let his head nod with the force of her hands, back and forth until the blows grew stronger and each was marked by the noise of her palm against his beard, a slapping sound that gradually grew into the dull pain accompanying each blow; and then finally his head was snapping from side to side.

"For Christ's sake, Emily." He had grabbed her wrists and was holding them away.

"Didn't you like that?"

"Sure. But you know."

"I know, Mr. Vogel. I mean it's hard seeing someone after two years of not seeing them at all. On the one hand you feel as if you've always been together, familiar, you know what I mean? But then there's another part of you, just a hiding scared part that feels, oh well, this person is a stranger. A stranger. Have you ever gone to bed with a stranger, Mr. Vogel?"

"I don't know," Sam said. "I didn't think so."

"If, for example, you went to bed with Janet. Did you ever go to bed with Janet?"

"No," Sam said. "Did you?"

"Yes."

"What was it like?"

"It was all right," said Emily Gathers. "You know what I mean. It drifted along, nothing special, and then it was over. But she didn't fire me or anything. I mean she was married but she didn't have a wife."

"You're angry," Sam said. "That's all right. Just get angry. Don't give me all this indirect bullshit." He pushed up and slid her off him, so they were both sitting naked on the rug. He looked down the slope of his belly and saw hair, grizzled and thick, ridged muscles going sideways, a waist that was defined under only a thin layer of fat. Even his arms had become shapely and defined. It was years since he had smoked a cigarette or a cigar. He hardly ever drank coffee or alcohol. In the morning he swallowed vitamins with his orange juice and at noon he ate only salad and skim milk.

"That's right," Emily said. "You're looking good. You're not dead yet, though you pretend to be. For example, you make me feel alive. Does anyone make you feel alive?"

"You do," Sam said. And it was true. Once more, her voice had pierced his defences and his heart rode on her every word. His chest was so open to her he ached, he could feel the blood rushing through him, rushing through his chest, his limbs, the aching places in his head where she had slapped him. And for the first time in two years, he wondered what it would have been like if he had stayed curled up in her bed, her hot breath on his neck, given himself up to his own feelings.

"Do it to me."

"Don't talk like that. I'm sorry I couldn't leave my wife."

"I'm sorry I dirtied your carpet, Mr. Vogel. But look what you've done to mine."

"You're bitter," Sam said. "I should have restrained myself."

"No," said Emily. "You should have let yourself go." She stood up: slim, blonde, supple – she was the exact image of herself.

"Well, Mr. Vogel. This is it."

"All right," Sam said. "I don't want to argue." He stood. His bones were sore, his loins too sweet and exhausted to care what words were being exchanged. "I was faithful to you," Sam said. "Do you know that?"

"No. But I think it's disgusting. I mean, you did stay with your wife."

"That's right," Sam said. He looked away from her and his eye was caught by a table lamp. He kept staring at it, distracted, until the glare began to hurt and join the dull ache in his face. And then, his head turned away, he was blinking: caught on the edges of his vision were small fleeting shapes: hands, feet, fingers long and curled, monkey's limbs. And, looking down at himself, Sam saw that was what he had been changing into, not a horse but a monkey, a spare and hairy monkey who was growing old, his back stooped and tired, his long arms folded across himself.

And then Emily was moving away from him and he was sitting on the couch, sorting through pants, socks, underwear, gradually getting dressed until finally he was facing her in street clothes.

"I didn't mean to get so angry. I mean it's late. You can stay here if you're afraid to go home."

"I'm not."

"Goodbye, Sam. Take it easy."

He spent the night in a downtown hotel. They charged him 42 dollars, and although he had no luggage, the porter insisted on accompanying him to the room. "Is there anything you need, sir?"

"A drink," Sam said.

"I'm sorry, sir. Room service is closed. I could try to arrange a bottle of rye."

"That's okay," Sam said.

He locked, chained, and bolted the door. With the lights off, he undressed again, afraid to see himself, and then took a bath in the darkness, washing her off him, soaping himself twice and then finally showering, standing in the dark afraid to close his eyes because he knew that when he did he would only see her leaning over him, her face close to his, her palms caressing his cheeks.

The next morning, he went straight to his store, Vogel's Haberdashery, an old-fashioned Jewish clothing store on Spadina. It was noon before Alison called.

"I worked late. I was so tired I went to sleep at the Park Plaza."

A long silence. Breath being held. Then a sigh. "You feel better? Maybe you should see the doctor."

"I'm all right."

"My brother is coming for dinner tonight, you remember. Are you planning to come home?"

"I'll be there at seven. You want me to pick up some wine?"

"Red," Alison said. "For passion."

At five o'clock Sam left the store and drove to the health club, where he began jogging his five miles. In the morning at the hotel, all day at the office, he had found himself reaching for his wallet, looking at the photo of his high school graduation class. There were things he had in common with this former self, details he could list, but whoever had lived inside that picture, whoever had walked around with whatever forgotten obsessions, had been buried in circumstance.

"So," Sam said. "What the hell! Times change. Goodbye." And now, on the track, that picture began to transform itself into him running, into his strong thrusting legs, his made-over arms and forcibly narrowed waist. He could feel his own blood surging through him, a fast and sudden gripping in his chest. And it was in the middle of such a perfect stride, confident and exact, when his back was straight and his legs were pumping, that the two pictures finally melted together. And as he went down he saw himself from a great distance, as if from the sceptical eyes of Henry Weinstock or Emily Gathers. He saw himself falling, slowly, his body gradually curling, his knees moving into his chest. And felt his heart burst open.

CRAIG DAVIDSON

THE RIFLEMAN

Let me tell you, the pure shooter's a dying breed. We're talking pretty much extinct: think snow leopard. Komodo dragon, manatee. The dunk shot more or less killed the pure shooter: nowadays everyone wants to be a rim-rocker, shatter the backboard to make the nightly highlight reel. You got kids with pogo-stick legs leaping clear out the gym but these same kids *cannot* hit a jump-shot to save their life. Blame Dominique Wilkins, Michael Jordan, Dr. J. A few shooters still haunt the league, scrawny white riflemen hefting daggers from beyond the three-point arc; most Euros have a deft touch, skills honed in some backwater –vakia or –garia with no ESPN on the dial. A damn shame, because few things in life are as sweet as the sound a basketball makes passing through an iron hoop: we're talking dead through the heart of the net, no rim, no glass. Called a *swish*, that sound, but truly it exists somewhere beyond human description – if heaven has a soundtrack, man, that is *it*.

My son's going to change all that. Jason'll make it cool to be a pure shooter again; once he's chewing up the NBA you'll see kids practicing spot-up j's instead of windmill dunks. I take credit for that silky-smooth jumper of his: feet set in a wide stance, knees bent and elbows cocked at eye level, smooth follow-through with the wrist. We drilled for hours on the driveway net until the mechanics imprinted themselves at a cellular level. Read in the newspaper he went off for 37 against Laura Secord High; those numbers'll attract scouts from Div I programs, believe-you-me. Jason's a Prime Time Player – a *PTP'er*, Dick Vitale would say, ole Dicky V with his zany catchphrases and kisser like a pickled testicle. My boy can *tickle the twine for two, baby!*

The Mikado's the only bar open on Saturday mornings. The TRW skeleton crew usually heads down after the shift whistle blows to knock the foam off a few barley pops. While I'm not *technically* employed there anymore I still like to hit the Mik for a Saturday morning pick-me-up, shake off the cobwebs and start the weekend on a cheery note. This particular Saturday it's about noon when they kick me out. I say "they" though in truth there's but a single bartender, a joyless moonfaced hag named Lola. I say "kicked out" but in point of fact I'd run dry and Lola isn't known to serve on the house. Once you reach a critical impasse like that, you'd best pack up shop.

The day bright and warm in a courtyard hemmed by the office buildings of downtown St. Catharines, the squat trollish skyline aspiring to mediocrity and falling well short. A warm June breeze pushes greasy fast food wrappers and pigeon feathers over the cracked concrete of an empty pay-n-park lot between a tattoo parlour and a discount rug store. Sunlight reflects off office windows with such intensity I'm forced to squint. Got to assume I'm drunk: downed eight beers at the Mik and polished off 20 ounces of gin watching infomercials last night. Haven't slept in days but in high spirits nonetheless, though I must admit somewhat alarmed by what appear to be tongues of green, gold, and magenta flickering off the tips of my spread fingers.

A trash-strewn alleyway to my left empties onto King Street. Catching human movement and the echo of up-tempo music, I wander off in that direction.

King is closed off for a two-block stretch to host a 3-on-3 basketball tournament. Ball courts staggered down the road, three-point arc and foul stripes etched in sidewalk chalk. Mammoth speakers pump out rap music: guttural growls and howls overlaid with occasional gunshots and the clinkety-clink sound slot machines make paying off. Players sit along the curb in knee-length shorts, sleeveless mesh tops, and space-age sneakers, checking out the competition or waiting to be subbed in. The staccato rhythm of ball chatter underlies all other sound: *D-up! Get a hand in his face! My bad, my bad. You got that guy, man; you own him! Give you that shot – you can't stick that shit! All day, son, all damn day. And one! And ONE!*

Weave through duffel bags and water bottles and teams talking strategy, stop at a long corkboard to scan the tournament brackets. No names, just teams: Hoopsters, Basket-Maulers, Santa's Little Helpers, Highlight Reelers, Dunks Inc. If Jason was playing, he'd've given his old man a call, right? I went to every one of his high school games, didn't I? I say "went," past tense, due to the incident occurring at a preseason game out in Beamsville. I say "incident," but I suppose I might as well say "brawl," that broke out when a few Beamsvilleians – and when I say "Beamsvilleians," I mean, more accurately, "inbred hill-people" – took offense at my distinctive style of encouragement. I guess some punches were thrown. Well, the whole truth of the matter is that punches *were* thrown, first by me, then at me. Let me tell you, those bumpkins pack a mean punch – even the *bitches!* Thankfully, when you're three sheets to the wind you don't feel a whole lot of anything. Coach Auerbach politely insisted I curtail my attendance.

Meander down the sidewalk checking out the games. The majority are tactless, bulling affairs: guys heaving off-balance threes and clanging running one-handers off the front iron, banging bodies under the boards for ugly buckets. It's really quite a painful ordeal for me: a classically trained pianist watching chimpanzees bash away on Steinway pianos. Stop to watch

an old-schooler with Abdul-Jabbar eyegoggles and socks hiked
to his knees sink crafty hook-shots over a guy half his age; the
young guy's taking heat from his teammates for the defensive
lapses.

The final court has drawn a huge crowd; can't see more than
flickering motion between the tight-packed spectators, but from
what little I do it's clear this is serious. A true student of the game
can tell right off: something about those confident movements,
that quickness, the conviction that lives in each and every gesture.

Push through the crowd and there's my son.

He's at the top of the three-point arc. Long black hair tied
back with a blue rubber band, the kind greengrocers use to bind
bunches of bananas. Apart from giving you the look of a pansy,
long hair has a habit of getting in a shooter's eyes. But the boy
refuses to cut it so one time I chased him around the house with
a pair of pinking shears, screaming, *Swear to Christ I'm gonna cut
that faggot hair off!* I was gassed at the time; you tend to do crazy
things when you're gassed. He locked himself in the bathroom.
I told him I'd cut it off as he slept. He passed the night on the
floor, those hippie locks fanned out over the pissy tiles.

He takes the ball at the top of the key and bounces a pass to
Al Cousy, a thick-bodied grinder on Jason's high school team.
Al's a bruiser with stone hands who's going nowhere in the sport.
Way I see it, the sooner he comes to grips with this, the sooner
he can make an honest go at something more suitable: he'll make
a great pipefitter with those strong mitts. However it works out,
years from now Al can say, hunched over beers or gutrot coffee
at some union meeting, he'd once played ball alongside Jason
Mikan – yeah, *that* Jason Mikan.

Al pivots around his defender, gets blocked, shovels the
ball out. Jason catches it a few feet beyond the three-point line,
throws a head-fake to shake his defender, steps back and lofts

a shot. The ball arcs through sparkling June air, a flawless parabola against a blue-sky backdrop, dropping through the centre of the net.

"Nice bucket!" I call out. "Thattaboy!"

Jason looks over, spots me, glances away and claps his hands for the ball.

Watching that shot, the unstudied perfection of it, I think back to all the time we spent practicing together. Every day in good weather we'd be out on the driveway hoop, shooting until the sun passed behind the house's high peaked roof. Before Jason could quit he had to make 15 foul shots in a row; he'd sink 12 or 13 easy before getting the jitters. I even built a pair of defending dummies, vaguely human plywood cutouts with outstretched arms. These I mistakenly destroyed: stumble home less than sober and spy two menacing shapes in your unlit garage – who wouldn't kick them to splinters? One night I came back a little greased and dragged Jason out of bed. It was cold – had to knock a glaze of ice off the net – Jason there in his PJs and I chucked him the ball. *Every minute you're not practicing is a minute some other kid is. You got to* work, *son – hard and every day. Now can that fucker!* My neighbour Hal Lanier, beetle-legged and bucktoothed, sidled out onto his front stoop.

"Hey," he said. "You two mind calling it a night?"

"What business is it of yours, bud?"

Hal pulled a housecoat shut over a belly pale as a mackerel's. "Trying to sleep, is my business. Got your boy out here in his fuggin' jammies, screaming like a lunatic, is my business."

"Telling me how to raise my kid?"

"Telling you I got kids of my own trying to sleep."

"Why not come say that to my face, ya fat prick ya."

I'll admit to being a bit surprised when Hal took me up on this offer, crossing the frost-petaled lawn in his slippers to where I stood in my grease-smudged overalls, hitting me square in the face. Well! Down on the grass we go, rolling around chucking knuckles. *Shoot that goddam ball!* I kept screaming at Jason. *Fifteen foul shots before you go back to sawing logs!*

Jason's team is up 20-13 when he hits a fadeaway jumper from the elbow to win. The teams shake hands and head to the sideline, gathering duffels and water bottles. I trot over to Jason, who's speaking to a guy with a clipboard. For a moment I'm struck dumb with terror at what appears – and I feel a distinct need to stress this – what *appears* to be a cone of ghostly flame dancing atop the man's bald head. Whoa!

"Hey," I say a bit shakily, "great game there, kiddo."

"Yeah," says Jason, "thanks."

"This your father?" The fire on clipboard-guy's head is now mercifully extinguished. "Your son's a helluva player."

"Don't think I don't know it." I clamp a hand around Jason's neck, give a friendly squeeze. "Gonna redefine the game, this kid. Aren't you?"

Wincing, Jason shrugs out of my grip. "When do we play next?"

"Championship game goes in about 45 minutes."

"Alrighty then," I say once clipboard-guy has wandered off. "What do you say me and you grab a bite to eat before the big game."

"I don't know. We were gonna set things up – defensive assignments, rotations, that sort of thing."

Dart a glance at Jason's teammates, big Al and lanky Kevin Maravich. "Boys don't mind if I steal this guy for a bit, do you?"

The two of them shrug in that mopey sceptical way kids their age have: as though, instead of asking could I take Jason to lunch, I'd suggested enrolling him in seminary college.

"Great! Have him back in time for the game. Honest injun."

We head to the Mikado and find seats on the patio. Afternoon sunlight hits the scalloped glass tabletops, splintering in blazing pinwheels and fanwise coronets. Tempered light falls through the patio umbrella, touching the beaded perspiration on Jason's upper lip.

Lola's dog, a nasty-looking Rottweiler chained to the patio's wrought-iron fence, yammers as its owner waddles outside.

"Back again, mister?" Lola's sun-blotting bulk towers above me, Lola tapping a toothmarked Dixon Ticonderoga against an order pad. "What'll y'have?"

"A Bud and a shot a rye. This fella'll have a Bud, too."

"He gots ID?"

"Dad, I got a game."

"Sweet Jesus, Lola, he's got a game!" Suddenly I'm angry – furious, really – at Lola for permitting my son to drink before a ball game. "Get him a Coke and a grilled cheese – you *do* grilled cheese, don't you?"

"Kin whip one up."

"Fine. Wonderful." Shake my head, disgusted. "He's got a *game*, for Christ's sake. The *championship*."

Lola shrugs and wanders off to fill the order. I say, "Hey, got any grape soda?"

"Nope," Lola says without turning back. "Coke and ging-a-ale."

I wink at Jason. "Never hurts to ask. Know how much you love your grape pop."

An inside joke of ours. A few years back Jason and some buddies had a pickup game going when I returned from a morning shift. Head to the kitchen for something to wet the whistle and on the counter spy a bottle of grape pop I'd bought earlier that week – *dead empty*. Don't know why, but this pissed the almighty hell out of me; guess maybe I'd been thinking about it at the drill press – a tall cool glass of grape soda, all purple and bubbly. Sounds ridiculous, but at the time I could've spat nails and thundered outside brandishing the empty bottle.

"Which one a you shits drank my pop?"

The driveway game ground to a halt, everyone standing about staring at their sneakers. After a moment Jason said, "I did, Dad. Hardly any left, really."

I stalked over and rapped his head with the bottle. Thin plastic made an empty *wok* off his skull.

"You drank it *all?* Couldn't leave a goddam glassful for your old man?"

"There wasn't even a glassful left." Jason rubbed his scalp. "There was like, only enough that it filled those dents, the, the *nubbins* at the bottom of the bottle. And it was flat, anywa—"

Hit him again – *wok!* – and again – *pok!* – and for good measure – *tok!* Silence except for big Al Cousy dribbling the basketball and the hollow glance of plastic off my son's head. Jason's eyes never left mine, though they did go a bit puffy at the edges, skin above his cheeks pink and swollen as though some horrible pressure were building there.

"It's not the grape pop," I said, intent on teaching my son a valuable life lesson. "It's the… *principle.* Now get on your horse – I mean *right now* – ride down to Avondale and pick up a fresh bottle."

Jason pulled his bicycle out of the garage. "Guys oughtta head home."

"Yeah, why don't you boys skedaddle. Jason's got an errand to run."

He rode down the street round the bend. I stood rooted like a stump until he came back, bottle swaying in a plastic bag tugged over the handlebars. By then my anger had ebbed so I only swatted him good-naturedly and made him sink 20 three-pointers. Pretty silly, when you think back on it – I mean, *grape pop*, right? Which is why we can make a joke of it now.

Lola comes out with the drinks. Bolt back the shot of rye, suck down half a bottle of Bud, lean back in my chair. Feeling a little calmer, more inside myself, breathe deeply and smile.

"How come you didn't tell me about this – know how I like to watch you play."

"Sort of a last-minute thing." Jason cracks an ice cube between his molars. "The other guy came down sick. Didn't want to, but they were in a bind."

"Well, good thing – woulda got creamed without you."

"Didn't *want* to," he says with emphasis. "They were hard up."

"Yeah, the whole tourney's below your skill level; you're too good for these chumps. So, any offers from down south yet? About that time of year."

"One, from Kentucky-Wesleyan." A shrug. "Like, partial scholarship or something."

"Kentucky-Wesleyan? But... they're Div II."

Jason stares out across the courtyard, telephone wires bellied under a weight of blackbirds. "Yeah, Div II. Maybe nobody's gonna come calling. So what? There's other things I could do."

"Other things. Like what?"

"I dunno... could be, like, a nutritionist or something."

"A nutritionist? What, with the carbs and proteins? The food pyramid and... oh god, the *wheat grass*. Don't be an idiot. This is just the start. You're gonna want to hold off for the best offer – and hey, might even want to declare straight out of high school."

"Declare for what?"

"Declare for what, he says – the *draft*, dopey. The NBA draft."

Jason shakes his head and for a split second I want to reach over and haul off on him. Instead I finish my beer and when Lola comes out with the sandwich order another.

"How's your ma doing?"

"Fine." Jason takes a bite of grilled cheese. "She's fine."

"Must be weird," I say hopefully, "the two of you roaming around that big ole house all by your lonesome."

"Not really."

Jason's mother and I are experiencing marital difficulties. The crux of the problem seems to lie in the admission I may've married her with an eye towards certain features – her articulate fingers, coltish legs, strong calves – that, united with my own physical makeup, laid the genetic groundwork for a truly spectacular ball player. She claims our entire relationship is "false-bottomed," that I ought to be ashamed for aspiring to create some "Franken-son" with little or no regard for her "feelings." She refuses to accept my apology, despite my being tanked and overly lugubrious at the time of admission. I feel this not only petty of her but verging on un-motherly, what with our boy at such a crucial juncture in his development.

"Who's gonna string up the Christmas lights this year, huh?" I ask, despite having gone derelict on this particular household duty for years. "You'll be away at school."

"Do it before I go, Mom asks me to."

Lola arrives with another beer. "Well anyway, this'll all come out in the wash. Me and your ma just need some time apart. Lots of couples go through it, don't worry."

"I'm not worried."

Something in his tone gets my dander up: it's the tone of a truth-hoarder, a secret-keeper and now I really *am* going to smack the taste out of his mouth but my hand's arrested by the arrival of a pretty young thing who strikes up a conversation with Jason. Short but amply endowed – *built like a brick shithouse*, my old TRW crony Ted Russell would say – leaning over the patio rail in lavender tubetop, cheeks dusted with sparkling glitter, she says, "Hey there, cutie," in a high breathy voice. My son smiles as they ease into typical adolescent conversation: what so-and-so said about so-and-so, so-and-so's having a bush party tonight, so-and-so's an angel, so-and-so's a creep but drives a Corvette and all the while I'm staring – say "staring," but I suppose "leering" is more apt – at the girl, picturing her a few years down the road, that knockout body grinding up and down a brass pole or something. Leering at a ditzy cocktease no older than your son, a man is forced into one of two admissions: either (*a*) your son is more or less grown up, or, (*b*) you're a lecherous perv.

"Look at my boy," I say, brimming with drunken pride. "All grown up and talking to girls."

"C'mon, Dad," Jason says nervously, as though addressing the drunken uncle gearing up to spoil a wedding. The girl, who up 'til now has treated me with the brusque inattention reserved for houseplants, seems baffled and somewhat sickened to learn Jason is the fruit of my loins: like discovering the Mona Lisa was painted by a mongoloid.

"Got to see a man about a horse." Swaying to my feet, I add, "Forgot to hit the bank. Spot your old man a few shekels, wouldya?"

Jason sighs in a manner that suggests he'd been expecting this all along. Reaching into his duffel, he lays a 20 on the table.

"That's a good lad. Knew your ma wouldn't send you out empty-handed."

"It's *my* money, Dad. I like, earned it. At my *job*."

"Sure you did, sonny boy." Tip him a wink. "Sure you did."

Stumbling through the patio doors, I hear the girl say: "So that's your dad? *Weird*."

Bathroom walls papered in outdated concert flyers and old cigarette signs. Piss rises wick-like up the drywall in hypnotic flame-shaped stains. A fan of dried puke splashed round the base of the lone commode, dried and colourful gobbets. Disgusting, yes, but I cannot say with utter certainty I am not the culprit: the sequence of this morning's events remain hazy.

Relieving myself, my eyes are drawn to a snatch of graffiti on the stall: *For Sale: Baby Shoes. Hardly Worn.* Beneath this is written, *How about 10 bucks?*, and under that a crude etching of a droopy phallus with what appears to be a flower growing out the pisshole. Stare up at a light bulb imprinted with blackened silhouettes of charred insects, which for some reason remind me of the holographic shadows burnt onto brickwork at Hiroshima and Nagasaki. Standing there in the piss and puke and dim unmoving puppetshow thrown by the bug-tarred bulb, a sense of grim desolation draws over me — a sensation of *psychological dread.* Through the smeared casement window phantom shapes dart and cycle, dark tongues licking beneath the warped frame. The stall presses in upon me, walls buckle-crimping like the lungs of some great primordial beast. A trilling voice invades my skull: *Weird-Weird-Weird-Weird-Weird.* Reel from the stall and in the crack-starred mirror glimpse my eyes punched out and dangling on sluglike stalks and there deep in the cratered sockets spy another pair of eyes, red and raw and slitted lengthwise like a cat's, peering back without pity or remorse.

The episode passes and everything's a bit cheerier when I get back outside. Jason and the girl are gone. Lola's cleared away the bottles and settled the bill. Pocket the change, leave no tip. The Rottweiler barks wrathfully — has it been trained to sniff out skinflints like those airport drug dogs? "Hush'n, Biscuits," comes Lola's voice from inside.

With a few minutes to spare before Jason's game, pop into the liquor store. A homeless man squats outside the door begging bus fare. Where's the guy need to get to so badly? He doesn't ask anything from me. Wander air-conditioned aisles, past cognacs and brandies and aged scotch whiskies, arriving at a cooler stocked with screw-top Rieslings, boxed Chardonnays and malt liquors. Settle on a smoky brown bottle, label stamped with a snorting bull: a pluck malt best enjoyed on those occasions one finds oneself a bit down at the heel. Paying the cashier with the coins my son hadn't bothered to pick up, it strikes me I may've hit a new low.

It's not kosher to drink in public so I hunt through the liquor store dumpster. An empty Big Gulp cup – bingo! A wasp inside, big angry bastard must've crawled down the straw to get at the crystallized globes of Orange Crush clinging to the waxed insides. It buzzes away as I pour in the contents of the brown bottle, re-fasten the lid, and step onto the sidewalk well pleased with this subterfuge. Sucking merrily on the neon pink straw, I pause to consider who else's lips it may've come in contact with. Could've been anybody, you got to figure – a bum's, Christ, some scabby diseased *bum*, cracked lips rich with fungal deposits and now I'm wondering if 7-Eleven even *sells* soda to the homeless, if they conduct a brisk trade with this sort of clientele, and while I come to the reasonable conclusion that no, they clearly do *not*, I cannot help but feel the earlier sense of lowness I experienced was merely a staging area, a jumping-off point for this profound, near-subterranean, even lower low.

A teeming throng rings the championship court. Shove through the mob with an air of boozy entitlement – it's *my son* they're gawking at, isn't it? – to find the game's already started. Jason's team is matched against a trio of blacks whose voices betray an upper New York lilt: "trow" for throw, "dat" for that, "dere" for there, "dear" for dare, so what you here is *Trow dat shit up dere – go on, I dear ya!* Up from Buffalo with their dusky sunpolished skin, cornrowed hair and trash talk, figuring they'll take these pasty Canucks to school. Some bozo with a megaphone, the announcer I guess, does not call the game so much as cap each play with an annoying catchphrase: "Boo-*YA!*" or "Boom-shaka-laka!" or "Dipsee-doo dunkaroo!" or "Ye-ye-ye-ye-ye-ye-*YEAH!*" or just "Ohhh, *SNAP!*"

The other team is up 7-4 when Jason takes the ball at the top of the key. He dribbles right and bounces a pass to Al Cousy on the low block. Al rolls off his man, elevates and fires a one-legged jumper that clanks off rim.

"Don't pass to stone hands!" I cry. "Jesus, son – use your *head!*"

The other team's point guard executes a smooth crossover dribble – an *ankle-snapper* – catching Jason flatfooted. Kevin Maravich shuffles over on helpside defence but the guard flicks the ball to Kevin's check, who dunks two-handed and gorilla-hangs on the rim.

"Biggedy-*BAM!*" hollers the announcer.

Jason keeps passing to his tits-on-a-bull teammates. Kevin gets blocked twice and big Al puts up enough bricks to build a homeless shelter. Their opponents dish out a constant stream of trash: *Don't go bringing that weakass shit in here, bitch – this is my house! Hope you got an umbrella, son – I'm gonna be raining on you all day! Boy, my game's so ill I make medicine sick!* The ref, a balding old shipwreck in frayed zebra getup, lets the Yanks get away with murder: pushes, holds, flagrant elbows. I give it to him both barrels.

"Hey ref, if you had one more eye you'd be a Cyclops!"

"Hey ref, Colonel Mustard called – he said get a clue!"

"Hey ref, if your IQ was any lower someone'd have to water you!"

Spectators snorting and laughing, a beefy mitt slams be-tween my shoulder blades and someone says, "Thattaboy – stick it to the man!" Take a haul on my drink and for a long vacant moment feel nothing but relentless seething hatred for the ref, the opposing team, Jason's teammates, anyone and everyone trying to stop him from reaching the goal he's destined for, stifle the gift that'll take him out of this rinkydink town, far from the do-nothing go-nowhere be-nobody yokels surrounding me.

The score's 13-4 and Jason hasn't taken a shot. He kicks the ball to Al who kicks it back, a stinging bullet hitting Jason in the chest. "What are you doing? *Take it*, man." Jason stab-steps his defender, gives him a brisk shake-n-bake, shoots. As soon as the ball leaves his hands, you know it's good. It passes through so clean the net loops up over the hoop and that *sound* – dear god, almost *sexual*.

"This guy's dialled in long distance!" the announcer brays.

Jason picks the point guard's pocket on the next possession, clears beyond the three-point arc, fires. *Swish.* 13-9.

"He's shooting the lights out folks!"

The point guard muscles past Jason but Kevin gets a hand in his face and the shot misses short left. Al gobbles up the rebound and shovels it to Jason. The defensive rotation's slow and he gets a clean look from 22 feet, burying it. 13-12 and now the other team's a bit frazzled; "C'mon, naa," the point guard says. "D-up. We gut these bitches."

But it's too late: Jason's entered some kind of zone. Wherever he is on the court, no matter how tight the coverage, he's draining it. Running one-hander from the elbow – good. Fadeaway three-ball with a defender down his throat – good. High-arcing teardrop in traffic – good. In my head I'm hearing Marv Albert, longtime New York Knickerbockers play-by-play man and pur-loiner of women's undergarments: *Mikan takes the ball at the top of the circle, shakes his man, hoists up a prayer – YESSSSS!* Twisting circus shot around two defenders – good. Step-back three launched from another zipcode – good. The lead's flipped,

22-17; the Yanks' faces are stamped with grimaces of utter disbelief.

"This cat's got the *skills* to pay the *bills*, ladies and gentlemen!"

Throughout this shooting display Jason's expression never
changes: a vacant, vaguely disgusted look like he's sniffed something rank. He doesn't follow the ball after it leaves his hand, as
though unwilling to chart its inevitable drop through the hoop.
If you didn't know any better, you'd almost think he *wants* to
miss. Scan the crowd for a familiar face, my shitheel supervisor
Mr. Riley maybe – *See that, asshole? That's my son! My good genes
MADE that! What did your genes ever make, Riley? Oh, that's right
– a few stains on the bedsheets and a PUSSY TAX CONSULTANT!*

The game-winning shot's a doozy. Jason passes down to Al,
who is blocked but corrals the ball and shuttles it to Jason. The
other point guard's tight to his vest and Jason backs off, dribbling the ball high. Maybe it's just the malt liquor but at this
moment he appears to move in a cocoon of beatific light: glowing, sundogs and sparkling scintillas robe his arms and legs. He
goes right but so does his defender, swiping at the ball, almost
stealing it. They're down along the baseline, Jason's heels nearly
out of bounds and he shoots falling into the crowd, a dozen
arms outstretched to cradle him and as he's going down I hear
him say, in a small defeated voice, "Glass." The ball banks high
off the backboard and through the net.

"The dagger!" screams the announcer. "Oh Lord, he hits
the *dagger!*"

The crowd breaks up, drifting away in twos and threes to
bars and parks and restaurants. A work crew dismantles the nets
and sound equipment, packing everything into cube vans to
truck to the next venue.

"Great game, son." Somehow I've managed to slop beer
down myself so it looks I've pissed my pants. Try to pawn it off

as excitement. "A real barnburner – look, you got me sweating buckets."

Jason's sitting on the curb with his teammates. "Yeah, guess it was a pretty good one."

To Kevin and big Al: "Lucky Jason was here to drag your asses out of the fire, huh?"

They don't reply but instead pull off their shoes and socks, donning summer sandals. Big Al's toenails thick yellow and thorny, curling over his toes like armour plating.

"What say I take you boys out for dinner?" I offer breezily. "A champion's feast."

"That's okay," Jason says. "Kev's parents are having a barbecue. They've got a pool."

"A pool? How suburban." Jam one hand in my pocket, scratch the nape of my neck with the other. "So Kev, where's your folks' place at?"

Kevin hooks a thumb over his shoulder, an ambiguous gesture that could conceivably indicate the city's southern edge, the nearest town, or Latin America.

"Could I tag along?"

Jason sits with his legs spread, head hanging between his knees. "I don't know. They sort of, like, only did enough shopping for, y'know, us three."

"Well, wouldn't come empty-handed. I could grab some burgers, or… Cheetos."

"You see, it's like, we kind of got a full car. Y'know, Al and me and all our gear and stuff. Kev's only got a Neon, right?"

"We could squeeze, couldn't we? Get buddy-buddy?"

"I don't know. Gotta do some running around first."

"I love running around. It's good for the heart."

Without looking up, Jason says, "Dad, listen, Kev's still on probation – his license, right? – so, it's like, he can't have anyone in his car who's been drinking. If the cops pull us over, Kev'll get his license suspended."

"Oh. Alrighty then." Stare into the sky, directly into the afternoon sun. Close my eyes and the ghostly afterimage burns there as a sizzling imprint, searing corona dancing with winking fairy lights.

The boys gather their bags and water bottles. Shake Kev and Al's hands, hug my son. His skin smells of other bodies, the sweat of strangers. Used to love the smell of his hands after practice, the scent of sweat and leather commingled. When I let him go the flesh around his eyes is red and swollen and it gets me thinking of that distant afternoon, grape soda and a sense of horrible pressure.

"Great game," I tell him. "You're gonna show 'em all one day."

He walks down the street, hitching the duffel up on his shoulder. Charting his departure, it's as though I'm seeing him through the ass end of a telescope: this tiny figure distorted by an unseen convex, turning the corner now, gone. Sun high in the afternoon sky, brilliant and hostile, beer's all gone and it's the middle of the day though it feels like it should be later, much later and near dusk and it dawns on me I've nothing to do, nowhere to be, the day stretching out bright and interminable with no clear goal or closure in sight.

Nighttime at the Knightwood Arms subsidized housing complex. My bedroom window overlooks a dilapidated basketball court, tarmac seized and buckled, nets rotted from the hoops. Early mornings I'll head down and shoot baskets beneath a lightening sky, mist falling through the courtyard's arc-sodium lamp to create a cool glittering nimbus. Often someone'll crack a window in one of the overhanging units, *Knock it off with the damn bouncity-bounce.* Don't make much fuss anymore, just go back to my room.

Eleven o'clock or so and the bottle's almost empty when the phone rings.

"Hey," Jason says. "It's me."

"Glad to hear it."

"Yeah, well, wanted to talk to you about something."

Good news, I'm guessing: Duke, Kentucky, UConn. "Your old man's all ears."

"Well, it's like, I've decided to not play ball."

"You mean you're going to take the year off?" Try to remain calm. "Don't know that's the best idea, kiddo – gonna want to keep in the mix."

"No, I sort of mean, like… *ever.* I mean, *forever.*"

"Forever? Don't get you."

The mouthpiece is shielded. Jason's muffled voice, then his mother's then Jason's back on the line. "I'm sick of it. Sick of basketball. Don't want to play anymore."

"Well," I struggle, "that's… sort of a childish attitude, son. I don't always like my job, but it's my job, so I do it. That's the way the world… *works.*"

A sigh. "You know, there are other things in life. Lots of jobs out there."

"Yeah, well, like what?"

"I don't know," he says. "I was thinking maybe… a vet?"

"You mean… a veterinarian?"

"Uh-huh. Like that, or something."

"Oh. Well, that's… y'know… that's grand. The sick cats and everything. A grand goal."

"Anyway. Just thought I'd tell you."

"Yeah. Well… thanks. What say you sit on it a bit, Jason, let it stew awhile. Who knows – might change your mind."

"No, I don't think so. Alright, goodbye."

"All I'm saying is—"

But the line's already dead. Hang up and lie back on the mattress, stare out at the starblown sky.

When Jason was a kid I bought him this mechanical piggy bank. You'd set a coin in the cup-shaped hand of a metal basketball player, pull the lever to release a spring and the player deposited the coin in a cast-iron hoop. Jason loved the damn thing. Sit him on the floor with a handful of pennies: hours of mindless amusement. Every so often I'd have to quit whatever I was doing to unscrew the bottom, dump the coins so Jason could start over. The *snak-clanggg!* of the mechanism got annoying after the first half-hour and I would've taken it away if Jason wasn't so small and frail and I so intent on honing that fascination. There were other toys, a whole closetful, but he *chose* basketball. Right from the get-go. And yeah, I encouraged it – what's a father supposed to do? Guide his kid towards any natural inclination, gently at first, then as required. If that's what your kid's born to do, what other choice do you really have?

All I'm saying is, I'm no monster, okay? As a father, you only ever want what's best for your boy. That's your job – the greatest job of your life. All you want is that your kid be happy, and healthy, and follow the good path. That's all I did: kept him on the good path. I'm a great father. A damn fine dad. Swear it on a stack of bibles.

So my boy wants to be a veterinarian, does he? Well it's a tough racket, plenty of competition, no cakewalk by a long shot. Don't I know a guy out Welland way who's a taxidermist? Sure, Adam somebody-or-other, stuffs geese and trout and I don't know – bobcats? Ought to shoot him a call, see if me and Jason can't pop by, poke around a bit. I mean, you want to be a doctor, got to know your way around cadavers, right? It's the same principle. Adam's one easygoing sonofabitch; doubt he'll mind.

Yeah, that's just what I'll do. Finish off this bottle, hunt up that number, make the call. I mean, hey, sure it comes as a shock, but nobody can call Hank Mikan a man of inflexible fibre. When life hands you lemons, make lemonade. Life offers sour grapes, make sweet wine. A veterinarian, huh? Well, that's *noble*. Damn *noble*. And hey, money ain't half-bad either.

Let's finish this last swallow and get right on the blower. It's a long road ahead.

Like the shoe commercial says, right? Just Do It. Hey!

BRIAN FAWCETT

MY CAREER WITH THE LEAFS

I'll explain how I came to play hockey for the Toronto Maple
Leafs. It was surprisingly easy, and other people with similar
ambitions to play in the Big Leagues might be able to pick up
some valuable tips. I'm a poet, you see, and one of the things
we do as part of our job is an occasional public reading. I had a
reading to do in Toronto, and one of the first things I did when
I got there was to drop down to Maple Leaf Gardens. The day
I went, the Leafs happened to be practicing.

As I sat in the stands watching the Leafs skate around the
rink I got an idea. I walked down to the equipment room, and
politely asked a man who turned out to be the trainer if it
would be okay if I joined the practice.

"Sure thing," he told me, just like that.

I asked if I could have a uniform to wear.

"Sure," he said. "What number would you like?"

"How about number 15?" I said innocently.

The number belonged to Pat Boutette at the time, but he
was injured and I knew he wouldn't be around. I felt a surge of
ambition – maybe I could beat him out of a job! Minutes later
I was out on the ice with the Toronto Maple Leafs.

I skated around for a while, carefully declining any involvement in the passing and shooting drills while I tried to get my
floppy ankles to cooperate. Instead of cooperating they were
beginning to hurt, so I drifted in the direction of the coach,
Red Kelly, who was yelling instructions at the players. I leaned

casually on my stick the way I'd seen Ken Dryden do on television, and looked down at my skates. I watched the drills for two
or three minutes until the ache in my ankles started to fade, then
edged closer to Kelly.

"Mind if I take a turn?" I asked as evenly as I could.

"Not at all," he replied. "Let's see what you can do."

Somebody pushed a puck in front of me and as I reached for
it I tripped on the tip of my left skate and fell flat on my face.
What to that point had almost been a dream turned abruptly
into a nightmare. I lay on the ice for a second, peering at the
puck as if it had tripped me, and wondered why I couldn't wake
up. I thought about quitting then and there.

I had nothing to lose, so I didn't quit. I got up, picked up
my stick, and looked Red Kelly in the eye. He didn't move a
muscle – didn't laugh or anything. I pushed the puck forward
and skated after it in the direction of the goalie – it was Gord
McRae I think – slowly gathering speed. About 15 feet from the
net I deked to my left without the customary deke to the right.
The deke took McRae with it, and I cut to the right. The net was
wide open and I shovelled the puck into it on my backhand.

All of this is incredibly difficult for a left-shooting skater to
do. In fact, the whole manoeuvre is an impossible one, and
everyone who saw it knew, including Kelly, who was staring at
me with his mouth open. For my part, I had no idea how I'd
done it, except that it had been awful easy.

"No bad," Kelly shouted. "Not bad at all."

If scoring that first goal had been easy, the rest of the practice wasn't. I'm not a great skater at the best of times, and I was
not in shape. I seemed able to score goals almost at will, but I
had difficulty with the defensive drills, particularly the ones that
involved things like skating backwards. I fell several times, and
one time I went into the boards so hard that Kelly skated over
and told me to take it easy.

As the practice ended, he asked me if I could drop by his office after I showered. I told him I'd be pleased to, and after a shower I can't remember at all, I was sitting in a stuffed red naugahyde chair staring across a big desk at Red Kelly and Jim Gregory, the General Manager of the Leafs.

Kelly was writing something on a pad of yellow foolscap. Gregory did the talking.

"You've got some interesting moves out there," he said. "I caught the whole thing from up in the box. Where'd you learn your hockey?"

I decided to tell them the truth.

"Well," I replied, "I really haven't played organized hockey since I was about twelve. I watch *Hockey Night in Canada*, of course, and I guess I've learned a lot from that."

"Where do you come from?" he asked.

"That's kind of a hard question," I replied, trying to figure out what the truth was. "I'm from the West Coast. Well, not the coast, actually. I'm from up north."

"What brings you to Toronto?"

"I'm a poet," I said, "here on business, for a public reading."

"No kidding," he said, looking reasonably satisfied with my answer.

"I guess you know Rota. He's from up there."

I was stumped. I didn't know any writer from up north named Rota. Kelly saw my confusion.

"New kid," he said. "Plays for Chicago."

"I've heard of him," I shrugged. "But I never played with him. He's a bit younger than I am."

There was a silence, as if the two of them were trying to decide which of them should speak. Finally, Gregory stood up and cleared his throat.

"How would you like to play hockey for the Toronto Maple Leafs?" he said.

"I'd really like that," I said quickly. "I'd prefer to play just the home games, though. I hate travelling."

Gregory seemed puzzled by my request, but he agreed to it, probably because I didn't ask for anything else.

"We play Boston Monday night," he said. "We'll see you at the rink at 6 p.m." He paused. "Make that 5:30, and you can get in an extra half hour of skating."

I stood up. "I can probably use it," I smiled.

Kelly grunted, and then grinned, and I followed him out of the office and down the long concrete corridors of Maple Leaf Gardens to the players' entrance. He shook my hand.

"Good to have you with us," he said, with a lot of sincerity.

"It's good to be part of an organization that takes chances," I said, with even more sincerity. "Toronto treats its visitors well."

Kelly smiled and waved goodbye as I stepped through the open door into a fine early winter blizzard.

The next thing I knew I was sitting in the Leafs' dressing room beside George Ferguson, suiting up for the game. Kelly came in and announced the player assignments.

"Fawcett here is going to be playing home games for us," he shouted, pointing vaguely in my direction. "He'll play on the wing with Ferguson and Hammerstrom for a while, and we'll see how things go. Any questions?"

To my surprise, a fair number of the players knew who I was, and it turned out that some of them had even read my work. Out of the corner of my eye I saw the two Swedes, Hammerstrom and Salming, exchange glances. Maybe they thought having a poet on the team might take some of the heat off them. They were still relatively new in the league, and they were taking a lot of physical and verbal abuse from the rednecks and goons who were worried about foreigners changing the game and taking their jobs. The rap on the Swedes was that they were chicken, particularly Hammerstrom, who the papers were saying was allergic to the boards. Personally I thought his skating more than made up for those faults.

I wondered a little at Kelly putting me on a line with him, but decided that he was trying to compensate for my poor skating. Every team in the league would stick their goons on our line, that was certain. Kelly probably figured Hammerstrom would skate his way out of trouble, and I would talk my way out.

We'd see soon enough. It was nice to be able to play with Ferguson, who I thought was one of the smarter centres to come into the league in a while. I planned to do what any rookie should – keep my head up and my mouth shut. It would be a new way of working, that was for sure.

The first period of that game was nothing to remember. My check, predictably, was Wayne Cashman, probably the dirtiest player in the league. I went up and down my wing without incident, partly because Cashman wasn't much of a skater either. He cut me with his stick several times, but I didn't bleed much, and I ignored it when he got me with the butt end just as the period ended. I waited until I could breathe again and skated off to the dressing room with the rest of the team.

Early in the second period Lanny McDonald and Don Marcotte were sent off for trying to remove one another's vital organs, and Kelly sent me out with Hammerstrom on a 5-on-5. The Bruins sent out Greg Sheppard and Cashman. The faceoff was in our end, and Hammerstrom won it, got the puck back to Ian Turnbull, and he banked it around on the boards to where I was waiting. I circled once, almost lost my balance, and headed up the ice. As I crossed the red line, I saw Cashman skating toward me with a gleam in his eye. I kept going toward Orr at the blue line, did the deke to my left as if to move between Orr and the boards, and then cut sharply right. Orr went for the first deke and so did Cashman, who by this time was right behind me prodding at my liver with his stick. When I deked to the right,

Cashman ran into Orr and both of them went heavily to the ice. I had a 2-on-1 with Hammerstrom, and I slid the puck over to him. He drew Al Simms over, passed back, and I had only Cheevers to beat. I did it again; deked left, cut right, and plunked the puck over the bewildered netminder into the upper right corner of the net.

I stuck my stick up in the air the way I'd seen it done on television, and was trying to honk my leg when I ran into Hammerstrom and we both fell down. Turnbull came over to congratulate me and Salming skated over to dig the puck out of the net. He handed it to me, grinned, and said something in Swedish I didn't understand. Hammerstrom grinned at me the same way and pointed to Cashman, who was skating in small circles at centre ice with his head down.

It was a tight-checking game, and the score was still 1-0 halfway through the third period. That was as far as I got that night. I skated into the corner for a Ferguson pass, Cashman went in behind me, and only Cashman came out.

Eventually I came *to*, but that was well after the game was over. The Leafs had won it 2-0. Cashman got a penalty for hammering me, and Sittler scored on the ensuing power play. That's what they told me anyway.

I made it to the practice the next afternoon, none the worse for having spent the night in the hospital to make sure I didn't have a concussion. I didn't get much sleep because the interns kept coming in every half hour to see if I was going to go into a coma.

"Are you there?" they asked, and lifted my eyelids with one finger to flash their penlights at my pupils. About 4 a.m. a very young intern came in. He was a hockey fan.

"You're the new guy with the Leafs, eh?" he asked.

"Yeah," I croaked.

"Nice move you made on that goal you scored," he said. "Where'd you learn that?"

"Watching television," I answered, telling the truth.

"I hear you write poetry, too," he said.

My head hurt, so I just grimaced.

"Pretty strange," he said. "Watch out for Cashman."

He checked my eyes so carefully I thought he was looking for poems, but he said I'd probably be able to leave in the morning.

At the practice the next day, Ferguson told me to watch out for Cashman, too.

"You were lucky," he said. "Cashman spent two periods setting you up. We all knew it was coming, but I guess you had to pass the test like anyone else."

"Some test," I complained. "All I can remember about it is my bell ringing when it was over."

I played the three games in that home stand, scoring again in the last one against the Rangers, and setting up a goal by Ferguson. The team was away for the next three games, and then back for three more. While they were away I worked on my skating, circling the rink again and again until my ankles were too sore for me to move anymore. I tried skating without a stick, but found, as I had when I was a kid, that skating that way was beyond me. I needed the stick for balance and without it I could barely stand.

When the team came back, I confided to Ferguson that I couldn't skate without a stick.

"You're kidding," he said.

"No," I told him. "It's true. I only got skates every three years, and the first year they were too big and the third year they were too small."

Ferguson had a good eye for details. "What about the second year?" he asked.

"I had weak ankles back then."

"You still have week ankles," he said.

"I use the stick for balance," I said, as we went on circling the rink.

Ferguson was skating backward to tease me. "Skating is easy," he laughed. "For me it's like breathing."

"I feel that way about some other things," I replied, "but not about skating."

"You don't look as if breathing is very easy right now," he pointed out.

While we unlaced our skates after practice, he asked me cautiously what it was like to be a writer.

"It's my way of breathing," I said.

"How'd you get into it?" he asked with genuine curiosity.

"I guess I was about thirteen," I said. "Right after I quit playing minor league hockey."

Ferguson and I became friends. He taught me a lot of the basics of pro hockey and I gave him books to read in return. I was interested in Rilke and an American poet named Jack Spicer at the time, and he pored through everything I lent him. I always had books in my equipment bag, and he dug through it regularly to see what was there. He asked me if Canadian writers were as good as Americans.

"The old guys are pretty tame," I said, "but there's a few writers under forty who might turn out to be interesting."

"Jeez," he said, "how long does it take to get good at it?"

"Usually about 15 years of hard work," I said. "A few get good earlier than that because they have special attentions or come from environments that encourage them," I went on.

"But that's rare. Most of us have to learn pretty well everything about the culture twice, and that takes time. After that, there's the job of keeping on top of it as it changes. A lot of writers get one good review of their work and they have to please their public, or, worse, they decide that they're geniuses, and don't have to listen to anything. So they imitate themselves until they lose their ability to learn. After that they just get drunk, or academic, or spend all their time trying to please the reviewers and filling out grant applications."

He wanted to know about the grants, so I explained to him the economics of trying to be a serious artist in a country that wants to have serious art without having to put up with the inconvenience and cost of paying the artists.

He looked sceptical. "Except for that, hockey is pretty much the same," he said after a moment's thought. "Only hockey players get screwed up more easily and a lot faster."

"That's because there's more people paying attention," I said, "and there's more money involved."

That home stand was a good one. I scored my third goal, drew assists on one of Ferguson's, and another on the power play, passing from behind the net to Sittler in the slot. Only four goals had been scored while I was on the ice, and after seven games I was plus five. Then the Leafs were off again on a five-game road trip and I went back to my solitary skating, circling the ice over and over again until slowly, very slowly, my skating began to improve. I skated clockwise first, and then counter-clockwise. Going counter-clockwise was easier, maybe because on the corners my stick was closer to the ice. But I couldn't quite master skating backward, and stopping remained a problem unless I was close to the boards. But I developed reasonable speed skating straight ahead, and during games I combined my lack of stopping skill with my speed to provide the team with some excellent bodychecking.

Ferguson and I went out on the town the night after the team flew in from Los Angeles. He showed me the important sights of Toronto, like Rochdale and Don Mills, and later that night we walked down to Lake Ontario and threw rocks at all the empty milk cartons floating in the water. There had been a thaw, and it was like spring – dirty snow was piled up everywhere, abandoned cars were being towed off the streets, and the curious sensation I'd had of being in Middle Earth began to dissipate. There were lovers everywhere, discussing Parliament, and kissing and fist-fighting as the fog rolled in from the lake to meld with the darkness coming up from the East.

We played our only other home date of the season with the Bruins several weeks later. As the game approached, I got a lot of good-natured ribbing from the guys about what to do with Cashman.

"Check him into the boards with a powerful metaphor," advised Sittler.

"And then slash him with an internal rhyme," someone else chimed in.

I laughed at the gags, but deeper down I was worried. The press had picked it up and were amusing themselves, mostly at my expense. Alan Abel in *The Globe & Mail* wrote something about it being a test of whether the stick is mightier than the pen, and in an interview, Cashman noised it around that he not only disliked my style, he detested poetry. Anybody who wrote poetry, he said, had to have something wrong with their hormones. That wasn't all he said, either. He told the interviewer he was going to show the fans that there was something fishy about me, promising to make fillets out of me *and* my poetry.

As I skated out for the pre-game warm-up, Cashman gave me the evil eye, so I gave the fans a demonstration of how fast I could skate through the centre ice zone. Kelly, out of kindness I guess, kept our line away from Cashman's as the game began, but on the second shift I saw the Bruin right-winger head for the bench right after the faceoff, and Cashman came over the boards. Somebody froze the puck, and as we lined up for the faceoff deep in Bruin territory, Cashman skated up to the circle, and around me once with his stick about a quarter of an inch from my nose.

"I hope you got a nice burial poem written for yourself," he sneered. "You skinned my behind and I'm gonna carve yours off and throw it to the crowd."

I looked him right in the eye and mustered up all my powers of language.

"Suck eggs," I said.

On the faceoff Ferguson drew the puck back to Salming and I skated to the corner to wait for a pass. Cashman ignored the puck and followed me. I ducked an elbow. It missed me, but the Ref didn't miss it, because I slid down the boards as if I'd been pole-axed. Cashman got whistled for an elbowing penalty, and then got a misconduct penalty when he tried to chase me into the stands. I skated away from him, and three of my teammates stayed between us to make sure I stayed alive. Kelly kept me on for the power play and I banged Sittler's rebound past Gilles Gilbert to make it 1-0.

When I got to the bench, Kelly told me Howie Meeker wanted to interview me after the first period. It was Saturday, and the game was being televised nationally.

I'd forgotten it was *Hockey Night in Canada*. You get like that in the Pros – you forget everything that makes the world tick for real people. You also pay a price. The price I was going to have to pay for my forgetfulness was an awful one. I hadn't brought any poems in my equipment bag. I was being handed the largest audience any poet in this country ever dreamed of and I wouldn't have a thing to read.

A few minutes later I was sitting in front of several television cameras with the customary towel over my shoulder, watching Howie Meeker introduce me to the nation and thinking that the dream was going to turn into a nightmare if I couldn't think of something quickly. My mind was a blank.

"We've got Toronto left winger Brian Fawcett here in the *Hockey Night in Canada* studios at Maple Leaf Gardens," Meeker announced in a voice that sounded more nasal in real life than on television.

He was hunched toward the cameras and I noticed he sat closer to them than I did. I hadn't seen a brush cut for years or, for that matter, as much makeup as he had on his face, and I was sorting through all that novelty without listening to what he was saying. Luckily, he was babbling as inanely as usual at the camera and ignoring me completely:

"...nice to see a young player come up to the NHL with a good grasp of hockey fundamentals and play sound, heads-up positional hockey the way you've been doing. Gee whiz, but I just get thrilled when I see a young kid with his mind on the game skate away from a player like Wayne Cashman. And it pays off, don't you see? It must have been less than a minute before you scored that beautiful goal like you were born with a stick in your hand and skates on your feet."

He hadn't actually asked me a question, but he seemed to have finished.

"Actually, Howie," I said, too nervous to do anything but tell the truth, "I haven't played much hockey since I was twelve or thirteen years old, and I'm thirty, so I'm not much of a kid any more. I've been mainly concerned with language, and more specifically with disjunction in poetry, for the last few years. You might say I've been learning the tools of an extremely complex trade."

Meeker appeared not to have understood. Maybe he thought I was speaking French. He ignored everything I said, and went off on another rant.

"Well, Brian, how do you like being with a team like the Leafs, eh, with their tradition of ruggedness and hard work?"

"Well, Howie," I said, still not sure if he realized that I understood English, and pretty sure he didn't know I was a poet. "I find the ruggedness something of a problem. Northrop Frye and Margaret Atwood created a problem a few years ago by writing some books about the importance of Nature and the frontier, and a lot of similarly empty glamour nonsense about rugged Canadian pioneers, and as a result a lot of the writers in this country now go around wearing logging boots and punching people for no reason. I used to do it myself, actually."

Meeker was staring at me, his jaw somewhere down around his navel. I took this as a signal to continue.

"I mean, violence may be natural, but Nature isn't a very good model for behaviour. It's been really overestimated."

I knew I was gesticulating too much, and starting to yap. I'd forgotten about the cameras – it was Howie Meeker I wanted to convince. I couldn't stop.

"Art is really about civilization," I said, "not about Nature. All Nature does is overproduce, then waste most of it, and then resort to violence when the garbage starts to stink. When human beings follow Nature, you get guys like Hitler."

I was really flying, so I went to Meeker's question about hard work next.

"Hard work, like you say, is really important, Howie. The more I know about this game, the more I begin to realize that the real secret is hard work. I guess that goes for hockey as well."

Meeker, for some reason, seemed to have lost his voice, so I went right on.

"If you'd given me a little more notice, I could have brought some work here to read, but I guess these interviews are a bit too short to give the folks at home any real idea of what's going on, let alone a sense of the breadth and skill and variety of good writing going on in this country today."

Meeker stuttered back to life.

"Ah, ahhh… Yes, well… Well, Brian, I wish you and the Leafs the best of luck in the upcoming second period," he said, regaining a measure of control that didn't show in his face.

"Back to you, Dave Hodge!" he said hoarsely.

I smiled politely at the camera until fade-out. I'd seen a few guys start to pick their noses when they thought they were off-camera, and I wanted people to remember what I'd said.

Meeker turned on me. "What was that all about, you crazy sonofabitch?"

I began to explain, but he walked out of the studio without listening to my answer.

The dressing room was oddly silent when I returned. I sat down next to Ferguson and pulled the towel from around my neck. He was sitting with his head between his knees, as if he were air-sick.

"Didn't you know about Meeker?" he asked incredulously.

"Know what?" I said, stuffing the towel into my equipment bag as a souvenir. "He seemed kind of ticked off when I talked about writing, but then he did ask those dumb questions, and he didn't stop me from answering them the way I wanted to."

"Geez man, that's the unwritten law of hockey," Ferguson said. "You're supposed to pretend you're really dumb."

It was my turn to be incredulous.

"Darryl thinks there's some kind of agreement between the owners about it," he said. "When you get out of Junior hockey, you're given a sheet of things you can say to the press. You talk dumb, talk about teamwork, and all that crap."

My head was reeling. When I was a kid I believed that the world was full of secret rules and conspiracies, but this was real life – the Big Leagues. I couldn't believe what I was hearing.

"I mean, a few years ago," he continued, "when Kenny Dryden started getting interviewed, he used all kinds of literate words like 'tempo' and so on, pronounced all the words properly, and there was a terrific uproar. But he was in law school and they had to accept it. I dunno. They may get him yet – force him to retire."

Ferguson shrugged, and a note of hopelessness entered his voice. "Rumour is," he said, "that this whole business about us being stupid and inarticulate is an explicit policy of the Feds – right from the top."

I looked around me to see if he was kidding. A couple of guys just nodded and looked the other way, but most of them were glaring at me. Kelly looked really angry.

"Aw, come on, you guys," I said to no one in particular. "Why put up with this? I've seen what's really true. Look at the books lying around the dressing room."

Several players slipped large hardbound books into their equipment bags. Sittler, everyone knew, was a big Henry James fan – said it helped his passing game. And Tiger Williams had come up from Junior already heavily into Artaud. The league had its share of jerks, it was true, but unless you noised it around, you were left alone if you had intellectual interests. I guessed they were mad at me because they thought I might have let the cat out of the bag. Hockey, Kelly told me later, was in enough trouble.

There was a TV set in the dressing room, and we watched as Meeker came on the screen to do the highlights of the period. My goal wasn't one of them. A few of the guys exchanged significant looks, but everybody remained seated, as if they were watching something very sad.

When a commercial came on, I asked Ferguson who'd died.

"You did, dummy," he said.

"Aw, come on," I said. "Why? Is it that bad? All I did was to get Howie Meeker mad at me."

"It's a lot worse than you think. You'll be blacked out," he said, grimly. "No radio perks, no television interviews, and as little newspaper coverage as they can give you. What you *will* see will all be bad."

"That's okay," I said, philosophically. "I'm pretty used to that."

I scored the winning goal in the third period by going around the defense in the usual way, and I didn't even get third star. I went up and down my wing against Cashman, took his checks, many of which were flagrantly vicious and should have drawn penalties, and I threw a couple of my own in his direction. Cashman was given third star, actually, and Meeker said he was the one Bruin on the ice who had dominated his opponent.

Ferguson and I had a few beers after the game. I invited the rest of the guys, but nobody seemed interested.

"You're really a goof," Ferguson said cheerfully. "Do you know that?"

"How was I supposed to know?" I said, irritably. It seemed like everybody knew the rules but me.

"Look," I said, "I didn't go through the system like you guys did. For me it was all watching the tube, and thinking about it.

How was I supposed to know – I mean, I've never believed much of what I've seen on televisions, but I did think *Hockey Night in Canada* at least was for real."

Ferguson grunted. "Rules are rules," he said. "Nobody but you believes they're supposed to be just."

"I'd settle for knowing what they are," I said bitterly.

"Would you really?"

"I'm not sure," I admitted. "I guess I really want to know who the big shots are who make them."

I didn't find out who the big shots were, that night or on any of the ensuing nights that season. I played my hockey as well as I could, and I played it in more or less the kind of obscurity I had been warned to expect. I scored nine goals and built 12 assists in 27 games, and I was invited back for training camp the following season even though I played increasingly less often toward the close of the season.

As I was packing up to go home, the two Swedes came over and mentioned how much they'd enjoyed my presence during the home games, and asked if I'd be able to visit them in Sweden during the summer.

"I've got a lot of writing to catch up on," I told them. "My season's really just starting now."

Salming grinned that same grin I'd seen in my first game.

"I understand this," he said. "No fun to go to Sweden if you're interested in the Pros in English language."

"Something close to that," I admitted.

He and Hammerstrom left the dressing room laughing. They sure weren't like the Scandinavians I knew from watching Ingmar Bergman movies. I wandered over to where Ferguson was packing his equipment, and said goodbye. His bag was full of books, and he was having a hard time getting them all in.

Finally, he had to give up, and he left with a pile of them under one arm. He turned at the door.

"I'm going to try to write some stuff myself this summer," he said. "Mind if I send you some of it?"

"Do," I replied. "You've got my address?"

"Sure have," he smiled. "Well, see you. Stay in shape."

"You too," I said. But I was talking to his shadow. He'd disappeared.

That summer passed in a flash, and by mid-September I was back skating and shooting again with the Leafs. The season started, and by December I had four goals and as many assists and, I thought, I was doing okay.

But the team wasn't doing well at all. We were fourth in our division, and Ballard could be heard snorting and snuffling all the way to Buffalo.

Then, before a practice right after a road trip that had gone badly, King Clancy walked into the dressing room, announced that Kelly had been fired, and that John McLellan was the new coach. Two days later Ferguson was traded to Pittsburgh. The day after that, McLellan called me into his office.

"Brian," he said, "I talked things over with Jim, and we, uhh…"

He seemed to be stumbling for the right words.

"We don't think your heart is really in this game. You're not skating…"

"I can't skate," I cut in, but he ignored that and went on.

"We want you to retire."

"I'm practically a rookie!" I sputtered.

"You're thirty-one," he said, "and you're not going to get any better. Meeker is still after your behind, and you're a target for every goon in the league. Both Jim and I spent some time over the summer reading you work. You're a better poet than a hockey player. You've got to go for that."

I fussed and fumed, but I ended up agreeing with him. I had two, maybe three years of good hockey in me. With poetry I had maybe 40 years, and I would only get better. I'd miss the crowds and the attentiveness of the critics, even though they'd done a good job of ignoring me. But I wouldn't miss Toronto and its bars, and I wouldn't miss the poetics, which, try as I did to ignore them, are as venal and profit-oriented at Maple Leaf Gardens as they are in the English departments of the nation's universities. If more poets were to play hockey instead of pretending flowers or vacant lots are really interesting, things might get better. But I wasn't going to hold my breath.

"You're right," I told McLellan. "I'll retire right now."

And I did. I walked out the way I had come in, gave back the blue on white and the number 15, and stepped out into the dull Toronto streets as if it were the next morning and not the next year I'd awakened to.

Three weeks later I got a letter from Ferguson, postmarked Atlanta. In it was this poem:

> It's cold in Pittsburgh, colder still
> in Philly. The north wind blows all night
> from Canada, and these raucous crowds
> that hoot and holler for our blood, Hey!
> They're the coldest thing of all.
> Skate and shoot, the coaches tell us
> Skate and shoot. But masked men block the goals
> and I am checked at every turn.
>
> Each year more miles to go
> More senseless contests of the will.
> My heart is like the puck; often frozen
> too often out of play, too often
>
> stolen by the strangers
> in the crowd.

KATHERINE GOVIER

ETERNAL SNOW

It was late afternoon when we arrived at the parking lot halfway up the mountain. The gondola terminal rose out of the snow, a space station, bright orange and blue girders like mechanical arms reaching up through the slash where the trees had been. I stretched in the thin air.

"Last chance to change your mind."

My voice was loud and hollow. Bill said nothing, so I slammed the car door: beside me, several little balls of snow separated themselves from the overhanging lip and rolled down to the packed road bed, a miniature avalanche. It reminded me of how my stepfather Harvey used to go shooting avalanches with the ski patrol. They'd ski across to the danger spots and then raise their guns, firing blanks, and the loud retorts would bring down perhaps a ton of snow.

"The snow looks great," I added.

"There's enough of it."

Bill had never been there before.

We lifted our suitcases and our skis out of the trunk of the car. I shouldered my skis the way I'd been taught to when I was six. This year I had fancy new bindings with brakes; they dug in behind my collarbone and hurt. But I picked up the suitcase in the other hand. Bill had his skis and the Adidas bag we'd filled with liquor for our week at the top of the mountain.

It was beginning to snow thickly, in tiny dry flakes. The man who sold us our tickets for the gondola said that it had come down like this every night for a week.

On the platform we watched gleaming egg-shaped capsules swing down from the slope and into the terminal, caught in their bobbing by boys in orange parkas, who walked them to a stop. People who worked at ski resorts always looked the same: ruddy faces, bleached-out hair, the genial, bland expressions of beach bums. I'd known kids from high school in Calgary who'd turned out like that: they went to live in Banff and took jobs as chambermaids or tow attendants just so they could have free skiing on their off hours. They'd be nearly thirty now. I wondered what became of old ski bums.

It used to be that you parked your car here and rode the next few miles in an old glass-topped tourist bus. The bus drivers spoke to one another over a crackling radio. "Fifty-seven at number six, coming around." The turns in the road were numbered. Sometimes you had to pull over and let another bus pass, going the other way. Back then, Sunshine was a private domain for the hardy mountaineers in leather boots and woollen pants which bloused at the ankle. The change had been gradual: metal skis, buckle boots, more cars, a day lodge, and then the hotel. This Swiss gondola was the latest, new this year. It was supposed to be the longest in North America, with four separate cables and two mid-stations along its course. It brought all these spacemen in their padded jumpsuits and their moulded plastic boots which looked like they were filled with lead to help the wearers cope with zero gravity.

The orange-parka boy gestured us to a cab and held the outside rail to steady it as we stepped in. The doors shut with an electric clap. It was meant to seat six, but we were alone inside: only hotel guests went up at this hour of the day. We sat on opposite sides and stretched our feet into the centre to touch.

I wanted Bill to know all of what I was thinking, to see how this place had been in the past. But he came from the east where I lived now, and he couldn't help but be a tourist, like the Japanese, the Americans. I felt the huge inertia of my unspoken emotions, a swelling resentment. I hadn't told him much. I wanted him to just know. It seemed to me that once no words had been needed. I had an image of being beside a man and having perfect, unspoken understanding.

The boy let go of the gondola and we jolted ahead. Looking out the plastic window I saw briefly the brown edges of old snow around the cuts for the road. Then we lifted high over the gulches and the spindly tops of half-buried trees. The ones with narrow forked tips we'd called "spinsters."

The white surface was 40 feet below us: the snow cover, who knew how deep, over the ground. All you could see was white. I could tell Bill was disappointed in the view. I was too. I had liked it better from the road. I remember looking out the window of the bus. I would have been eight or nine and Harvey was sitting beside me. "Is that eternal snow?" I had asked him, repeating a phrase from my geography book. Eternal snow lasted through all seasons: it never melted. I knew he would be pleased that I had heard of it. He gave me a quick look but didn't acknowledge – he never had – my cleverness. He looked straight ahead. "Not here," he said, "but a little further up."

Our room was smaller than I had imagined. Bill took one look at the little window, the double bed pushed into an alcove, and single chair beside it and suggested that we go to the lounge for a drink. The lounge was called the Chimney Corner. It was dominated by a two-storey stone fireplace. A three-piece rock group was playing "American Pie." *"Bye, bye Miss American Pie, Drove my Chevy to the levy but the levy was dry…"* Around the table sat the skiers, with their boots yawning open, buckles clacking. The day was over; these were the overnight guests, staying for the week as we were.

Firelight reflected triangles of red cheeks, thick necks, everywhere the arrow-head shape of bodies bulging out of unzippered jackets, turtlenecks. I wondered if Bill realized what it was to come to a chalet at 10,000 feet on a snow-driven pile of rocks in March with only a gondola that stopped at 6:00 p.m. for escape. When the light went off the mountain, there would be no place to come but here. These people would be our companions.

The roomful of faces was like an abstract painting. I saw the colours, the metallic lines, human shapes broken into bits. I knew it would change by the end of the week; it would be as if I had stood in the museum long enough to know the hidden objects in the work – lunchbox pear, table leg, glove. I would recognize every face and know the person it presented; at least I would know that facet of a person that he chose to be during a week's holiday with strangers.

But now we knew no one. We found a seat as near the fire as possible and ordered bloody caesars – in honour of the west. We held hands across the table. I looked outside. The tow had closed now, and the last skiers struggled up the slope to the lodge. Directly below us there used to be a small log cottage called Snowflake. We stayed there as a family in the fifties. When my father was alive, my mother used to go skiing with us. I was too young to remember much, but when I think back, I see myself walking out the door of that cottage, the snow on either side of the path as high as my parents' heads. After my father died and my mother married Harvey, only he and I went skiing. I think I loved Harvey more than my mother did. Often at Sunshine we would meet a woman who worked in Harvey's office. I would see her standing in the lift line and pretend that

I didn't. "Oh look," Harvey would say in a tone of false surprise, "there's Miss Corbett."

The music stopped, and a tall dark woman in a green sweater, her matching jacket hanging from a crooked finger, walked into the lounge. Everyone looked at her, not only because she timed her entrance so well, but because she was over six feet tall and her black hair hung down to the middle of her shoulder blades. She walked between the tables and found a seat right in front of the fire, a single seat. The back of her head was between Bill and me. Her hair was so shiny it was blue, like steel. She ordered a drink, and within minutes a man was leaning over to speak to her. She answered him but kept staring into the fire. Then another man came up and tried.

"You know what she is?" Bill whispered.

"What?"

"A skiing prostitute."

"You're not serious."

"Sure. They'd have to have them, in a place like this. You get your wealthy businessmen up here, they want to do something for the night. You can't get down the mountain, so... The management would know that she was here; they'd probably even give her special rates. She'd have just come one weekend and decided to stay. High-class prostitute. You can tell by the clean hair. Men like these would be worried about disease. The clean hair would reassure them."

Snow, when you poked a hole down six inches with your ski pole, is blue. Harvey used to say it reflected the sky, but I've noticed it's blue even when there are clouds. The sun did not shine that week, but the fresh snow kept coming, covering the hills every night with powder. The experts were ecstatic: in the morning you could ski over great trackless fields that swallowed your skis whole and let you skim like a bird over water, throwing up a cockscomb of the fine white stuff. I had never been able to ski powder well, though. You have to forget about edging, holding back; you just have to let your skis lie flat, keep your weight low, and stay close to the fall line. It takes nerve. I remember following Harvey straight downhill in the deep powder: I got going too fast and couldn't turn so I opened my arm and skied into a tree.

"Don't unweight," my instructor told me. "Just give in to it." He was a man of about fifty, with red hair and a grizzled face. He had a trucking business in northern Manitoba, but he came here every year to teach skiing for six weeks. It was the only way he ever stayed married to his wife, or so he told me. He had a sign on his fanny pack that said "Skiers make better lovers."

Bill and I were in the same class. I had more experience but he had less fear; in the powder we both floundered and fell a lot. We tried hard for the first three days. We had a lot of scotch that night and became living proof that high altitude increases the effects of alcohol: more was the only solution to our hangovers. On the fourth day we took up a wineskin of port. We tried a slope that was called the Great Divide. If you drew a line among the peaks following the height of land, you'd have found the Divide: on the one side all the water flowed west to the Pacific and on the other it flowed east. The Great Divide coincided with the border here. We passed signs that said "Leaving Alberta, Welcome to Beautiful British Columbia!" and then two minutes later a sign that said "Welcome Back to Sunny Alberta!" Bill took pictures from our chair.

On the way down we stayed on the sides. In a sheltered place we propped up our skis and began to drink. We laughed and I started pushing him around. He's a lot bigger than I am; he pushed me back into the drifts so that I sank past my waist and couldn't get up. I struggled out and into my skis, feeling very huffy, and we went down for lunch.

By then we knew a lot of faces in the dining room. They belonged to lawyers and accountants and Canadian Tire dealers and their wives with four sons. The women had been librarians until their second child was born and now were so busy and so game that everyone marvelled. There was a bachelor stockbroker who touched up his skiing every summer in the Andes and a doctor alone with his two children, who said his wife didn't like to ski. He made me think of Harvey. Ronald was his name, and on the first day he developed a crush on me. He'd barge in on the lines to share a chairlift. Bill and I had thought it was funny.

"There's your beau."

"Who, Ronald? He's not. Look, he's dropped me."

It appeared to be true. Ronald, who'd gazed at me across the dining room, who'd come over with his sullen daughter to eat with Bill and me only the day before, was gracing the next table, rubbing elbows with the tall woman with the blue-black hair. Bill put his arm around me to draw me out of my bad humour.

"He still likes you. He's just trying to make you jealous."

I looked at Ronald's daughter. Once in Banff Harvey and I had gone for dinner with Miss Corbett from his office, and he had taken me back to the hotel room first. "I'll just see Miss Corbett home," he had said. I had just lain in my bed waiting for him to come for an impossibly long time. We shared a room; that was the type of economy Harvey was given to, although he had no need. Finally I had fallen asleep. In the morning he'd been just the same as before. I couldn't see Ronald's daughter anywhere.

"I'm sick of skiing," I said.

"I think I might take a lesson in the powder."

"Good idea." I didn't want to take a lesson. I knew I could not give myself up to that edgeless snow. It was like asking me to jump out of an airplane. No thanks.

"Maybe I'll go down the gondola and see how Banff has changed."

He didn't react to the way I'd excluded him but, typically, turned to the bus schedule.

"Just make sure you get back before the gondola closes at six."

"I'll take a cab."

It was the first time we'd been apart all week. I wore my knee-high sheepskin boots and beige cords and felt all unfettered after the ski gear. I was happy, sinking back on the gondola seat alone. Bill didn't take to Sunshine well. I noticed there were things I didn't like about it now too, but I had my loyalties to the past, and I wanted him to feel the specialness of the place even if it was gone. Unfair, wasn't it?

I looked down at the chairlift as I passed over and saw my admirer, Ronald, waiting in the line with the tall dark-haired woman. She was leaning forward on her poles, sliding her long legs back and forth along the snow. Switch, switch, switch. "You know what men call legs like that?" Bill had said. "Skullcrushers." He liked to say these things and see the combined shock and glee on my face. I didn't want to believe half of it, but I loved hearing what men said among men, echoes of a forbidden world. Because of the legs, we had taken to calling the woman in green Miss Tongs.

Miss Tongs sat every night in front of the hearth. A stream of men approached her. First guests, then instructors, then the employees of the lodge. She spoke to them all. Sometimes she got up and left the room, apparently following one of them. She always came back alone. Maybe Bill was right about her. Probably she was just what Ronald needed, I thought furiously from my gondola, my gaiety dissolving. Ronald had no pride. I couldn't understand this lack of pride in men. My best friend once told me that she had gone to meet her father in a New York hotel and had caught him on the telephone summoning a prostitute. "They all do it," she said. Do they? In places like this? If Harvey did, what did that make me – a victim or an accomplice?

Banff had changed from a mountain village to a tourist town in the years since I spent summers and school holidays there. The buffalo paddock still stood and the carved wooden bear by the museum, but new motels and condominiums built of cedar lined Banff Avenue, and the old hotel where the bus station was had burnt and had a new front. The Banff Café was still there. I went in and had a bowl of chicken noodle soup because I was cold. Once I'd been sitting there with a friend and the waitress had brought me a milkshake which I hadn't ordered. She said it was a gift but wouldn't tell me which of the boys at the counter had sent it. Later my friend and I walked out on the street, and the telephone rang in a booth on the corner. I answered it: it was for me. The same boy. He was across the street and wanted to ask me for a date. Boys had always liked me, and I had never been sure why. Similarly, I didn't seem to know if I liked them or not.

I went to the Quest shop and bought some earrings just to remind myself that this was today, not 10 years ago, to prove that I existed now. Then I got a cab back to the parking lot.

It was after five o'clock. Snow was falling. The light had grown extremely flat earlier, and already most of the skiers had given up. I was glad I'd arrived before six; you never knew if they might shut down the gondola early, and then I would have been stuck in Banff for the night. Lonely and tired of memories, I was anxious to see Bill all of a sudden.

I was the only person going up. Four gondolas stood in line and the cable wasn't running. I chose the front cab. I could hear the boys talking in the control box.

"Won't it? It did that last time. Just throw it harder. Harder."

The gondola jolted forward three feet and then stopped. My cab moved just beyond the edge of the platform: below me was the road past the brown snow. The car swung. I was still close enough to hear the voices.

"I don't know – sometimes it stops and sometimes it goes." One boy pulled on a lever while the other laughed and boxed at his back.

I turned away, and then I was off. It was cold already, and the early mountain darkness was coming fast. I was hoisted over the disused bus route and into miles of snow. At first there were faces in the descending cabs on my right, the last skiers going out. Then there was no one. I was the only living thing.

The mountain was completely silent except for the low running of the electric cable, a sound like the purr of a refrigerator. I had never been alone on a mountainside before. I almost cried, I was so impressed by the hugeness of the rock and the whiteness of the snow, the thick sky over it. Suddenly the gondola seemed right. This was the visit I wanted with my landscape. I knew that snow so well. Moving over top it all I felt I was being carried to something stupendous. Then the purr stopped. My gondola swung just a little and was still.

I dangled there. Moments passed, and a sense of abandonment dawned. I coached myself not to panic. In ski class, Ronald had told a story about a man left overnight on the chairlift at Mount Tremblant. We'd also heard about the daredevil who went over a cliff right here on Brewster Rock. When they found him, the largest piece of his boot was the size of a potato chip. Or so people said. Ski stories involved putting oneself in danger of health, flirting, skirting the uninhabitable areas of earth, surviving where you couldn't survive; that was the whole idea. I wiggled my toes. The sheepskin boots were good but the cord pants a disaster: I had no long johns on either. The cable stretched in front of me, motionless.

Perhaps the gondola had been shut down for the night. Perhaps the operators had forgotten I was on it: they'd looked pretty careless. I don't wear a watch, but I could feel time passing in my numbing toes, my stiffening fingers. My backside was turning to ice. The man on Mount Tremblant had lived, but it couldn't have been this cold.

When we used to ride up on the bus, we would get stuck. Sometimes we had to get out and push the vehicle out of the drifts at the side of the road. It would slant and heave, the skis stowed in racks along its sides clanging. But we always got out of the drift, we arrived at the lodge safely. The gondola was different, massive, electronic, impervious to human intervention. Should I close or open the window? Perhaps I could force open those electrically sealed doors and jump. It looked to be about 30 feet down at this point. But I had no skis. What if the snow was bottomless? I might sink over my head and not be able to move.

In any case, I wouldn't know which way to go once I got off. I didn't remember now on which side of me the road lay. If I found it, I could simply walk uphill and know that I would eventually reach the lodge. But what if I couldn't find it? Or what if I jumped and hit a rock and broke a leg? I'd have to judge the odds. Stay in the gondola and freeze helplessly or jump and risk the other dangers on the chance of reaching warmth. I decided it was too early to make a decision. Hold on, I told myself, you'd be really mad if you jumped and then the gondola began to move.

The purr started suddenly and the gondola jerked ahead. I was relieved, but not fully. I had the feeling that I'd glimpsed the face of my death and that he was circling to return. I passed the first way station. There was an orange-parka boy in there, clapping his huge mitts together. He saluted me merrily in my freezing bubble. I did not open the window or speak. I did not try to get out.

When the gondola stopped a second time, I wondered why I had done that, why I had gone meekly past the person who might be my last possible rescuer. Perhaps I was already suffering from hypothermia and had lost my judgement. This time I was dangling near a support pole. I began to wonder if I could reach the pole by climbing over the top of the gondola, as I had seen people do in a James Bond movie. Then I could climb down the pole into the snow. But I felt so cold I didn't think I could grip the rails. I had let the moment pass. If I died, what would the story be? Harvey hated people who postponed decisions until it was too late to make one.

I fingered my small paper bag with silver earrings made by someone in the Quebec Charlotte Islands. Perhaps instead it would become a story about a vain woman who had lost herself for the sake of a trinket, a narcissistic version of "Gift of the Magi"? I had bought earrings to show Bill I was able to enjoy myself without him. I had known as I bought them that to him they would be a reproof. A lover's quarrel ends in freezing death.

Was it time to jump now? I was very cold. Once I had frozen my feet black while skiing with Harvey. He wouldn't listen when I had said I was cold. "Tough it out," he had said. In which way was I to tough it out? If I jumped and succeeded, I would be a heroine. If I jumped and failed, a fool. If I waited and died, a helpless victim. If I waited and survived, merely another epic ski story.

At least I should have had the wineskin. And why not do exercises? I stamped my feet, and the gondola started.

I went up and up, the empty cars streaming past me on their way down. They looked almost like company now. When I passed the second station, I waved to the orange parka and again asked no questions. The gondola stopped two more times on the last leg of the journey. Each time was less frightening than the time before. My death began to lose credibility; the truth was, the danger now seemed like a fantasy.

When I reached the platform my feet were like cubes of wood, and I stumbled out of the cab. The orange parka asked me if I had had a pleasant ride.

It was cocktail hour at the Chimney Corner. I could hear the rock group with its tired repertoire. "...*drinkin' whiskey and rye, singin' this will be the day that I die.*" I giggled a little, passing the door. I saw all the faces, known quantities now – Ronald and Miss Tongs and my drunken instructor. It was only six o'clock, and although I had been in the gondola for almost an hour, it was not even late enough for Bill to be worried. I knocked on the door of the room and he opened it. I walked two steps to the bed and fell. He was buoyant, reaching to pull off my boots.

"You won't believe," he said. "I went up the chair with Miss Tongs. She's not a hooker at all. She's an aeronautical engineer from Orlando, Florida and she's never been on skis before in her life. What's the matter? Wasn't Banff the same?"

I was so cold I couldn't undress myself. He rubbed my feet and ran a hot bath. He held me while I lowered myself by inches into the steaming water. I remember I hurt more as the warmth invaded each cell than I had when the cold took over.

LINDA GRIFFITHS

A GAME OF INCHES

It's the bottom of the ninth and I'm standing at the plate, and thousands of people are chanting "Hit that ball! Hit that ball! Hit that ball!" My teammates behind me in the dugout are chanting, "Hit that ball! Hit that ball! Hit that ball!" It's all resting on me. And I know I'm not going to hit that ball. As I lay there alone in my bed, I realized I'd had my very first baseball nightmare. And I thought, surely now he'll call.

The light changed that day. There was the wet rain and the damp and the sliding about on the packed icy surface, but it did seem that an almost imperceptible change occurred, like the turning up of a dial of light. The turning of the season. The time when John used to look for the very first baseball magazines. You know what I mean? They're not very good, they're made of newsprint and they herald the later abstracts and larger tomes that come out throughout the season. These magazines were like daffodils or tulips to him, because, of course, they meant spring training.

I knew he wouldn't call in winter. I knew he wouldn't call Valentine's Day. Ridiculous, the way it comes right in the armpit of winter. There's no more depressing time of year. No, he has no use for those kinds of occasions, the bleeding hearts in the store windows, the silly, humorous cards, "If you break my heart, I'll break your face," and so on. No, I knew he wouldn't call then. He'll call in the spring. Or the summer. Or at the very latest, fall.

I'm aware that it's ridiculous, being a virgin at my age. I should have just gone out and done it a long time ago and got it over with. But oh no, I had to wait. Still, I don't know why everything has to be done at once. Painters don't paint masterpieces all at once. They begin with a triangle, a circle, a square. They move onto a bowl of fruit, an apple, a pear, eventually a banana and then they go on to paint *Boy Blue* and *Pinkie*. Of course it's possible that some people just aren't very highly sexed. As if there was a kind of gauge with "nymphomaniacs" on the top, then "highly sexed," "very sexed," just plain "sexed," "lightly sexed," all the way down to "barely sexed."

When I told my psychiatrist my baseball nightmare, he said something I know he's been dying to say for a very long time. He said that this dream might mean that I was gay. This disturbed me, not because of any prejudice, but because I've never felt particularly gay. But I told him that I'd be willing to seek a second medical opinion and if they concurred, I would be willing to work on becoming gay, with qualified professionals, for several years if necessary. Still, it didn't feel quite right.

It's true, I never had boyfriends as such. Of course, I had the experience of "that dance." You know the one I mean. My mother spent 300 dollars on a dress. In the fifties they had those dresses with the crinolines that stuck straight out. In bright green taffeta and I weighed 204 pounds. Then came the snow boots, large brown galoshes with soles as thick as bricks. I clomped into that dance carrying my shoes in a little bag. I saw the girls, batting their eyelashes and giggling and listening to the boys talk about sports, pretending interest the way women do. I wasn't going to do that. I made for the couch and sat there watching like a giant frog. I wasn't going to eat anything. I wasn't going to drink anything. I wasn't going to take my boots off. I just sat there and waited until it was over and then I went home.

This is all that's left: a giant house, some mouldy antiques, a small annuity. I've always liked to keep a room in my house empty, actually, not a room, an entire floor. I thought that if I filled up the whole house with things – with my voluminous collection of books on the female orgasm, the works of the modern French feminists – *Angst, Volumes One Two and Three* – with lamps and tables and things, then there would be no room for *him* when *he* came. I thought a lot about it that spring three years ago, inviting John to come and stay. I'd had my eye on him, but then I'd had my eye on other fish before. I thought, "This is the way it's done. The woman has the nest and provides, and the man is in between things, he doesn't have much money, he moves in and that's the way it's done." So I said to John, "Well, if you don't have a place to stay, you can always stay at my house, you can pay me 250 dollars or nothing." And he said, "Sure." The way they do. "Sure."

I sat in my kitchen waiting for him to come and I wish I had known then about Sadaharu Oh. Sadaharu Oh was perhaps the most successful hitter ever. He hit more home runs than Hank Aaron or Babe Ruth. A Japanese man, he was a high school star until he made the major leagues and went into a giant slump. He just couldn't hit the ball. He's in despair. Finally his teacher comes to him and says, "Oh, you must learn to concentrate on *ki*. *Ki* is the point of spirit energy in the body." Now, I would have thought that this point of *ki* would have been located somewhere at the top of the head, or the forehead or the mouth or, at the lowest, the chest. But no, it appears this point of *ki* is located all the way down, about two inches below the navel. Sadaharu Oh learned to concentrate on his point of *ki* and balance his spirit energy and still he couldn't hit the ball. His teacher came to him and said, "Oh, you must understand and eliminate the *mah*. *Mah* is energy between opponents." In this case the pitcher and the batter. Sadaharu Oh had to learn never to think of the pitcher as his enemy. He had to think into the eyes of the pitcher, through his own eyes in a giant circle thus eliminating the *mah* between them. And he learned to do this and still he couldn't hit the ball. Then, it's terrible, they're about to throw him off the team and he has one last game. He's in despair and his teacher comes to him and says, "Oh, you are a piece of shit," the way they do. "You have one last chance. You must hit the ball standing on one leg." Sadaharu Oh thinks he's crazy but he doesn't have anything to lose, so he agrees.

He goes out to the stadium to face the fans. They are so used to him striking out that every time he comes up to bat, they chant, "Oh, strike out! Oh, strike out! Oh, strike out!" But he quiets them in his mind, concentrates on his point of *ki*, eliminates the *mah* between himself and the pitcher, and raises himself on one leg in the now familiar "flamingo stance." He waits for the perfect moment, hits the ball with a resounding crack, it arches up and out of the park! He runs around the bases, hits home plate, and flings his arms up in his only gesture of emotion for the next 22 years. And the crowd chants, "Oh! Oh! Oh! Oh! Oh… Oh… Oh… Ohh… Ohhhhhhh… Ohhh… Oh."

I sat in my kitchen, waiting for John to come, with some lapsang souchong tea in a perfect china cup, and a fresh strawberry tart with whole wheat crust, of course made from scratch, and I heard the doorbell ring. I looked down the long hallway and saw him through the glass, a huge black shadow with a suitcase. I waved him in and he walked down the hallway, coming closer and closer, looming larger and larger, seeming to cut out all the light behind him and all of a sudden all I can see is the enemy!

A man a man a man! With his man smell smell smell, his penis penis penis! A rapist! A war-monger! An oppressor, a brute! I know all I'll want to do is serve and serve and serve. I see 45 years in one fell swoop. He is old and bald and has cancer and I'm changing his colostomy bag. I want to take a piece of chalk and draw a giant circle around me and say, "No! You can't come here. This is me! This is my mind, I fought for it! This is me, you can't come here!"

Instead, I say, "Come on in. Take a beer from the fridge." I've stocked the fridge and the cupboards and the freezer with enough food to last seven nuclear wars. I know that he must feel my panic and yes, my revulsion. But how could I tell him that although these things are true, he is also my beloved?

He moves in up to the third floor where he creates unbelievable devastation. I seem pulled by my very genes up to the third floor just do a bit of dusting, not to move anything around. I see his dirty laundry scattered on the floor. I'm tempted to pick up one of his shirts and smell that unbelievable combination of polyester blend and sweat. Just to get used to him, you understand. I'm further tempted to gather up the shirts, not the socks, only the shirts, and carry them downstairs and wash them and then say casually, "Yes, no trouble really, I had to do a black wash anyway."

It is as if we've lived together for 40 years, it's that comfortable, that ordinary, at the same time there is an unspeakable tension between us. Then one day he comes in and says, "Do you mind if I watch the game?" Game? What game? "The Blue Jays and the White Sox." I say, "Sure," the way I do now. "Sure."

We are in the living room and as I turn on "the game," I hear that hard–edged announcer's voice. The sound of all little girls being separated from their fathers. The voice says, "The Blue Jays are in the Skydome and they've opened the roof, they've closed the roof, and they're opening, they've closed, yes they've opened, no they've closed the roof…" But I can't watch the game. I am only aware of him behind me on the couch, it's as if the back of my head has eyes. I know he's wondering whether or not he can put his boots up on the couch. I want to beam out to him, that I dearly want him to feel comfortable enough to put his boots up on the couch. At the same time, I feel that if he does, I'll chop his feet off. Finally he gives a contented sigh, stretches himself out on the couch, and puts his boots up. I tell myself, "You see, the world hasn't fallen apart, the boots are up, so what?" But I still can't watch the game. All I can think of is, "Does he want tea, coffee, pound cake, lemon meringue? Any of the enormous meal I've prepared and hidden in the back of the fridge?" No, I can't watch the game. Then I think, "Is it possible that perhaps at this moment, he is also thinking of me?" I glance at him. Wrong, wrong, wrong. He, of course, is watching the game.

I don't know how many games went on like that, without my seeing a single one. I began to plot and plan the way women do, checking ahead in the television guide to see when the games were on, so that when he came in, he wouldn't have to say, "Do you mind if I watch the game?" Because the game would already be on. But we were, maybe only I was, exhausted with the tension of the unspoken between us. Then one night I was just fed up. He wasn't home but I put the game on anyway and sat staring blankly at the screen. I heard him come in and get a beer from the fridge and I thought, "No, everything's fine. This is how they do things. They come in, they get beers from fridges, they crack them open, they flop on the couch, they fart, and they watch the game."

But this night, for some reason, I wasn't thinking so much of him. It was as if a glow of light began to illuminate my mind and for the first time I saw these players, these White Sox. A bunch of men dressed in what looks like long underwear with numbers on them, loping about chewing wads of cud that stick out of their mouths like tumours, scratching and spitting gobs of phlegm and tobacco juice and spit into some kind of trough that must be in front of them. A gang of fairly ordinary fellows, all shapes and sizes. Then, in come the Toronto Blue Jays — warped and introverted and miserable. I think, "What's wrong with them? What have we done to them? What have they done to themselves?" The entire team looks like it's in its second year of psychotherapy.

As the game progresses, I understand more and more, until finally I know that it's the top of the ninth. All baseball stories begin with, "It's the bottom of the ninth" or "It's the top of the ninth." It's the top of the ninth and the game is tied and the bases are loaded and there are two down and the White Sox are up to bat and the Blue Jays are in the field. The Blue Jays' pitcher appears to be losing his mind, quite literally coming apart at the seams. He gets a tragic, haunted look in his eyes and starts to twitch and shake in an almost Parkinsonian manner. Then he starts to pull at himself. And as if on cue, all the other players start to pull at themselves too. The other players are more circumspect, they pull down and a little to one side, but this Dave Stieb, he goes right for it. Then he starts to talk to himself and it appears everything is going to disintegrate until a calm comes over the entire stadium. The coach, Cito Gaston, the classiest man in baseball, has come out to talk Dave down. He gets to the mound, but before he begins to speak, you can see the tension start to drain away from Dave's face. He begins to regain control of his limbs, and to do fairly ordinary things with his hands, like play with the ball. We don't know what Cito has said. We only know it's perfect. A job well done, Cito goes back to the dugout, sitting like Yul Brynner in *The King and I*.

Dave strikes the batter out. The Blue Jays are up, and out comes George Bell, the Butcher of San Pedro, the most hated man in baseball. Clearly, George is a man used to boos. Booo

booo booo! "Eeeef the Canadian faaans don't like me, they can keees my purple butt!" "Booo. Booo. Booo." But today, the fans aren't booing. They're quiet, almost kind. It's not putting George in a good mood at all. He looks like he wants to eat the plate, the bat, the ball and the pitcher. He swings, misses, and his statistics come up on the television set before you. You know everything. You know he's been in a giant slump, that he needs an eye operation, that his shoulder's gone, his elbows are gone, his knees are gone, his ankles aren't very good either, we know his contract is up, that he'll ask for too much money. Meanwhile the announcers are saying, "Perhaps George will get a single today." And George raises his bat, big as a fence post, hacks and hews the empty air, strikes out, throws his bat to the ground and stalks off in a snit.

Then in comes a large chin followed by curling blond hair coming to the nape of the neck, Kelly Gruber. Most young boys want to be baseball players and end up being policemen. Kelly wanted to be a policeman and became a baseball player. He's holding his pinkie finger at an unusual angle and his skin is stretched thin and taut over his cheekbones. It seems he's also been in a slump and the fans are booing him too. With the black chalk marks smeared under his eyes, he looks like that rock singer, Alice Cooper. He bends over the plate, his lips thin with tension, and cracks the ball for a stand-up triple. As he arrives on third base, you can hear him thinking, "Just let them call me 'Mrs. Gruber' now."

Then there is a curious dragging sound, a player appears to be dragging a giant cross onto the field and on his face are tears from his latest appearance on VisionTV. Tony Fernandez is a man clearly tormented by the wounds of Christ. And I want to beam into the television set, "Tony, of course it's all right to believe in Jesus and be tormented by the wounds of Christ. Just not right now, it's the bottom of the ninth." He clearly hears me because he seems to solidify. Underneath his torment we see a body as neat and graceful as a young gazelle. He comes to the plate with no unnecessary panache, waits for the perfect moment, almost invisibly whacks the ball and drives Gruber in!

We win! We win! At least, they win. The Blue Jays win. I win. John and I win. Yeah, team! We're very excited, John and I, because of the game of course, and it's ten o'clock at night and it seems that something more could happen, that the evening could extend. But we don't seem to be able to engineer it and I get almost Dave Stiebian in my twitches as I say, "Coffee?" "No." "Tea?" "No." "Pound cake?" "No." "Chicken breasts? Broccoli with hollandaise sauce?" "No." Things are about to come apart at the seams when a calm comes over the living room. I turn and there is Cito Gaston, handing me a pack of cards. And Kelly Gruber has found the candles. And Tony Fernandez wipes the coffee table clean. John and I play Crazy Eights by candlelight till four o'clock in the morning. Then dawn starts to alter the light, we are tired, yet it seems that something more could happen with the evening, something more. A long silence. I look at John, of course I don't speak. Finally he says, "Well, I guess I'd better crash."

"Yes. You should crash." I should crash. We all should crash. We say goodnight, he goes down the hallway to the bathroom to leave the toilet seat up, then climbs the stairs to the third floor. Lying alone in my bed, I hear his heavy body fall on the mattress on the floor above me and I ache the way women ache when they want something they can't ask for.

Then I hear a very curious sound. Like ice cracking. I follow the sound into the living room, and there, sitting on the couch, is George Bell. He's crying in a heartbroken manner and burbling, "Sheeet, man. Sheeet. Everyone knows, man. They think I'm feeneeesh. I'm not feeneeesh. I got two years left in me, two years, and my contract is up. I gotta go out there and act like a king. My eyes are gone. My shoulder is gone. My knees gone. My ankles aren't very good. Cito, he says, keep our eye on the ball. I can't see the goddamn ball."

Smooth as silk, I go up to him and help him take the chips off his shoulders. First the left one then the right, which is even larger. Then I am in his arms, his hands are huge and calloused like bear paws and they are travelling travelling over me, finding places I didn't know existed. All the moves I thought I would have to learn by rote or with professionals are coming through me in waves. He is no longer the Butcher of San Pedro, these are not butcher's arms, but blacksmith's arms and they are holding me so gently. He touches me with the sweetest part of his bat and we are at first base, we are at second base, at third base, oh ohhhhhh home. Then I am curled in his arms and he is tickling me with his moustache.

Now I don't know if that was a proper orgasm. I don't think anyone really knows what an orgasm is, certainly not in all the books I've read. All I know is that I was very pleased and I didn't want to do it anymore.

As I helped George strap the chips back on his shoulders, he said, "Pamela, they say I'm a pretty shitty guy, maybe that's true, maybe that's not true. But I tell you one thing, don't you worry about this John. Just play your natural game." And he was gone.

I had such a moment of peace, even the French feminists within were peaceful. Yes, of course, just play your natural game. But how to be natural with *him?* I was becoming more and more unnatural. Seemingly unbidden, I was giggling, batting my eyelashes, wiggling odd parts of my body in coy ways. My voice had gone up octaves, I was running around like Betty Crocker in heat.

Natural? It seems natural when he goes out to say, "When are
you coming home?" Just like that, "When are you coming
home?" But when I say it, it comes out like an order born of brutality and desperation. I want to grab the words back. If I don't
say, "When are you coming home?" there is a unnatural conver-
sational gap. There is no natural left. I'm just a schemer now. I
think, "What he needs is a good shirt. It would look just like his
other shirts, except it would cost 250 dollars. He wouldn't be
able to tell, they can't, you know. But 15 years down the road,
when he's with someone a little closer to his own age, all the
things from this time will have disintegrated, except for that one
shirt and he will think of me."

Just after the all-star game, John said that he was "getting it
together" to look for a place again and that pretty soon he would
be off my hands. Again there was that silence. I just wanted to
say, "Oh don't be so ridiculous. Marry me. Marry me. Marry me.
I'll nail your feet to a perch. I'll nail mine to one. We'll stay there
frozen forever, locked in this beautiful prison!" But then I
thought, "No, that can't be quite right." Sometime after the Blue
Jays lost the playoffs, he said that he was a little closer to getting
a place and he pretty well had a line on one.

It's the bottom on the ninth. Joe DiMaggio is standing at the
plate. It's all resting on him. If he hits, the team will win the
Series, he will break all the records. The crowd is electric, insane.
The ball comes toward him, he waits for the perfect moment,
swings, hits it with a resounding crack and it arches high over the
park. He's done it! The crowd cheers wildly, everybody gets up
to leave, the game is over... except for one outfielder standing by
the wall. The ball's already travelled over the wall several feet

when this outfielder makes the most astounding leap. He jumps up, arches back, reaches out that extra impossible quarter of an inch and catches the ball! The photograph of this moment shows the fans with their jaws dropped open, with their coats and hats half on. That outfielder never played baseball again. He opened a bar. Baseball stories are like that. They always seem to have that twist of lemon.

Just after the World Series, which was hard to watch because, of course, the Jays had "choked in the clutch," an expression I truly despise, John said that he had found a place and he couldn't thank me enough and he owed me dinner. Even as he spoke I thought I caught something out of the corner of his eye, something that seemed to ask for something, but no, I was probably wrong.

He is standing in the hallway with his suitcase and I am standing in front of him. It's an awkward moment. I see this nose coming toward me, looming larger and larger. I get what's supposed to happen. I do understand the physics of it. Something has to occur so that our lips can touch. He comes closer and closer, and then, I don't know why I did it, but I turned my head. I turned my head just a quarter of an inch and his lips brushed my ear awkwardly and a wall went up between us. A wall as cold and as grey as a Toronto sky in February. We try to reach our hands over the wall. I say, "Don't worry about the rent." He says, "I'll give you a call."

I am standing under the ball. It's one of those moments when there's no question the outfielder will make the catch. The ball comes closer and closer, looming larger and larger, and then, for some reason, it slips between the mitt and my hands. It's one of those ridiculous bloopers. There I am with my bum in the air, searching for the ball between my legs. I finally find it, too late to throw to third base. A couple of inches, one way or another. I hear the door close gently behind him.

You can imagine what a meal the French feminists would make of such a moment. They're very good in the politics, but about male/female relations, very dicey, very dicey indeed. You can just hear them. "Oh, Philippe, Philippe, I am woman. You are man. I am cunt. You are penis. I am penis, You are cunt. Oh, please fuck me. Oh, don't fuck me. I hate you, I love you. I hate you. Ooooh, I will die if you leave. You will die if you stay. You must come, come, go, go, oh fuck me."

Well, I am not like that. I didn't get hysterical, instead I hid for a year, never leaving the house. My hibernation ended one morning when I woke up, threw open the window and smelled mud under the frost. I turned on the radio and heard that George Bell was signing copies of his book – imagine George writing a book – at the World's Biggest Bookstore. I knew I had to see him again. The World's Biggest is not where I usually buy my books, but I ventured into a warehouse-like building, with screaming bargain signs and hideous lighting. There were crowds of schoolchildren milling about but it was easy to see George. At the end of a long line, there he was, a nattily dressed Dominican man with a moustache and large sunglasses, flanked on one hand by a security guard with a gun, on the other hand by an over-wrought, overachieving woman publicist. The schoolchildren were waving bits of paper, chanting "I got his autograph. I got his autograph."

A stack of books announced the apt title of George's book, *Hardball*. I clutched a copy to my chest and lined up, the one adult in a mass of children. When I finally got to George, I waited for some sign of recognition but it was impossible to see his eyes behind the shades. To ignite his memory, even though my voice was shaking, I boldly asked, "Would you mind writing 'to Pamela' in my book?" I wanted something personal after all.

The overwrought, overachieving woman publicist screeched, "No! He's only going to write his name!" George flexed his gold-ringed fingers and signed his name, smiling at me in an innocuous way. I retreated to a vantage point near a large section on the royal family. The Queen and her corgis were everywhere. George knew I was watching him. A lumpy fourteen-year-old who'd wanted to have his baseball signed but wasn't allowed, joined me, recognizing a good spot when he saw one. The two of us stood in companionable silence as George signed his way to the end of the line. Still no acknowledgement. I intuited that the lumpy lad was living in some suburban hell, camped out in his parents' basement, trying to keep his mind alive by quoting baseball statistics. Our bond grew as the clock struck twelve-thirty, the hour when the book signing was to end. As George left he had to walk right by us. As he came closer and closer, I began to fear he would leave without any signal of our past acquaintance when at the last moment he leaned towards me and said, "If you're ever in the Windy City, look me up." Windy City? My lumpy friend explained that George had been traded to the Chicago Cubs. Traded? Not a Blue Jay? "Yeah, didn't you know? A whole bunch of last year's team are gone, like Tony Fernandez." Tony of the cross? Gone? I felt as if the ground beneath my feet was dissolving. What can it mean? They were our team, those particular Blue Jays, not just any jays flying about the city. Is there no loyalty? Can this mean John won't call? I am ten years old again and my best friend has moved away and the world is cracking and there's nothing left. But somehow I pull myself together. My only refuge is knowledge. I resolve to learn, to research, to be practical and thereby come to an understanding as to how the game is played in all its aspects. The lumpy fourteen-year-old takes me over to the baseball section and I buy 357 dollars worth of baseball books, give him my signed copy of *Hardball* to begin training.

In the spring of my training, I watched the Blue Jays build their new team. As I saw them bring in Joe Carter, his face splitting with an enormous smile that filled up the Skydome whether the roof was open or not, I worked on balancing the spirit energy of my *ki*. I was still having considerable difficulty eliminating the *mah* between myself and just about everybody else as I watched a peculiar energy begin to take hold of our Jays. By midsummer I was speed-reading through the wisdom of Yogi Berra who once said, "Baseball is 90 percent mental, the other half is physical."

He didn't call.

I intensified my training. Halfway through the season I could stand on one leg for considerable lengths of time. My knowledge increased. I knew Babe Ruth once ate a hat. Lou Gehrig was obsessed with his mother. Walter "The Big Train" Johnson, master of the fastball, used to give young batters a break, the catcher whispering, "The Big Train likes you today," and somehow the ball would be right over the plate. All of this was in tandem with the strengthening of the new team. I didn't forget those players who had gone and missed them deeply, but still I welcomed the sight of Roberto Alomar, like a young bear cub, playing the game with such ease it made me want to weep. Alomar took over Dave Stieb's position as the player most likely to pull at himself. Nineteen times in one game, I noted.

And still he didn't call. Even though I felt fairly certain that the *mah* between me and the world had significantly diminished.

A World Series win began to be a tangible goal, one that fueled the imagination and inspired sold-out games. The stands were full, the team moving together like a dream. Veteran Dave

Winfield was brought in to clinch the win. The Jays' management was spending money, critics said they were buying a Series rather than building a true team from within. Big Dave Winfield didn't care. One night he strode to the front of the stands, raised his mighty hands like a conductor and yelled, "More noise!" The crowd roared back. I managed a yell myself, all the while maintaining my flamingo stance.

There was a *soupçon* of a frenzy or what passes for one in this city and of course the detractors were doing their best to squash it. Journalists droned on with macabre delight about "choking in the clutch" and the "curse of the Blue Jays." I sensed that this was a delicate moment and called Cito Gaston into the living room for a chat. "Cito, we all know what you're trying to go. You want the big win, the World Series, entry into the Hall of Fame. We all do. But it can't all be about winning and losing, it must be about how you play the game. If it isn't, then I am a loser and I won't accept that. Take it from me, no one ever won by thinking about winning all the time. You can't play your natural game then. You can't push to win, pray to win, think to win, plan to win – you can only be ready to win. Prepared. Tell them it's about waiting for the perfect moment, balancing your spirit energy, eliminating the *mah*, playing your natural game, and having the courage to… the courage to…

Only then does the obvious occur to me. Daringly, carelessly, I pick up the phone and dial the number I'd carried on my back like a cross for two seasons. Of course he was home, of course he was. "Hello John? It's Pamela. Yes, I've been watching. I think they just might take the Series this year. Next year too? Oh, don't be silly." And I laugh my natural laugh.

STEVEN HEIGHTON

A Right Like Yours

He is short but he has shoulders and I think he wears the flattest
shoes going, cheap sneakers of some kind, and that is attractive,
that he doesn't try to elevate himself in any way. His look is shy
though, maybe cold, with green eyes that don't meet your eyes
but look at your mouth or chin in the same way as, when you're
in the ring, the other girl will stare a little below your eyes. So
maybe he does it to practice. Always be in the ring, Webb Ren-
ton tells us.

I choose to think he is just somewhat shy.

It started because I was training for my fifth fight and my
sparring partner had hurt that ligament in the knee that's called,
I think, cruciate but we just say crucial because that's what it is.
The other girls at the club are either on the little or the huge size
and Trav is about the same weight as me, though he is shorter,
and toward the end of a workout Webb yelled at him to get in
there and give me a couple rounds. Trav's face then – like someone told him to throw himself on a grenade. People started gathering ringside. Like I said, it was the end of the night, and I
would have been interested too. I don't think the coach had ever
put a girl and guy in to spar that way.

So the bell sounds, he comes out as if being shoved from
behind and he is ogling my chin as usual, as if meaning to clock
me there, but his eyes don't have that focussed, violent shine. He
sets his hands high with the forearms upright in an old-fashioned stance and he peeks from between them like he's behind

bars – a guy who just woke up in jail and has no idea how he got there. I fling a few jabs at his face to see what he will do, which turns out to be nothing, so I hook low to his gut and then I follow with a loaded right and there's this sound like an air mattress just sprang a leak and he takes a seat on the canvas and looks down at his lap with a puzzled frown. In a way it feels good I've knocked down such a solid and experienced little guy but mainly I feel bad. He was not trying. "Get up, send something back at her now, she's training!" yells Webb from my corner. Trav's cheeks inflate with air which he now puffs out through his mouth in a serious way and he gets to his feet slowly and we begin.

Next day I see him downtown after my shift at the Ramada where I work in the office. He is walking out of a camera store looking down at some photos and he has this warm, wide-open smile, just the opposite of his awkward frown last night in the ring. I stand in his road so he will have to collide with me or stop. He stops, looks up from his photos. The smile dies. He'd looked beautiful before, thinking no one could see.

"That's a shiner, all right," I say idiotically, even pointing. "Nice photos?"

He mumbles something and he's not staring at my chin but into my eyes! Well, my left eye.

"Damn," he says now. "Sorry."

"You know what Webb says about fighters apologizing."

"That's just in the ring. I never gave a girl a black eye before."

"Yours is blacker," I argue. "And I dropped my left."

He nods and develops a thoughtful frown. "It's a bad habit."

"Not anymore. I won't drop it in my fight and that's thanks to you."

The shiner is a sexy touch on him, like a pirate eye patch on a pretty boy face.

I think he wants to leave but I would like a few more seconds here.

"Your photos turn out?"

His face unfists, almost smiles. My knees waver like from a scoring blow.

"Sure," he says, "they're fine."

"They of you in the ring?"

"Family," he says, shaking his head, and he looks down at his shoes which I notice he always does after he answers a question, like he's hoping that when he looks up again, you won't be there.

"Parents?" I can't believe how nosy I am being.

"Uh, kids. Son and daughter. Four and three."

I stare from his face to the stack of photos and back again. I cock my head. In a slow, wary way he passes the top photo toward me like he's surrendering his credit card to a mugger. It's Trav, no shiner, pushing his grinning face (!) between the faces of the little girl and boy who are laughing in a wide stretchy way on either side. There's a cake too. The girl's face has been made up as a black and orange butterfly. The faces are a bit blurred, and the pupils are diabolically red, but there's no missing the joy here.

"Birthday?"

"Nicole's third. At the five-pin lanes up on the base."

"Beautiful," I say. "You look young to have a family. I mean, kids."

"Boy came when I was eighteen."

He shuffles. I think he knows what I want to ask.

"It's a shared arrangement," he says, and the look on his face is like somebody tricked him into speaking.

It can be as tempting to hit a face that attracts you as to hit one you hate, if the liked face is not replying to your attraction. At the Friday night workout we spar three rounds and he again pulls his punches but not too much now. A couple times after I score on him he retaliates instantly and for a second there is an exciting gleam in his eyes and he almost meets my gaze. He avoids hitting me in the chest guard, though. Breast shots really kill so I guess I could see this as a sign of budding affection, though I realize it might just be courtesy.

After, I ask if he will walk me to my car and he growls, "With a right like yours, a chaperone's the last thing you need." He walks me anyway. We cross the parking lot and he slows up as we approach each car, then glances at me as we continue.

"Farther," I say. "I parked over there." I nod up the dark service road toward the beer store on the far side of the diamonds.

"Why so far?"

"The lot was packed when I got here," I lie.

"I've never seen this lot packed."

"And like Webb tells us… got to fill those legs up with mileage before a fight."

Several hours later, it feels like, he says, "I think you're ready. Guess you'll taper back on the sparring, next couple weeks."

"Oh I don't know," I say quickly. "That'll be Webb's call."

The service road lacks lighting. I glance over but can't read his face. I have butterflies, like before a fight, and it makes me walk faster though I am trying to slow down.

"Maybe when you're training for your next fight," I blurt out, "he'll put us together again. Give you some extra rounds!"

"I doubt it," he says. "I mean, I'd be *training*."

I will knock him down again next week. He is short and pale and uncommunicative. He needs a shave. When we clinched tonight, he smelled of, I think, garlic bread.

Now he mumbles, "That was rude of me. Sorry."

All of a sudden we're at my ruin of a Lada which I parked under a crackling amber streetlight in a corner of the beer store lot. It sounds like a zillion volts are running through this light. I know the feeling. There is a ticket under the car's front wiper. Trav removes it carefully and hands it to me with a sympathetic frown. He looks almost apologetic.

"Can I give you a lift," I say strongly.

"I don't want you to go out of your way, Trina."

"It's no trouble! Get in! Don't mind the mess."

There is no mess. This morning I vacuumed and lint-picked the interior and before the workout I took the car through a car-wash where the asshole attendants actually offered me raingear and then (I watched them in the rear-view) bent over laughing as I drove slowly in.

"Thanks," he says, and my heart for a moment there, till he says, "but I'll walk. Like you say. Got to get mileage into these legs."

"Yup," I say with an idiot's grin. "For sure. That's very true."

I renew my oath to knock him down Monday.

"Anyway, I live close. Near the No Frills." He points in a vague way, like he is embarrassed to live in the neighbourhood, or he just prefers not to locate himself too clearly.

Webb says I headhunt too much and he needs me to work on my body shots. He also thinks Trav needs to work on *taking* body shots if he is serious about turning pro. For a round at the end of each workout he makes Trav become a human punching bag and sicks me on him. Trav never looks pleased about these dates of ours. He leans back on the ropes with his blue gloves by his scrunched-up face, elbows glued to his ribs, and my job is to find openings and work his body. He is permitted to move but not to punch, which basically means I can have my way with him. Since he is short, with long, thick arms, it can be hard to find undefended parts of his flesh to pound and I am very careful about not hitting below the belt – though at times I get the urge. Sometimes I feel him flinching, too. He must be concerned that even one of my hard punches could land foul, by accident or otherwise.

Tonight he smells of, not garlic bread, just bread. He works in a bakery, four in the morning till noon, five days a week. He likes it there. He was just promoted. It is easier to pry personal information out of him now and I am getting opportunities because after the last two workouts he has let me drive him home. To extend the drive, since he only lives a few blocks from the gym, I park some distance in the other direction on the service road, which also means we get to walk first to my spotless wreck of a car. Naturally he is silent on these outings and I have to talk for both of us. I think maybe he is annoyed about the extra walking but he still does it with me and I choose to see this as hopeful.

We are filling our legs with mileage.

When my arms get too heavy to plant the punches Webb is yelling at me to throw, I have no option but to lean in on Trav and clinch, for a pleasant rest. Would anyone notice if I sampled the fresh sweat on his neck? I think Trav would notice. Tonight for the first time *he* initiates a clinch. On Webb's command I have been throwing repeat right hooks at his solar plexus, trying to pry through his guarding elbows, then I do get through and his stomach is solid, though with a slight layer over it, I guess from all those baked goods. It's so satisfying to connect. He grunts and gasps softly and sags and envelops me and my punches stop dead. He is humid, panting. Webb hollers at him to break and get back on the ropes.

My roadwork is a 40-minute run each day at the traditional hour for fighters in training. It's a struggle to get out of bed but once you are up and out, you can sprint straight down the middle of Princess Street if you want to. I do that sometimes. I have been known to sing at the top of my lungs while doing that.

I would like to sing at the top of my lungs this morning but this morning I will play it cool because *this morning Trav is running with me.* It's the first day of his weekend, Tuesday. You'd think he would choose to sleep in but he says he is used to getting up for work and besides he wants time to get his place ready for his kids, who stay over on these days. Runs With Man is his morning alarm, he says. Runs With Man is a pound rescue dog, Jack Russell and malamute, a furry barrel with a wolf's head and stub legs who trots at Trav's side without a leash.

I would feel more encouraged by Trav's presence if he hadn't said, when I asked him to run with me, that Tuesday is his "usual day for a run anyway."

Like I say, I love running through the city in the last dark with the streets wide and empty and all to myself, but this morning after we do some of that, Trav asks me to run across the causeway to the fields and hills around the old fort. "The sunrise," he says and it sounds like a romantic proposition maybe, except as usual he mutters it from the side of his mouth. But we run across and there's this mist on the river from the night's chill and with the lake still warm from the summer. "Let's go," he says, and frowns at his watch. He has a good idea exactly when the sun shows its face every day because he works at an east window, and to me there is something so appealing about a guy who sees every sunrise.

We put on a surge as we run up the middle of the road that climbs to the hilltop fort. Trav's face knots up with the strain. When we get there he is winded. This embarrasses him, I think – that he is somewhat unfit or maybe that I am fitter.

He mumbles that he can just run once or twice a week, because of his hours.

Runs With Man flops on the grass and his tongue lolls like a pulled muscle.

"So are you really going to turn pro?" I ask, hoping the question won't offend.

"Coach still wants me to, but there's no way," he tells the patch of dirt at his feet.

To my surprise his words are a relief. To my greater surprise I realize I am not serious about turning pro either, though I have talked about it like I am.

"I saw a couple friends turn pro," he says. "Used to think it might be a way to support the kids. Not a chance." He turns to watch the coloured clouds at the horizon as if trying to figure the odds on our sunrise. To me, the view up the river and west over the big lake is enough. This view of Trav in profile is enough. He says, "I'm not good enough to win big prize money and not bad enough to get work as a bleeder for rising stars."

"They love you at the bakery, though."

"For some reason I'm good at it."

I shift my feet downhill so my eyes are at his level, even a bit lower. Will this help? I am almost ready to suggest we start back down the hill when he taps the dog in the butt with his shoe and says, "Go, boy, get that squirrel." The dog's ears prick up and it pelts away downhill toward the water.

"I didn't see a squirrel," I say.

He looks me plumb in the eye and shows his still-good teeth and steps toward me. The sun is up. Clouds are in the way but sunlight sneaks through a momentary opening and it is enough to turn the grassy hill and the fort and the calm river and lake a rosy gold, like in a religious poster. Then it's gone and I am glad because I see that the flush in his cheeks and spreading up to his hairline and down to his throat is not a reflection of the sun at all.

Like Webb says, the one that gets you is the one you don't see coming.

"Just wanted us to be alone for a second," he says, and as I open my arms the hill pulls him down to me.

MARK JARMAN

THE SCOUT'S LAMENT

You're the GM, you bring in 60 bodies. But only 20 you want to see, I mean really look at.

The next 20 have a chance. Say you show them something they like. Say you're drilling holes in goalies. Knocking them down, a hot streak.

Then there are the last 20. The last 20 are filler, warm bodies, keep a scrimmage going.

Now, do you know which 20 you are? You've *GOT* to find out.

Say the coach comes to your house, or a scout. Or maybe they don't come to your house. Get a feel. Phone them up. They treat you rotten you know that's how they'll treat your kid. You want your kid there? No, you don't want your kid there.

Ask them what your kid should do for conditioning over the summer. *One*, this shows interest. *Two*, you see how they react, whether they could give a hoot. It's important. *Three*. I forget three. Go with your instincts.

And *politics*. It's brutal. Some kid will make the team and you'll say WHAT THE HELL!? Whoa, whose nephew is that? It's really bad. And remember they get money for a draft choice from the NHL, so they're always looking at that. Factors. Certain traits they want, right or wrong. Some get pushed into steroids, get out the needles, bulk up, get in a 'roid rage, screw up their kidneys. They think it's their only chance at a barrel of cash and a hot car with local tarts crawling on it. Guys can't see past the end of their dick so they find someone at the gym can get 'roids and hypos. Backroom deals and politics like crazy. Not everyone's a star or a rocket scientist. Not everyone has a million choices.

Go to Portland, you walk in you're handed clean sweats, towel, the whole nine yards. You feel like a human. They phone, you listen. They got money and they'll spend it. Good food, good hotel.

The Cougars are a different can of worms. Cougars: bad food, bad rink, bad cans, housed poorly. Last year half of them got mono. No leadership. Coach of the week club.

They screwed kids on eligibility. Traded their best players to Kamloops.

No. Forget the Cougars. Go down to Cornell or Harvard, Notre Dame, Ivy League, or NCAA, do a degree, good degree, use your brain, play some hockey at the same time. It's impressive. You'll get invited anywhere after. Like Manderville with the Leafs.

You have to teach them something. Not just to brawl. Some of these guys, they are not kings and counsellors. Three-time losers in nylon jackets. Gumchewers, can't organize a lay in a whorehouse with free labour. That coach we had there was too hard on them, knocking heads for no reason, pointless drills where they're getting injured, killing them, demolishing them; jeez they hated him.

Kent Manderville is a funny case. Told – not tough enough kid. His ma pulled him out. His ma. Now look, toughest on the team. Well maybe second or third toughest. College kid, Cornell, Ivy League, good degree, nice kid from Victoria, and now he's bashing and crashing with the Leafs. They want a berserker, make him into Curt Brackenbury. If he wants to stick. Same choice as when he was a kid. But he's not really like that. More a finesse guy. Maybe you get to like being a berserker. Never can tell. I still haven't learned to read minds. I tried though, tried to learn. I tried to read minds.

Some of these coaches got their certificate out of a Crackerjack box. You have to teach the kids *something*. You have to deal with kids' *heads*. Million miles from home, from their families. Fifteen, sixteen, they're *babies* really. Long road trips. Junk food. Blizzards, whiteouts, black ice all over the roads. Fall off the team bus with no legs and that instant you have to play some humungous farmboys waiting to knock your frigging block off. Things not going well. Bunch of strangers giving each other the greasy eyeball. Buses breaking down or going in the ditch on their side, like those Swift Current kids that died. Collecting stitches, broken noses, broken hands. The Philly flu. Psychology is a big thing. Some kids party like there's no tomorrow, go out and drink right after practice, boozehounds pissing it all away, soup to nuts. Or doing coke. They get a rep that's hard to ditch. And some kids just never fit in. What if your kid gets traded to Fernie, Podunk, Nowheresville? His best buddy gets cut from the club? What if your kid gets cut? They're out there, they're out there on their own, hung out to dry. It's hard on the kids. *Really* hard. You have to deal with kids' heads.

Lots of jerks out there, too. Believe me. Lots of jerks. Guy here ran minor hockey and now in jail for molestation. I tried to punch his lights out in '69. I tried to take him out. Know what I mean? Guy hangs around injuries, all concerned. "Need sharper skates," he says to the kid. "Let me do them," he says.

Bring them to your house. *Jeez*. Good service. Molesting eight-
or nine-year-old boys on the hockey teams. Imagine what that
did to their game, their love of the game.

You're asking. You're worried about your kid. It's *good* you're
asking about this. Go with your instincts. There'll be tough
times. I tell you no one but no one knows how hard it is to
make it. Even to the minors or Europe. No one knows. We
just see the guys that make it so we think no prob. Watch TV
and think, I could do that. It's a long shot for anyone, no
matter how good. I remember going through this. You're the
skinny rookie, you're the new guy at camp they say to a veteran, *Run him*. See what you're made of. Tell the vet: run the
new guy. Maybe the new guy makes the team the vet doesn't.
Blindside you in a scrimmage, cheap shot to the face. Try to
get up he knocks you down. Creams you you spear him back,
slit open his face, chop him upside the head – hey, no ref at
a camp. No penalties. Other guy'll be pissed big time but
coach'll be happy. He sees what you're made of. You go after
the other guy no matter he's the size of a fucking ape. You
can't back down. You must *retaliate*. Helluva thing but there
you go. Carve him a new asshole need be. Dig down, find
that old-time religion.

I can give you a name – Tommy Black. Your kid'll have to join
the Y. Tommy won't show him how to fight but how to defend
himself. Nice guy. How to defend himself. Can't get away from
it. Your skinny kid here goes into the corners he needs to worry
about the puck, not the other guy. He needs to know he can
take care of himself. Confidence is important to any athlete.
Call Tommy Black. Firefighter, in great shape. Fifty-five and he

looks half that. Friends with the Courtnall boys, coached them when they were kids. Went down to Los Angeles when the younger one married that movie star.

I've never been to Los Angeles. I've scouted for the Montreal Canadiens and the Whalers and some ragtag WHA outfits along the way. I knew Rocket Richard and Gordie Howe and his sons. I almost got on the same plane with Bill Barilko, yeah that one that crashed, and I've caught a lot of salmon over the years up in Campbell River. I shot a moose in Newfoundland and I've been treed by a grizzly in the Rockies. But I've never been to L.A. Seems kind of scary to me actually. I know some tough young players in L.A. and they got mugged at a Wendy's. Knife to the heart. Maybe someday I'll get down, see a game at the Duck Pond.

My boy was about twelve, small for his age. Gets levelled by a guy way bigger, knocked right on his can. But he springs right up and BAM BAM BAM!

All over the guy. I was surprised, I didn't know he was like that. Little Tasmanian devil. You never really know.

Four years later some gorilla charges in full steam from the blue line – running him. My kid comes around behind the net with the puck, fast, BAM!! Into the boards. Then gloves off and drills my boy in the face going down. Brutal. Face a fucking mess. This time he didn't spring right up.

The needle moving through his cheek. I could read his mind this time.

My boy says to me while they're sewing up his face, "This isn't worth it. I don't like this game anymore."

He works with numbers now, an accountant. Handles money. Not a puck. He won't even watch hockey on TV anymore.

I watch. My job is to watch. I see a prospect, I put in a word. Hope the big club will listen. Hope I'm right. I've sent them some good ones.

My boy had wheels, too. Afterburners. And hands; make that puck get up and talk. Deke you in a phone booth. I still remember that needle and thread moving through his cheek. I don't like this game anymore, he says. And I still love it. Helluva thing.

But like I say, 20 get a legit look-see, 20 have an outside chance, and 20 are filler, nothing, losers.

Which are you? Which 20 are you right this moment? Do you ever know? Do you ever *really* know for sure? All my life. All my life I wonder this.

W.P. KINSELLA

DIEHARD

I remember good old Herky saying many a time, "The only way to kill an old catcher is to cut off his head and then hide it." We'd always laugh even if it was the hundredth time over the years that Herky had said it and I had heard him say it. We'd laugh, me and Herky and whoever else was around the big table at Bronko's Polish Falcon Bar. Bronko's ain't the Hyatt-Regency, if you know what I mean. But then Superior, Wisconsin ain't San Francisco, and me and Herky and the boys at Bronko's Polish Falcon ain't lawyer and stockbroker types, so it all evens out.

Herky grew up right here in East Superior, not a dozen blocks from Bronko's. He was German. Arnold Waldemar Herkheiser was his full handle. The house where he grew up still stands, a sad, old two-storey place, covered in imitation brick the grey sooty colour of a melting snowbank.

When we came home in the fall from our first year in Triple A baseball Herky married Stella Piska, who lived next door to St. Wenceslaus Church there on Fourth Street. The year Herky hit the Bigs for the first time him and Stella bought the old Wasylinski place, right after the old folks had to go into a nursing home. I helped Stella and Herky clean the junk out of that little house: tons and tons of Polish newspapers, *Life* magazines, *Collier's*, *Saturday Evening Posts* by the hundreds. The whole second bedroom was stacked right to the ceiling and the basement was stuffed full, some magazines stacked so close to the furnace it was a wonder the place hadn't burned down years before.

Stella still lives there. Their kids are married now; the girl lives in Seattle, the boy in Minneapolis. I've always been half in love with Stella, and, what with my Margie bein' gone goin' on four years now, I figure after a decent period of time I'll propose to Stella. I figure we can have a pleasant old age together. But that's the future. What we got here is a problem in the present: what to do with Herky's ashes.

The service was at St. Wenceslaus' yesterday. There'd been a viewing time down at Borowski's Funeral Home on Tuesday night. They laid Herky out real nice. He looked good, his silver hair combed up in a big pompadour the way he liked, that broken beak of his about a half inch to starboard, the way it had been since he slid into Sherm Lollar's knee at third base in, what would it have been, the '44 season? And his hands, those big mitts of his were resting on his belly; at one time or another he must have broke every knuckle he owned. The first time I cried for Herky was when I looked at those great, scarred hands, the right thumbnail split down the middle, ridged like the peak of a roof. I knew I was crying for me as much as for Herky. I'd lost a friend I'd known all my 62 years.

Stella had laid out Herky's catching gear on the bottom half of the coffin. Pretty cruddy stuff compared to what catchers have today, the thin shin guards, the small mask, the old cowhide mitt the size of a plate with the round indentation in the middle. It added a nice touch. The Red Sox remembered and sent their Midwest scout to the funeral – a classy organization. Walt Dropo and Mel Parnell, teammates of ours on the Red Sox, came; and Swede Tenholm drove down from Hibbing, Minnesota, where he manages a mine there in the Iron Range.

"Geez, Hector, he looks better than you do," the other old ballplayers said to me, after viewing the body. "All you'd have to do is lie down and we could have a double funeral," said Swede.

They kidded me some more about my playing days. I'd been a good field, no hit infielder for four seasons with the Red Sox. I put in five more years in the minors; in those days you could play your way up and down in the minor leagues. Now, if you're not a true major league prospect, you're driving a truck by the time you're twenty-five.

We went back to Stella's after the service. Neighbours brought tons of food and the place was crowded. The living room seemed so small; nobody sat in Herky's chair, that square box of a chair covered in maroon velvet with a raised-leaf pattern, ferns in concentric swirls. Both arms of the chair were worn bald from Herky hanging first one leg and then the other over the sides. There were food stains, grease, and beer can rings on the arms and seat cushion of that chair. Stella furnished the rest of the room at least three times over the years but Herky's chair dated back to when they got married, 1943. He was 20, Stella was 18. The wedding picture hangs in the dining room, right above the silver chest on the buffet. I swear we were never that young: me and Herky fresh-faced, our hair brushcut and watered; Herky's brother in his Marine uniform; Stella not as good looking as she is now, all sharp angles and frizzy hair, made almost ugly by the wartime women's fashions.

The children and grandchildren said their goodbyes. The son and his family would take the sister to Minneapolis for a day before she flew home to Seattle. The neighbours trickled away one family at a time, with much hugging and reassuring. Stella and I were left alone.

We sat at the kitchen table drinking coffee laced with Irish whiskey. Old Tennis Shoes, as Herky called it. Herky's ashes sat across the room on the kitchen counter, amid cake boxes, and plates of sandwiches draped in wax paper. Borowski the undertaker had said, "Why don't you drop over next week and pick up the ashes," but Stella insisted she wanted them that day. Borowski delivered them himself, early that evening.

We had several drinks mainly in silence; the kind of silence lifelong friends share with comfort. Finally, it was Stella who looked over to where the blue, long-necked urn sat like a heron among rocks.

"What should I do?" she asked.

"Some women keep their husband's ashes on the mantel-piece, or in their bedroom." Stella shook her head. "The attic? The basement? The garage?" At each suggestion Stella continued to shake her head gently.

"I don't have any desire to keep them. They're not Herky. I've got my memories here inside me." She patted her dress just below her breasts. Stella's yellow hair is greying now, her face is thinner, her eyes sharper. But she's still a beautiful woman. "I think it's sad to keep something like that," she went on. "It's the kind of thing dreary old movie has-beens do to seek sympathy."

"I could scatter them the next time I go for a walk," I said. "Herky and I must have walked the tracks and the trestle out by the flour mill a thousand miles or more. That was his favourite place in the world, walking across the trestle looking down at the fields of marsh grass, especially if the moon was out and glinted off the tracks and the water in among the grass."

"It's an idea," said Stella, "but I'd like something special, someplace special."

Though we both played for the Boston Red Sox, once our playing days were over we were never more than interested fans. We followed the standings in the newspapers and watched *The Game of the Week* on Saturday, but we didn't have the money to travel to Boston, in fact neither of us was ever back there again. We went down to Milwaukee once in a while, but we mainly watched minor league baseball until 1960 when the Minnesota Twins came into being.

On Saturdays and Sundays we could jump in the car right after breakfast and get to Met Stadium in time for batting practice. The four of us, hundreds and hundreds of trips down Interstate 35 to the Twin Cities. The Met was a lot like Fenway Park, a solid, friendly stadium with natural grass and open spaces. We even bought season tickets one year, but it proved too much for us, getting home at 2:00 a.m. and having to get up to go to work, then drive back to Minneapolis the next night, sometimes not arriving until the second or third inning. But what a season it was. That magical year when Minnesota won their only pennant.

The Season. The Season was what we called that year. We went to the World Series, and it was more exciting than playing in one. Both Herky and I were with the Red Sox in 1946 when we lost to the Cardinals and Harry Brecheen in seven games. Herky caught two of those games and I got to pinch hit twice, 0-2, and play three innings as a substitute second baseman. But if any one of us mentioned The Season, we all knew it was 1965, the year the Twins went to the World Series.

They were 102-60, first by seven games over the White Sox. Sam Mele was manager. And they had Don Mincher, Harmon Killebrew, Tony Oliva, Frank Quilici, Zoilo Versalles. Earl Battey was the catcher. Jimmy Hall hit like crazy; he never had another good season.

And the pitchers: Mudcat Grant, Jim Kaat, Jim Perry, and Camilo Pascual, who at 9-3 (.750) had the best winning percentage of his 18-year career.

Oh, we loved those Twins. Sometimes after a game we'd go down to the clubhouse and Herky would talk catching with Earl Battey.

Then there was the Series. Los Angeles had such pitching. Tony Oliva, the American League batting champion, hit only .192, poor Earl Battey was at .120, Don Mincher .130. Only

Killebrew and Versalles were able to hit. But the Twins took them to seven games anyway. Jim Kaat against Sandy Koufax.

The seventh game! Two lousy runs!

"Two runs," Herky would cry, and he'd actually have tears in his eyes. "Two runs away from the World Championship."

We were disappointed but not bitter. It was just that Koufax was so good. Herky would shake his head and marvel at the speed of his fastball, the fade of the curve.

"What a joy it would be to be rooting for him instead of against him," Herky said.

"Stella," I said, after maybe the fourth Irish coffee, "I just thought of something. You know Herky and me never talked about him dying. I wish we could have. If we could have talked about death we could have really said goodbye…" As I said that I thought of Herky, pale as his white hospital shirt, too weak to raise his head from the pillow.

"I know," said Stella, "we didn't talk about it either."

"One thing I remember, Stella, was a night at the Met in Minneapolis; it was one of those perfect baseball nights; the air was soft and warm, there wasn't a hint of a breeze. When we looked up past the blaze of floodlights, the stars winked silver and gold, like bits of tinsel floating in ink. The Twins were winning; all was right with the world. Herky leaned over and said to me, 'You know, Hec, if there's anything after this life, the first words I want to hear when I wake up are Play Ball!' That's the closest we ever came to having a talk about life."

"We lived it, Hec," said Stella. "We didn't have to talk about it."

"What I was thinkin', Stell, was maybe the stadium, you know, the Met. Maybe all across the outfield. I'm sure that would make Herky feel good."

"But they're gonna tear the Met down in a couple of years. Soon as the new stadium is ready."

Stella was right. They were just nicely getting started on the new stadium. They'd play both football and baseball there. It was going to be enclosed. There'd been a lot of controversy, letters to the editor and such, a lot of people hated the idea of an enclosed stadium. But Herky had been philosophical about it.

"I've caught games in snow storms in April and May. I've seen a whole week of games rained out at the Met. I've seen football games played in a blizzard, the field frozen hard as concrete. We need both kinds of stadiums, not that it will ever happen. When the weather's warm, and sweet and perfect, play at the Met, but move inside when the weather's terrible.

"You know what's gonna happen, Hec? In a few years, like 30 or 40, all the stadiums will have retractable roofs. It will be the best of both worlds – green grass, blue skies, but a nice clear dome to keep the rain and wind out."

"What about the new stadium?" I said to Stella. "How about getting Herky a seat behind home plate in the new stadium?"

"I think you've hit on a good one," Stella said, and she reached across the kitchen table and squeezed my hand.

We talked for another hour about the idea. The liquor and our emotional exhaustion after the funeral combined to produce a crazy euphoria, a giddiness, like the four of us used to get sometimes on the long drive home from Minneapolis after a big Twins win. We'd be singing, joking, happy as children. But there were only the two of us now.

"Secrets are so much fun," laughed Stella.

I slept on the sofa, fully clothed.

"You know what my daughter had the nerve to suggest?" Stella had said the night before, just before she went to bed. "'You know, Mama, now that Daddy's gone, it isn't proper for Hector to stay over, even in the spare room. What will people think?' 'Let them think any damn thing they want,' I said to her. 'I guess Hector's stayed here a few times over the years, so him and your dad could get up at 3:00 a.m. to go duck hunting. I stayed at Hector's many a night when poor Margie was dying. If anybody thinks anything about it they can go straight to hell.'"

The letdown the next morning was so solid we could feel it. The sky was low and waxy. Our hangovers had a life of their own. Stella fixed me a big breakfast: fried eggs, toast, bacon, coffee. But all either of us was able to manage was the coffee.

Though we didn't talk about it, we were both wondering if we were doing the right thing. I stopped at my place to change clothes, and I thought of suggesting we rethink our idea. But I could see Stella sitting grimly in the front seat of my car; I took two aspirin and a deep breath and pointed the car toward the interstate and the long drive to the Twin Cities.

We didn't have much to say on the 150 miles to Minneapolis. Stella sat over by the door; the urn with Herky's ashes sat between us. It was a reverse of the situation when he was alive; Stella always sat in the middle; whoever owned the car drove, while the other one sat by the window.

I had a difficult time finding a parking spot near to where they were building the new stadium, the Metrodome. Talk was they were gonna name it for that little yap Humphrey. If the Democrats had had a real candidate in 1968 Nixon never would have got elected. I glanced over at Stella. She looked drawn and tired; her face was the same pale colour as her hair.

The paved streets were breaking up and were covered in dirt tracked out of the construction site by trucks. It had rained overnight and the streets were slick. We'd both dressed sensibly, me in my green workpants, boots and a mackinaw. Stella in jeans and a carcoat. We walked on past the yellow-lettered sign that said: *Hardhats Must Be Worn Beyond This Point.*

Cement trucks rumbled by, groaning like dinosaurs. A crane passed back and forth overhead, slabs of concrete dangling from its beak. Finally we heard a voice above the melee shouting,

"Hey! Hey!" From a wooden construction shack a beefy man emerged; he was wearing a red-and-black checkered jacket, steel-toed boots and a scarred and dented silver hardhat. Stella and I waited for him to catch up to us.

Stella, waving the long-necked urn in her left hand, had to yell to be heard. My head ached and the construction noises were like someone whittling little pieces off the back of my head with a jackknife.

"I suppose there's nothin' wrong with it," the man said. Then he smiled, a loose-lipped, lopsided smile. "This does give a whole new meaning to a guy saying, 'I'd die for a front row seat at all the Twins games.' No offense."

"None taken," I said. "He was a real diehard fan of the Twins. There's nothin' Herky would have liked better than season tickets behind home plate, with nothing foolish like workin' for a living to interrupt his enjoyment of baseball."

"A hell of an idea," the foreman said. "I'm more of a Vikings fan myself. But, by God, if I die before this place is finished I'll have my old lady plant me on the 50-yard line."

"Where is home plate gonna be?" asked Stella.

The man stopped and stared around him; he looked puzzled for a moment as if trying to get his bearings.

"Come on back to the shack and we'll look at the blueprints to make sure," he said.

At the shack he fitted us each with a bulky yellow hardhat with *Visitor* stencilled across the crown.

He held the blueprints up to the light, making them look like ghostly writing on a midnight blue background.

"See, the press box goes here," he said, marking a section with a dirty thumbnail, "so the plate would be here," and he pointed out another squiggle on the blueprint.

The three of us picked our way across the muddy site. Bulging cement trucks pregnant with concrete grumbled past us. Stella cradled the indigo-coloured urn in the crook of her left arm.

"The first row of seats will be right along here," the foreman said.

The odours of freshly sawn wood, of wet cement, of old fires, filled the air. The cloud cover lightened a bit and though we still couldn't see the sun, the intensity of light quickened dramatically.

"First row, Hector, what do you think?" said Stella. "An aisle seat. Herky can put his feet on the screen, chug a beer, spill mustard down the front of his shirt while he tries to eat a hot dog, keep score, and tell the catcher how to call the game."

"Looks good to me," I said.

The concrete forms were held together by aluminum-coloured industrial staples. The foreman caught the attention of a cement truck driver heading for a spot 50 yards away. He walked out, and as the truck labouriously backed up, a safety instrument bleating annoyingly at every turn of a wheel, he directed it to a standstill next to us. He yanked the spout down and positioned it for pouring.

"You got to put it down if you want us to cover it up," the foreman said.

"Oh, my," said Stella.

The close sky, the raw, chilling air, the confusion about us all took their toll on our resolve.

"There was no place Herky loved more than a ballpark," I said. "Even after they close this one in he'll still have a choice view of Twins games, until long after either of us will care about it anymore."

Stella smiled a wan smile, and leaning over stared into the dark recesses of the concrete form.

"If you want, this will be our secret," I said. "Tell the kids you did something more conventional."

"Our secret," said Stella, and squeezed my hand.

The foreman banged on the back of the truck, and a slide of concrete rushed into the void. He steered the spout down a six-foot length of form, banged on the truck again and the flow stopped.

"Now," he said.

I put my arm around Stella's waist; we each gripped the blue-glazed urn. Together we lowered it as deep into the form as our arms would allow. Stella closed her eyes and grimaced as we released it. The urn dropped less than two feet before it met the wet cement.

"Thanks," we said.

The foreman nodded, signalled the truck again, and a second rush of cement was released into the form, filling it to the brim.

"Play Ball," I said softly, as Stella and I picked our way back toward the construction shack and the street.

STEPHEN LEACOCK

THE OLD, OLD STORY OF HOW FIVE MEN WENT FISHING

This is a plain account of a fishing party. It is not a story. There is no plot. Nothing happens in it and nobody is hurt. The only point of this narrative is its peculiar truth. It not only tells what happened to us – the five people concerned in it – but what has happened and is happening to all the other fishing parties that at the season of the year, from Halifax to Idaho, go gliding out on the unruffled surface of our Canadian and American lakes in the still cool of early summer morning.

We decided to go in the early morning because there is a popular belief that the early morning is the right time for bass fishing. The bass is said to bite in the early morning. Perhaps it does. In fact the thing is almost capable of scientific proof. The bass does *not* bite between eight and twelve. It does *not* bite between twelve and six in the afternoon. Nor does it bite between six o'clock and midnight. All these things are known facts. The inference is that the bass bites furiously at about daybreak.

At any rate our party were unanimous about starting early. "Better make an early start," said the Colonel when the idea of the party was suggested. "Oh, yes," said George Popley, the bank manager, "we want to get right out on the shoal while the fish are biting."

When he said this all our eyes glistened. Everybody's do. There's a thrill in the words. To "get right out on the shoal at daybreak when the fish are biting," is an idea that goes to any man's brain.

If you listen to the men talking in a Pullman car, or a hotel corridor, or better still, at the little tables in a first-class bar, you will not listen long before you hear one say— "Well, we got out early, just after sunrise, right on the shoal." ...And presently, even if you can't hear him you will see him reach out his two hands and hold them about two feet apart for the other man to admire. He is measuring the fish. No, not the fish they caught; this was the big one that they lost. But they had him right up to the top of the water: Oh, yes, he was up to the top of the water all right. The number of huge fish that have been heaved up to the top of the water in our lakes is almost incredible. Or at least it used to be when we still had bar rooms and little tables for serving that vile stuff, scotch whiskey and such foul things as gin Rickeys and John Collinses. It makes one sick to think of it, doesn't it? But there was good fishing in the bars, all winter.

But, as I say, we decided to go early in the morning. Charlie Jones, the railroad man, said that he remembered how when he was a boy, up in Wisconsin, they used to get out at five in the morning – not get up at five but be on the shoal at five. It appears that there is a shoal somewhere in Wisconsin where the bass lie in thousands. Kernin, the lawyer, said that when he was a boy – this was on Lake Rosseau – they used to get out at four. It seems there is a shoal in Lake Rosseau where you can haul up the bass as fast as you can drop your line. The shoal is hard to find – very hard. Kernin can find it, but it is doubtful – so I gather – if any other living man can. The Wisconsin shoal, too, is very difficult to find. Once you find it, you are all right; but it's hard to find. Charlie Jones can find it. If you were in

Wisconsin right now he'd take you straight to it, but probably no other person now alive could reach that shoal. In the same way Colonel Morse knows of a shoal in Lake Simcoe where he used to fish years and years ago and which, I understand, he can still find.

I have mentioned that Kernin is a lawyer, and Jones a railroad man and Popley a banker. But I needn't have. Any reader would take it for granted. In any fishing party there is always a lawyer. You can tell him at sight. He is the one of the party that has a landing net and a steel rod in sections with a wheel that is used to wind the fish to the top of the water.

And there is always a banker. You can tell him by his good clothes. Popley, in the bank, wears his banking suit. When he goes fishing he wears his fishing suit. It is much the better of the two, because his banking suit has ink marks on it, and his fishing suit has no fish marks on it.

As for the railroad man – quite so, the reader knows it as well as I do – you can tell him because he carries a pole that he cut in the bush himself, with a ten-cent line wrapped round the end of it. Jones says he can catch as many fish with this kind of line as Kernin can with his patent rod and wheel. So he can, too. Just the same number.

But Kernin says that with his patent apparatus if you get a fish on you can *play* him. Jones says to Hades with *playing* him: give him a fish on his line and he'll haul him in all right. Kernin says he'd lose him. But Jones says *he* wouldn't. In fact he *guarantees* to haul the fish in. Kernin says that more than once (in Lake Rosseau) he has played a fish for over half an hour. I forget now why he stopped; I think the fish quit playing.

I have heard Kernin and Jones argue this question of their two rods, as to which rod can best pull in the fish, for half an hour. Others may have heard the same question debated. I know no way by which it could be settled.

Our arrangement to go fishing was made at the little golf club of our summer town on the verandah where we sit in the evening. Oh, it's just a little place, nothing pretentious: the links are not much good for *golf;* in fact we don't play much *golf* there, so far as golf goes, and of course, we don't serve meals at the club, it's not like that – and no, we've nothing to drink there because of Prohibition. But we go and *sit* there. It is a good place to *sit,* and, after all, what else can you do in the present state of the law?

So it was there that we arranged the party.

The thing somehow seemed to fall into the mood of each of us. Jones said he had been hoping that some of the boys would get up a fishing party. It was apparently the one kind of pleasure that he really cared for. For myself I was delighted to get in with a crowd of regular fishermen like these four, especially as I hadn't been out fishing for nearly 10 years: though fishing is a thing I am passionately fond of. I know no pleasure in life like the sensation of getting a four-pound bass on the hook and hauling him up to the top of the water, to weigh him. But, as I say, I hadn't been out for 10 years: Oh, yes, I live right beside the water every summer, and yes, certainly – I am saying so – I am passionately fond of fishing, but still somehow I hadn't been *out.* Every fisherman knows just how that happens. The years have a way of slipping by. Yet I must say I was surprised to find that so keen a sport as Jones hadn't been out – so it presently appeared – for eight years. I had imagined he practically lived on the water. And Colonel Morse and Kernin – I was amazed to find – hadn't been out for 12 years, not since the day (so it came out in conversation) when they went out together in Lake Rosseau and Kernin landed a perfect monster, a regular corker, five pounds and a half, they said: or no, I don't think he *landed* him. No, I remember, he didn't *land* him. He caught him – and he *could* have landed him – he should have landed him – but he *didn't* land him. That was it. Yes, I remember Kernin

and Morse had a slight discussion about it – oh, perfectly ami-
cable – as to whether Morse had fumbled with the net – or
whether Kernin – the whole argument was perfectly friendly –
had made an ass of himself by not "striking" soon enough. Of
course the whole thing was so long ago, that both of them
could look back on it without any bitterness or ill nature. In
fact it amused them. Kernin said it was the most laughable
thing he ever saw in his life to see poor old Jack (that's
Morse's name) shoving away with the landing net wrong side
up. And Morse said he'd never forget seeing poor old Kernin
yanking his line first this way and then that and not knowing where to try to haul it. It made him laugh to look back
at it.

They might have gone on laughing for quite a time but Charlie
Jones interrupted by saying that in his opinion a landing net is
a piece of darned foolishness. Here Popley agrees with him.
Kernin objects that if you don't use a net you'll lose your fish at
the side of the boat. Jones says no: give him a hook well
through the fish and a stout line in his hand and that fish has
got to come in. Popley says so too. He says let him have his
hook fast through the fish's head with a short stout line, and
put him (Popley) at the other end of that line and that fish will
come in. It's *got* to. Otherwise Popley will know why. That's the
alternative. Either the fish must come in or Popley must know
why. There's no escape from the logic of it.

But perhaps some of my readers have heard the thing discussed before.

So as I say we decided to go the next morning and to make
an early start. All of the boys were at one about that. When I
say "boys," I use the word, as it is used in fishing, to mean people from say forty-five to sixty-five. There is something about

fishing that keeps men young. If a fellow gets out for a good morning's fishing, forgetting all business worries, once in a while – say once in 10 years – it keeps him fresh.

We agree to go in a launch, a large launch – to be exact, the largest in the town. We could have gone in row boats, but a row boat is a poor thing to fish from. Kernin said that in a row boat it is impossible properly to "play" your fish. The side of the boat is so low that the fish is apt to leap over the side into the boat when half "played." Popley said that there is no *comfort* in a row boat. In a launch a man can reach out his feet, and take it easy. Charlie Jones said that in a launch a man could rest his back against something and Morse said that in a launch a man could rest his neck. Young inexperienced boys, in the small sense of the word, never think of these things. So they go out and after a few hours their necks get tired; whereas a group of expert fishers in a launch can rest their backs and necks and even fall asleep during the pauses when the fish stop biting.

Anyway all the "boys" agreed that the great advantage of a launch would be that we could get a *man* to take us. By that means the man could see to getting the worms, and the man would be sure to have spare lines, and the man could come along to our different places – we were all beside the water – and pick us up. In fact the more we thought about the advantage of having a "man" to take us the better we liked it. As a boy gets old he likes to have a man around to do the work.

Anyway Frank Rolls, the man we decided to get, not only has the biggest launch in the town, but what is more, Frank *knows* the lake. We called him up at his boat house over the phone and said we'd give him five dollars to take us out first thing in the morning provided that he knew the shoal. He said he knew it.

I don't know, to be quite candid about it, who mentioned whiskey first. In these days everybody has to be a little careful. I imagine we had all been *thinking* whiskey for some time before anybody said it. But there is a sort of convention that when men go fishing they must have whiskey. Each man makes pretence that the one thing he needs at six o'clock in the morning is cold raw whiskey. It is spoken of in terms of affection. One man says the first thing you need if you're going fishing is a good "snort" of whiskey: another says that a good "snifter" is the very thing and the others agree, that no man can fish properly without "a horn," or a "bracer" or an "eye-opener." Each man really decides that he himself won't take any. But he feels that in a collective sense, the "boys" need it.

So it was with us. The Colonel said he'd bring along "a bottle of booze." Popley said, no, let *him* bring it; Kernin said let him: and Charlie Jones said no, he'd bring it. It turned out that the Colonel had some very good scotch at his house that he'd like to bring: oddly enough Popley had some good scotch in *his* house too; and, queer though it is, each of the boys had scotch in his house. When the discussion closed we knew that each of the five of us was intending to bring a bottle of whiskey. Each of the five of us expected the others to drink one and a quarter bottles in the course of the morning.

I suppose we must have talked on that verandah till long after one in the morning. It was probably nearer two than one when we broke up. But we agreed that that made no difference. Popley said that for him three hours' sleep, the right kind of sleep, was far more refreshing than ten. Kernin said that a lawyer learns to snatch his sleep when he can, and Jones said that in railroad work a man pretty well cuts out sleep.

So we had no alarms whatever about not being ready by five. Our plan was simplicity itself. Men like ourselves in responsible positions learn to organize things easily. In fact

Popley says it is that faculty that has put us where we are. So the plan simply was that Frank Rolls should come along at five o'clock and blow his whistle in front of our places, and at that signal each man would come down to his wharf with his rod and kit and so we'd be off to the shoal without a moment's delay.

The weather we ruled out. It was decided that even if it rained that made no difference. Kernin said that fish bite better in the rain. And everybody agreed that a man with a couple of snorts in him need have no fear of a little rain water.

So we parted, all keen on the enterprise. Nor do I think even now that there was anything faulty or imperfect in that party as we planned it.

I heard Frank Rolls blowing his infernal whistle opposite my summer cottage at some ghastly hour in the morning. Even without getting out of bed, I could see from the window that it was no day for fishing. No, not raining exactly. I don't mean that, but one of those peculiar days – I don't mean *wind* – there was no wind, but a sort of feeling in the air that showed anybody who understands bass fishing that it was a perfectly rotten day for going out. The fish, I seemed to know it, wouldn't bite.

When I was still fretting over the annoyance of the disappointment I heard Frank Rolls blowing his whistle in front of the other cottages. I counted 30 whistles altogether. Then I fell into a light doze – not exactly sleep, but a sort of *doze* – I can find no other word for it. It was clear to me that the other "boys" had thrown the thing over. There was no use in my trying to go out alone. I stayed where I was, my doze lasting till ten o'clock.

When I walked up town later in the morning I couldn't help being struck by the signs in the butchers' shops and the restaurants, FISH, FRESH FISH, FRESH LAKE FISH.

Where in the blazes do they get those fish anyway?

BARRY MILLIKEN

RUN

"Uhnee-peesh e-zhaayin?" my mother asks. She has been watching me since I came downstairs, and, now that I have eaten, she knows that I'm going.

"Up the road," I say. That is all I tell her because that is all I know. She doesn't say anything for a minute, just stands by the noisy old wash machine looking grumpy and feeding wet clothes into the wringer. Her hair is tied by a rubber band at the back, but many strands are loose and hang like little droopy antennas beside her face. I see many lines that weren't there before my father died. In her eyes there is sadness that makes me mad when I see it, just like everything seems to do lately. I know what she is going to say next, and I turn away as she does.

"When you gonna be back?"

For a minute I stand like that with my back to her, feeling suddenly like I want to cry. But I am fifteen so I will not.

"Peter?"

A loud bump, and then my sister's laughing comes from above me. The mad feeling gets worse. I shrug my shoulders.

"Are you going to Budge's?"

I shrug again and hear her sigh; I know that some of the sadness in her eyes is because of me.

"If you're going to Budge's, I want you to take something to her."

Finally, I turn halfway around and nod.

She goes to the cupboard, and from the edge of my vision, I see her reach up to the top shelf. My sister's baby starts to cry in his high chair. My mother comes to me and holds out her hand. Without looking up, I take the thing and shove it into my back pocket.

"Don't forget," she says. I turn and go, feeling her eyes on me. As I reach the front door, I think I hear her say my name, but when I turn she has gone into the kitchen and I hear the high chair bang as she lifts the baby from it.

Out on the porch I can see without looking the mess of beer bottles and cigarette butts around me on the floor. After the washing, and after the baby is cleaned up, my mother will come like a servant woman and clean up this mess my sister and her friends made last night. Her and Tucker.

Above me the clouds look like blankets, dark and light, a big unmade bed.

In front of the house is Tuck's car, which sits exactly as he left it yesterday about four o'clock. That's when he and my sister's friends arrived. All around it the ground is bare and oily, littered with tools, flattened old cigarette packages, beer bottles from other days and yesterday. The trunk and one door are open. On a table beside the car there is a part of a carburetor and beside this Sacha our cat, is sprawled. As I come down the porch steps, she gets up yawning and stretching. A car comes along the road and stops in a big cloud of dust. It backs up, then comes up our laneway with the wheels spinning, throwing dirt and stones behind it and sending Sacha running. I recognize who it is before the car comes to a stop about three feet from Tuck's. They are two of his friends, Manny and Sly. One look and I know they have been drinking all night. Manny's eyes are only half open, as he tilts his head out the window. The idling car makes a mean gurgling sound.

"Hey Pee-pee," he says and leans his head back on the seat. His mouth is twisted into a half-smile, and he looks about ready to pass out.

"C'mere."

When I go up beside the car, he lifts his arm and lets it rest along the top of the door. In his hand is a half-full bottle of beer.

"Wanna drink?"

I say no and stare at a tattoo he has put on his arm himself, the shape of a star with letters at the points. With his head still back, he squints up at me.

"Where's Tuck?"

I look toward the lake and shrug my shoulders.

"Sleeping, I guess," I say.

He repeats the word "sleeping" so softly I can hardly hear it. His eyes close and for a minute I think he is gone. But then, in a voice louder and harder, he says:

"Don't you know?"

His eyes half open and fix on me. There is white stuff around the corners of his mouth.

"Nope," I say, and bend forward, letting a gob of spit fall to the ground beside the car. For a minute again his eyes close and he says nothing, then when I glance down I see a little smile has come to his face.

"Hey, Pee-pee, I hear you're a fast runner."

His smile gets bigger. "Nother fu'n Longboat, I hear."

I shrug and say nothing. Sly laughs from his side of the car, and Manny rolls his head to look at him.

"Nother fug'n Longboat," he says again.

They laugh harder. I turn and walk away and see the black shape of my dog back along the treeline. He stops and looks up when I whistle and comes towards me as I start to trot along the path leading south from home. Their laughter reaches me like high, strange barking, pushing me faster. Boog comes jumping through the high grass and reaches the road the same time as me. There is dust and pieces of dry grass on his black fur. Once free of the grass he leaps high beside me, then runs ahead. He will stop and sniff around a tree or pole until I pass, then run on again. He was a present from my father for my tenth birthday. Now he's the best friend I have.

At first, as I run, the road feels hard; I hear my feet on the gravel which lies along both sides. There are bumps in the middle where I never go except to cross, and now I find the smooth part which lies just beside the gravel. My feet under me go faster; the air hits harder, cleaning me, crashing away the sound behind me.

Because it is Sunday morning, there is no one around and no cars in sight. The lake on my right doesn't sparkle the way it does when the sun is out, but it doesn't matter. I fall into a good pace, and I know that soon nothing will matter. The ground lies out flat and straight, my feet flash under me, and I am filled with something that washes everything else away. It is a power that makes me know that when I run I am strong, and there is nobody who is better. That's the way it has been since the first time the strangeness happened nearly two years ago when I had just turned fourteen.

People were just starting to notice how fast and far I could run, although I hadn't yet raced against Simon Cloud who was known to be the fastest runner on the reserve.

An older boy bet me that I couldn't run from his place, out to the highway and back in less than an hour. I told him I had no money to bet, but I knew, too, that I hesitated because I wasn't sure I could do it. The distance he talked about was four and a half miles each way. I had never gone more than six miles without a rest, and never against a clock. I also knew that my mother wouldn't want me getting into something like that.

Nine miles without a rest. It scared me all right. But the more I thought about it, the more I wanted to try it.

Carman Fisher was there, and, rather than see a good bet go down the drain, he covered the other boy's money then told me that if I could do it, I'd get 10 dollars.

It was very hot that day, and 15 minutes after I started I was wishing that I had put if off till evening. But I found a pace that I knew I could keep until at least the halfway point, and although it seemed like an hour before I reached the highway, someone yelled as I started back that 24 minutes were gone.

I had done better than I thought, but now as I ran the sun seemed like a torch that hung too close above me, the road stonier than I ever remembered it. I knew that it was because I was afraid. Please God, I said inside, don't let me fail and shame myself. Don't let it happen that they laugh at me.

But as I ran, my arms and legs went away from me and became only things I saw faintly, at the edges of my vision. My breath became a useless noise that flew in and out of my open mouth. Sweat flew from me and into my eyes, until I had to close them. *Please*, I said again. Then ahead of me the road blurred and a brightness flashed that seemed to go into me like a shock, and suddenly, not as much in vision, but in feeling as strong as the flash of light had been, my father was there, around me and in me. The tiredness was gone, the road and the air helped me again. But more than that was the joy I felt that my father had come back to me.

All I knew about Carman Fisher before I made that run was that he was about three years older than me, he had a car, and he worked at the lumberyard in town. After that day, he'd honk his horn if he passed me on the road, or sometimes he'd stop and talk a little.

One day he asked if I'd like to go for a ride. I felt important and honoured to be considered a friend by someone who was working and had his own car. We went to the beach where he met some people he knew – older kids, like him. When they offered him a beer, he said, "I hope you got one for my buddy here. We're gonna be watchin' him in the Olympics one day." Everybody laughed, but Carman looked at me and winked as if to say, "You'll show 'em."

After that I didn't see him for a long time, then I heard he had found a job in the city and was living there.

It was around then that the trouble at home started. When my father died, he took something that had made everything good for our family. After he was gone, we couldn't seem to talk, but instead, we each took our sorrow to a different part of the house, not willing to share it.

My sister quit school and started going with Tuck, who is a good-for-nothing drunk. The next thing I knew, he was living with us and sharing my sister's bed every night. She had a child one year after my father died. The boy is a symbol of the shame she has brought to our family. He cries and messes, and it is my mother who sees to him, and cooks the meals, and cleans up.

"We need the money Glenda gives me," she says. "You want us to live on welfare?"

I want to tell her that it wouldn't be any worse to have that shame than it is to have the shame of living the way we are. At least then she'd be able to tell them to get out. But of course I don't say it, because I know she wouldn't do it. That's the real shame. She has let it happen. She has betrayed my father. And that's why I have to go. Now, as I run, I have decided. I will do what has been in the back of my mind to do for a long time. It's a good day for running and I have a good start. Almost 50 miles to the city, almost two marathons.

Something I remember, too, makes me more excited. A while ago I saw Carman when he was back for a weekend, and though I didn't write it down, I remember his address because he joked about it.

"Just think of 13 turtles walking down the road," he said. That was it, 13 Turtlewalk Road.

Now that I have decided to go, I want to save all the time and distance I can. Two miles along the lake road, I turn east following a creek that winds through the bush. Though the path is rocky in parts and I have to watch my step, most of it is smooth and wide.

Boog runs past me and disappears into the bush up ahead. Seeing him makes me sad, because I know how hard it's going to be to leave him behind. I tried to think of some way I could take him with me, but I know that he would never be happy in the city. Then I remember Aunt Budge once saying that if she had a dog she would want it to be like Boog. He'll be happy there, because he likes her, too.

Out of the bush and onto a dirt road that takes me to her place, I notice that something isn't right. My wind? My stride?

Before I can think any more about it, I am there, and as I go up the lane, I see that her car is gone. Boog circles the house, barking loudly. Although I want to see her before I go, I'm relieved that she's gone to church. I know it would be hard not to let her talk me out of it. This way is sneaky, but at least I'll be gone.

Her back door is padlocked, so I look in the shed for what I need. Because there are no windows, I leave the door open and Boog comes in to sniff around. I find a piece of cardboard, but there is no rope. After watching him for a minute, I know what I have to do, although it's not what I wanted. He comes like a black ghost out of the darkness when I call. Already as I bend to say goodbye my throat is tight, my eyes full of tears. I say no words, but circle his neck with my arms. As if starting to know what is happening, he whimpers. I tell him to stay, then go to the door. When I turn to close it he takes a step toward me, confused. Quickly I close and hook it, then stand for a minute listening. He knows I'm still here and waits quietly to see what game we're playing. For the first time since deciding to go, I am unsure, and for a while longer I stand. Am I really doing this — locking Boog up in a shed so I can run away? It seems wrong. But then I think about home, and it's enough to get me moving again. I dig in my pockets for the pencil stub I keep and come across what my mother gave me for Aunt Budge. It's a photograph of my parents that must have been taken just before my father died, one that I haven't seen before. They stand beside my father's car, my father looking at the camera, my mother looking at him. Aunt Budge probably took the picture. It looks as if she has just called to my father, because the camera has caught him with a look that he hardly ever had — serious, maybe even sad. My mother, too, is caught with a faint smile and a brightness in her eyes, her hand in mid-air just above my father's arm. Suddenly, I can't look any longer. I stand, jamming the picture back into my pocket and start to print a message on the cardboard. My hand shakes, the pencil barely shows up, but it will do. Boog whimpers in the shed, then barks. I print, *Aunt Budge, left because I have to. Can't take home any longer. Boog is yours now, I'll be with a friend — don't worry. Love, Peter.*

I fold it and wedge it in beside the door handle, then, after glancing again toward the shed, I trot back down the laneway to the road, hearing Boog bark and rattle the door as he jumps against it.

The highway is good to run on, like the track at school, my feet barely seem to touch it as I go. But after a while, I start to have the feeling again that something is wrong. I have only come about four miles, and my breathing already is too hard and quick. Another mile. I concentrate on what Mr. Quinto, my track coach, teaches me: *Use your mind to beat the distance. Distract yourself from the tiredness.* I see myself in the last miles before the city, still strong and sure in my stride, still with the power. I try to bring it back, to feel it come into me now, but it won't. There is only the pain of going on. Six miles, but it feels like 60. I go on until the highway becomes a haze. I see the photograph again: my father looking straight at me; the great love in my mother's eyes as she looks at him. Great love where there is only sadness now. My body burns; my feet pound as I make them go.

L.M. MONTGOMERY

NATTY OF BLUE POINT

Natty Miller strolled down to the wharf where Bliss Ford was tying up the *Cockawee*. Bliss was scowling darkly at the boat, a trim new one, painted white, whose furled sails seemed unaccountably wet and whose glistening interior likewise dripped with moisture. A group of fishermen on the wharf were shaking their heads sagely as Natty drew near.

"Might was well split her up for kindlings, Bliss," said Jake McLaren. "You'll never get men to sail in her. It passed the first time, seeing as only young Johnson was skipper, but when a boat turns turtle with Captain Frank in command, there's something serious wrong with her."

"What's up?" asked Natty.

"The *Cockawee* upset out in the bay again this morning," answered Will Scott. "That's the second time. The *Grey Gull* picked up the men and towed her in. It's no use trying to sail her. Lobstermen ain't going to risk their lives in a boat like that. How's things over at Blue Point, Natty?"

"Pretty well," responded Natty laconically. Natty never wasted words. He had not talked a great deal in his fourteen years of life, but he was much given to thinking. He was rather undersized and insignificant looking but there were a few boys of his own age on the mainland who knew that Natty had muscles.

"Has Everett heard anything from Ottawa about the lighthouse business yet?" asked Will.

Natty shook his head.

"Think he's any chance of getting the app'intment?" queried Adam Lewis.

"Not the ghost of a chance," said Cooper Creasy decidedly. "He's on the wrong side of politics, that's what. Er rather his father was. A Tory's son ain't going to get an app'intment from a Lib'ral government, that's what."

"Mr. Barr says that Everett is too young to be trusted in such a responsible position," quoted Natty gravely.

Cooper shrugged his shoulders.

"Mebbe – mebbe. Eighteen is kind of green, but everybody knows that Ev's been the real lighthouse keeper for two years, since your father took sick. Irving Elliott wants that light – has wanted it for years – and he's a pretty strong pull at headquarters, that's what. Barr owes him something for years of hard work at elections. I ain't saying anything against Elliott, either. He's a good man, but your father's son ought to have that light as sure as he won't get it, that's what."

"Any of you going to take in the sports tomorrow down at Summerside?" asked Will Scott, in order to switch Cooper away from politics, which were apt to excite him.

"I'm going for one," said Adam. "There's to be a yacht race a'tween the Summerside and Charlottetown boat clubs. Yes, I am going. Give you a chance down to the station, Natty, if you want one."

Natty shook his head.

"Not going," he said briefly.

"You should celebrate Victoria Day," said Adam, patriotically. "Twenty-fourth o' May's the Queen's birthday, ef we don't get a holiday we'll all run away, as we used to say at school. The good old Queen is dead, but the day's been app'inted a national holiday in honour of her memory and you should celebrate it becoming, Natty-boy."

"Ev and I can't both go, and he's going," explained Natty. "Prue and I'll stay home to light up. Must be getting back now. Looks squally."

"I misdoubt if we'll have Queen's weather tomorrow," said Cooper, squinting critically at the sky. "Looks like a northeast blow, that's what. There goes Bliss, striding off and looking pretty mad. The *Cockawee's* a dead loss to him, that's what. Nat's off – he knows how to handle a boat middling well, too. Pity he's such a puny youngster. Not much to him, I reckon."

Natty had cast loose in his boat, the *Merry Maid*, and hoisted his sail. In a few minutes he was skimming gaily down the bay. The wind was fair and piping and the *Merry Maid* went like a bird. Natty, at the rudder, steered for Blue Point Island, a reflective frown on his face. He was feeling in no mood for Victoria Day sports. In a very short time he and Ev and Prue must leave Blue Point lighthouse, where they had lived all their lives. To Natty it seemed as if the end of all things would come then. Where would life be worth living away from lonely, windy Blue Point Island?

David Miller had died the preceding winter after a long illness. He had been lighthouse keeper at Blue Point for 30 years. His three children had been born and brought up there, and there, four years ago, the mother had died. But womanly little Prue had taken her place well, and the boys were devoted to their sister. When their father died, Everett had applied for the position of lighthouse keeper. The matter was not yet publicly decided, but old Cooper Creasy had sized the situation up accurately. The Millers had no real hope that Everett would be appointed.

Victoria Day, while not absolutely stormy, proved to be rather unpleasant. A choppy northeast wind blew up the bay, and the water was rough enough. The sky was overcast with clouds, and the May air was raw and chilly. At Blue Point the Millers were early astir, for if Everett wanted to sail over to the mainland in time to catch the excursion train, no morning naps were permissible. He was going alone. Since only one of the boys could go, Natty had insisted that it should be Everett, and Prue had elected to stay home with Natty. Prue had small heart for Victoria Day that year. She did not feel even a thrill of enthusiasm when Natty hoisted a flag and wreathed the Queen's picture with creeping spruce. Prue felt as badly about leaving Blue Point Island as the boys did.

The day passed slowly. In the afternoon the wind fell away to a dead calm, but there was still a heavy swell on, and shortly before sunset a fog came creeping up from the east and spread over the bay and islands, so thick and white that Prue and Natty could not even see Little Bear Island on the right.

"I'm glad Everett isn't coming back tonight," said Prue. "He could never find his way cross the harbour in that fog."

"Isn't it thick, though," said Natty. "The light won't show far tonight."

At sunset they lighted the great lamps and then settled down to an evening of reading. But it was not long before Natty looked up from his book to say, "Hello, Prue, what was that? Thought I heard a noise."

"So did I," said Prue. "It sounded like someone calling."

They hurried to the door, which looked out on the harbour. The night, owing to the fog, was dark with a darkness that seemed almost tangible. From somewhere out of that darkness came a muffled shouting, like that of a person in distress.

"Prue, there's somebody in trouble out there!" exclaimed Natty.

"Oh, it's surely never Ev!" cried Prue.

Natty shook his head.

"Don't think so. Ev had no intention of coming back tonight. Get that lantern, Prue. I must go and see what and who it is."

"Oh, Natty, you mustn't," cried Prue in distress. "There's a heavy swell on yet – and the fog – oh, if you get lost—"

"I'll not get lost, and I must go, Prue. Maybe somebody is drowning out there. It's not Ev, of course, but suppose it were! That's a good girl."

Prue, with set face, had brought the lantern, resolutely choking back the words of fear and protest that rushed to her lips. They hurried down to the shore and Natty sprang into the little skiff he used for rowing. He hastily lashed the lantern in the stern, cast loose the painter, and lifted the oars.

"I'll be back as soon as possible," he called to Prue. "Wait here for me."

In a minute the shore was out of sight, and Natty found himself alone in the black fog, with no guide but the cries for help, which already were becoming fainter. They seemed to come from the direction of Little Bear, and thither Natty rowed. It was a tough pull, and the water was rough enough for the little dory. But Natty had been at home with the oars from babyhood, and his long training and tough sinews stood him in good stead now. Steadily and intrepidly he rowed along. The water grew rougher as he passed out from the shelter of Blue Point into the channel between the latter and Little Bear. The cries were becoming very faint. What if he should be too late? He bent to the oars with all his energy. Presently, by the smoother water, he knew he must be in the lea of Little Bear. The cries sounded nearer. He must already have rowed nearly a mile. The next minute he shot around a small headland and right before him, dimly visible in the faint light cast by the lantern through the fog, was an upturned boat with two men clinging to it, one on each side, evidently almost exhausted. Natty rowed cautiously up to the one nearest him, knowing that he must be wary lest the grip of the drowning man overturn his own light skiff.

"Let go when I say," he shouted, "and don't – grab – anything, do you hear? Don't – grab. Now, let go."

The next minute the man lay in the dory, dragged over the stern by Natty's grip on his collar.

"Lie still," ordered Natty, clutching the oars. To row around the overturned boat, amid the swirl of water about her, was a task that taxed Natty's skill and strength to the utmost. The other man was dragged in over the bow, and with a gasp of relief Natty pulled away from the sinking boat. Once clear of her he could not row for a few minutes; he was shaking from head to foot with the reaction from tremendous effort and strain.

"This'll never do," he muttered. "I'm not going to be a baby now. But will I ever be able to row back?"

Presently, however, he was able to grip his oars again and pull for the lighthouse, whose beacon loomed dimly through the fog like a great blur of whiter mist. The men, obedient to his orders, lay quietly where he had placed them, and before long Natty was back again at the lighthouse landing, where Prue was waiting, wild with anxiety. The men were helped out and assisted up to the lighthouse, where Natty went to hunt up dry clothes for them, and Prue flew about to prepare hot drinks.

"To think that that child saved us!" exclaimed one of the men. "Why, I didn't think a grown man had the strength to do what he did. He is your brother, I suppose, Miss Miller. You have another brother, I think?"

"Oh, yes – Everett – but he is away," explained Prue. "We heard your shouts and Natty insisted on going at once to your rescue."

"Well, he came just in time. I couldn't have held on another minute – was so done up I couldn't have moved or spoken all the way here even if he hadn't commanded me to keep perfectly still."

Natty returned at this moment and exclaimed, "Why, it is Mr. Barr. I didn't recognize you before."

"Barr it is, young man. This gentlemen is my friend, Mr. Blackmore. We have been celebrating Victoria Day by a shooting tramp over Little Bear. We hired a boat from Ford at the harbour head this morning – the *Cockawee*, he called her – and sailed over. I don't know much about running a boat, but Blackmore here thinks he does. We were at the other side of the island when the fog came up. We hurried across it, but it was almost dark when we reached our boat. We sailed around the point and then the boat just simply upset – don't know why—"

"But I know why," interrupted Natty indignantly. "That *Cockawee* does nothing but upset. She has turned turtle twice out in the harbour in fine weather. Ford was a rascal to let her to you. He might have known what would happen. Why – why – it was almost murder to let you go!"

"I thought there must be something queer about her," declared Mr. Blackmore. "I do know how to handle a boat despite my friend's gibe, and there was no reason why she should have upset like that. That Ford ought to be horsewhipped.

Thanks to Prue's stinging hot decoctions of black current drink, the two gentlemen were no worse for their drenching and exposure, and the next morning Natty took them to the mainland in the *Merry Maid*. When he parted with them, Mr. Barr shook his hand heartily and said: "Thank you, my boy. You're a plucky youngster and a skillful one, too. Tell your brother that if I can get the Blue Point lighthouse berth for him I will, and as for yourself, you will always find a friend in me, and if I can ever do anything for you I will."

Two weeks later Everett received an official document formally appointing him keeper of Blue Point Island light. Natty carried the news to the mainland, where it was joyfully received among the fishermen.

"Only right and fair," said Cooper Creasy. "Blue Point without a Miller to light up wouldn't seem the thing at all, that's what. And it's nothing but Ev's doo."

"Guess Natty had more to do with it than Ev," said Adam, perpetrating a very poor pun and being immensely applauded therefore. It keyed Will Scott up to rival Adam.

"You said that Irving had a pull and the Millers hadn't," he said jocularly. "But it looks as if 'twas Natty's pull did the business after all – his pull over to Bear Island and back."

"It was about a miracle that a boy could do what he did on such a night," said Charles Macey.

"Where's Ford?" asked Natty uncomfortably. He hated to have his exploit talked about.

"Ford has cleared out," said Cooper, "gone down to Summerside to go into Tobe Meekins' factory there. Best thing he could do, that's what. Folks here hadn't no use for him after letting that death trap to them two men – even if they was Lib'rals. The *Cockawee* druv ashore on Little Bear, and there she's going to remain, I guess. D'ye want a berth in my mackerel boat this summer, Natty?"

"I do," said Natty, "but I thought you said you were full."

"I guess I can make room for you," said Cooper. "A boy with such grit and muscle ain't to be allowed to go to seed on Blue Point, that's what. Yesser, we'll make room for you."

And Natty's cup of happiness was full.

SUSANNA MOODIE

BRIAN, THE STILL HUNTER

O'er mem'ry's glass I see his shadow flit,
Though he was gathered to the silent dust
Long years ago: —a strange and wayward man,
Who shunn'd companionship, and lived apart.
The gleamy lakes, hid in their gloomy depths,
Whose still, deep waters never knew the stroke
Of cleaving oar, or echoed to the sound
Of social life – contained for him the sum
Of human happiness. With dog and gun,
Day after day he tracked the nimble deer
Through all the tangled mazes of the forest:
                                        —Author

In the early day, in the fall of 1832, I was alone in the old
shanty, preparing breakfast for my husband, and now and then
stirring the cradle with my foot, to keep little Katie a few minutes longer asleep, until her food was sufficiently prepared for
her first meal – and wishing secretly for a drop of milk, to make
it more agreeable and nourishing for the poor weanling – when
a tall, thin, middle-aged man, walked into the house, followed
by two large, strong dogs.

Placing the rifle he carried across his shoulder, in a corner of
the room, he advanced to their hearth, and, without speaking,
or seemingly looking at me, lighted his pipe, and commenced
smoking. The dogs, after growling and snapping at the cat, who

had not given the strangers a very courteous reception, sat down on the hearth-stone, on either side of their taciturn master, eyeing him, from time to time, as if long habit had made them understand all his motions. There was a great contrast between the dogs: the one was a brindled, grey and white bulldog, of the largest size – a most formidable and powerful brute; the other, a staghound, tawny, deep-chested, and strong-limbed. I regarded the man and his hairy companions with silent curiosity. He was between forty and fifty years old: his head, nearly bald, was shaded at the sides by strong, coarse, black, curling hair. His features were high, his complexion brightly dark; and his eyes, in size, shape, and colour, resembled the eyes of a hawk. The expression of his face was sorrowful and taciturn; and his thin, compressed lips, looked as if they were not much accustomed to smiles, or, indeed, often served to hold communication with any one. He stood at the side of the huge hearth, silently smoking, his keen eyes fixed on the fire; and now and then he patted the head of his dogs, and reproved their exuberant expressions of attachment, with – "Down, Chance! Down, Music!"

"A cold, clear morning," said I, in order to attract his attention, and draw him into conversation.

A nod, without raising his head, or taking his eyes off the fire, was my only answer; and turning from my unsociable guest, I took up the baby, who just then awoke, sat down on a low stool by the table, and commenced feeding her. During this operation, I once or twice caught the stranger's keen eye fixed upon me; but word spoke he none; and presently after, he whistled to his dogs, resumed his gun, and strode out.

When M— and Monaghan came in to breakfast, I told them what a strange visitor I had; and they laughed at my vain attempts to get him to talk.

"He is a strange, mysterious being," I said. "I must find out who, or what he is."

In the afternoon, an old soldier called Layton, who had served during the American war, and got a grant of land, about a mile in the rear of our location, came in to trade for a cow. Now, this Layton was a perfect ruffian – a man whom no one liked, and whom all feared. He was a deep drinker, a great swearer, and a perfect reprobate, who never cultivated his land, but went jobbing about, from farm to farm, trading horses and cattle, and cheating in a pettifogging way. Uncle Joe had employed him to sell M— a young heifer, and he had brought her for him to look at.

When he came in to be paid, I described the stranger of the morning; and as I knew that he was familiar with every person in the neighbourhood, I asked if he knew him.

"No one should know him better than myself," he said. "'Tis old Brian, the hunter, and a near neighbour of yours. A sour, morose, queer chap he is, and as mad as a 'March hare.' He's from Lancashire, in England, and came to this country some 20 years ago, with his wife, Deb, who was a pretty young lass in those days. He had lots of money, too; and he bought 400 acres of land, just at the corner of the concession line, where it meets the main road – and excellent land it is; and a better farmer, while he stuck to his business, never went into the bush. He was a dashing, handsome fellow too, and did not hoard the money either. He loved his pipe and his pot too well; and, at last, he left off farming, and stuck to them altogether. Many a jolly booze he and I have had, I can tell you. But Brian was an awful passionate man; and when the liquor was in, and the wit was out, as savage and as quarrelsome as a bear. At such times, there was no one but Ned Layton dared go near him. We once had a pitched battle, and I whipped him; and ever after he yielded a sort of sulky obedience to all I said to him. After being on the spree for a week or two, he would take fits of remorse, and return home to his wife – would go down upon his knees, and ask for her forgiveness, and cry like a child. At other times, he would hide himself up in the woods, and steal home at night, and get what he wanted out of the pantry, without speaking a word to any one. He went on with these pranks for some years, till he took a fit of the 'blue devils.'

"'Come away, Ned, to the Rice Lake, with me,' said he. 'I'm weary of my life, and I want a change.'

"'Shall we take the fishing-tackle,' says I: 'The black bass are in prime season; and F— will lend us the old canoe. He's got some capital rum up from Kingston. We'll fish all day, and have a spree at night.'

"'It's not to fish I'm going,' says he.

"'To shoot, then? I've bought Reckwood's new rifle.'

"'It's neither to fish nor to shoot, Ned: it's a new game I'm going to try; so, come along.'

"Well, to the Rice Lake we went. The day was very hot, and our path lay through the woods, and over those scorching plains, for 16 miles; and I thought I should have dropped by the way; but all that distance, my comrade never opened his lips. He strode on before me, at a half run, never once turning his hard leather face.

"'The man must be the devil,' says I, 'and accustomed to a warmer place, or he must feel this. Hollo, Brian! Stop there: do you mean to kill me?'

"'Take it easy,' says he; 'you'll see another day after this: I've business on hand, and cannot wait.'

"Well, on we went, at this awful rate; and it was mid-day when we got to the little tavern on the lakeshore, kept by one F—, who had a boat for the convenience of strangers who came to visit the place.

"Here we got our dinner, and a good stiff rum to wash it down: but Brian was moody; and to all my jokes he only made a sort of grunt; and while I was talking with F—, he slips out, and I saw him crossing the lake in an old canoe.

"'What's the matter with Brian?' says F—; 'all does not seem right with him, Ned. You had better take the boat, and look after him.'

"'Phoo!' says I, 'he's often so; and grows so glum nowadays, that I will cut his acquaintance altogether, if he does not improve.'

"'He drinks awful hard,' says F—, 'there is no telling what he may be up to at this minute.'

"My mind misgave me, too; so I e'en takes the oars, and pushes out, right upon Brian's track; and, by the Lord Harry! if I did not find him, upon my landing on the opposite shore, lying, wallowing in his blood, with his throat cut.

"'Is that you, Brian?' says I, giving him a kick with my foot. 'What upon earth tempted you to play F— and me this dirty, mean trick; to go and stick yourself like a pig – bring such a discredit on the house – and you so far from home, too, and those who should nurse you!'

"I was so wild with him, that, saving your presence, ma'am, I swore awfully, and called him names that would be undecent to repeat here; but he only answered by groans, and a horrid gurgling in his throat.

"'It's choking you are,' said I; 'but you shan't have your own way, and die so easily either, if I can punish you, by keeping you alive.' So I just turned him upon his belly, with his head down the steep bank; but he still kept choking, and growing black in the face. I then saw that it was a piece of flesh of his throat that had been carried into his wind-pipe. So, what do I do, but puts in my finger and thumb, and pulls it out, and bound up his throat with my handkerchief, dipping it first in the water to stanch the blood. I then took him, neck and heels, and threw him into the bottom of the boat, and pushed off for the tavern.

Presently, he came to himself a little, and sat up in the boat, and, would you believe it? Made several attempts to throw himself into the water. 'This will not do,' says I: 'you've done mischief enough already, by cutting your wizzand: if you dare to try that again, I will kill you with the oar.' I held it up, threatening him all the while; and he was scared, and lay down as quiet as a lamb. I put my foot upon his breast. 'Lie still, now, or you'll catch it.' He looked piteously at me, but he could not speak; but he seemed to say – 'Have pity upon me, Ned; don't kill me.' Yes; this man, who had cut his throat, and who, twice after that, tried to drown himself, was afraid that I should knock him on the head, and kill him. Ha! Ha! I never shall forget the work F— and I had with him.

"The doctor came, and sewed up his throat; and his wife – poor crater! – came to nurse him; and he laid bad there for six months; and did nothing but pray to God to forgive him; for he thought the devil would surely have him, for cutting his own throat. And when he got about again – which is now 12 years ago – he left off drinking entirely, and wanders about the country, with his dogs, hunting. He seldom speaks to any one, and his wife's brother carries on the farm for him and the family. He is so shy of strangers, that it is a wonder he came in here. The old wives are afraid of him; but you need not heed him: his troubles are to himself: he harms no one."

Layton departed, and left me brooding over the sad tale he had told in such an absurd and jesting manner. It was evident, from the account he had given of Brian's attempt at suicide, that the hapless hunter was not wholly answerable for his conduct – that he was a harmless maniac.

The next morning, at the very same hour, Brian again made his appearance; but instead of the rifle across his shoulder, a large stone jar was suspended by a stout leathern thong. Without speaking a word, but with a truly benevolent smile, that flirted slowly over his stern features, and lighted them up, like a sunbeam breaking from beneath a stormy cloud – he advanced to the table, and, unslinging the jar, set it down before me, and in a low, gruff, but not unfriendly voice, said:

"Milk, for the child," and vanished.

"How good it was of him! – how kind!" I exclaimed, as I poured the precious gift, of four quarts of pure new milk, out into a deep pan – "and I never asked him – never said that the poor babe wanted milk. It was the courtesy of a gentleman – of a man of benevolence and refinement."

For weeks did my strange friend steal silently in, take up the empty jar, and supply its place with another, replenished with milk. The baby knew his step, and would hold out her hands to him, and cry – "Milk!" and Brian would stoop down and kiss her, and his two great dogs lick her face.

"Have you any children, Mr. B—?"

"Yes, five; but none like this—"

"My little girl is greatly indebted to you for your kindness."

"She's welcome, or she would not get it. You are strangers; but I like you all. You look kind; and I would like to know more about you."

M— shook hands with the old hunter, and assured him that he should always be glad to see him.

After this invitation, Brian became a frequent guest. He would sit and listen with delight to M—, while he described to him elephant-hunting at the Cape; grasping his rifle with a determined air, and whistling an encouraging air to his dogs. I asked him one evening what made him so fond of hunting?

"'Tis the excitement," he said: "it drowns thought, and I love to be alone. I am sorry for the creatures, too, for they are free and happy; but I am led, by an impulse I cannot restrain, to kill them. Sometimes the sight of their dying agonies recalls painful feelings; and then I lay aside the gun, and do not hunt for days. But 'tis fine to be alone, with God, in the great woods – to watch the sunbeams stealing through the thick branches – the blue sky breaking in upon you in patches; and to know that all is bright and shiny above you, in spite of the gloom that surrounds you."

After a long pause, he said, with much solemn feeling in his look and tone:

"I lived a life of folly for years – for I was well born and educated before I left home for the woods, and should have known better; but if we associate long with the depraved and ignorant, we learn to become even worse than them. I felt I had become the slave to low vice and sin. I hated myself; and in order to free myself from the hateful tyranny of evil passions, I did a very rash and foolish action. I need not mention the manner in which I transgressed God's laws – all the neighbours know it, and must have told you long ago. I could have borne reproof, but they turned my sorrow into indecent jests; and, unable to bear their ridicule, I made companions of my dogs and gun, and went forth into the wilderness. Hunting became a habit – I could no longer live without it – and it supplies the stimulant which I lost, when I renounced the cursed whiskey bottle.

"I remember the first hunting excursion I took alone in the forest, how sad and gloomy I felt. I thought that there was no creature in the world so miserable as me; I was tired and hungry, and I sat down upon a fallen tree to rest. All was still as death around me; and I was fast sinking to sleep, when my attention was aroused by a long, wild cry. My dog – for I had not Chance then, and he is no hunter – pricked up his ears, but instead of answering with a bark of defiance, he crouched down, trembling, at my feet. 'What does this mean?' I said; and I cocked my gun, and sprang upon the log. The sound came nearer upon the wind. It was like the deep baying of a pack of hounds in full cry. Presently, a noble deer rushed past me, and fast upon his trail – I see them now, like so many black devils – swept by, a pack of 10 or 15 large fierce wolves, with fiery eyes and bristling hair, and paws that seemed scarcely to touch the ground, in their eager haste. I thought not of danger, for, with their prey in view, I was safe; but I felt every nerve within me tremble for the fate of the poor deer. The wolves gained upon him at every step: a close thicket intercepted his path; and rendered desperate, he turned at bay. His nostrils were dilated, and his eyes seemed to send forth long streams of light. It was wonderful to witness the courage of the beast – how bravely he repelled the first attack of his deadly enemies – how gallantly he tossed them to the right and left, and spurned them from beneath his hoofs; yet all his struggles were useless, and he was quickly torn to pieces by his ravenous foes. At that moment, he seemed more unfortunate than me; for I could not see in what manner he had deserved his fate. All his speed and energy, his courage and fortitude, had been given to him in vain. I had tried to destroy myself; but he, with every effort vigorously made for self-preservation, was doomed to meet the fate he dreaded. Is God just to his creatures?"

With this sentence in his throat, he started abruptly from his seat, and left the house.

One day he found me painting some wild flowers, and was greatly interested in watching the progress I made in the group. Late in the afternoon of the following day, he brought me a large bunch of splendid spring flowers.

"Draw these," said he: "I have been all the way to the Rice Lake Plains to find them for you."

"Oh! pretty, pretty flowers," lisped Katie, grasping them with infantine joy, and kissing, one by one, every lovely blossom.

"These are God's pictures," said the hunter; "and the child, who is all nature just now, understands them in a minute. Is it not strange, Mrs. M——, that these beautiful things are hid away in the wilderness, where no eyes but the birds of the air, and the wild beasts of the woods, and the insects that live upon them, ever see them? Does God provide, for the pleasure of such creatures, these flowers? When I am alone in the forest, these things puzzle me."

Knowing that to argue with Brian was only to call into action the slumbering fires of his fatal malady, I asked him why he called the dog Chance?

"I found him," he said, "40 miles back in the bush. He was a mere skeleton. At first I took him for a wolf, but the shape of his head undeceived me. I opened my wallet, and called him to me. He came slowly, stopping and wagging his tail at every step, and looking me wistfully in the face. I offered him a bit of cooked venison, and he soon became friendly, and followed me home, and has never left me, night or day, since. I called him Chance, after the manner I happened with him; and I would not part with him for 20 dollars."

Alas! for poor Chance! he had, unknown to his master, contracted a private liking for fresh mutton; and one night he killed no less than eight sheep that belonged to Mr. D——, on the front road; who, having long suspected, caught him in the very act; and this mischance cost him his life. Brian was very sad and gloomy for many weeks after his favourite's death.

"I would have restored the sheep, four-fold," he said, "if he would but have spared the life of my dog."

All my recollections of Brian seem more particularly to concentrate in the adventures of one night, when I happened to be left alone, for the first time since my arrival in Canada. I cannot now imagine how I could have been such a fool, as to give way for four and 20 hours to such childish fears; but so it was, and I will not disguise the truth from my readers. M—— had bought a very fine cow of a black man named Mollineux, who lived 12 miles distant through the woods, and one fine, frosty spring day, he and John Monaghan took a rope and the dog to fetch her home. M— said that they should be back by six o'clock in the evening, and to mind and have something cooked for supper when they returned, as their long walk and the sharp air would give them a great appetite. This was during the time that I was without a female servant, and lived in old Mrs. H—'s shanty.

The day was so bright and clear, and Katie was so full of frolic and play, rolling about the floor or toddling from chair to chair, that the day passed on without my feeling remarkably lonely. At length the evening drew nigh, and I began to expect the return of my beloved, and to think of the supper I was to prepare for his reception. The red heifer came lowing to the door to be milked, but I did not know how to milk in those days, and was terribly afraid of the cattle. Yet as I knew milk must be had for the tea, I ran across to Mrs. Joe, and begged that one of her girls would be so kind as to milk for me. My request was greeted with a rude burst of laughter from the whole set.

"If you can't milk," said Mrs. Joe, "it is high time you should learn. My galls are above being helps."

"I would not ask you but as a favour; I am afraid of cows."

"*Afraid of cows!*" Here followed another horse laugh; and indignant at the refusal of the first request I had ever made, when they had all borrowed so much from me, I shut the door, and returned home.

After many ineffectual attempts I succeeded at last, and bore my half pail of milk in triumph to the house. Yes! I felt prouder of that milk than the best thing I ever wrote, whether in verse or prose; and then it was doubly sweet, when I considered that I had procured it without being under any obligation to my ill-natured neighbours.

I fed little Katie and put her to bed, made the hot cakes for tea, boiled the potatoes, and laid the ham cut in nice slices in the pan, ready to cook the moment I saw the men enter the clearing, and arranged the little room with scrupulous care and neatness. A glorious fire was blazing on the hearth, and everything was ready for their supper, and I began to look out anxiously for their arrival. The night had closed in cold and foggy, and I could no longer distinguish any object a few yards from the door. Bringing in as much wood as I thought would last me for a few hours, I closed the door, and for the first time in my life, found myself in a house entirely alone. Then I began to ask myself a thousand torturing questions, as to the reason of their unusual absence. "Had they lost their way in the woods? could they have fallen in with wolves? – one of my early bugbears – could any fatal accident have befallen them?" I started up, opened the door, held my breath, and listened. The little brook lifted up its voice, in loud hoarse wailing, or mocked, in its bubbling to the stones, the sound of human voices. As it became later, my fears increased in proportion. I grew too superstitious to keep the door open; and not only closed it, but dragged a heavy box in front of it. Several ill-looking men had asked their way to Toronto during the day; and I felt alarmed lest such rude wayfarers should come tonight, and find me alone and unprotected. Once I thought of running across to Mrs. Joe, and asking her to let one of the girls stay with me until M— returned; but the way in which I had been repulsed in the evening deterred me. Hour after hour wore away, and the crowing of the cocks proclaimed midnight, and yet they came not. I had burnt out all my wood, and I dared not open the door to fetch in more. The candle was expiring in the socket, and I had not courage to go up into the loft, before it went finally out, to set up another. Cold, heart-weary, and faint, I sat in the middle of the floor, and cried. The furious barking of the dogs at the neighbouring farms, and the cackling of the geese upon our own place, made me hope that they were coming; and then I listened, till the beating of my own heart excluded all other sounds. Oh! that weary brook! how it sobbed and moaned, like a fretful child! What unreal terrors, and fanciful illusions, my too active mind conjured up, while listening to its mysterious tones! Just as the moon rose, the howling of a pack of wolves, from the great swamp in our rear, filled the whole air. Their yells were answered by the barking of all the dogs in the vicinity; and the geese, unwilling to be behind hand in the general confusion, set up the most discordant screams. I had often heard, and even been amused, during the winter, particularly on thaw nights, by the howls of these formidable wild beasts; but I had never before heard them alone, and my fears reached a climax. They were directly on the track that M— and Monaghan must have taken – and I now made no doubt that they had been attacked, and killed, on their return, and I wept and cried, until the grey cold dawn looked in upon me through the small dim windows. I have passed many a long, cheerless night; but that was the saddest and longest I ever remember. Just as the day broke, my friends, the wolves, set up a parting benediction, so loud and wild, and so near the house, that I was afraid that they would come through the windows, or come down the chimney, and rob me of my child. But the howls died away in the distance; the bright sun rose up, and dispersed the long horrors of the night; and I looked once more timidly around me. The sight of the uneaten supper for a few minutes renewed my grief, for I could not divest myself of the idea that M— was dead. I opened the door, and stepped forth into the pure air of the early day. A solemn and beautiful repose still hung, like a veil, over the face of nature. The mists of night still rested upon the majestic woods; and not a sound, but the flowing of the waters, went up in the vast stillness. The earth had not yet raised her matin hymn to the Throne of the Creator. Sad at heart, and weary and worn in spirit, I went down to the spring, and washed my face and head, and drank a deep draught of its icy waters. On returning to the house, I met, near the door, old Brian the hunter, with a large fox across his shoulder, and the dogs following at his heels.

"Good God! Mrs. M——, what is the matter? You are early up, and look dreadfully ill. Is anything wrong at home? Is the baby or your husband sick?"

"Oh no!" I cried, bursting into tears: "I fear he is eaten by the wolves."

The man stared at me, as if he doubted the evidence of his senses, and well he might; but this one idea had taken such strong possession of my mind that I would admit no other. I then told him, as well as I could, the cause of my alarm, to which he listened very kindly and patiently.

"Set your heart at rest, Mrs. M——, he is safe. It is a long journey, on foot, to Mollineux's, and they have stayed all night at his shanty. You will see them back at noon."

I shook my head, and continued to weep.

"Well, now, in order to satisfy you, I will saddle my mare, and ride over to Mollineux's, and bring you word, as fast as I can."

I thanked him sincerely for his kindness, and returned in somewhat better spirits to the house. At ten o'clock, my messenger returned, with the glad tidings that M—— was safe, and on his way home.

The day before, when half the journey was accomplished, John Monaghan had let go the rope by which he had led the cow, and she had returned to her old master; and when they again reached his place, night had set in, and they were obliged to wait until the return of day.

Brian's eldest son – a lad of fourteen – was not exactly an idiot, but what, in the Old Country, the common people designate a *natural*. He could feed and assist himself; and even go on errands to and from the town, and to the neighbouring farmhouses; but he was a strange creature, who evidently inherited, in no small degree, the father's malady. During the summer months he lived entirely in the woods, near his father's house, and only returned to obtain food, which was generally left for him in an outhouse. In the winter, driven home by the severity of the weather, he would sit for days together moping in the chimney corner, without taking notice of anything passing around him. Brian never mentioned this boy – who had a strong active figure, and rather a handsome, though perfectly inexpressive, face – without deep sigh; and I feel certain that half his own dejection was caused by painful reflections, occasioned by the mental aberrations of his child.

One day he sent the lad with a note to our house, to know if we would purchase the half of an ox that he was going to kill. There happened to stand in the corner of the room, an open wood-box, into which several bushels of apples had been thrown; and, while M— was writing an answer to the note, the eyes of the idiot were fastened, as if by some magnetic influence, upon the apples. Knowing that they had a very fine orchard, I did not offer him any, because I thought it would be useless to do so.

When the note was finished, I handed it to him. The lad grasped it mechanically, without removing his fixed gaze from the apples.

"Give that to your father."

The lad answered not: his ears, his eyes, his whole soul, were concentrated in the apples. Ten minutes elapsed; but he stood motionless, like a pointer at a dead set.

"My good boy, you can go."

Still, he did not stir.

"Is there anything you want?"

"I want," said the lad, without moving his eyes from the objects of his intense desire, and speaking in a slow, pointed manner, which ought to have been heard to be fully appreciated – "I want apples!"

"Oh! if that's all; take what you like."

The permission once obtained, the boy flung himself upon the box, with the rapacity of a hawk upon its prey, after being long poised in air, to fix its certain aim. Thrusting his hands to the right and left, in order to secure the finest specimens of the coveted fruit, scarcely allowing himself time to breathe, until he had filled his old straw hat and all his pockets. To help laughing was impossible; while this new "Tom o' Bedlam" darted from the house, and scampered across the field, for dear life, as if afraid that we should pursue him, to rob him of his prize.

It was during this winter, that our friend Brian was left a fortune of 300 pounds per annum; but it was necessary for him to return to his native country, and county, in order to take possession of the property. This he positively refused to do; and when we remonstrated with him on the apparent imbecility of this resolution, he declared, that he would not risk his life in crossing twice the Atlantic, for 20 times that sum. What strange inconsistency was this, in a being who had three times attempted to take away that life which he dreaded so much to lose accidentally!

I was much amused with an account, which he gave me, in his quaint way, of an excursion he went upon, with a botanist, to collect specimens of the plants and flowers of Upper Canada.

"It was a fine spring day, some 10 years ago; and I was yoking my oxen to drag in some oats I had just sown, when a little, fat, punchy man, with a broad, red, good-natured face, and carrying a small black leathern wallet across his shoulder, called to me over the fence, and asked me if my name was Brian. I said, 'Yes; what of that?'

"'Only, you are the man I want to see. They tell me that you are better acquainted with the woods than any person in these parts; and I will pay you anything in reason if you will be my guide for a few days.'

"'Where do you want to go?' said I.

"'Nowhere in particular,' says he. 'I want to go here, and there, in all directions, to collect plants and flowers.'

"'That is still-hunting with a vengeance,' said I. 'Today I must drag in my oats. If tomorrow will suit, we will be off.'

"'And your charge?' said he: 'I like to be certain of that.'

"'A dollar a day. My time and labour just now, upon my farm, is worth that.'

"'True,' said he. 'Well, I'll give you what you ask. At what time will you be ready to start?'

"'By daybreak, if you wish it.'

"Away he went; and by daylight, next morning, he was at my door, mounted upon a stout French pony.

"'What are you going to do with that beast?' said I. 'Horses are of no use on the road that you and I are to travel. You had better leave him in my stable.'

"'I want him to carry our traps,' said he. 'It may be some days that we shall be absent.'

"I assured him that he must be his own beast of burden, and carry his axe, and blanket, and wallet of food, upon his own back. The little body did not much relish this arrangement; but as there was no help for it, he very good-naturedly complied. Off we set, and soon climbed the hills at the back of your farm, and got upon the Rice Lake Plains. The woods were flush with flowers; and the little man grew into such an ecstasy, that at every fresh specimen he uttered a yell of joy, cut a caper in the air, and flung himself down upon them, as if he were drunk with delight.

"'Oh! What treasures! What treasures!' he cried. 'I shall make my fortune!'

"It is seldom I laugh," quoth Brian, "but I could not help laughing at this odd little man; for it was not the beautiful blossoms that drew forth these exclamations, but the queer little plants, which he had rummaged for at the roots of old trees, among the moss and long grass. He sat upon a decayed tree, which lay in our path, for an hour, making a long oration over some greyish things which grew out of it, which looked more like mould than plants; declaring himself repaid for all the trouble and expense he had been at, if it were only to obtain a sight of them. I gathered him a beautiful blossom of lady's slipper; but he pushed it back when I presented it to me, saying:

"'Yes, yes; 'tis very fine: I have seen that often before; but these lichens are splendid!'

"The man had so little taste, that I thought him a fool, and left him to talk to his dear plants, while I shot partridges for our supper. We spent six days in the woods; and the little man filled his wallet with all sorts of rubbish, as if he wilfully shut his eyes to the beautiful flowers, and chose only to admire the ugly, insignificant plants, that even a chipmunk would have passed without noticing, and which, often as I had been in the woods, I never had observed before. I never pursued a deer with such earnestness as he continued his hunt for what he called 'specimens.' When we came to the Cold Creek, which is pretty deep in places, he was in such a hurry to get at some plants that grew under the water, that he lost his balance, and fell, head over heels, into the stream. He got a thorough ducking, and was in a terrible fright; but he held on to the flowers which had caused the trouble, and thanked his stars that he had saved them, as well as his life. Well, he was an innocent man," continued Brian – "a very little made him happy; and at night he would sing and amuse himself, like a little child. He gave me 10 dollars for my trouble, and I never saw him again; but I often think of him, when hunting in the woods that we wandered through together; and I pluck the wee plants that he used to admire, and wonder why he preferred them to the fine flowers."

When our resolution was formed to sell our farm and go upon our grant of land, in the backwoods, no one was so earnest in trying to persuade us from our ruinous plan, as our friend Brian, who became quite eloquent in his description of the trials and troubles which awaited us. During the last week of our stay, he visited us every evening, and never bade us good-night without a tear moistening his eyes. We parted with the hunter as with an old friend, and we never saw him again.

His fate was a sad one. He fell into a moping melancholy, which ended in self-destruction – but a kinder or warmer-hearted man, while he enjoyed the light of reason, has seldom crossed our path.

LISA MOORE

THE STYLIST

The stylist stands behind you and leans in. She scrunches your hair in her fists, testing bounce. She lifts it to the sides like wings, tugging her fingers through the snags.

She says, What's the idea here?

The idea is I want to look good.

You want a change, she says. Your husband left you. Your husband left you. Your husband left you.

Uncross your legs, she says. You adjust your posture. She spreads her hands on your shoulders, meets your eyes in the mirror.

Now listen, you'll have to sit up straight.

You have hunched since the competitive diving at the Aquarena when you were twelve and grew breasts. Your bathing suit, the frosty green of the old Ford. The green of leaves covered with short silver hair, lucent grapes. You wore this bathing suit every day after school. The chlorine wearing the lycra thin, fading the sheen. When the bathing suit was wet your nipples were visible. The colour of your nipples.

You hunch your shoulders. You aren't like the older girls whose breasts are a fact.

Your breasts are tender, a rumour, the beginning of a long story, a page-turner. It's the worst when you're speaking with your coach. The bathing suit transparent as the skin of a grape you peel with your teeth.

The lineup for the ladder is the worst. Long enough for the warm lights to make the beads of water on your arms creep to a standstill, chlorine tingles your skin. Under the water nobody can see your nipples. Diving practice enchants you. You fall asleep as soon as you get home. Asleep before the soaps, drooling on the cushion. Over your fried eggs and beans, the ketchup screaming on the white plate.

This is what the table looks like: placemats with illustrations of a fox hunt. Red riding jackets, top hats, hounds. A silver water pitcher, greasy with condensation. An ashtray with a smoking cigarette. Your father's empty chair. His placemat, without the cutlery. Your mother is likely to cry. She cries every night. Sometimes while watching the news, sometimes over supper. These are her specialties: sweet-and-sour ribs with tears, spaghetti with tears, steak, baked potato, tears. Mom, hold the tears.

This is what you see out the window: hideous icicles, a row of fangs. You dream you kiss your coach.

A kiss so ripe and desperate, nothing else will ever come close.

He kisses you and cups his hand under your chin and one of your front teeth drops into his open palm. Blood seeps from the fleshy hole. You know at once it isn't a baby tooth. Now you must go through life like this. Icicles crash from the eaves.

In the morning you run your tongue and run your tongue. Your mother and you live in the mouth of winter, waterlogged. The sky is a ravenous mink, the spruce trees raking its wet fur underbelly. You have become enchanted. Your coach lifting weights in the chrome gym, wiping his glistening neck with a white towel, rolling his shoulders, sweat in his eyelashes. He lies on his back, a leg on either side of the black vinyl bench. The leg of his shorts gapes and you see the white perforated cotton inside and the bulge of his penis, pubic hair. You have never seen. This is something else. Something else again. When he stands up the foggy print of his sweat in the vinyl, his spine, his shoulder blades like the wings of a dragonfly. Rank gym, feet, the iron smell of clanking weights, chlorine, boiling hot dogs from the hot air vent, the tangy liniment. The slap of his hand against his wet neck. The smell of his liniment. Like laundry dried in the wind and licorice, coniferous.

How fickle the water is. You slip in from a great height and the blush in your cheeks cools. The water unzippers your new-girl body, your breasts, the hunch. The water peels you. The saddest thing you've ever seen is the back of your father's green Ford raising clouds of dust that make the alders unshiny. The saddest thing is that Ford turning the corner.

Or the pool rises up in a fist and mangles your face.

A month ago you blackened both your eyes. They swelled shut. Two plums sitting neat. Sockets like eggcups. A blow so stunning it seemed ordained. The fangs snapped shut. Mink savaging the hind leg of a cloud. Your mother kneeling near your head on the concrete.

Next we'll see the macaroni, she says.

You vomit chlorine and macaroni. Where has she come from? She was supposed to be at work. How long have you been out? She would have had to come across the city. The back of her hand on your cheek. She would have had to know without being told.

But here you are again, toes curled over the edge of the ten-metre board. It's warm up here because you're near the lights. You're in the rafters. Far away, at the other end of the Aquarena, an aerobics class.

Your coach could turn on the bubbles. No matter what, it will be okay if he turns on the bubbles, which cost money, which aren't allowed at the Nationals, which make the water as welcoming as whipped cream.

He wants to see a triple.

You want the bubbles but you don't ask. You are in love, the black Trans Am with a flame that bursts over the hood, the megaphone. He's sitting in a canvas chair by the side of the pool and he's wearing black flip-flops with red plastic flowers. He speaks to you.

Shoulders, he says. Although it's a megaphone, his tone sounds bedroomy. He calls you by your last name.

Fo*cus* Malone.

It's strange, but you are very good at diving. You are the youngest on the provincial team. You will go to the Nationals. You have come to suspect you can do absolutely anything. It's intoxicating, this glimmer of your will. The pool crunches your ribs like a nutcracker, the board nicks your shin, unspooling a ribbon of blood in the water, a love tap on the left shoulder so you can't lift your arm.

Or the pool plays dead. It doesn't matter, you keep doing it. Doing begets doing. You could go on like this forever.

You unhunch. It's a magic trick, the triple. The action doesn't happen until it's over. It happens in the future and you catch up. A triple is déjà vu. Trusting the untrustable.

The key: give yourself over/over/over.

The stylist reams a finger around your cape collar, loosening. Takes a steel comb, flicks it against her hipbone. You are thirty-four and you've been to a stylist a handful of times. Maybe six, not ten.

She says, That length is doing nothing for you.

She whips your swivel chair: slur of mirror, porcelain, chrome, fluorescent nettles stick themselves to the glass. Droning hair dryers, running water, phones.

The stylists talk. A mazey, elliptical daisy chain of talk. They adhere to nothing. Vacation packages, electric toothbrushes, blind dates. (He's got to be kidding: *coffee*. Going for coffee equals *death*. Night skiing, spritzers, bowling, sea-kayaking, I'm like, Okay. Let's go. But coffee? He's kidding, right?) They are the experts on every topic. Hair is a mild distraction. Hair happens.

She flicks the steel comb and it whirs near her hip. She's drawing a conclusion.

Your hair: upkeep, damage, regrowth, definition, product, lifestyle, frost, frizz, product, streaks, foils, body, cut. Where you're a small person. Where you've got a round face.

Outside, the storm slows traffic like a narcotic. You haven't seen a winter like this since. The equipment is breaking down. Bring in the army, they're saying. At night the snowplows crash into the drifts and stagger backward like dazed prizefighters. The windshields have bushy eyebrows. Cars stuck on the hills, smoking tires, engines squealing like dolphins. You haven't seen anything like this since you were a kid. You and your mother, the icicles, the lake catching over, the wind circling the glassy trees like a wet finger tracing a crystal rim. Her sleeping pills, the alarm clock blaring near her ear. Stumbling from your room at dawn to wake her so she can drive you to diving practice. The smell of chlorine in your skin always, your hair.

You like your driveway to be scraped down to the pavement since your husband left you. You get out there early ever Saturday morning. The children watch from the living room window. Your little daughter taps the glass. She waves. Your son puts his lips against the glass in a big gummy kiss.

The hospital room zings. Your husband says he wants a smoke. His forehead is gleaming, his eyebrows raised. He's feral, acute with stillness. His hazel eyes, flecks of rust, hair white as a fresh sheet of paper. He's socking one fist gently into his open palm.

You breathe. The minute hand reverberates each time it moves, a *twang*. You wait, wait for it, wait. The minute hand moves. Your mother lays an icy towel on your forehead. A drop of water moves down your temple and into your ear. The moving drop is exquisite in every way. The contraction recedes. The nurse is driving a spaceship in her sleep. She's gripping the arms of the chair, leaning slightly forward, snoring.

Go have your smoke, you say. Nothing's happening yet.

But it starts to happen while he's in the parking lot. He tells you later about his moment: how he will never be the same. He's standing on a slab of concrete near a loading entrance at the back of the hospital. The door is tied open with a piece of rubber tubing. The smell of cold food, sausage, powdered egg, the churning of dishwashers, spilled cutlery. It's a foggy night and he can smell the harbour and something bitter, pigeon shit. He's bewildered, hardly able to remember how he got where he is.

When he goes back to your hospital room his son's head is visible, becomes visible with each contraction and disappears again. It's the most awesome, unlovely, soul-quaking thing he has ever seen. He cups one of your heels in his hand, your mother holds your other heel. The baby is mauve coloured, smeared darkly with guck, and crying.

Your hair will be by Suzanne.

They're single or have just eloped, the stylists, young or staving off age with fashion, trend. The best one-room apartments in the city.

Do you have children, Suzanne?

Nope. No. Thank. You.

And you don't ever?

You got that right. Kids are *so expensive*. Why would you?

Suzanne knows what she doesn't want. Sometimes desire is forged by the process of elimination. Your husband wanted golfing and hockey, a new tent, to celebrate his Native heritage (hitherto unmentioned during seven years of marriage), to become a theologian, to hunt seals. (There's a white mask the Inuit hunter holds to his face while approaching the seal basking at the edge of an ice floe. Everything is white, the hunter's white furs, the ice, the air. When he lifts the white mask he's obliterated. Your husband, the empty landscape, your husband, the empty landscape.) You prefer oblique dreams but you are too tired to manufacture the oblique. He wanted to be a vegetarian. (There are foods you can't face anymore. Basil you can't eat because of him. Even the smell of it.) To add on an apartment. (He got to keep the house through a conspiracy inspired by his mother.)

Then he realized what he didn't want. To be married anymore. To you. And now he's with Rayleen, an airhead.

The idea is to look good, you tell the stylist. That's the idea.

Things the stylists insist upon: a fireplace, a cappuccino maker. Toronto once a year, loyalty, techno music. A stuffed toy.

What's going on out there?

Suzanne: Still snowing.

The streets have become impossibly narrow. Snowbanks muscling the cars like ululating throats. The stylists win dance contests. Drink B52s, martinis.

You are here to learn how to become vulnerable again. How to give yourself over. They like a nice glass, fruit. They like their drinks to be blue, orange slices; they tip flamboyantly. There's a big, decaying city in their past. Havana, maybe. Venice. They have no past.

The stylist absolutely insists upon silence at certain hours. Watching the February snow make the sky listless, the slob ice on the harbour lifting in swells so gentle it seems the couch moves beneath them. Hand-knit socks. Original art. Brand names: Le Château, Switch, Paderno. To watch the dusk settle. Soap operas. The primacy of their cats.

Suzanne has one item in her fridge: dehydrated miniature crabs. She can see the whole city from her window in the Battery.

Your mother has been begging you for years to get your hair streaked. You have breakfast together and she puts down her fork.

Enough, your mother says. She leans over the table and touches your cheek with the back of her hand. You have been going with the salt over the eggs. You stop. And you go and go and go with the salt. Then you toss it across the kitchen.

You have made everything soft for him, like whipped cream.

There he is in the La-Z-Boy, hungover, misty-eyed.

I made a mistake, he says, I fucked someone.

Enough you say.

Your mother cannot understand, nor will she accept, that you don't want streaks. You had no money in law school. Sometimes you were hungry. You left home, and your mother had to shovel. Sleeping pills. It got dark so early. There aren't even streetlights out that way. Her asthma. She'd have to walk through waist-deep snow and stop to use her inhaler. Icicles glinting. Leaks in the roof. You hear her smoke over the phone. A pause while she smokes. You hear the whir of the microwave, the bell. You hear the ice in her glass of scotch. You hear the icicles dripping outside. You hear her crying. What will make you stop crying, Mom?

She says, Have you thought about streaks?

Your husband wants to be an actor. He wants to give up his career as a bank manager. He wants a break from the kids. He wants the kids in his arms. He wants to go bankrupt, be a filmmaker. He has begun to identify with the clients whose assets he's been forced to seize. They aren't such bad guys.

The stylist takes a pair of scissors from the jar of blue liquid. Snaps them twice, flicking drops.

Suzanne's hair is short, stucco-like in texture, blonde with ironic roots. Black-framed glasses. The bones of her hips pressing the red plastic jeans. Her shirt is clingy, reveals her belly button, a piercing. There are two kinds of hair, you've been told. The long and wispy: fuck-me hair. The short and androgynous: fuck-you hair.

You don't have the money now nor will you ever have the money to get your hair done every four months, which is how often you must in order to keep the roots from showing. You do not like roots. You hate them. You will not incur the extra expense just now when your bastard prick of a husband, who has run up every jointly owned credit card, who has spent the nest egg saved to help your mother retire early and not have to wade through snowbanks with her inhaler. The bastard prick has a spending disorder, in fact, hitherto unmentioned, and has left you with half his debt, which is the law, and is seeing an airhead, and you can't trust him to come up with his half of the money. You won't incur the extra expense for anything because you had to buy a new house and a second-hand car, the engine of which is tied together with dental floss.

Suzanne says, You're thinking colour.

Yes I am.

You need colour.

Yes I do.

I'm thinking streaks.

So am I.

When you are in your ninth month with Adrian, a youth hurls his chair across the courtroom at you. You see one metal leg blur past your temple. You've prosecuted this kid several times.

Perhaps five. His sister also. Almost all the girls who appear in youth court are named Amanda. They are named after Rachel's daughter on the discontinued soap opera *Another World*. Most of the boys are named Cory. The boy leaps onto a table and is striding across the backs of the fixed seating. The judge has a button on his desk for moments like these. He presses the buttons, his black robes puff with air, and the safety door clicks quietly closed behind him. You can see him in the small square window of the door peering out to watch the action.

You think: Judge Burke has saved himself. You are taken up with giddiness. Judge Burke strikes you as humorously prissy. You are trembling with a fit of suppressed giggles. But as the boy gets closer, your initial feeling about Judge Burke changes. You realize his decision to save himself and leave you, along with the handful of spectators, three security guards, three more youth also scheduled to appear before him this morning – Judge Burke's decision is a sound one. Certain men, given the appropriate circumstances, will behave with decisive and thorough self-centredness that smacks of sound judgement. Burke is elderly, completely unable to defend himself against a physical attack. Batty, even. His pronouncements are usually unsound. You often have to say, Judge Burke, I can see you're angry because your face is getting red, and I can tell by the tone of your voice that you are upset because you are speaking very loudly, but I feel I have to continue. You say things like this for the benefit of the court stenographer so the records will reflect Judge Burke's demeanour, should he come to the batty conclusion that he should charge you with contempt. Right now Judge Burke is nowhere to be seen. Right now a young man named Cory is going to kill you just before you give birth to your son, Adrian. As far as you know there have never been any Adrians on *Another World*. The youth is leaping, you have a contraction that doubles you, the security guards have him, water pours down your legs.

The male stylists are openly gay, mavericks, blithe, built. But it's the women who interest you. The women are beautiful, or look beautiful, stubbornly independent, current, childless. They enter and win lip-sync and wet T-shirt contests. At home in airports. Their families make allowances. They don't shovel. At Christmas they are the most extravagant, most deflated by the aftermath of unwrapped presents. They are the babies in the family. They're allowed to pick at the turkey. Suzanne brings you to the porcelain sink with the scoop for the neck. You lean back, close your eyes. You are determined to enjoy this.

She says, You don't have to hold your neck like that.

You have been holding your neck. You let your neck go loose. You are submitting. You let go. The salon falls away. Your scalp is a grass fire. You would kiss something if you could, or drift to sleep. The long, greying hair is such a weight. The hose makes you tingle all over. A hot, delicate raking. She's raking you to the surface of yourself. She drops the hose. Squirts a thread of viscous cherry over your scalp and begins with her fingers. She lets her nails graze. No one has touched you like this since your husband left. You almost kiss the snow white inside of Suzanne's wrist.

You are alone. It's your husband's night with the kids. Since your husband left, you have been falling asleep early in the evening. You haven't bought a TV. You got to keep the CD player but you only have a handful of CDs. You have listened to Cat Stevens' *Greatest Hits* so often you can. At first you kept the radio on all the time. A cheap radio in every room. Then you got tired of the radio. You listen hard but there's nothing to hear. A row of icicles falls from the eaves startling you so badly you almost. You don't turn on the lights. You see your neighbour across the street pull into his driveway, his headlights lighting up falling snow. He can't see you in your window because the lights are off. He has asked you over for a glass of wine.

Once you awoke to the sound of him shovelling your driveway. He gets out of the car and the light over his porch comes on. He looks up into the sky. He's standing in his driveway with his hands in his pockets, his head tilted back. He stays that way. Your fridge cuts in. Nothing moves on the street for a long time, no cars, just the snow. Your neighbour goes inside and you are alone. You are very much alone.

Suzanne fits a rubber skullcap over your head. The skullcap is full of holes and she tugs strands of hair through each hole with a metal hook. It hurts so much you think you might cry. Then you do cry. Suzanne doesn't make a big deal of it. She's seen all this before. She keeps pulling your hair.

That's the price, she says. She paints your hair with a foaming chemical. It's an awful stink, poisonous and angry. It makes you feel exuberant.

Everyone has left the Aquarena because of the storm and your mother hasn't come. Your coach switches off all the lights. They make a thwack noise when they go off, and the filaments burn pink then blue. The pool is empty and has gone still. The pool is a chameleon and it has changed its skin so it resembles nothing more than a swimming pool. It has become invisible. Your thirteenth birthday is coming and very soon you will lose interest in diving. One day you can think of nothing else, you are haunted. The next day diving hardly exists. You can't remember anything about it. You let your mother sleep in.

The storm has closed roads. Where is your mother? Your coach drives you home. The Trans Am flies through whiteouts. You lose the road. The flame on the hood swallowed by the mouth. You have been saying. Talking. Telling him. Your eyes two soft plums, and a soft plum in your throat. Your heart is aching, but your heart is your eyes and you have two and they are bruised and weeping. Your coach pulls over. You pull over into Lovers Lane together. The trees slap the windows, paw the roof. He cups his hand under your chin and he kisses you. He gently sucks a bright plum from your throat. He kisses and kisses. You have never. Nothing will ever be as wonderful as this. You give yourself over/over/over.

You want Suzanne to give you some advice before you leave, and she does. She tells you that from now on you must use a round brush. She holds a mirror behind so you can see how sharp the cut is. You can see your neck. You don't recognize yourself from this angle. She's sprayed you and blown the whole thing dry so your hair feels as hard as a helmet. The blonde is called ash and it glints like a tough metal.

MARGUERITE PIGEON

ENDURANCE

The hallucination happens late on Day 4. A man appears, weaving through the trees on shore in a red jumpsuit, keeping pace with her, peering from around trunks, the eyes popping 3D like tennis balls from a machine – yellow and big as eggs. He chuckles – or are those branches snapping? Is that wind? She thinks she hears her name tickle her ear: Anick.

Panic. Her snowshoes fly through the powder on the ice surface, the sled bouncing behind on its tethers. Schwonk-schwonk. Schwonk-schwonk. Her chest burns. Her breath comes in short, loud bursts. *Stay calm*, she thinks. She reminds herself that other notable hallucinations have come sooner: Day 2 of the Death Valley Ultra-Triathlon, Day 3 1/2 of the Race Across the Alps. *You got through those*. But she doesn't quite convince herself the same will be true this time. *I've pushed too hard. I'm in trouble. I want Saturday morning bacon and eggs with Michael.* This rush of thoughts takes her by surprise. She hates doubt. Hates people who favour sleeping in and fatty pork dishes. This is her world. Right now. A frozen lake. The race. Alaska. Four-fifths of the way to the finish. She needs to remain in control. *You've hypnotized yourself is all.* It's the only logical answer. But the red figure is still sailing along in the corner of her eye.

She's been watching her snowshoes – the ones Michael handed her at Christmas with a stupid grin and so much reverence for their long-tailed, duckbill design – because the lake ice has become brittle and feels like it could give out. To cut back to shore would've cost her too much time. So she's stayed the course, watching and calculating, her feet appearing and disappearing below her. So many factors are important: time of day, indications that the powder has melted and refrozen, her own stride, on top of all her normal considerations of body temperature, position, energy level, hydration... *I'm just dazed with all of it*, she concludes again, but suspects something worse could happen if she doesn't snap out of this. She could lose sight of what's important, of the win.

It's Michael, she complains inwardly. The thought of him 3,000 miles away, training alone for the Race Across America, the fact that she never wished him luck. *He's messing me up.* She forces herself to break pace, closes her eyes hard, and tries to slow her heart rate. She blinks them open again a moment later, pushing the frost from her lashes with her glove. Quick as that, the red jumpsuit recedes between shadowed mounds of snow on shore. The hallucination is over. She changes tacks, keeping her eyes up.

Now there is only wind, metal cold pine-blown air, inky snow, hot, regular puffs of her breath, and the forest, like a locked-down prison all around the lake. She feels angry, cold, then hot again, and likes it: her blood's back. She falls into a rhythm and is grateful to see a faint light across the lake. Camp. *Thank fucking God*, she thinks, and shuffles the snowshoes to a more brisk beat. Schwonk-schwonk.

❧

She unhooks her sled and pushes into the large tent with numb hands. Inside, it's not much warmer but she flushes anyway, with the change in temperature, but more with relief at the sight of other human beings. A half dozen competitors are lying around on their sleeping bags, plus support people. It's not her style to admire others more than herself, however, and the relief is overlaid, almost immediately, by hunger for rank – she might still get to teach these bastards a thing or two about endurance. *If I can keep my goddamned marbles.*

Within minutes, the warmer air brings back the pain that Anick has ignored all day, sets a match to her earlobes, tugs hard at her thigh muscles like at broken elastic bands. She pulls off her running shoes but is most afraid of all to know what's happened to her feet, so she doesn't dare touch her socks. Mac promised the new shoes would perform maximally. Now she thinks they might cost her a toe. "God himself would wear these to win Alaska," he said, more than once. Mac and his twisted love of prototypes, his stupid G5, his pale skin and flabby middle, his eyes already weak from his years of computer-generating high-tech gear. *What would you or God know about racing? You avoid hell!* she always thinks, but hasn't said so aloud. Mac, after all, has been with her before the first big racing win, before people started lining up to pay her bills for being an elite guinea pig.

She lies back now and begins her visualization of the next day's performance. She pictures her arms and legs moving easily, in harmony; imagines her breathing, her blood moving into the very tips of her fingers and toes. She experiences the joy of finding out she's placed in the top three. She finishes by telling herself there will be no further hallucinations or distractions. Also, she will manage her pain.

Pain. It's all around her. Several of the competitors are having their shoulders or calves or feet rubbed by team support, filling the tent with the smell of ointment. Anick watches them dispassionately. She's alone – only runs Solos. It's how she likes it. Bigger prize money, more prestige, more sponsorship deals. Besides, she's always hated groups. Can barely handle Mac.

Nearby, someone is crying and she turns to look with what is suddenly a huge effort. It's Ola, the Russian. Her short damp hair is stuck to her forehead like weeds. The team doctor is crouched beside where she's sitting in her skinny black jump-suit. He points at Ola's eyes and shakes his head. Ola drools and babbles in protest. But Anick concurs: the eyes are too dark, fixed in misery. *Ola's out*, thinks Anick. *She's out and her team is fucked.*

"Anick?"

She turns and flinches as her neck muscles resist the sudden movement like cold plasticine. Last year's Men's Solo winner, Reg Rogers, a Texan, is sitting on his sleeping bag two crumpled competitors away.

"What?"

Reg gets up awkwardly. *He's too thin this year*, she thinks, noticing his twin, chicken-like collarbones. *Overtrained bastard!*

"You got any spare performance bars?" he asks, and his voice sounds odd, like he both is and isn't addressing her in par-ticular.

"No." *Jesus. You don't pack your own food now?*

Reg, who has come to stand over the place where she sits in her bare socks, reaches down towards her headband. "Your ears are burned."

"Yeah. Yesterday." *Fuck you*, she thinks and pulls away.

"I shit myself around hour three."

"Reg, I gotta eat."

He glares at her with hatred. He's on the edge. Anick can tell. He looks crazed, like a child nearing a tantrum, or a soldier coming off a bad tour of duty. She wonders if he even knows who he is. She does: he's an ego in expensive gear, an ultra-marathoner, an ultra-prick. They ran into one another a few months ago at a dinner for the Endurance Runners of North America in Arkansas. While Michael was in the bathroom, Reg came to stand much too close, said to her, "I race because it gets me off."

"Gets you off what?"

"Don't be so butch, Anick. You're too pretty for that."

"Butch sells. Ask my sponsors." She thought then of the shot they'd chosen for the Ultra-Bar ad: she was hunched over her handlebars in a splashy one-piece, the skin of her cheeks stretched unnaturally, like dough in a wind tunnel.

"Why don't you come train at the farm? Find your softer side in the South."

"No can do. Rode that right off on the Devil Mountain Double."

Michael walked back then, smiling broadly. "Drinks, anyone?"

You can practically outrace a horse, but you can't tell when someone's trying to pick me up, she thought, not without sympathy for Michael's naïve belief in people's good intentions.

Now, Reg looks like an X-ray of the man who hit on her that night. He seems about to topple over her, but manages to plod back to his sleeping bag, where he kneels and eases himself horizontal. She watches him for another moment, then turns away in disgust. Sleep – the enemy, the thing she most wants – claws at the back of her eyes. She used up too much last night though. *Two hours will have to do*. She can rest when she's dead. And so the moment of truth has arrived: gingerly, she pulls off her long "mega-breather" socks (another Mac trial).

Oh fuck, she thinks. As she's feared, early-stage frostbite has spilled like powder across both sets of toes. Her right foot is bleeding pretty badly, especially the big toe. She lost the nail in her third race across the Sahara and the toe's been left vulnerable, black around the cuticles, and prone to bleeds. Right now it looks like a thick worm with the end chopped off.

Carefully applying cream, she recalls that event – meeting Michael there. Night 4, she stumbled into the nine-man tent, unrolled her crinkly silver sleeping sheet beside his, and mumbled hello. As she was getting herself ready for sleep, she couldn't help but notice something unusual about this compact man who was carefully shaking out and folding away his desert head gear. He had the familiar yellowing eyes, wind-burned skin, and vine-like leg muscles of the other racers, but none of their frantic fervour – none of hers. She's always felt that somewhere inside, something invisible holds a gun to her heart, generating the will – the fear – to go on. *What else could?* she wondered, watching him. But the longer she looked, the more untouched he seemed by the tough talk and posturing she was so used to. She found it irritating. *Pure tactics.* As if he could really afford to care about that filthy paisley scarf and the linen hat with its rumpled flaps!

By Night 5, she was in serious pain, nearly hypothermic from the dramatic loss of body heat after the sweltering day. Her big toe was blackening. Around 3:00 a.m., with the desert wind howling across the open-ended tent, she started, against training and disposition – against everything she believes in, actually – to cry. A voice nearby said, very gently, "You need rest." It was Michael. He offered to bring over his sleeping bag and lie closer to her – double the heat. With a wet gulp she agreed. They lay that way, like battered spoons, for three full hours.

Two days later, the race over (he came 10th, she 17th – worse than she'd counted on), they had coffee in the dusty market in Ouarzazate. He told her about his ex-wife, his job in Silicone Valley, his rock garden, his love of "world music." He hauled out the signposts of his life like someone discovering them for the first time. They were the offerings of an amazed child begging her for approval. The Moroccan stall owner returned over and over with more tiny, full cups.

❧

Feet creamed, her shrunken stomach stretched to capacity by a peanut-butter sandwich, handfuls of dried apricots, and a pre-mixed vial full of vitamins, Anick zips herself, caterpillar-like, into her narrow, orange sleeping bag. Mac promised her its weave of new materials couldn't fail – no matter how sweaty she became or how cold the conditions were. But so far he's been wrong. She freezes every night. As she lies awake, shivering and damp, panic finds her again, crawls in and tingles all over. Her feet. The hallucination. The doubt. Michael.

Stop it. Shut the fuck up.

She blinks and the world finally goes dark, lost as though under a wave of black milk, washing away the sound of Ola's moaning.

❧

A moment later it's morning – 4:00 a.m. She's up, snapping closed the high stiff neck of her jacket, strapping on her sleigh harness. Reg brushes by her, his rear end like matched loaves of bread painted into royal blue stretch pants. He pretends she doesn't exist.

She pushes off and does three hours on the snowshoes, makes great time. The weather is good: bitter cold, but dry and windless. Tall, short-branched spruce rush past her in their green-black silence. Snow fleas grey the snow in the depressions left by other racers. At one point, a crow startles her by flying low across her path, nearly blue in the gauzy, heatless sunlight.

She makes it to the juncture with the "road" (not a road at all, but not a forest or a lake or a swamp either, something like a straight stretch, and so the name has stuck among racers) and switches to her bike around 10:00 a.m., taking the break she promised herself, then pulling her custom-made frame and tools from the sleigh, adjusting the tire pressure, and screwing in place wheels, handle bars, and seat. The bike is perfect. *You rock, Mac.* She glides down the path that was never meant for cycling, certain she's easily in fourth place.

But just one hour later, fatigue lands in her lap like an anvil. She stops and throws up. Two French teammates hover for a moment as they pass on the trail, insectile in their covered boots and black balaclavas. "*Vous auriez besoin d'un medecin?*" calls one flatly.

"*Non, ça va.*" Stuck-up assholes.

They pedal away in a fierce display of kneecaps. Alone again, Anick pulls out her tube of espresso-flavoured energy gel and sucks the bittersweet goo. *Let's go.*

Back on the bike, struggling up an icy incline of exposed roots, her mind drifts again to Michael. It was just a week after the Sahara race when he emailed her the invitation to his cottage in Ontario. *For–get it!* she said to herself, rolling her eyes with a chuckle that surprised her with its tone of genuine regret. But she couldn't go. She wasn't good with vacations and worse with men. There had been moments when she'd thought she'd been in love. A cold winter in Whistler with an Australian ski instructor. A bike builder in Nevada who wanted her to quit racing and go into the dog breeding business with him. It was all so exhausting, such responsibility. To her, sex was like a dangerously long break between races: after a while, you could forget it was just a pleasant waste of time. Alone, she'd been at her best. Could defy fear. Win more races.

She emailed Michael.

Can't make it. Back in Jasper and we've got a group of German businessmen putting us through our paces. Besides, I'm the Lone Ranger type when it comes to training – Anick

He replied immediately.

I understand, but this invitation is NOT to a training week, it's for a COTTAGE week. We can fish. Think marinaded STEAKS! – Michael (xo)

A carnivore, like herself. A bad speller too. Reading it, she felt an inkling of the strange difference about Michael that she'd noticed in the desert. She weakened.

❦

Michael turned out to be as amazed with sex as he was with everything else, eager to explore the mechanics of it all. He didn't bug her with too many questions or gush about nature. He filleted the measly pickerel she caught. Most days, he was satisfied to make love and breakfast. He did tell her endurance racing made him feel "spiritual." She let out a snort and immediately regretted it, seeing his face fall. "I just didn't know it could," she said, and it was true. From the first time she put on running shoes, she's simply wanted to get as far as possible from weakness. Everything, it seems to her – her whole career – has just flowed from that.

Afterwards, Michael came to visit several times, emailing her marked-up calendars with races they could do together. The Mount Diablo. The Belle Isle Ultra. They attended the Arkansas dinner, spent Christmas in Colorado. He gave her the snowshoes. On New Year's Eve day, they tested them out, doing seven hours out and back into high, fluffy snow country. But she found herself getting annoyed when he wanted to stop along the way to talk or to slide a gloved hand up the back of her jacket. She pulled ahead significantly, but slowed down again when she looked back and saw that he looked small, sadness settled on his shoulders. She stopped, kissed him, felt under his toque for a patch of bald head to rub.

But on New Year's Eve, at their cabin, the inevitable.

It began when she refused some champagne he'd surprised her with. The outing had got her thinking about the Alaska race and she was worrying about her nutrition.

"Anick," he said, letting the unopened bottle sink back down into the melting ice of its bucket.

"Yes?"

"I have to train really hard for the Race Across America. I want the Solo."

"So go Solo!" She stuck a finger in his ear and gave it a wiggle.

"Right. Well, that's what I was considering... Would you think about leaving Alaska until next year? I mean, we would do it together then."

Her finger stopped. A silence stretched. "Michael," she said finally, "if you want me to chase after you while you do the R.A.A., you should've given me a sponsor's van and a cheerleader's uniform for Christmas instead of snowshoes."

She stood up from the couch where she'd been lying, not sure what to do with herself.

"It's not that I don't want you racing," he said, exasperated, burying his head under a pillow on the floor. "It's just that I thought we could take turns: you come with me this year and I go up North with you next."

"I don't need a goddamn shadow. I need to race," she said, feeling less sure about this than she let on.

It was their last night together. She landed back in Canada in the middle of a soupy snowstorm feeling equal parts emotional exhaustion and anticipation. The next day, 3:00 a.m., serious training resumed.

❧

Now it's 10:00 p.m. The lit northern night sky like purple ink with sparkles mixed in. She is beyond exhaustion, has passed over to a fuzzy state where pain, cold, and damp jostle for space in her mind like clowns inside a tiny car. She places the beam from her headlamp on the spot just ahead of her front tire.

The bike, it turns out, isn't perfect – she's had to stop four times to adjust tire pressure so far. *You suck, Mac.* Her health, too, sucks – another vomiting session about 3:00 p.m., numbness in the toes that she can't ignore any more. And the weather has turned windy and snowy. But the worst, as of 10 minutes ago, is she has no idea where she is.

She laughs out loud at her tedious pace – really a crawl – as she cycles through a narrow bank of trees, but the sound comes out like an old recording in the hush of falling snow. She hasn't seen anyone since lunchtime and suddenly she feels very alone. Hunger overwhelms her despite near-constant doses of supplements. A longing rekindles for Michael's breakfast: bacon and eggs, with slices of melon.

No more Michael! No hallucinating! she orders. She wants to put on another layer of clothes or switch back to the snowshoes, but can't bring herself to stop and pry open the closed-topped sleigh with her frozen hands. *Fuck. Stay calm*, she thinks. *Calm. Calm.* Camp must be close. *I can still win.*

She is pushing through snow damp and chunky enough to suggest a creek below, trying to get her bearings, when her wheels catch in some especially gummy thickness and she has to dismount to grind through to the next rise. Gloved fingers wrapped around her light, narrow handlebars, pushing hard from the thighs, she works forward in slow, deliberate steps, but gets light-headed from the effort. Nearly through, she looks up and is stunned still by what she sees: it's Reg, kneeling in the snow, his back to her, the tails of his silver snowshoes pointing straight into the sky, his sleigh, unhooked, off to one side.

She drops her bike, unhooks her sleigh and runs. She grabs his shoulders and turns him around. Reg looks at her wild-eyed, searching her face with the fervour of a child lost in a department store. His hands come up to touch her shoulders. "Uhm vehry tttired. Zts' not – camp's not herrre."

"Okay. Ssshh. It's there. Just calm down, Reg."

She pushes her stiff hand into her jacket, digging for the miniature flare she keeps in the inner pocket, but with snow falling in streaks all around like wet cotton, it takes forever to get it out. She launches the little rocket and watches it zing – a blur of orange-red riding up into the grey sky, then back down onto an icy pond nearby.

She clicks open the latches on Reg's sleigh and pulls out all the clothes she can find as well as Reg's sleeping bag. She forces him to sit on a Gore-Tex shell, pushes more layers over his head, and after popping off his snowshoes and yanking off his trail shoes, tugs extra socks over his frozen feet. The effort further drains her, and only fear keeps Reg in focus – ghostly and waxy white in the beam of her headlamp.

She inches the sleeping bag over his feet, her slow-working mind evaluating the situation. *Way worse than Ola.* And Reg isn't even shivering. *How long before someone comes?* With much tugging she zips him in, right to the armpits, like into a shroud. She grips Reg's whole body then, unsure how much heat she has left to give. His arms, inside the sleeping bag, are stiff as a toy soldier's.

"I knowww jjyyou," says Reg, delirious, his chin against her shoulder.

She shifts and their cheeks touch.

She has an experience then, of seeing herself from above. She is sure, suddenly, that this is Michael. Here, lying beside her.

"No, you don't," she answers, feeling something sharp in her chest, poking her from the inside.

Suddenly, she cannot be there a moment longer. She gets up and goes to her bike, pulling it up to standing, then turning it around and hauling it, with the sleigh coasting behind, her breath an exaggerated wheeze, back to where Reg is lying. She drops the bike, gets on her knees, and does what she resisted doing earlier: pulling back the fingers of her gloves, she works open the sleigh's frozen hinges until its top half is completely released. She then chucks all of its contents – all her expensive clothes and tools and gear – into the snow, leaving just the empty bowl of the sleigh bottom. She unhooks it from her bike and places it lengthwise beside Reg.

She has not even told herself that these are the steps she must follow. She simply follows them, pushing Reg's side up off the ground now, howling aloud with the effort, seeing spots float into her field of vision, her hands like heavy, dumb oafs she cannot communicate with. Somewhere in her mind, a question calls out: *what about the win?* But it is like an echo of her own voice, and she can barely make out the words. She tips Reg's weight over the lip of the sleigh and tries to slide the rest of him in, but fails several times. Once, she simply collapses over him. *Fucking ridiculous.*

Finally, on her fifth try, Reg, miraculously, slips into the bowl of the sleigh, the bottom half of his sleeping bag dangling off the end like a tongue. Anick, tears freezing on her cheeks, hooks the sleigh back to the bike, pulls up her handlebars and, holding them straight, begins to push ahead, back over the roots and rocks and snow she came through just minutes ago. It is farcical. Fuzzy. Fantasy and dream begin to converge as they did just before the man in the red jumpsuit appeared yesterday.

"I know you," says Reg, again, and she is grateful for the shock of reality his words bring. But she also sorely wants to tell him to shut up so she can concentrate.

Then her foot catches a root and she falls in such a way that the small bolt between her handlebars smacks her on the nose and blood spurts out. She tries to get up, but the snow is like muck. She is trapped. Soaked. Fatigued to the core of her being. Her toes have begun a revolt inside her shoes. She recalls the night in the desert with Michael, how little pain she'd felt during those three hours. She'd felt nothing, really. Like sitting in a boat on a lake when there's no wind.

Her eyes, through frozen lashes, search the trees, looking for camp, for the single jerky light of the search and rescue snowmobile that will spot them.

"I know me," she says, in response to Reg's comment. Then she grabs her handlebars, the blood spotting the snow beneath her, and tries again.

MORDECAI RICHLER

PLAYING BALL
ON HAMPSTEAD HEATH

Summer.

Drifting through Soho in the early evening, Jake stopped at the
Nosh Bar for a sustaining salt-beef sandwich. He had only managed one squirting mouthful and a glance at the unit trust quo-
tations in the *Standard* (S&P Capital was steady, but Pan
Australian had dipped again) when he was distracted by a
bulging-bellied American in a Dacron suit. The American's
wife, unsuccessfully shoehorned into a mini-skirt, clutching a
London A to Z to her bosom. The American opened a fat credit-
card-filled wallet, briefly exposing an international medical
passport which listed his blood type; he extracted a pound note
and slapped it into the waiter's hand. "I suppose," he said, winking, "I get 24 shillings change for this?"

The waiter shot him a sour look.

"Tell your boss," the American continued, unperturbed,
"that I'm a Galicianer, just like him."

"Oh, Morty," his wife said, bubbling.

And the juicy salt-beef sandwich turned to leather in Jake's
mouth. It's here again, he realized, heart sinking, the season.

Come summer, American and Canadian show business
plenipotentiaries domiciled in London had more than the usual
hardships to contend with. The usual hardships being the
income tax tangle, scheming and incompetent natives, uppity
au pairs or nannies, wives overspending at the bazaar (Harrod's,

Fortnum's, Asprey's), choosing suitable prep schools for the kids, doing without real pastrami and pickled tomatoes, fighting decorators and smog, and of course keeping warm. But come summer, tourist lines and jets began to disgorge demanding hordes of relatives and friends of friends, long (and best) forgotten schoolmates and army buddies, on London, thereby transmogrifying the telephone, charmingly inefficient all winter, into an instrument of terror. For there was not a stranger who phoned and did not exude warmth and expect help in procuring theatre tickets and a night on the town ("What we're really dying for is a pub crawl. The swinging pubs. Waddiya say, old chap?") or an invitation to dinner at home. ("Well, Yankel, did you tell the Queen your Uncle Labish was coming? Did she bake a cake?")

The tourist season's dialogue, the observations, the complaints, was a recurring hazard to be endured. You agreed, oh how many times you agreed, the taxis were cute, the bobbies polite, and the pace slower than New York or, in Jake's case, Montreal. "People still know how to enjoy life here. I can see that." Yes. On the other hand, you've got to admit... the bowler hats are a scream, hotel service is lousy, there's nowhere you can get a suit pressed in a hurry, the British have snobby British accents and hate all Americans. Jealousy. "Look at it this way, it isn't home." Yes, a thousand times yes. All the same, everybody was glad to have made the trip, it was expensive but broadening, the world was getting smaller all the time, a global village, only next time they wouldn't try to squeeze so many countries into 21 days. "Mind you, the American Express was very, very nice everywhere. No complaints in that department."

Summer was charged with menace, with schnorrers and greenhorns from the New Country. So how glorious, how utterly delightful, it was for the hardcore show biz expatriates (those who weren't in Juan-les-Pins or Dubrovnik) to come together on a Sunday morning for a sweet and soothing game of softball, just as the Raj of another dynasty had used to meet on the cricket pitch in Malabar.

Sunday morning softball on Hampstead Heath in summer was unquestionably the fun thing to do. It was a ritual.

Manny Gordon tooled in all the way from Richmond, stowing a fielder's mitt and a thermos of martinis in the boot, clapping a sporty tweed cap over his bald head and strapping himself and his starlet of the night before into his Aston-Martin at 9:00 a.m. C. Bernard Farber started out from Ham Common, picking up Al Levine, Bob Cohen, Jimmy Grief and Myer Gross outside Mary Quant's on the King's Road. Moey Hanover had once startled the staff at the Connaught by tripping down the stairs on a Sunday morning, wearing a peak cap and T-shirt and blue jeans, carrying his personal Babe Ruth bat in one hand and a softball in the other. Another Sunday Ziggy Alter had flown in from Rome, just for the sake of a restorative nine innings.

Frank Demaine drove in from Marlow-on-Thames in his Maserati. Lou Caplan, Morty Calman, and Cy Levi usually brought their wives and children. Monty Talman, ever mindful of his latest twenty-one-year-old girlfriend, always cycled to the Heath from St. John's Wood. Wearing a maroon track suit, he usually lapped the field eight or nine times before anyone else turned up.

Jake generally strolled to the Heath, his tattered fielder's mitt and three enervating bagels filled with smoked salmon concealed under the *Observer* in his shopping bag. Some Sundays, like this one, possibly his last for a while, Nancy brought the kids along to watch.

The starting line-up on Sunday, June 28, 1963 was:

AL LEVINE's TEAM	LOU CAPLAN's BUNCH
Manny Gordon, *ss.*	Bob Cohen, *3b.*
C. Bernard Farber, *2b.*	Myer Gross, *ss.*
Jimmy Grief, *3b.*	Frankie Demaine, *lf.*
Al Levine, *cf.*	Morty Calman, *rf.*
Monty Talman, *1b.*	Cy Levi, *2b.*
Ziggy Alter, *lf.*	Moey Hanover, *c.*
Jack Monroe, *rf.*	Johnny Roper, *cf.*
Sean Fielding, *c.*	Jason Storm, *1b.*
Alfie Roberts, *p.*	Lou Caplan, *p.*

Jake, like five or six others who had arrived late and hung over (or who were unusually inept players), was a sub. A utility fielder, Jake sat on the bench with Lou Caplan's Bunch. It was a fine, all but cloudless morning, but looking around Jake felt there were too many wives, children, and kibitzers about. Even more ominous, the Filmmakers' First Wives Club or, as Ziggy Alter put it, the Alimony Gallery, was forming, seemingly relaxed but actually fulminating, on the grass behind home plate.

First Al Levine's Team and then Lou Caplan's Bunch, both sides made up mostly of men in their forties, trotted out, sunken bellies quaking, discs suddenly tender, haemorrhoids smarting, to take a turn at fielding and batting practice.

Nate Sugarman, once a classy shortstop, but since his coronary the regular umpire, bit into a digitalis pill, strode onto the field, and called, "Play ball!"

"Let's go, boychick."

"We need a hit," Monty Talman, the producer, hollered.

"*You* certainly do," Bob Cohen, who only yesterday had winced through a rough cut of Talman's latest fiasco, shouted back snidely from the opposite bench.

Manny, hunched over the plate cat-like, trying to look menacing, was knotted with more than his usual fill of anxiety. If he struck out, his own team would not be too upset because it was early in the game, but Lou Caplan, pitching for the first time since his Mexican divorce, would be grateful, and flattering Lou was a good idea because he was rumoured to be ready to go with a three-picture deal for Twentieth; and Manny had not been asked to direct a big-budget film since *Chase*. *Ball one, inside*. If, Manny thought, I hit a single I will be obliged to pass the time of day with that stomach-turning queen Jason Storm, 1b., who was in London to make a TV pilot film for Ziggy Alter. *Strike one, called*. He had never hit a homer, so that was out, but if come a miracle he connected for a triple, what then? He would be stuck on third sack with Bob Cohen, strictly second featuresville, a born loser, and Manny didn't want to be seen with Bob, even for an inning, especially with so many producers and agents about. K-nack! *Goddammit, it's a hit! A double, for Chrissake!*

As the players on Al Levine's bench rose to a man, shouting encouragement—

"Go, man. Go."

"Shake the lead out, Manny. Run!"

—Manny, conscious only of Lou Caplan glaring at him ("It's not my fault, Lou"), scampered past first base and took myopic, round-shouldered aim on second, wondering should he say something shitty to Cy Levi, 2b., who he suspected was responsible for getting his name on the blacklist years ago.

Next man up to the plate, C. Bernie Farber, who had signed to write Lou Caplan's first picture for Twentieth, struck out gracefully, which brought up Jimmy Grief. Jimmy swung on the first pitch, lifting it high and foul, and Moey Hanover, c., called for it, feeling guilty because next Saturday Jimmy was flying to Rome and Moey had already arranged to have lunch with Jimmy's wife on Sunday. Moey made the catch, which brought up Al Levine, who homered, bringing in Manny Gordon ahead of him. Monty Talman grounded out to Gross, ss., retiring the side.

Al Levine's Team, first inning: two hits, no errors, two runs.

Leading off for Lou Caplan's Bunch, Bob Cohen smashed a burner to centre for a single and Myer Gross fanned, bringing up Frankie Demaine and sending all the outfielders back, back, back. Frankie whacked the third pitch long and high, an easy fly had Al Levine been playing him deep left instead of inside right, where he was able to flirt hopefully with Manny Gordon's starlet, who was sprawled on the grass there in the shortest of possible Pucci prints. Al Levine was the only man on either team who always played wearing shorts – shorts revealing an elastic bandage which began at his left kneecap and ran almost as low as the ankle.

"Oh, you poor darling," the starlet said, making a face at Levine's knee.

Levine, sucking in his stomach, replied, "Spain," as if he were tossing the girl a rare coin.

"Don't tell me," she squealed. "The beach at Torremolinos. Ugh!"

"No, no," Levine protested. "The civil war, for Chrissake. Shrapnel. Defense of Madrid."

Demaine's fly fell for a homer, driving in a panting Bob Cohen.

Lou Caplan's Bunch, first inning: one hit, one error, two runs.

Neither side scored in the next two innings, which were noteworthy only because Moey Hanover's game began to slip badly. In the second Moey muffed an easy pop fly and actually let C.

Bernie Farber, still weak on his legs after a cleansing, all but foodless, week at Forest Mere Hydro, steal a base on him. The problem was clearly Sean Fielding, the young RADA graduate whom Columbia had put under contract because, in profile, he looked like Peter O'Toole. The game had only just started when Moey Hanover's wife, Lilian, had ambled over to Al Levine's bench and stretched herself out on the grass, an offering, beside Fielding, and the two of them giggling together and nudging each other ever since, which was making Moey nervy. Moey, however, had not spent his young manhood at a yeshiva to no avail. Not only had he plundered the Old Testament for most of his winning *Rawhide* and *Bonanza* plots, but now that his Lilian was obviously in heat again, his hard-bought Jewish education, which his father had always assured him was priceless, served him splendidly once more. Moey remembered his David ha'melech: *And it came to pass in the morning, that David wrote a letter to Joab, and sent it by the hand of Uriah. And he wrote in the letter, saying, Set Uriah in the forefront of the hottest battle, and retire ye from him, that he may be smitten, and die.*

Amen.

Lou Caplan yielded two successive hits in the third and Moey Hanover took off his catcher's mask, called for time, and strode to the mound, rubbing the ball in his hands.

"I'm all right," Lou said. "Don't worry. I'm going to settle down now."

"It's not that. Listen, when do you start shooting in Rome?"

"Three weeks tomorrow. You heard something bad?"

"No."

"You're a friend now, remember. No secrets."

"No. It's just that I've had second thoughts about Sean Fielding. I think he's very exciting. He's got lots of appeal. He'd be a natural to play Domingo."

As the two men began to whisper together, players on Al Levine's bench hollered. "Let's go, gang."

"Come on. Break it up, Moey."

Moey returned to the plate, satisfied that Fielding was as good as in Rome already. May he do his own stunts, he thought.

"Play ball," Nate Sugarman called.

Alfie Roberts, the director, ordinarily expected soft pitches from Lou, as he did the same for him, but today he wasn't so sure, because on Wednesday his agent had sent him one of Lou's properties to read and – Lou's first pitch made Alfie hit the dirt. That settles it, he thought, my agent already told him it doesn't grab me. Alfie struck out as quickly as he could. Better he put down for a rally-stopper than suffer a head fracture.

Which brought up Manny Gordon again, with one out and runners on first and third. Manny dribbled into a double play, retiring the side.

Multi-coloured kites bounced in the skies over the Heath. Lovers strolled on the tow paths and locked together on the grass. Old people sat on benches, sucking in the sun. Nannies passed, wheeling toddlers with titles. The odd baffled Englishman stopped to watch the Americans at play.

"Are they air force chaps?"

"Filmmakers, actually. It's their version of rounders."

"Whatever is that enormous thing that woman is slicing?"

"Salami."

"*On the Heath?*"

"Afraid so. One Sunday they actually set up a bloody folding table, right over there, with cold cuts and herrings and mounds of black bread and a whole bloody side of smoked salmon. *Scotch. Ten and six a quarter, don't you know?*"

"On the Heath?"

"Champagne *in paper cups*. Mumm's. One of them had won some sort of award."

Going into the bottom of the fifth, Al Levine's Team led 6-3, and Tom Hunt came in to play second base for Lou Caplan's Bunch. Hunt, a Negro actor, was in town shooting *Othello X* for Bob Cohen.

Moey Hanover lifted a lazy fly into left field, which Ziggy Alter trapped rolling over and over on the grass until – just before getting up – he was well placed to look up Natalie Calman's skirt. Something he saw there so unnerved him that he dropped the ball, turning pale and allowing Hanover to pull up safely at second.

Johnny Roper walked. Which brought up Jason Storm, to the delight of a pride of British fairies who stood with their dogs on the first base line, squealing and jumping. Jason poked a bouncer through the infield and floated to second, obliging the fairies and their dogs to move up a base.

With two out and the score tied 7-7 in the bottom half of the sixth, Alfie Roberts was unwillingly retired and a new pitcher came in for Al Levine's Team. It was Gordie Kaufman, a writer blacklisted for years, who now divided his time between Madrid and Rome, asking a 100,000 dollars a spectacular. Gordie came in to pitch with the go-ahead run on third and Tom Hunt stepping up to the plate for the first time. Big black Tom Hunt, who had once played semi-pro ball in Florida, was a militant. If he homered, Hunt felt he would be put down for another buck nigger, good at games, but if he struck out, which would call for rather more acting skill than was required of him on the set of *Othello X*, what then? He would enable a bunch of fat, foxy, sexually worried Jews to feel big, goysy. Screw them, Hunt thought.

Gordie Kaufman had his problems too. His stunning villa on Mallorca was run by Spanish servants, his two boys were boarding at a reputable British public school, and Gordie himself was president, sole stockholder, and the only employee of a company that was a plaque in Liechtenstein. And yet – and yet – Gordie still subscribed to the *Nation*; he filled his Roman slaves with anti-apartheid dialogue and sagacious Talmudic sayings; and whenever the left-wing pushke was passed around he came through with a nice check. I must bear down on Hunt, Gordie thought, because if he touches me for even a scratch single I'll come off a patronizing ofay. If he homers, God forbid, I'm a shitty liberal. And so with the count 3 and 2, and a walk, the typical social-democrat's compromise, seemingly the easiest way out for both men, Gordie gritted his teeth, his proud Trotskyite past getting the best of him, and threw a fast ball right at Hunt, bouncing it off his head. Hunt threw away his bat and started for the mound, fist clenched, but not so fast that players from both sides couldn't rush in to separate the two men, both of whom felt vindicated, proud, because they had triumphed over impersonal racial prejudice to hit each other as individuals on a fun Sunday on Hampstead Heath.

Come the crucial seventh, the Filmmakers' First Wives Club grew restive, no longer content to belittle their former husbands from afar, and moved in on the baselines and benches, undermining confidence with their heckling. When Myer Gross, for instance, came to bat with two men on base and his teammates shouted, "Go, man. Go," one familiar grating voice floated out over the others. "Hit, Myer. Make your son proud of you, *just this once.*"

What a reproach the first wives were. How steadfast! How unchanging! Still Waiting For Lefty after all these years. Today maybe hair had greyed and chins doubled, necks had gone pruney, breasts drooped and stomachs dropped, but let no man say these crones had aged in spirit. Where once they had petitioned for the Scottsboro Boys, broken with their families over mixed marriages, sent their boyfriends off to defend Madrid, split with old comrades over the Stalin-Hitler Pact, fought for Henry Wallace, demonstrated for the Rosenbergs, and never, never yielded to McCarthy... today they clapped hands at China Friendship Clubs, petitioned for others to keep hands off Cuba and Vietnam, and made their sons chopped liver sandwiches and sent them off to march to Aldermaston.

The wives, alimonied but abandoned, had known the early struggling years with their husbands, the self-doubts, the humiliations, the rejections, the cold-water flats, and the blacklist, but they had always remained loyal. They hadn't altered, their husbands had.

Each marriage had shattered in the eye of its own self-made hurricane, but essentially the men felt, as Ziggy Alter had once put it so succinctly at the poker table. "Right, wrong, don't be silly, it's really a question of who wants to grow old with Anna Pauker when there are so many juicy little things we can now afford."

So there they were, out on the grass chasing fly balls on a Sunday morning, short men, overpaid and unprincipled, all well within the coronary and lung cancer belt, allowing themselves to look ridiculous in the hope of pleasing their new young wives and girlfriends. There was Ziggy Alter, who had once written a play "with content" for the Group Theatre. Here was Al Levine, who used to throw marbles under horses' legs at demonstrations and now raced two horses of his own at Epsom. On the pitcher's mound stood Gordie Kaufman, who had once carried a banner that read *No Pasarán* through the streets of Manhattan and now employed a man especially to keep Spaniards off the beach at his villa on Mallorca. And sweating under a catcher's mask there was Moey Hanover, who had studied at a yeshiva, stood up to the committee, and was now on a sabbatical from Desilu.

Usually the husbands were able to avoid their used-up wives. They didn't see them in the gaming rooms at the White Elephant or in the Mirabelle or Les Ambassadeurs. But come Brecht to Shaftesbury Avenue and without looking up from the second row centre they could feel them squatting in their cotton bloomers in the second balcony, burning holes in their necks.

And count on them to turn up on a Sunday morning in summer on Hampstead Heath just to ruin a game of fun baseball. Even homering, as Al Levine did, was no answer to the drones.

"It's nice for him, I suppose," a voice behind Levine on the bench observed, "that on the playing field, with an audience, if you know what I mean, he actually appears virile."

The game dragged on. In the eighth inning Jack Monroe had to retire to his Mercedes-Benz for his insulin injection and Jake Hersh, until now an embarrassed sub, finally trotted onto the field. Hersh, thirty-three, one-time relief pitcher for Room 41, Fletcher's Field High (2-7), moved into right field, mindful of his disc condition and hoping he would not be called on to make a tricky catch. He assumed a loose-limbed stance on the grass, waving at his wife, grinning at his children, when without warning a sizzling line drive came right at him. Jake, startled, did the only sensible thing: he ducked. Outraged shouts and moans from the bench reminded Jake where he was, in a softball game, and he started after the ball.

"Fishfingers."

"*Putz!*"

Runners on first and third started for home as Jake, breathless, finally caught up with the ball. It had rolled to a stop under a bench where a nanny sat watching over an elegant perambulator.

"Excuse me," Jake said.

"Americans," the nurse said.

"I'm a Canadian," Jake protested automatically, fishing the ball out from under the bench.

Three runs scored. Jake caught a glimpse of Nancy, unable to contain her laughter. The children looked ashamed of him.

In the ninth inning with the score tied again, 11-11, Sol Peters, another sub, stepped cautiously to the plate for Lou Caplan's Bunch. The go-ahead run was on second and there was only one out. Gordie Kaufman, trying to prevent a bunt, threw right at him and Sol, forgetting he was wearing his contact lenses, held the bat in front of him to protect his glasses. The ball hit the bat and rebounded for a perfectly laid down bunt.

"Run, you shmock."

"Go, man."

Sol, terrified, ran, carrying the bat with him.

Monty Talman phoned home.

"Who won?" his wife asked.

"We did. 13-12. But that's not the point. We had lots of fun."

"How many you bringing back for lunch?"

"Eight."

"*Eight?*"

"I couldn't get out of inviting Johnny Roper. He knows Jack Monroe is coming."

"I see."

"A little warning. Don't, for Chrissake, ask Cy how Marsha is. They're separating. And I'm afraid Manny Gordon is coming with a girl. I want you to be nice to her."

"*Anything else?*"

"If Gershon phones from Rome while the guys are there please remember I'm taking the call upstairs. And please don't start collecting glasses and emptying ashtrays at four o'clock. It's embarrassing. Bloody Jake Hersh is coming and it's just the sort of incident he'd pick on and joke about for months."

"I never coll—"

"All right, all right. Oh, shit, something else. Tom Hunt is coming."

"The actor?"

"Yeah. Now listen, he's very touchy, so will you please put away Sheila's doll."

"Sheila's doll?"

"If she comes in carrying that bloody golliwog I'll die. Hide it. Burn it. Hunt gets script approval these days, you know."

"All right, dear."

"See you soon."

DIANE SCHOEMPERLEN

HOCKEY NIGHT IN CANADA

We settled ourselves in our usual places, my father and I, while the singer made his way out onto the ice and the organist cranked up for "O Canada" and "The Star Spangled Banner." Saturday night and we were ready for anything, my father half-sitting, half-lying on the chesterfield with his first dark rum and Pepsi, and I in the swivel chair beside the picture window with a box of barbecue chips and a glass of 7Up.

My mother was ripping apart with relish a red and white polka dot dress she hadn't worn for years. There were matching red shoes, purse and a hat once too, but they'd already been packed or given away. Trying to interest someone in her project and her practicality, she said, "Why, this fabric is just as good as new," pulling first one sleeve, then the other, away from the body of the dress.

But the game was starting and we were already intent on the screen and each other.

"They don't stand a chance tonight," I said, shaking my head sadly but with confidence as the players skated out.

My father grinned calmly and took a drink of rum.

"Not a chance," I prodded.

"We'll see, we'll just see about that." Even when they played poorly for weeks on end, my father remained cheerfully loyal to the Chicago Blackhawks, for no particular reason I could see, except that he always had been. He must have suffered secret doubts about the team now and then – anyone would – but he never let on. I, having no similar special allegiance and wanting to keep the evening interesting, always hoped for the other team.

We were not violent fans, either one of us. We never hollered, leaped out of our chairs, or pounded ourselves in alternating fits of frustration and ecstasy. We did not jump up and down yelling, "Kill him, kill him!" Instead, we were teasing fans, pretend fans almost, feigning hostility and heartbreak, smirking and groaning gruesomely by turns, exaggerating our reactions mainly for the benefit of the other and sometimes just to get a rise out of my mother, who was by this time humming with pins in her mouth, smoothing pattern pieces onto the remains of the dress, and snipping merrily away with the pinking shears, while scraps of cloth and tissue paper drifted to the floor all around her.

The dress, I discovered, was to be reincarnated as a blouse for me, a blouse which, by the time it was finished (perfectly, seams all basted and bound, hem hand-done), I would probably hate. Between periods, she took me into the bathroom for a fitting session in front of the full-length mirror. I did not breathe, complain or look as she pinned the blouse together around me, a piece at a time, one sleeve, the other, half the front, the other half, back, collar, the cold silver pins scratching my bare skin just lightly.

By the time we got to the three-star selection after the game, my mother was off to the back bedroom with the blouse, whirring away on the Singer.

When her friend Rita was there, my mother at least played at watching the game. Whenever the crowd roared, my father groaned and Rita began to shriek, my mother would look up from her stamp collection, which she was endlessly sorting and sticking and spreading all over the card table, and smile encouragement at the TV.

"Who scored?" she asked innocently, as she put another page in her album and arranged another row of stamps across it. Russia was her favourite country for collecting, the best because their stamps were bigger and grander than any, especially ours, which looked stingy and common by comparison. The Russians had hockey players, cosmonauts, fruits and vegetables, wild animals, trucks and ballerinas, in red, blue, green, yellow, even shiny silver and gold. We had mainly the Queen in pastels. My mother's everyday fear and loathing of Communists did not enter into the matter.

"Just guess, Violet, just you guess who scored!" Rita crowed.

"Don't ask," my father muttered.

"Most goals, one team, one game," Rita recited. "Twenty-one, Montreal Canadiens, March 3, 1920, at Montreal, defeated the Québec Bulldogs 16 to 3."

"Ancient history," said my father. "Besides, who ever heard of the Québec Bulldogs anyway? You're making it all up, Rita. Tell me another one."

"Fewest points, one season," Rita chanted. "Thirty-one, Chicago Blackhawks, 1953/54, won 12, lost 36, tied 4."

"Not quite what I had in mind." My father rolled his big eyes and went into the kitchen to fix more drinks, one for himself and one for Rita, who took her rum with orange juice, no ice. I said nothing, not being sure yet whether I wanted to stick up for my father or fall in love with the Canadiens too.

Rita had followed the Montreal team for years. Unlike my father and me, she was a *real* fan, a serious fan who shrieked and howled and paced around the living room, calling the players by their first names, begging them to score, willing them to win with clenched fists and teeth. She did not consider her everyday dislike of those Frenchmen (as in, "I've got no use for those Frenchmen, no use at all") to be contradictory. Hockey, like stamp collecting, it seemed, was a world apart, immune to the regular prejudices of race, province and country – although she did sometimes berate my father for siding with a Yankee team.

When the Blackhawks lost another one, Rita and I (for I'd been won over after all by her braying) took all the credit for knowing the better team right off the bat, and heaped all the blame upon my father who was now in disgrace along with his team – a position he took rather well. When they did win, as far as he was concerned, it was all or mainly because he'd never given up on them.

After the game my father and I usually played a few hands of poker, a penny a game, with the cards spread out on the chesterfield between us. My mother and Rita were in the kitchen having coffee and maybe a cream puff. The hum of their voices came to me just vaguely, like perfume. I wanted to hear what they were saying but my father was analyzing the last power play and dealing me another hand. I won more often than not, piling up my pennies. For years after this I would think of myself as lucky at cards. In certain difficult situations which showed a disturbing tendency to repeat themselves, I would often be reminded of Rita's teasing warning: "Lucky at cards, unlucky at love."

Later, after Rita had gone home, I would find the ashtray full of lipstick-tipped butts which I pored over, looking for clues.

My mother had met Rita that summer at Eaton's where Rita was working at the Cosmetics counter. Rita still worked at Eaton's, but she was in Ladies Dresses now, having passed briefly through Lingerie and Swimwear in between.

To hear Rita tell it, you'd think their whole friendship was rooted in my mother's hair.

"I just couldn't help myself," Rita said, telling me the story. "There I was trying to convince this fat lady that all she really needed was a bottle of Cover Girl and some Midnight Blue mascara and up walked your mother with her hair."

Patting her hair fondly, my mother said, "I couldn't figure out what she was staring at."

I already knew that before Rita had come to live in Hastings, she was a hairdresser in Toronto. She'd been to hairdressing school for two years and still took the occasional special course in cold waves or colouring. She was about to open her own beauty parlour just when her husband Geoffrey killed himself and everything was changed. It was not long after that that Rita gave up hairdressing and moved to Hastings to stay with her younger sister, Jeanette. Six months after that Jeanette married a doctor and moved back to Toronto. But Rita stayed on in Hastings anyway, bought herself a second-hand car and rented an apartment downtown in the Barclay Block above an Italian bakery (which was the very same building my parents had lived in when they were first married, a fact that I found significant and somehow too good to be true).

My mother always did her own hair, putting it up in pincurls every Sunday night so that it lay in lustrous black waves all around her face and rolled thickly down past her shoulders in the back. But what Rita meant was the streak, a pure white streak in the front from the time she'd had ringworm when she was small. Even I had to admit it looked splendid and daring, although there were times when we were fighting and I wanted to hurt her and tell her she looked like a skunk. Rita's own hair was straggly and thin, half-dead from too many washings, a strange salmon colour, growing out blonde, from too many experiments. Her bangs hung down almost to her eyebrows. Sometimes she wore them swept back with coloured barrettes, revealing the delicate blue veins in her temples.

"Anyway," Rita said, pausing to light another cigarette with her Zippo, "I finally got rid of the fat lady and your mother and

I got talking. Just seeing her hair gave me the itch again — I could just picture all the things I could do with that hair. We went up to the cafeteria for coffee—"

"And we've been friends ever since," my mother said in a pleased and final-sounding voice, the way you might say, And they all lived happily ever after.

My mother had never really had a friend of her own before. Oh, there was a neighbour lady, Mrs. Kent three doors down, who would come over once in a while to borrow things that she never returned — the angel food cake pan, the egg beater, the four-side cheese grater. And so my mother would go over to Mrs. Kent's house occasionally too, to get the things back. But it was never what you would call a friendship, so much as a case of proximity and Mrs. Kent's kitchen being sadly ill-equipped.

I had never seriously thought of my mother as wanting or needing a friend anyway. Friends, particularly best friends, I gathered, were something you grew out of soon after you got married and had children. After that, the husband and the children became your best friends, or were supposed to.

But then she met Rita and it was as though Rita were someone she had been just waiting for, saving herself up for all those years. They told each other old stories and secrets, made plans, remembered times before when they might have met, had just missed each other, almost met, but didn't. Rita was at least ten years younger than my mother. I suppose I thought of her as doing my mother a favour by being her friend. In the way of young girls, I just naturally imagined my mother to be the needy one of the two.

When Rita was in Cosmetics, she would bring my mother makeup samples that the salesmen had left: mascara, blusher, eyebrow pencils, and sometimes half-empty perfume testers for me. And her pale face was perfect. Once she moved to Ladies Dresses, she hardly ever wore slacks anymore, except when the weather turned cold. She was always trying out bold new accessories, big belts, coloured stockings, high-heeled boots. I could only imagine what she'd bought while she worked in Lingerie – the most elegant underwear, I supposed, and coloured girdles (I didn't know if there were such things for sure, but if there were, Rita would have several), and marvellous gauzy nightgowns.

On her day off during the week Rita was usually there in the kitchen when I came home from school for lunch. While my mother fixed me a can of soup and a grilled cheese sandwich, Rita sipped black coffee and nibbled on fresh fruit and cottage cheese. This was the first I knew of dieting as a permanent condition, for although Rita was quite slim and long-legged, she was always watching her weight. My mother, who was much rounder than Rita anyway, had taken up dieting too, like a new hobby which required supplies of lettuce, pink grapefruit and detailed diet books listing menus, recipes and calories. She'd begun to compliment me on my extreme thinness, when not so many years before she'd made me wear two crinolines to school so the teachers wouldn't think she didn't feed me. How was it that, without changing size or shape, I had graduated from grotesque to slender?

"How's school going this week?" Rita would ask, offering me a tiny cube of pineapple, which I hated.

She listened patiently, nodding and frowning mildly, while I told her about Miss Morton, the gym teacher who hated me because I was no good at basketball; and about my best friend Mary Yurick who was madly in love with Lorne Puhalski, captain of the hockey team and unattainable; and about everybody's enemy, Bonnie Ettinger, who'd beat up Della White on Monday in the alley behind the school.

It was easy to get carried away with such confidences in the hope that Rita would reciprocate, and I almost told her that I was in love with Lorne Puhalski too, and that Bonnie Ettinger was going around saying she'd knock my block off if she ever got the chance. But I talked myself out of it at the last minute. I wanted so much to have Rita all to myself but somehow it never was arranged.

With Rita there, my mother could listen to my problems without worrying too much or wanting to do something about them. She and I probably learned more about each other from those kitchen conversations with Rita than we ever could have any other way.

Sometimes it was as though they'd forgotten all about me. One day when I came home for lunch my mother was sitting wrapped in a sheet on the high stool in the middle of the kitchen while Rita gave her a cold wave, something she'd been threatening to do for weeks. I made my own sandwich.

My mother was saying, "I was so young then, and every-body said I was pretty. We were in love but when they found out, they shipped him off to agricultural school in Winnipeg. I still think Sonny was my own true love."

"What about Ted?" Rita asked, wrapping pieces of hair in what looked like cigarette rolling papers and then winding them nimbly onto pink plastic rods.

"Oh, Ted."

Ted was my father of course, but it was strange to hear my mother call him by his name when usually she called him "Dad" or "your Dad."

"Yes, well, Ted. That was different. I was older. I'm even older now. I didn't tell Ted about Sonny until long after we were married."

I went back to school that afternoon with a picture of my mother as another person altogether, someone I had never met and never would now. This woman, mysterious, incomplete and broken-hearted, pestered me all day long. The stink of the cold wave chemicals lingered too, bitter but promising.

At other times it was as though my mother could tell me things through Rita that she could never have expressed if we were alone.

One Saturday night after the hockey game I left my father dozing on the chesterfield and went into the kitchen.

Rita was saying, "When Geoffrey hung himself, his whole family blamed me. They said I'd driven him to do it. They kept bringing up the baby who died and then Geoffrey too, as if I'd murdered them both with my bare hands. I had a nervous breakdown and they said it served me right. It was then that I realized I would have to leave town." She spoke calmly, looking down at her lap, not moving, and a sense of young tragic death wound around her like scented bandages, permanent and disfiguring, the way Japanese women used to bind their feet to keep them dainty. She was doomed somehow, I could see that now, even though I'd never noticed it before.

"You have to be strong, we all have to be so strong," my mother said without looking at me. "We're the women, we have to be stronger than they think we are."

I could hear my father snoring lightly in the other room, no longer harmless. The kitchen was snug with yellow light. The window was patterned with frost like feathers or ferns and it was just starting to snow. My mother pulled the blind down so no one could see in. We could have been anywhere, just the three of us, bending in together around the kitchen table, knowing things, these sad things, that no one else knew yet.

That night Rita slept over. An odd thing for grown-ups to do, I thought, but I liked it.

After I'd gone to bed, it reminded me of Christmas: something special waiting all night long in the living room: the tree, the unopened presents, Rita in my mother's new nightie wrapped up in an old car blanket on the chesterfield.

Around the middle of December, Rita flew to Toronto to have Christmas with her sister Jeanette and her doctor husband. My mother had somehow not considered exchanging presents with Rita and was horrified when she appeared the morning she left with three gaily-wrapped boxes, one for each of us. Even more surprising was my father, who handed Rita a little package tied up with curly red ribbons. She opened it on the spot, still standing in the doorway, and produced a silver charm of the Montreal Canadiens' crest.

On Christmas morning we opened her presents first. She'd given my mother a white silk scarf handpainted with an ocean scene in vivid blues and greens. My father held up a red Chicago Blackhawks jersey with the Indian head on the front and the number 21 on the back. I got a leather-covered date book for the new year in which I immediately noted the birthdays of everyone I could think of. Rita's presents were the best ones that year.

After dinner, we called all our relatives in Manitoba and then my mother took some pictures of the tree, of my father in his new hockey sweater and of me eating my dessert behind the chicken carcass. My friend Mary called and we told each other everything we got. I thought Rita might call later but she didn't.

Between Christmas and New Year's my mother went out and bought a braided gold necklace to give to Rita when she got back. The silver charm was never discussed in front of me.

Not long after Rita returned from her holidays, she was moved from Ladies Dresses into Ladies Coats. Now when she came over she wore a knee-length black coat trimmed with grey Persian lamb at the collar and cuffs. She always hesitated before taking it off, caressing the curly lapels, picking invisible lint off the back, giving my mother and I just enough time to notice and admire it again. She knew a lot about mink and ermine now, how the little things were bred and raised on special farms, how vicious they were, how many tiny pelts it took to make just one coat. She lusted uncontrollably, as she put it, after one particular mink coat in her department but had resigned herself to never being able to afford it and seemed both relieved and disappointed the day it was bought by some doctor's wife.

"Just between you and I," my mother said right after Rita phoned to say she'd sold the fabulous coat, "I think mink is a waste of money. It's only for snobs. I wouldn't wear one if you gave it to me." Ten years later, my father bought her a mink jacket trimmed with ermine and she said, hugging him, "Oh, Ted, I've always wanted one."

It was an extravagant winter, with new records set for both snow and all-time low temperatures. My father seemed to be always outside shovelling snow in the dark, piling up huge icy banks all around the house. He would come in from the cold red-cheeked and handsome, trying to put his icy hands around my neck. Rita came over less and less often. She said it was because her car wouldn't start half the time, even when she kept it plugged in.

On warmer days when Rita wasn't working, my mother often took the bus downtown to her apartment. When I came home from school at three-thirty, the house would be luxuriously empty. I curled up on the chesterfield with the record player on and wrote in the date book Rita had given me or worked on the optimistic list my friend Mary and I had started: "One Thousand Things We Like." Well into its second spiral notebook, the list had passed 700 and was coming up quickly on 800 with

> *cuckoo clocks*
> *Canada*
> *lace*
> *my mother's hair*

> *comfortable underwear and*
> *having a bath without interruptions*

being the most recent additions.

My mother returned just in time to start supper before my father got home from work. She was distracted in a pleasant sort of way, all jazzed up and jingling from too much coffee or something, gabbing away gaily as she peeled the potatoes. Rita had given her some old clothes which could be made over into any number of new outfits for me. There was a reversible plaid skirt I'd always admired and wanted to wear right away but my mother said it was too old for me.

One Saturday afternoon when we had been out shopping together, my mother suggested we drop in on Rita before catching the bus home. I had never been to her apartment before and as we walked up Northern Avenue to the Barclay Block, I tried to imagine what it would be like. Small, I supposed, since Rita lived alone – and was, in fact, the only person I'd ever known who did. Such an arrangement was new to me then, a future possibility that became more and more attractive the more I thought about it. The apartment would be quite small, yes, and half-dark all the time, with huge exotic plants dangling in all the windows, shedding a humid green light everywhere. The rooms smelled of coffee and black earth. The furniture was probably old, cleverly draped with throws in vivid geometrics. The hardwood floors gleamed and in one room (which one?) the ceiling was painted a throbbing bloody red. I thought that Rita and I could have coffee there just the two of us (my mother having conveniently disappeared) and she would tell me everything I needed to know. Why did Geoffrey hang himself, what happened to the baby, do you go out with men sometimes, do you think I'm pretty, do you think I'm smart? She could tell my future like a fortune.

We climbed a steep flight of stairs up to the second floor.

The smell of baking bread rose up cheesy and moist from the Italian bakery below. I'd forgotten that my parents had lived here once too, until my mother said, "I always hated that smell, we lived in 3B," and pointed to a door on the left. I could not imagine anything at all about their apartment.

My mother knocked loudly on Rita's door. Further down another door opened and a woman in her housecoat leaned out into the hall, expecting somebody, I guess, or maybe just spying. "Oh, it's you, hi," she said and ducked back inside.

My mother knocked again, and then once more.

"Maybe she's working," I offered.

"No, she's not. She definitely told me she was off today."

"Where can she be then?" I was pretty sure I could hear a radio going inside.

"How would I know?" my mother said angrily and sailed back down the hall.

Only once did I find my father and Rita alone in the house. I came home from Mary's late one Saturday afternoon and they were drinking rum at the kitchen table, with the record player turned up loud in the living room. They seemed neither surprised nor sorry to see me. There was something funny about Rita's eyes when she looked up at me though, a lazy softness, a shining, which I just naturally assumed to be an effect of the rum. She poured me a glass of 7Up and we sat around laying bets on the playoffs which were just starting, Montreal and St. Louis, until my mother came home from shopping. As it turned out, the Canadiens took the series four games straight that year and skated back to Montreal with the Stanley Cup.

Rita stayed for supper and then for the game. I went back over to Mary's and then her father drove us downtown to the Junior A game at the arena. Rita was gone by the time I got home and I went straight to bed because I'd had one shot of rye in Lorne Puhalski's father's car in the arena parking lot and I was afraid my mother, who still liked to kiss me goodnight, would smell it.

They were arguing as they got ready for bed.

"She lost her son, Violet, and then her husband too," my father said, meaning Rita, making her sound innocent but careless, always losing things, people too. But he was defending her, and himself too, protecting her from some accusation, himself from some threat that I'd missed, something unfair.

"Well, I *know* that, Ted."

"Don't forget it then."

"That's no excuse for anything, you fool."

"I didn't say it was."

"Be quiet, she'll hear you," my mother said, meaning me.

RUDY THAUBERGER

GOALIE

Nothing pleases him. Win or lose, he comes home angry, dragging his equipment bag up the driveway, sullen eyes staring down, seeing nothing, refusing to see. He throws his bag against the door. You hear him, fumbling with his keys, his hands sore, swollen and cold. He drops the keys. He kicks the door. You open it and he enters, glaring, not at you, not at the keys, but at everything, the bag, the walls, the house, the air, the sky.

His clothes are heavy with sweat. There are spots of blood on his jersey and on his pads. He moves past you, wordless, pulling his equipment inside, into the laundry room and then into the garage. You listen to him, tearing the equipment from the bag, throwing it. You hear the thump of heavy leather, the clatter of plastic, the heavy whisper of damp cloth. He leaves and you enter. The equipment is everywhere, scattered, draped over chairs, hung on hooks, thrown on the floor.

You imagine him on the ice: compact, alert, impossibly agile and quick. Then you stare at the equipment: helmet and throat protector, hockey pants, jersey, chest and arm protectors, athletic supporter, knee pads and leg pads, blocker, catching glove and skates. In the centre of the floor are three sticks, scattered, their broad blades chipped and worn. The clutter is deliberate, perhaps even necessary. His room is the same, pure chaos, clothes and magazines everywhere, spilling out of dresser drawers, into the closet. He says he knows where everything is. You imagine him on the ice, focused, intense, single-minded. You understand the need for clutter.

When he isn't playing, he hates the equipment. It's heavy and awkward and bulky. It smells. He avoids it, scorns it. It disgusts him. Before a game, he gathers it together on the floor and stares at it. He lays each piece out carefully, obsessively, growling and snarling at anyone who comes too close. His mother calls him a gladiator, a bullfighter. But you know the truth, that gathering the equipment is a ritual of hatred, that every piece represents, to him, a particular variety of pain.

There are black marks scattered on the white plastic of his skates. He treats them like scars, reminders of pain. His glove hand is always swollen. His chest, his knees and his biceps are always bruised. After a hard game, he can barely move. "Do you enjoy it?" you ask, "Do you enjoy the game at least? Do you like playing?" He shrugs, "I love it," he says.

Without the game, he's miserable. He spends his summers restless and morose, skating every morning, lifting weights at night. He juggles absentimindedly; tennis balls, coins, apples, tossing them behind his back and under his leg, see-sawing two in one hand as he talks on the phone, bouncing them off walls and knees and feet. He plays golf and tennis with great fervour, but you suspect, underneath, he is indifferent to these games.

As fall approaches, you begin to find him in the basement, cleaning his skates, oiling his glove, taping his sticks. His hands move with precision and care. You sit with him and talk. He tells you stories. This save. That goal. Funny stories. He laughs. The funniest stories are about failure: the goal scored from centre ice, the goal scored on him by his own defenceman, the goal scored through a shattered stick. There is always a moral, the same moral every time. "You try your best and you lose."

He starts wearing the leg pads in September. Every evening, he wanders the house in them, wearing them with shorts and a

T-shirt. He hops in them, does leg lifts and jumping jacks. He takes them off and sits on them, folding them into a squat pile to limber them up. He starts to shoot a tennis ball against the fence with his stick.

As practices begin, he comes home overwhelmed by despair. His skill is an illusion, a lie, a magic trick. Nothing you say reassures him. You're his father. Your praise is empty, invalid.

The injuries begin. Bruises. Sprains. His body betrays him. Too slow. Too clumsy. His ankles are weak, buckling under him. His muscles cramp. His nose bleeds. A nerve in his chest begins to knot and fray. No one understands. They believe he's invulnerable, the fans, his teammates. They stare at him blankly while he lies on the ice, white-blind, paralyzed, as his knee or his toe or his hand or his chest or his throat burns.

To be a goalie, you realize, is to be an adult too soon, to have too soon an intimate understanding of the inevitability of pain and failure. In the backyard, next to the garage, is an old garbage can filled with broken hockey sticks. The blades have shattered. The shafts are cracked. He keeps them all, adding a new one every two weeks. You imagine him, at the end of the season, burning them, purging his failure with a bonfire. But that doesn't happen. At the end of the season, he forgets them and you throw them away.

You watch him play. You sit in the stands with his mother, freezing, in an arena filled with echoes. He comes out without his helmet and stick, skating slowly around the rink. Others move around him deftly. He stares past them, disconnected, barely awake. They talk to him, call his name, hit his pads lightly with their sticks. He nods, smiles. You know he's had at least four cups of coffee. You've seen him, drinking, prowling the house frantically.

As the warm-up drills begin, he gets into the goal casually. Pucks fly over the ice, crashing into the boards, cluttering the net. He skates into the goal, pulling on his glove and blocker. He raps the posts with his stick. No one seems to notice, even when he starts deflecting shots. They come around to him slowly, firing easy shots at his pads. He scoops the pucks out of the net with his stick. He seems bored.

You shiver as you sit, watching him. You hardly speak. He ignores you. You think of the cost of his equipment. Sticks, 40 dollars. Glove at 120. Leg pads, 1,300 dollars. The pads have patches. The glove is soft, the leather eaten away by his sweat.

The game begins, casually, without ceremony. The score-board lights up. The ice is cleared of pucks. Whistles blow. After the stillness of the faceoff, you hardly notice the change, until you see him in goal, crouched over, staring.

You remember him in the back yard, six years old, standing in a ragged net, wearing a parka and a baseball glove, holding an ordinary hockey stick, sawed off at the top. The puck is a tennis ball. The ice is cement. He falls down every time you shoot, ignoring the ball, trying to look like the goalies on TV. You score, even when you don't want to. He's too busy play-acting. He smiles, laughs, shouts.

You buy him a mask. He paints it. Yellow and black. Blue and white. Red and blue. It changes every month, as his heroes change. You make him a blocker out of cardboard and leg pads out of foam rubber. His mother makes him a chest protector. You play in the backyard, every evening, taking shot after shot, all winter.

It's hard to recall when you realize he's good. You come to a point where he starts to surprise you, snatching the ball out of the air with his glove, kicking it away with his shoe. You watch him one Saturday, playing with his friends. He humiliates them, stopping everything. They shout and curse. He comes in, frozen, tired and spellbound. "Did you see?" he says.

He learns to skate, moving off of the street and onto the ice. The pain begins. A shot to the shoulder paralyzes his arm for 10 minutes. You buy him pads, protectors, thinking it will stop the pain. He begins to lose. Game after game. Fast reflexes are no longer enough. He is suddenly alone, separate from you, miserable. Nothing you say helps. Keep trying. Stop. Concentrate. Hold your stick blade flat on the ice.

He begins to practice. He begins to realize that he is alone. You can't help him. His mother can't help him. That part of his life detaches from you, becoming independent, free. You fool yourself, going to his games, cheering, believing you're being supportive, refusing to understand that here, in the rink, you're irrelevant. When you're happy for him, he's angry. When you're sad for him, he's indifferent. He begins to collect trophies.

You watch the game, fascinated. You try to see it through his eyes. You watch him. His head moves rhythmically. His stick sweeps the ice and chops at it. When the shots come, he stands frozen in a crouch. Position is everything, he tells you. He moves, the movement so swift it seems to strike you physically. How does he do it? How? You don't see the puck, only his movement. Save or goal, it's all the same.

You try to see the game through his eyes, aware of everything, constantly alert. It's not enough to follow the puck. The position of the puck is old news. The game. You try to understand the game. You fail.

He seems unearthly, moving to cut down the angle, chopping the puck with his stick. Nothing is wasted. You can almost feel his mind at work, watching, calculating. Where does it come from, you wonder, this strange mind? You try to move with him, watching his eyes through his cage, and his hands. You remember the way he watches games on television, cross-legged, hands fluttering, eyes seeing everything.

Suddenly you succeed, or you think you do. Suddenly, you see the game, not as a series of events, but as a state, with every moment in time potentially a goal. Potentiality. Probability. These are words you think of afterwards. As you watch, there is only the game, pressing against you, soft now, then sharp, then rough, biting, shocking, burning, dull, cold. No players. Only forces, feelings, the white ice, the cold, the echo, all joined. A shot crashes into his helmet. He falls to his knees. You cry out.

He stands slowly, shaking his head, hacking at the ice furiously with his stick. They scored. You never noticed. Seeing the game is not enough. Feeling it is not enough. He wants more, to understand completely, to control. You look out at the ice. The game is chaos again.

He comes home, angry, limping up the driveway, victorious. You watch him, dragging his bag, sticks in his hand, leg pads over his shoulder. You wonder when it happened, when he became this sullen, driven young man. You hear whispers about scouts, rumours. Everyone adores him, adores his skill. But when you see his stiff, swollen hands, when he walks slowly into the kitchen in the mornings, every movement agony, you want to ask him why. Why does he do it? Why does he go on?

But you don't ask. Because you think you know the answer. You imagine him, looking at you and saying quietly, "What choice do I have? What else have I ever wanted to do?"

PRISCILA UPPAL

VERTIGO

Bottom right corner. Hit. *Bottom left corner.* Hit. *Top right corner.* Hit.

My accuracy is over 98 percent, even when the sessions run longer than one hour. I toss up the ball with my left hand, arch my back, bend my elbow over my head, and serve. *Top right corner.* Hit. *Bottom right corner.* Hit.

The researchers love it. Even the poor, tired, neurotic, twitchy graduate students, whose clothes don't fit, and whose responsibility it is to supervise the monotonous exercise, call out target locations on the tennis grid, and check off each time my serve falls within the lines and within a two-inch radius a "hit"; even they are visibly excited by my accuracy.

Good job, they say, and nod as I put down one of the research team's five tennis rackets – it doesn't seem to matter which I use, although I prefer bright neon yellow strings as they whip in front of my eyes, I still score the same – let them gather up all the neon green balls and head over to the shower stalls. *Good job*, like I've passed a test. When the truth is, I'm actually failing a test. And I have been for the last nine months.

I'm not a tennis player. I'm a diver. An Olympic-qualifying diver with a difficulty range of 3 to 3.6. An Olympic-qualifying diver who won't be going to the Olympics. Because I have vertigo.

⌘

My father had always encouraged me to play sports and didn't seem at all worried about my bat-swinging, ball-dribbling, bag-hitting, rope-climbing tomboy tendencies. In fact, he frequently took great pleasure in commenting on how fat and lazy the other kids on our street or at my school were. *People who sit still aren't really still at all. They're digging graves,* he'd say, and jump straight into the air tucking both knees, kicking out at the highest point (My mother lost weight without exercising. She could be found at all hours of the day in the kitchen, cooking up a storm, but ate like a bird. I figured she just grazed all day and never developed appetite for a meal. Meals, for my mother, consisted of spoonfuls from each bowl and tiny cuts of meat; passing the salt and pepper and tubs of sauces; finding the longest yet most elegant way to move a utensil from the table to the plate and then up to her small, bow-like mouth.) then bouncing on his toes once he'd hit the ground.

A man of close to fifty, but tight and trim, like a coat rack. My father was a runner. Not a professional runner, but a daily runner. *There he goes, light as a feather,* my mother would say, shaking her head as she peeled carrots or sliced onions or marinated thick rib-eye steaks (I need my protein) for dinner, or organized my schoolbooks in the morning. *Always running, running, light as a feather.* And she'd shake her head again. *The best part of running is the turn home,* my father would sometimes say as he glided back inside for a quick reappearance if my mother had sounded more resentful than habitual, if, as my father liked to joke, her Latin roots got the better of her. Athletes appreciate habit and ritual, but not resentment. Resentment is for those who can't run or dive. And he'd kiss her olive cheek. And then he'd kiss mine. *Jump, Dad, jump!* I'd scream as a little girl. And he'd jump. And jump higher again. *You're jumping over your grave, Dad! You're jumping over your grave.* And we'd jump up and down, tucking our knees and kicking out at the highest point over and over until mother scolded us. *Don't you two dare talk so casually about death!*

But what was death to me then? What's it to me now?

I cared only for sports then. And what was that? A form of order, probably. Something aesthetic. Something you strive for, work for, push your body and mind to the limits for, something so beautiful you are almost destroyed by its presence, but you keep hoping will take you on, as it keeps shifting, changing, betraying, keeping you guessing.

❧

After my shower, I'm expected to report to Dr. Melanie Burhauer's office located on the third floor of the university athletic centre. She is going to weigh me, check my blood pressure, and then ask me a series of questions. Then I'm going to lie down on a blue mat raised on a platform to the level of her waist and she's going to manipulate my head in several directions, while I stare at her freckled nose as this transpires so she can monitor my eyes and see if they lose focus or twitch. During this procedure, she will ask me the same series of questions again.

Dr. Melanie Burhauer does not like it when I weigh myself in the change room before stepping on the scale in her office – a storage space converted to office space beside the stationary bicycles room – such bad air circulation – you'd think grant money could fund something more modern and elaborate, but she says granting bodies don't care much for aesthetics, only for results, so I guess I'm a means to a result amidst rows of silver and black medical equipment on steel shelves. She does not like me weighing myself ahead of time in the change room because, no matter, the two numbers are never the same. The difference is usually two or three ounces (or points of a kilogram – we note both), but sometimes as much as two pounds. On my twenty-seventh birthday last month, four and a half pounds. Calls were made, adjustments, a new scale was brought in and installed in the women's change room. Everything was properly calibrated, the procedure supervised by four university researchers and two equipment technicians. Dr. Burhauer looked as if her cheeks were going to crack – I've never seen such a stiff face on a non-athlete in my life. I wanted to say, *Anomalies usually please you. Inconsistencies. Against-all-logic results, no? That's when there are breakthroughs.* But I didn't. People don't like to have their words used against then when they're scared. And I could tell, for whatever reason, Dr. Melanie Burhauer was scared, and she wasn't used to that emotion, though it rose to her cheeks and petrified there. Instead I said things like, *Could I be losing weight – or gaining it – over two flights of stairs? Maybe water is drying out of my hair? Maybe it's my hormones – I'm due for my period. Maybe it's the vertigo? I could be unbalanced every time I step on the scale.* Dr. Burhauer could usually be placated with the last comment, but not for four and a half pounds on my birthday. *Vertigo can't be the answer to everything,* she said incredulously, though mostly to herself it seemed and not to me. *It just can't be.* And then, *This has no bearing on our research, so let's forget about it.* Her equally-scared litter of graduate students, one of whom, the short Filipino girl who hiccups a lot, had just taken a cell phone photo of the scale reading as if it would not otherwise be believed at home, nodded to Dr. Burhauer and then to the others, but the nods had little conviction. Oh, I'm sure they all talk about me at home. I'm probably the subject of a great deal of dinner and transit conversation. I wish those conversations were part of the reports. Not that I get to read them. I refused to get off the scale. Four and a half pounds heavier. In less than 20 seconds. My birthday. With the same waist (28), hips (32), and chest (34) measurements. With the same shoulder-length wavy brown hair, and the same tight as a cannon ball calves. My shoulders, still broad from diving training, throbbed in strange excitement. My birthday. The day my mother gave me life. Four and a half pounds. Where was it? In my long neck, my flat abs, my size-seven feet, my oak-brown eyes, the yellowish mole on my left rib cage? The nausea was swishing in me like a rowboat tied to a rock at high-tide, but I refused to get off the scale. *Vertigo is not the answer*, said Dr. Burhauer, and the graduate students, including the short Filipino with her cell phone photograph, wrote this down.

But I know vertigo is the answer to a lot of things. It may even be a question too. But I'll leave that up to the professionals, the experts, the researchers. I'm no researcher. I'm just a damaged athlete taking work where I can get it. But I don't want to forget about it. Not like the way I want to forget about diving. I take a strange, secret pleasure when I slip off my shoes for a step on the stainless steel and watch the red numbers race to a plateau, waver, then rest in a stand-still position. The secret pleasure is in the knowledge that, in a few moments' time, before I can blink twice or serve an ace on the court, those numbers will change.

An athlete lives by numbers. And by belief in change. For better or worse, we're all a series of calculations.

❦

It was while running with my father through the ravines the autumn of my twelfth year that I told him I wanted to concentrate solely on diving. He broke his stride, and his arms dropped to his side. He never did that – broke proper running form – not even when I would insist on taking out the basketball to dribble here and there on our run and he'd be forced to pause at street corners and on sidewalks to wait up for me, his knees marching high as he counted how many seconds it would take me to sprint to catch up with a wayward ball smacked off a curb or rolling down to a sewer and then back to his side.

Anything but diving, was his response, and took a sip from his hip water bottle, an item he carried but only indulged in at specific landmarks on the route – the post office, the Hoppers' willow tree on Salter St., the red plastic slide at the park. He drank heartily at those points, as if he were filling his belly like a pool. I loved watching his Adam's apple bob up and down his throat with satisfaction.

Water is life, I said proudly, as if to my biology teacher, flashing him my newly retainered twelve-year-old teeth.

That's why it should be respected. Diving is a flashy sport. Arrogant in the face of nature. He resumed his running.

Without my basketball, and armed with youthful indignation, I caught up easily and began my offence. *So is running!* I held my head high as I kept to my father's steady rhythm on the long storefront pavement already two dozen streets away from our own.

No, it isn't, he replied firmly, his white skin erased of its usual flush, handing me his water bottle though I hadn't asked for it. *Running is an evolutionary advantage. Running prepares you for your finest human moment and to get you through the hardest human times. Diving will only get you into deeper waters.*

I was twelve. Without knowing exactly why, I started to cry. Tiny hot tears streamed speedily down my cheeks. I don't know why, because my father was never moved by my mother's tears to go against any of his fervent beliefs (my mother would say, *That man is from a race of Vikings. They just go from place to place, taking what they can. They don't miss what's not there.).* And I rarely, if ever, cried. (*Nerves of steel,* she'd say of me. *She doesn't listen to pain,* was my father's point of view.) For me, tears were just plain ugly, like crooked teeth – and I didn't want those either. And yet, there I was crying.

I have to dive! I'm really good. Coach Van der Berg says I can make provincials this year if I put in the extra training time! I was blubbering, talking and wiping my face along my sweatshirt sleeve at the same time. My breath was laboured now. My father's long strides were pulling away from me. *You're the one who signed me up for diving!*

My father kept running. And though I chased after him, I could not keep up. But I heard him. *Your mother signed you up,* he said, without looking over his shoulder, as he hurdled over a speed bump and into the park, *to make a point. And now she's made it.*

For at least a year, as I trained 15 hours a week – at the university pool on 1-metre and 3-metre diving platforms on weekdays, and then at a training centre a two-hour train ride away on weekends, the nearest facility with a 10-metre platform – I tried to figure out what point my mother had won by my choosing diving over all other sports. I begged her to tell me. She'd just shake her head and keep chopping potatoes or washing cabbage, and losing weight. With less flesh, her eyes looked bigger and bigger, taking me in whenever we faced each other. Her bow-like mouth remained mute on the subject. When I came in third place that year in provincials – to jovial cheers from both my parents – she exclaimed *You're so beautiful! You control gravity!* and I tried to decode her outburst for a clue to the puzzle, but I soon trained more hours per week, and more hours meant more competitions and less time for this sort of contemplation anyway. My mother didn't want to tell me. Fine. Neither did my father. Fine. Once something was decided, it was decided. I was a diver. That was that.

⟡

Did your vertigo subsist at any time during today's pole-vaulting session?

No, not that I am aware.

Was it better or worse at any point during the pole-vaulting session?

It was maybe worse at the beginning, but the difference between the start and the end is negligible, I think. I wouldn't know how to measure it.

What did you focus on?

Throwing my body weight.

Did you focus on the pole? Or on the bar?

Neither, as I said, I focussed on throwing my body weight over the bar.

But where did you let your eyes rest?

I'm sorry, I don't know.

You don't know what you were looking at?

Not really. The vertigo makes everything so skewed and blurry. I just tell myself what I have to do and I do it. I suppose I see something but...

Your scores today would qualify you for the Canadian nationals in pole-vaulting. Are you aware of that?

No.

It's time for another eye exam.

OK. But I need a washroom first.

Are you experiencing vertigo?

Always.

Are you going to throw up?

Yes.

That's three times this week. Here's a washcloth. We'll weigh you again after the exam.

❧

What I loved most about diving was the efficient beauty of it, the precision it necessitated from me. Calculation. Discipline. All muscles from my head to my torso down to my pointed toes all working together toward the common goal of entering the water – first, with the most joyous acrobatics, and then with the most exquisite lines. My father was right. It was flashy, arrogant, to approach water this way. And throughout my years of training, I did pay the price, many times, the sting of my skin slapping against her face, my nose ballooning with her spray, my forehead whipped by her palm. There were times I thought the water hated me.

But oh, when she would relent, when you had achieved the feat of a perfectly straight entry, you felt all her respect, you felt her welcoming you. You felt it by feeling nothing. The greatest moment in diving is when you've dived so precisely the water *parts* for you. You look wet, but you never feel wet. Not until the dive is fully executed and you've completed your last rotation under the water, in her arms, and are pushed up to the surface. You managed to manipulate all your weight into one common purpose and line. Weightless. Ideal displacement. That's why there's no splash. So exact, you weren't even there.

❧

This week the varsity track, basketball, water polo, and ringette players will be participating in some of Dr. Burhauer's experiments. I'm taking an extra 10 minutes in the shower, water as hot as the taps will allow, trying to relax my muscles – particularly those on my feet – reminding myself to breathe deeply. Most of the varsity athletes have heard of me, either because I was supposed to be going to the Olympics in two months – hailed as a medal hopeful – a great pride of the university and the city – or because they read the Faculty of Physical Education newsletter where semi-regular updates on the vertigo-suffering national champion who has offered her body up as a guinea pig while she tries to find herself another sport appear.

After reading about these experiments, the long gruelling athletic sessions, the tedious and sometimes painful scientific and medical exams and other corollaries, and the non-stop nausea, several of my former peers have stopped me: *Why are you putting yourself through this?*

As if training for the Olympics didn't push my body to unnatural extremes. *Maybe they'll learn something valuable. Maybe they won't. But I'll never dive again, so I need to find something else to do all day. And it pays. Pays better than diving.*

Then I usually laugh to put the questioner at ease.

What are they trying to prove?

They are trying to determine whether the vertigo can offer me any advantage – any evolutionary advantage, as my father would say – in any sport. I think the idea is that it's not only our strengths that can be cultivated to our advantage, but perhaps also our weaknesses. If only we pick the right arenas for them.

Do you believe that? many then ask.

I usually shrug, and say, *I'm excelling at sports I've never tried and failing at others that were once easy for me. This interests them immensely.*

They usually nod, nervously, as if it's expected but they have no idea what I've just said, but also a bit hopefully, the way people do when they simply want to believe in science and its results without any idea of why.

Usually, I nod back. Then I weigh myself.

❦

I always knew my mother felt left out of the athletic life, but I believed it was her choice. Her domain was the house, father's the streets, mine somewhere in the middle – the natural world contained indoors. If she wanted to run, she could put on a pair of shoes. If she wanted to swim, she could buy herself a one-piece and take classes in any one of the city's many community centres. *Who has time for such things?* she would say to me, which would always make me laugh, since I felt like the busiest person alive, running to the pools, to school, to competitions, to the dinner table, back to the pools, to gyms, to my father's arms. But we had time, because of her. She never said this, but I know it's true. Time is its own kind of weight. I'm learning this too, along with the new sports.

I used to think she was a bit lazy. Cooking was easy. You mixed ingredients, but you didn't have to do the work yourself – the food transformed, you just helped it along, like a coach. I thought my coaches were lazy too. Lazy because they had decided to stop competing.

Once though, I caught my mother, her black hair tied back into its usual black ponytail, with two golden carrots in her hand, staring off into the window, the water pot boiling over on the stove. The smell was smoky, stinging. Her apron was sprinkled with dots of water, but she didn't budge. *Mom, aren't you cooking? What are you cooking?* I said, about to take the carrots from her arms.

Memories, she said. *Memories.*

At the time I thought she was trying to tell me she got caught up in her memories and so had forgotten about her cooking. This was easy to understand. I would frequently get caught up in my training and not hear a bell or buzzer. Once the fire alarm had gone off at the pool, and I kept swimming lengths until my coach hit me on the head with a paddle board. But now I know she meant she was cooking memories. My mother was too busy to run or to swim. She was in her own training.

❦

My signature dive was the inward 3 1/2 somersault in the pike position, 1-metre tower. When I say *was* sometimes Dr. Burhauer (and the doctors I saw before her who thought they could cure the vertigo with pills and convoluted eye exercises) says *is*, but I know even though they don't know (or didn't know) I will *never* dive again, even if in the end they do manage to cure my vertigo as they have managed to cure my broken arm, three ribs, and my whiplash. I loved the inward dives, probably because when I first started diving they were the most feared. I hated fear. I hated its smell. Diving smells like fear to non-divers, but not to us. To us, diving smells like life. Not death. At least, it *did*. I am no longer a diver. I must remember that.

❦

Vertigo is not life-threatening, I am told by everyone who knows even a little about vertigo. *Neither are memories*, I want to shoot back, but don't. *They're not supposed to be.*

❦

My mother left a note:

My memory has succeeded in destroying me. My body has continued to perform the same basic bodily functions that I've trained it to perform, day in day out, but my memory is stronger than habit.

I feel ugly no matter how much I pretty myself. I feel heavy no matter how much weight I lose. I've tried arguing with death. I'm diving in.

She shot herself. With an old silver pistol that belonged to her father. I must admit, regardless of the news and movies, I really didn't believe that people shot themselves anymore. And certainly not women. Not women like my mother, who spent the better part of their days washing, peeling, chopping, and marinating in kitchens. I'd seen the gun once, in the basement, on a shelf beside old woks and camping gear, locked in its dusty case, and never thought about it. It was obvious my mother thought about it a lot. She aimed it at her head, near her right ear – perhaps where the memories were, smashing them to bits.

For the last month I've been trying to tell Dr. Melanie Burhauer about the visions, but she won't listen to me. And she has stopped weighing me personally. She must fill this part of her chart out though, I think, for the grant money, so one of her twitchy graduate students does it for her. I don't know why I think this exactly – I don't know how the money flows or doesn't flow through this research centre – but I believe that's the case. What I am sure about is that she no longer wants to know about me. The result I am becoming is not one she predicted, and not one she wants to continue working with. She's like a coach who wants to drop a player. Not because I'm not working hard, but because something has happened that makes her no longer objective, no longer able to do her work as professionally as before – as if she's become emotionally involved. She *is* emotionally-involved – I can attest to that – she's afraid. I'm now 50 pounds heavier than I was when we started this, although my body fat to muscle composition has barely changed and I should be, by our measurements, about 10 pounds lighter than when we began. The charts terrify her.

Last month, things went further. I told her that I'd been seeing things sometimes with my vertigo. Her eyebrows lifted. At
first she was visibly excited.

*What are you seeing? Spots of light? What colours? Dots?
Flashes?*

No. None of these.

*What are you seeing then? Do shadows appear on your eyes? Do
you have obstructed vision?* (She took out a new notebook.)

No. I'm not seeing shadows or dots or spots of light. I'm
seeing flashes of people, and objects, things that seem familiar
but I know I've never seen before. The man I see sometimes, he
looks a bit like my mother – his voice has similar inflections and
he has the identical forehead and wide nose – and he reaches out
to me a lot, his big olive arms, and I know I should like him,
care for him, he's smiling at me, and he smells like sweet pepper, but I feel... scared... really scared. Then I see things like
bags of potatoes and onions... I think I'm in the cellar, and I
feel pain shoot through my whole body like an electrical shock,
but when I look at my arms or my legs or my belly, I can't see
anything and it doesn't seem to be my body at all that's in pain.
Is this some kind of side effect of perpetual vertigo?

So, you are experiencing hallucinations?

I guess. But I don't think they are coming from my brain, if
that makes sense. I think they are coming from my body.

How long has this been going on?

Ever since I gained four and a half pounds on my birthday.
Before then, I had vague flashes – a second at the most – but I
figured it was just my brain processing these last months, trying
to get me to reorient myself – I've seen a blue pool for hours and
hours a week for the last 15 years – I thought it would go away
and was not worth bothering you about. But now, now it's for
20, 30 seconds at a time. This morning, one of these sessions
lasted about two minutes. I ran through a field, and could actu-

ally feel the nicks from rose bushes against my legs. I didn't care. I wanted those nicks. I enjoyed the blood trickling down my calves. I was crying, and when I looked down at my feet, I saw that I wasn't running at all, I had a stem in my hand and was beating my legs with it. What do you think?

I was seriously hoping that Dr. Burhauer would have some insight to share with me. She's a doctor after all. She does innovative research – at least that's what her website bio says – she must have experienced unexpected results before now. Before me. Perhaps she would start a new series of tests. Instead she reduced the tests we were already doing. I heard rumours about her funding decreasing.

I suggest you use your medical coverage and pay a visit to Dr. Flin's office.

Dr. Flin? Don't you mean Dr. Phillips' office, the neurosurgeon?

No. Dr. Flin. He's a psychiatrist. This is beyond the scope of my research. Your dealings with him should be kept confidential from mine. I don't want them to interfere with our tests.

That was three weeks ago. Yesterday, I had a session that lasted 47 minutes. I now recognize more of the people – they appear again and again – and the thoughts that take form in my head I'm sure are still not mine, but are very, very familiar. Sometimes I try to talk to the people in the visions, but it's hard for me, I'm not trained in this yet, and Dr. Flin doesn't want to encourage me. He keeps trying to prescribe drugs. Says I'm experiencing imbalance in all areas of my life – the vertigo is just one easy-to-spot physical symptom – which is making it difficult for me to cope. That I shouldn't be ashamed to be afraid.

I'm not ashamed to be afraid anymore. And I'm not ashamed about what's happening to me. I'm less afraid today than I was those three weeks ago in Dr. Burhauer's office. I'm gaining weight like crazy now. And I'm seeing things. I'm seeing things my mother left behind inside my body. That fateful day when I dove off the 10-metre tower. Inward 3 1/2 somersaults in the pike position. That's what was listed. I felt the tip of my forehead graze the edge of the platform, and then I stopped rotating. I just stopped. I fell hard on my stomach. Ten metres. The audience gasped and screamed.

I didn't yet know what had happened. Pain. Shock. A stretcher. An ambulance. My mother's body would be found by my father following his early evening run, and after the police arrived at the house, the telephone would ring and my coach would tell him to drive to the hospital to be with his daughter, who had experienced a serious diving accident. I didn't yet know that my mother was dead. What did that mean?

But I knew I had displaced something. Or something had displaced me. It wasn't the water. I know now it was my mother. Her memories. Now, they are mine. They are making me dizzy, but I'll learn to deal with it, just as I've always learned to adjust calculations for dives depending on what platform I'm on, how many rotations are required, how long it will take to reach the water. Many people get dizzy when they look down on a diving platform. I'm dizzy when I'm not. But I didn't have these memories before. My mother's memories. I must figure out a way to use them. I believe she left them to me to continue her training.

She didn't learn to run until it was too late, my father claimed, weeping into his hands at the memorial.

No, Dad, I thought, *she can run faster than the two of us put together.* But instead I stood there, my neck still in a brace, and my left arm and ribs in a cast. I stood there, not crying, not because I didn't listen to the pain, but because I was more afraid than in pain. Afraid for him. And afraid for the deep waters my mother had launched herself into.

Take my father. He still runs, but now he runs farther, without a water bottle, almost to the point of absolute exhaustion and dehydration. *It's shameful now to me that I return home. I shouldn't. I shouldn't want to live so much.*

Do athletes have a greater urge to live than most people? I've often wondered about this. Are we living at our fullest by testing the body, by making our various parts work as purposefully and efficiently and yet, as beautifully, as possible?

My father runs corners like no professional I've ever seen. His legs are like grass blades in the wind – he's all natural, as if the wind is pushing him lovingly around the city. Nothing has changed that. Nothing.

The main thing missing now is a destination. But we can't blame the wind for that.

⌒✖⌒

Dr. Melanie Burhauer is switching focus. I am to continue the experiments, in scaled-down versions, with Dr. Krissy Samson, a new tenure-stream professor, who doesn't yet have a large funding grant of her own.

At the moment, she is fascinated by my talents on the tennis court and in the pole-vaulting pitch, and she too is amazed by my weight – the two of us spent an entire afternoon stepping on the different scales all over the centre – hers consistent, mine going up, up, and up. I don't tell her about the visions though. I can see she's not ready for that. She's far too light – like my father. Apparently, my mother's memories don't create advantages or disadvantages in the athletic arena. I'm not sure they create advantages or disadvantages in any arena, but there we are. There is much I don't understand. It's what I used to love about diving. Unlike running, there is no rational explanation for it. And yet, it's still beautiful, still something that seemed worth striving for. Though I'll never get back on the platform again.

I secretly hope they are never able to cure my vertigo. But I do hope they'll find a purpose for it. With every memory, I get dizzier, dizzier. And yet, I feel steadier, calmer, closer to the woman who loved me, who was no athlete, but who cooked and wanted me to make a point to my father by my diving. The woman who displaced her brains by putting a gun to her head, who thought I could control gravity. I feel her there, welcoming me. Like I once felt the water. I feel her without feeling her at all. She's so exact, she's not even here.

GUY VANDERHAEGHE

THE MASTER OF DISASTER

The summer of 1968. Norman Hiller and Kurt Meinecke, both dreamers, and me caught sticky between them, the jam in the sandwich. Norman was the flashy type, the guy who collected followers, collected them the way he did baseball cards and Superman comic books. I was seventeen the summer he collected Meinecke, old enough to have said something, to have warned my mild and innocent friend, but I didn't.

Kurt Meinecke and I had one more year of high school left, we were going back to the books in September. Norman Hiller, in a manner of speaking, was already done. In June of that year Principal Koslowski had handed him the grade-ten diploma he hadn't earned on the promise that Hiller would never again darken the classrooms and corridors of R.J. Plumber High. Which made Norman Hiller the Seventh Wonder of the World. Nobody but Norman would have dared to make such a larcenous proposal to old Cougar Koslowski. What's more, he drove the bargain through. Whenever any one of us asked him what he intended to do now, all he said was, "I got some irons in the fire. I'm waiting on developments."

Of the two of them, Norman and Kurt, Norman had the more remarkable imagination. The movies were partly responsible. Norman was always crazy about the movies. Our town had just one theatre, the Empire, and Hiller was always in it. Sometimes he would see the same movie, three, four, even five times. In the theatre he kept strictly to himself, was always alone. If any of us tried to sit with him, he'd tell us to piss off, he didn't need anybody yapping and yammering next to him, ruining the show. Twenty years after the fact I can still see him slouching down the aisle to his seat floppy-limbed, a tall boy with huge feet and hands and long, restless fingers constantly twitching in his pockets; a narrow, nervous face with hot, black eyes, which turned lukewarm and bored whenever the conversation slid off into anything he wasn't interested in, which meant practically everything except money, sports, and the movies. It was that look which made people, teachers in particular, think he was stupid. They never stopped to consider why, if he was so stupid, he was always managing to get the better of them.

There was a ritual he performed at the movies. Before draping his gangly legs over the seat in front of him, he loosened his laces so his feet could breathe. Next his baseball cap came off and was hung on the toe of one of his shoes. The cap coming off was like the Pope making a public appearance in shorts. The Empire was the only place anybody ever saw Norman Hiller without his baseball cap on his head; he even wore it in school. Every teacher who had tried to threaten him out from underneath it had failed. The baseball cap was non-negotiable. The only reason it came off was because it interfered with Norman's line of sight to the big screen. It says something about his self-possession when you remember the year was 1968, and, despite The Beatles and everything they meant, eighteen-year-old Norman Hiller could still wear a baseball cap winter and summer without risk of being laughed at.

When the screen lit up, retrieving the faces of the waiting audience from that fleeting, profound moment of darkness before the projector began to whir, Hiller was utterly changed. The scurry abandoned his eyes and the fidget was wiped from his face, leaving it pale, smooth, and shining.

What were Hiller's favourite movies? He had a list of them. Norman was famous for his lists. "Okay," he'd propose, "name me the top policemen in the NHL, one to ten." Or rank the National League third basemen. It only followed that he had an All Time Greatest Movies list. By the summer 1968 this list included *The Magnificent Seven, The Guns of Navarone, The Dirty Dozen, The Devil's Brigade*, and, in his opinion, the world's ultimo primo flick, *Cool Hand Luke*. These were the films from which Hiller absorbed the arts of scripting and direction which put Murph and Dooey and Hop Jump and Deke and me under his spell, a cast of misfits who could be persuaded to identify themselves with the screwballs who populated the movies Hiller loved. We were all reborn in Norman's imagination. He turned Dooey, an edgy little shoplifter, into James Garner. What was Garner famous for in *The Great Escape?* Scrounging. He could rustle up whatever you required, even in a Nazi prison camp. Norman constructed Dooey into a legend in Dooey's own mind, until he became the consummate booster, the guy who could steal anything. "Fucking Dooey," Norman would say, "nothing the guy can't lift. Dooey could steal Christ off the cross and not disturb the nails. Couldn't you, Dooey? Fucking right. Because he's the best. Dooey is *it*."

If Cool Hand Luke gained undying fame just by swallowing 40 hard-boiled eggs, then wasn't glory in the cards for Hop Jump Benyuk? Because Hop Jump could stuff a whole baseball in his mouth. Encouraged by Norman, he even started carrying one around in his jacket pocket so he was always equipped to perform. "He ought to be on television," Hiller would exclaim. "How many guys can do what he can do? One in a hundred million? I doubt it. Maybe, just maybe – outside chance – one in two hundred million. The guy ought to be on Ed Sullivan."

And me, Bernie Beman, who was I? In the movies Norman admired I would have been the brain gone bad, the one the criminals nicknamed The Professor. Just possibly I was Donald Pleasance in *The Great Escape,* bird-watcher, egghead, forger. However, Norman was always a little bit uncertain of my dependability, my loyalty to the regime. He never forgot, or forgave me putting *Lawrence of Arabia* on my All Time Greatest Movies list.

"What!" he had cried, in open-mouthed disbelief. "A seven-hour movie about a bunch of camel-fucking Arabs?"

"Yes," I said, aware of Dooey, Murph, Deke, Hop Jump, all the other geeks, snorting their derision, already feeling the chill of exclusion.

"The only reason they had an intermission in that show was to go around and wake up everybody from the first half so's they didn't get bedsores. There something the matter with you, Beman?"

I didn't say. What was the matter with me was that I found it easier to identify myself with a tormented Peter O'Toole than a chiselled, brass-balled Charles Bronson or Clint Walker.

I pointed out *Lawrence of Arabia* had won a lot of Oscars.

"You ever think that those rug-riders didn't rig the Oscars?" said Norman. "Use your head. Those fucking Arabs are so rich their Lincoln, their Cadillac gets a full ashtray they walk away from it, buy a new one. I read that somewhere. They shit quarters and wipe their asses with ten-dollar bills. You think they couldn't buy themselves as many Oscars as they want? Even for such a loser as that?"

"There's no point in even talking to you, Hiller."

"No point in talking to me? No point in talking to you, Beman. No point in talking to *you.*" Which is what happened. Norman put the word out and nobody did talk to me. I was shunned, given the silent treatment for a month and a half before I managed to weasel my way back into Norman's good graces.

I was as susceptible to Hiller's manipulations as any of the others. When he was feeling magnanimous towards me, he made flattering predictions about my future as a lawyer (his choice of profession for me), extolled the notorious Beman vocabulary. With me as a lawyer, Hiller's clan would be untouchable, beyond the reach of the law. "How'd you like to be a lawyer and come up against a gunfighter like Beman there? Slinging those high words of his at you, words you hadn't even heard of? Fuck, the English teachers don't even know what Beman is talking about half the time when he starts firing off those yard-long words full of syllables. No shit, Beman reads the dictionary for fun. Don't you, Beman?"

"Yes." I couldn't help myself, I relished basking in the glare of Hiller's temporary spotlight, too. Just like Dooey or Hop Jump.

"Say one of your high words, Bernardo, my man."

"What?"

"Say one of those words no normal human being knows what they mean."

"Like what?"

"Come on, come on. A word, Beman. Give us one of those words of yours."

"Bastinado."

Hiller looking challengingly from Dooey to Murph to Hop Jump. "What's it mean? That word?"

Shrugs and sheepish grins.

"What'd I say? How you going to bear that man in court? How you going to argue against a guy when you don't even know what the fuck he's saying? Impossible."

Whatever I withheld from Hiller, whatever would have been unspeakable in the company of others (like an affection for

Lawrence of Arabia) was confided to Kurt Meinecke. Kurt and I had been friends since elementary school. What he listened to were secret, laughable ambitions. To be a journalist and report a war. To be drunk and cynical in a great city. To speak foreign languages like a native. With a patient, bewildered look on his face he heard me out nights as we tramped the dull, empty streets after the pool room shut, on the prowl until our knees ached, hoping against all previous experience that something exciting would happen and we would be there to witness it. But the only thing that ever happened was that a police cruiser would stop and the officers tell us it was three o'clock in the morning, get the hell home you two.

Kurt was possessed but he didn't look the way possessed people ought to, the way Norman Hiller did. Norman fit the bill because he was an exposed wire, sparking, jerking, snapping, hot with current. Kurt was the furthest thing from that. He was big and slow and solid. He walked like a man hip-deep in molasses, wading upstream against the flow of the current. But he was possessed.

Whenever I shut up long enough to give him an opening, he would jump in with something like, "I think I'll take up golf."

"Yeah?"

"Yeah. I think I'm suited to golf. All you need is hand-eye coordination and concentration. Concentration is my strong point."

"Sure it is."

"If I practiced real hard I should do good. I got what it takes."

"Right."

Hopeless.

For as long as I'd known him, Kurt Meinecke had been in search of his game, the one that would prove what he knew deep down inside – that he was an extraordinary athlete. He was a Meinecke, which meant that he had the bloodlines of a champion. His father and all his uncles had been locally celebrated athletes, renowned hockey players and baseball players and players of every other game that idle, foolish men will play. It was even said that his Uncle Rudy Meinecke would have made the NHL, if he hadn't caught his right hand in a power take-off which chewed four of his fingers off.

Kurt was a different story. It wasn't so much that he was bad at sports, only appallingly average. Yet his consistent failure to shine on the fields of glory did nothing to shake his bedrock, imperturbable self-confidence that he was destined for greatness. He always spoke of this as a given and obvious. And he tried everything, a hundred schemes to locate and free the springs of his talent. His batting problems would be solved if he switched from batting right-handed to left-handed. They weren't. He'd be a much better hockey player if he moved from forward to defence. He wasn't. A typical conversation with Kurt Meinecke might run something like this.

"It's too bad we don't play lacrosse around here. That'd be the game for me, you can get a running start and really pop somebody in lacrosse. That's my problem at football, from the down position I can't work up a good head of steam to pop anybody. I'm the kind of guy needs a head of steam to be effective."

There were times when this serene absence of self-doubt worked on my nerves terribly, festered until I believed there was no help for it, I was going to tell him. Of course, I never did. Truly sweet and gentle souls never get told what the rest of us do. Kurt Meinecke was so incorrigibly innocent that whenever I rehearsed the cynicism and world-weariness I intended to adopt when I was loosed upon the great cities of the world, he would smile uncomfortably, duck his head, and waddle along just a little bit more quickly in that goofy, toes-turned-out walk he had, as if seeking to put distance between himself and the nasty things being said.

Norman and Kurt weren't strangers, our town was too small for that, but they never had much to do with one another. Hiller wasn't interested in collecting the likes of Meinecke, someone who, on the surface, was as dull as ditch water and twice as murky. But then one afternoon Norman sensed a possibility, leaned over, peered into the ditch and saw all the way down, clear to the bottom. I was there when it happened.

Kurt and I were planted on a bench in the pool room. Meinecke was droning on and I was pretending to be preoccupied with a couple of senior citizens shooting a game of blue ball so I didn't have to wax too enthusiastic about Kurt's next adventure in the wide world of sports. That's when Norman Hiller slouched over to pay us a visit, jabbing his thumb in the direction of the pool table and delivering a typical sample of Hiller wit. "You know why they call it blue ball, eh? Because that's what the old farts who play it got dangling between their legs." Having delivered this line, he dropped down on the bench beside us and started to beaver a toothpick for all he was worth.

I laughed, but Hiller's sally only caused Kurt to blink a couple of owlish, solemn blinks before resuming his monologue. "I was thinking I'd go out for the wrestling team this year," he said. "I ought to be a pretty decent wrestler. I mean I got real strong fingers" – he held them up and flexed them under my nose – "and they say strong fingers are a must. I think I ought to make an okay wrestler."

I didn't say anything. Hiller did. He always had an opinion when it came to sports. "You don't want to wrestle," he said. "Wrestling is a homo sport, guys dry humping each other all over a mat. There are more queers in wrestling than there are in figure skating. Little known fact. You want to take up the personal combat line – go into boxing, Meinecke."

"Boxing?" I said. There was no boxing club in our town, nor any boxers that I knew of.

"Yeah, well, look at him," said Norman turning to me. "Look at the fucking neck on him. The guy's got a fucking neck like a tree trunk. Neck like that – works like shock absorbers on a car. You hit a guy with a neck like that, no way you could knock him out."

I cast Kurt a sidelong glance. I could see he was listening intently. Hiller could see it too.

"Neck and hands," continued Norman confidently. "That's what makes a fighter. Kurt here has the neck but does he have the hands? That's the 64,000-dollar question. Let's have a peek at the mitts, Meinecke."

Kurt showed the mitts, self-consciously displaying them on his knees where they lay immense, red, chapped, ugly. Norman prodded the knuckles with his index finger. "Look at them knuckles, Beman!" he urged. "Like fucking ball bearings. These are lethal weapons we're looking at. Stand back! Stand back!" he shouted theatrically, recoiling in mock alarm. "You don't want those exploding in your face!"

Apparently Kurt had it all, neck and hands. To hear Hiller talk we were in the presence of greatness. And greatness believed it. Norman shifted position on the bench and slipped his arm around Meinecke's shoulders. "Ducks were made for water," he said. "And you were made for the ring, Meinecke. You are a natural raw talent just waiting to be developed."

"But how? How do I get developed?"

"You got to have like a manager, a trainer. Somebody to get the best out of you."

"But who?" said Meinecke. "Who's a trainer around here?"

I knew. Before answering, Norman leaned a little closer.

The Meinecke training camp's headquarters was established at Deke's. Deke's daddy had disappeared about the time Deke turned fourteen, three years before, and the mattress which Deke's mom had drunkenly set on fire while smoking in bed, and which his father had hauled smouldering through the house to heave into the backyard, was still there, a map of interesting stains dominated by the charred, blackened crater whose flames Mr. Deke had extinguished with the garden hose that fateful day. Shortly after this incident Mr. Deke had taken off for parts unknown and Mrs. Deke, down in the dumps and remorseful over the turn her life had taken, fell prey to Jehovah's Witnesses and converted. Despite all these momentous changes, nobody got around to hauling the offending mattress off to the nuisance grounds and three years later it still lay where it had fallen. Which was convenient for Dooey, Hop Jump, Murph, and the rest of us because it provided a spot to loll about on while watching Hiller put Kurt through his paces. There amid the yellow grass, the run-over tricycle with the sow thistle growing up through the spokes of a twisted wheel, the greasy patch of lawn which Mr. Deke had killed by draining the oil from his car onto it every change, there amid all the other symptoms of neglect – scattered gaskets, a picket pulled from the sagging fence by Deke's brothers and sisters, a lid from a paint can, shards of vinyl from a broken record, a torn plastic diaper, a discarded hot plate whose two rusted elements seemed to regard the scene with blood-shot, whirling eyes – the training of Kurt Meinecke went on in a blistering July heat wave.

Meinecke jumping rope in the hottest stretch of the afternoon, Hiller roaring abuse and ridicule at him. "Knees higher! Get them knees up! No pain, no gain! I still see titty bouncing there! Bouncing boobies, Meinecke! Shame! No fighter of mine goes into the ring looking like he needs a brassiere! Knees up!"

Road work was even more brutal. Hiller conned Kurt into allowing himself to be tied to the bumper of Murph's reservation beater Chev with 20 feet of rope. The car was then driven at exactly six miles an hour down two miles of deserted country road with Kurt flailing along behind in the dust. If Meinecke didn't keep up he'd be dragged. When I protested, Norman said that it was the only way to get Meinecke to put out, he was such a lazy fuck. Anyway, boxing was survival of the fittest.

"But what if he trips and falls?" I asked.

"He's got no business tripping," said Norman.

The really bizarre thing was that Meinecke seemed grateful for the opportunity of being leashed to a bumper and towed up and down country lanes. "Like Norman says," he explained to me when I told him he was crazy, "no pain, no gain and another thing – which Norman also says – you don't know what you can do until you have to do it. Couple of times there on the road I wanted to quit awful bad, but when you know you can't... well, you don't. And then you're the better for it."

"Yeah, and after that fucking lunatic ends up dragging you a couple hundred yards behind a car, then you'll say you're the better for the skin graft too."

Norman was a genius of the stick-and-carrot school of psychology. For Meinecke, the carrot was the rapturous commentary which Hiller provided to accompany Kurt's daily thumping of the heavy bag dangling from Mrs. Deke's clothesline pole. There was no doubt about it, Meinecke could punch. Even with Murph clinging to the bag, bracing it, Meinecke could rock them both with one of his awesome right hands. A little praise from Norman and Meinecke looked like a cat full of sweet cream. "That's a boy, Kurtie! Look at that! That boy's what you call a banger. Your classic body puncher, your get down and get dirty George Chuvalo kind of fighter. Jab! Jab! Stick it in his face! Set it up! Go downstairs now! Hit him with the low blow! Crack his walnuts! All's fair in love and war, Kurtie, my man! You beauty, you!"

A typical July afternoon.

Each of Hiller's boys had a role to play in the making of a champion, nobody was left out. The pattern was the same as in *The Magnificent Seven, The Great Escape, The Dirty Dozen,* where each contributed according to his talents. Dooey was our equipment manager, shoplifting Vaseline, adhesive tape, gauze, iodine, Q-tips, copies of *Ring* magazine – all the props – from the local drugstore. Murph and his beat-up '57 Chev towed Meinecke through his road work. Deke's yard was our training camp. I was delegated corner man and masseur. To Hop Jump fell the honour of being appointed Meinecke's sparring partner, a seemingly perverse choice since the Hopper was notorious for his cowardice. This he cheerfully acknowledged with the frequent declaration, "I'm a lover, not a fighter." The truth was that he was neither, but everyone instinctively understood poetic licence and what he was getting at. Hiller was implacable; no amount of whining and pleading on Hop Jump's part got his sentence commuted. For the rest of us seated on the pulpy mattress, swigging Cokes and puffing cigarettes, the sparring match was the highlight of the day. We jeered and hooted "Beep! Beep!" as Hop Jump, the human roadrunner, ducked and dodged and scrambled all over Deke's backyard, dust puffing up out of the dead grass around his sagging white socks, Meinecke in awkward, earnestly determined pursuit.

Up and down, back and forth, from corner to corner, from pillar to post, around the clothesline pole and the smashed trike they went, Meinecke occasionally unleashing a looping roundhouse which nearly always missed the mark, or at best, landed a glancing blow to Benyuk's shoulder or back, pinching a

squawk of terror out of him and spurring him on to swifter
flight.

When I asked Hiller about this strange pairing, inquiring
why he had assigned Meinecke a sparring partner whose one aim
was to avoid an exchange of blows at all costs, he gave me a long,
steady look before answering. "I don't want Meinecke getting
used to getting hit – and Hop Jump isn't going to hit him. I don't
want Meinecke hitting nothing but the bag – nothing human –
and Hop Jump sure the fuck isn't going to let nobody hit him.
Perfect," he concluded enigmatically.

Meanwhile, the changes in Kurt were growing more and more
pronounced. It was bad enough that he did exactly what Hiller
told him to do when Hiller was there, but now he went even further, obeying his instructions to the letter even when Norman
had no way of checking up on him. Hiller had ordered him to
get lighter on his feet and now Kurt minced along on tippy toes.
Walking home with him was like taking a stroll with Liberace. It
didn't stop there. Each night he poured half a box of Windsor
salt into the bathroom sink filled with water and soaked his head
in it because Hiller had told him that fighters who cured their
skin in brine toughened it, making themselves harder to cut.

Kurt may have been having the time of his life, but for the
rest of us, the novelty began to wear off soon enough. Even Hop
Jump's scampers around the backyard weren't as funny as they
once were. We'd seen too many Road Runner and Coyote car-
toons, they'd begun to pall. Nobody said it, but all of us were
thinking of it. What was the point?

Norman, with his exquisite sense of timing, broke the news just
when interest was nearly dead. "Having just concluded extensive

and lengthy negotiations," he reported, "I am pleased to reveal that I have signed Meinecke for a fight."

"What?" I said. "You negotiated Hop Jump into a phone booth? Because that's the only way you'll get a fight going between those two."

Everybody laughed. Everybody but Hiller.

"I got him a fight with Scutter," he said flatly, in a tone that judges in the movies use to hand down a death sentence.

Nobody spoke. We all avoided looking at Meinecke. A kind of deadly hush embraced the seven of us.

"Nothing to worry about," Norman said calmly. "Scutter's a street fighter. This is way different. If Scutter can't flash the boots he ain't much – and he can't flash the boots in a boxing match. Never fear. He's soap on a rope. Our boy's got the training, our boy's got the know-how, our boy's got the neck and he's got the hands." Hiller gave us a significant look. "Our boy's got the *team*."

The team didn't say anything, the team was thinking of Blair Scutter. Scutter was unquestionably the most dangerous of the local psychopaths, a square, stocky kid with acne so bad that his head looked like a gigantic raspberry perched on a cigarette machine. When he was twelve he had given up terrorizing contemporaries and started picking fights with teenagers; when he was a teenager he graduated to brawls with miners at dances in the community hall. When Blair Scutter walked down one of the humanity-choked corridors at R.J. Plumber High, an avenue opened in the congestion, everyone shrinking back against the lockers so as not to risk brushing up against his brutish shoulders. Brushing up against Scutter was like rubbing shoulders with death.

Hiller could see we weren't convinced. "Everybody heard what I said?" he demanded, "I said we got the team. And the team backs Kurt here 110 percent. We all *think* positive. We all *do* positive. As President Kennedy said, 'Ask not what Kurt can do for you, but what you can do for Kurt.' Right?" He looked at each of us in turn, gouging out of us grudging nodes of agreement. What we were thinking went unvoiced.

I felt compelled to speak to Norman and hung around until everybody had left that afternoon.

"What is this?" I said to him. "You know he hasn't got a chance."

"He does if he does what I tell him," said Norman. "But the rest of you got to back me up. No fucking with his head, putting doubts in it. A right attitude is a winning attitude. Anybody gives him doubts is a traitor in my books." It was clear whom he was thinking of when he used that word. "Anybody's a traitor in our camp better watch out."

I felt that alone, tried another tack. "But why Scutter?" I asked. "Why start him with Scutter?"

"Box office," said Norman abruptly. "You promote a fight you got to have a draw. Scutter's a name attraction. I got a hall to fill."

Things were moving too fast. "What do you mean hall? What hall?"

"Kingdom Hall. That Jehovah Witness place a mile out of town. Deke's old lady has the key to it because she cleans it. So Deke'll steal her key and we have the fight out there on Thursday night. It being out in the country it won't attract too much attention if we borrow it a couple of hours. If somebody drives by and sees cars and lights they'll just figure the Jehovahs are having one of their singalongs or circle jerks or whatever they do out there."

"You're going to throw a fight in a *church?*"

"Hall," Norman corrected me, "The place is called Kingdom Hall. It isn't a church."

There was no debating with Hiller. Arguments with him were conducted in a twilight zone where normal mental operations were suspended and invalid. I switched tracks. I wanted to know what was in this for Scutter.

"Twenty-five bucks," said Norman. "I guaranteed him 25 to fight and 50 if he wins. But no sweat. We can charge two bucks a head at the gate for a fight like this. And there's no problem getting a hundred guys in there. I got Murph to drive me out so I could look in the windows yesterday. They don't have pews. Just those tin stacking chars. We can clear a space easy. It was made for us."

"And what about Kurt?" I asked. "What are you paying him? What does he get out of this?"

Norman gave me one of his dangerous stares, the kind in which his eyes went flat, unreadable. "Don't play stupid with me, genius. You fucking know as well as I do what Kurtie gets. He only gets what he's been begging for all along. Nothing else."

"So tell me, what's he been begging for?"

"Just what he's going to get," said Norman.

Maybe at seventeen I was already as cynical at heart as I hoped to be in those future haunts – London, Paris, Vienna, Rome – which I imagined for myself. When Hiller unveiled his fight plan naturally I assumed Meinecke was being set-up, jobbed. Norman claimed that the way to beat Scutter was to blow his mind the way Paul Newman had blown George Kennedy's mind in *Cool Hand Luke*. How had he done this? By absorbing all the punishment that Kennedy could hand out while proving that it was not enough to break him. This totally fucked a guy's head when he was giving you his best shots and you were laughing at them. "Meinecke will not even think of throwing a punch until he gets the nod from me," said Hiller. "Meinecke will let

Mr. Hardass wear himself out hitting him. He will inform Mr. Hardass that his sister can hit harder than that. He will Cool Hand Luke him. He will be trained for this. He is going to show Scutter that when you got the tree trunk neck, when you got the Floyd Patterson peekaboo defence, when you got the team behind you – then you are unstoppable. *You* are the hardest ass in town, none harder. You got the plan to twist all the bolts and nuts loose in Scutter's head. Once they are good and rattling I will turn Meinecke loose. He will execute."

I didn't point out the obvious to Kurt – that being forbidden to hit back in a boxing match is a handicap. I was busy trying to convince myself that he was asking for whatever he got. I felt disgust for his naked need, for his gullibility, for the soft, accommodating clay he had become under Norman's hands. In one of Hiller's favourite movies, *The Magnificent Seven*, a ruthless bandit, who had been robbing and terrorizing poor peasants, poses a question to Yul Brynner, the gunman who has become their protector. He asks: If God did not wish them to be shorn, why did he make them sheep?

A sheep myself, I still managed to muster contempt for the others in Hiller's flock, for their stupidity if nothing else. Didn't they know what was going on? When Hiller made his speech about how we ought to show team spirit by each handing over to him five bucks to bet on Meinecke, I knew what was up. The bet wasn't going on Kurt, it was going on Scutter. And when Scutter pounded the snot out of Meinecke those morons would believe their money was lost because Kurt had lost. Sure, lost. Lost in Hiller's pockets. Still, I didn't break ranks. He got my money too.

Five days before the fight Meinecke was christened. Hiller explained to us that his research proved there had never been a great fighter who didn't have a great ring name. Check it out. Archie Moore? The Mongoose. Beautiful. Jack Dempsey? The Manassa Mauler. A-one. Robinson? Sugar Ray. Sweetness itself. Ingemar Johansson? The Hammer of Thor. You had to love it. Joe Louis? The Brown Bomber. Outstanding.

For days now, he confessed, he had been racking his brains to come up with a moniker that would elevate Meinecke into the same class as Robinson, Moore, Dempsey, etc. And now he had it.

There was a stir of anticipation. I glanced at Kurt who looked like he was about to come in his pants.

"Yeah?" said Murph, unable any longer to contain himself. "So what is it?"

"Gentlemen," said Norman, making a sweeping gesture of introduction, "let me present, Kurt Meinecke, The Master of Disaster!"

Enthusiasm was unanimous. "Right on, like a mouse's ear!" "Fucking, aye!" "Leave it to Hiller." "The Master of Disaster! It's pissing!"

Kurt beamed.

I did not both to point out that the meaning of Master of Disaster was ambiguous. English Composition was never Norman's strong suit. Psychology was.

The big night arrived. As Murph headed his Chev out of town for Kingdom Hall, the streetlights were flickering feebly into life and then, one after another, exploding full strength in the failing light. Norman sat up front beside Murph. Kurt, in running shoes, shorts, and boxing gloves, was in the back seat wedged between me and Hop Jump like a prisoner under escort. Nobody said anything during the short drive, although Meinecke kept nervously clearing his throat and striking his gloves together, one

muffled pop after another. Deke and Dooey had gone on ahead
to open the hall and sell admissions to what Norman predicted
would be a standing-room-only crowd.

Hiller was correct, the turnout was prodigious. Forty-five
minutes before fight time and the parking lot was already
crammed with cars, many with their engines running and their
headlights left on to provide light to party by. When we pulled
into the lot, guys with beers in their hands were lounging on
fenders, perching on bumpers, saluting and insulting one
another, drifting about from one milling, jostling gathering to
the next. Nosing a car through the throng wasn't easy. Norman
stuck his head out the window and began to shout, "Make way!
Make way! Fighter coming through! Out of the way, pecker-
heads!" Every couple of seconds he lunged impatiently across
Murph to knock peremptory blats out of the horn with the heel
of his hand when people didn't hasten out of our path quickly
enough for him. Slowly we crept around to the back of Kingdom Hall, pale, excited faces with bottles tipped into them
looming out of the swiftly falling darkness; dust swaying and
shaking like smoke in the white-hot tracks of high beams; figures doubling over to gape through the windows of the car at
Meinecke huddled up between Hop Jump and me in the back
seat. As we edged along they thumped the hood of the car, gave
ear-splitting whoops and hollers, chanted a variation of Hiller's
announcement: "Corpse coming through! Make way! Dead
man coming through!" Hiller had been wrong about one thing.
No one passing by would have mistaken this congregation for
Jehovah's Witnesses.

At last Murph got us clear of the mob and drew the car up
to the back door. Norman gave everybody orders to stay put in
the vehicle and wait, except for me. I was to accompany him.
Inside, the hall was filling rapidly, growing warm with the
funky, animal heat of packed bodies; blue with cigarette smoke

and yeasty with the smell of beer. Like any promoter worth his
salt, Norman immediately made for the box office to check the
take. As he peered over Dooey's shoulder into the shoe box
holding the money, Deke began to gripe and bitch about the
behaviour of the crowd. Who had stolen the key? Who was
going to take any of the shit coming down if the premises got
damaged? Him. Deke. "They won't stop smoking," he said to
Norman in a whiny voice. "You got to lay the law down to
them, Norman. I mean Jehovahs don't smoke. You think they
aren't going to smell stale smoke and wonder how it got here?
And somebody spilled a beer on the floor. Already the place
stinks like a fucking brewery. You got to do something with
them, Norman…"

Norman wasn't listening. He turned to Dooey. "How
much?"

Dooey gave a shake to the box. "Close to 120 so far," he
said.

"All right," said Norman. "Shoo those assholes in the parking lot in here. That fucking carnival out there is going to attract
attention. I want this show on the road." Norman had an after-
thought. "And, Dooey, remember. No sticky fingers in the till.
Sticky fingers are broken fingers."

"Norman…" Deke began mournfully, trying to steer the
conversation back to his complaint, but Hiller was moving off,
double-time, flipping a roll of electrician's tape from hand to
hand. Lugging a plastic pail and a brown paper shopping bag
stuffed with a corner man's supplies, I trotted after him.

In the centre of the hall Norman commenced laying out the
boundaries of a ring on the floor with the black tape. There
were no ropes or posts, but he explained that if the crowd stood
flush to the tape that would keep the fighters hemmed in. I set
up chairs in opposing corners and unpacked the medical supplies Dooey had shoplifted: sponge, gauze pads, Vaseline.

Meanwhile Hiller had completed his chores and was on the prowl like a caged beast, pacing back and forth, jacking himself up on his tiptoes to scan late arrivals over the heads of the thick mob, muttering to himself. Scutter hadn't shown yet. Donald Broward, half-drunk, wandered over to get instructions from Norman. For a six-pack Hiller had hired him to referee, not because Broward knew anything about boxing, but, a lineman on the high school football team, he was big enough to pull Scutter off Meinecke and prevent a homicide if things got out of hand.

The multitude suddenly stirred and then there was a surprising drop in the volume of drunken noise. Scutter trooped into the hall, flanked by his brother and some other bad actors. As he advanced on the ring, a swell of encouraging murmurs trailed after him, accompanied by several shy pats to his shoulders and back which he, supremely indifferent, accepted without acknowledgement.

I heard Hiller whispering to himself as we watched him approach. "Yes," he said. "Yes. I've got you in my sights now."

From this point on, everything went forward in a dizzy rush. Hiller ordered me off to collect and ready Kurt. As I swung open the back door I heard him throwing himself into his highly coloured impersonation of a Madison Square Garden announcer.

"Tonight, from Kingdom Hall, Norman Hiller Productions presents the fight extravaganza of the century. The Collision of the Titans—" The closing door had choked him off.

In the last half hour all the headlights had been extinguished, night had overtaken us, and the yard was thick with darkness. After the brightness of the hall, it was difficult to see. All I could make out was the car parked at the bottom of the steps, more solidly black than the blackness which lapped it. I cast my words into this blackness, like a line into a pool. "Kurt, they're almost ready for you." There was movement near the car, a wrinkling of the skin of night. Hop Jump proclaimed, "He's just finishing up losing his cookies. Be with you in a sec." I waited. My eyes were becoming more and more accustomed to the darkness, I could make out Murph and Hop Jump now, their pale shirts focusing whatever light the dim air contained. Then Kurt stood up behind the car, his nakedness a white ghostly blur. Back in the hall, the din was increasing, growing stronger, more frantic, move violent.

"Hurry up," I said. "It's time."

The three of them filed up the steps, Meinecke wiping at his mouth with the back of a glove. Striking a match I looked in his face. "Are you okay?" He nodded. "You're sure?" He nodded again. Even in the flare of the match his face had that dirty, grey-white colour that a sink in a public washroom acquires with time.

"All right," I said. "You know the drill. Let's do it right, just like Hiller wants it, just like we practiced it."

They bumbled into place. Murph in front, Kurt in the middle with his hands on Murph's shoulders, Hop Jump behind him. I draped a towel over Meinecke's head, just the way Sonny Liston had worn his towels, so as to give his face a hooded, menacing look. Then I took up my position, point man, three steps ahead of the procession. From inside the hall we heard an overwhelming roar, Scutter's introduction was climaxing. I dodged catching Kurt's eye, stepped quickly to the door and opened it a crack so I didn't miss our cue. Norman's voice came drilling into the night, strident, straining to clamour above the bedlam it had incited.

"Please welcome, in the red trunks," he was shouting, "the challenger, your favourite and mine." I hustled into the hall, Murph and Meinecke and Hop Jump shuffling forward just the way Hiller had taught them, hands laid on the shoulders of the man in front, eyes lowered. "Kurt Meinecke!" Hiller screamed.

"The Maaassster of Diiisssassster! The Maaaassster of Diiss-sassster!" And right on cue, also as rehearsed, Deke and Dooey began to chant at the top of their lungs, "MASTER! MASTER! MASTER!"

I flung myself into the melee, shoving and pushing, cleaving the pack for the three scuffling behind me in tandem. Ahead of me, Norman was hopping about the ring like a fiend, pounding the air with his fist, urging the crowd to joint the chant. Here and there about the hall it was being taken up with a jokey, aimless excitement. "Master! Master!" they cried. And then more added their voices, on every side of us the crowd began to sway to the dull thunder of the refrain. "Master! Master! Master!" And there was Hiller, striding up and down the ring, grinning triumphantly, eyes glittering as he flourished his fist, whipping them into an even greater frenzy.

We fought through the rush and gained our corner. Kurt seemed in a daze, a trance, he looked as if he scarcely knew where he was when Hiller took him by the wrist and led him like a child to the middle of the ring to be introduced to his opponent. Scutter had stripped off shirt, shoes and socks and was wearing only his pimples and blue jeans. While the referee stumblingly repeated what Norman had coached him to say, Scutter, who couldn't hold a cigarette with boxing gloves on his hands, kept jerking his head at his brother, signalling for a drag on his. Each time his brother held the butt to his mouth for a pull, Scutter inhaled deeply, then expelled the smoke in Meinecke's face with a thin-lipped smile.

Broward ended his little speech. "Let's have a good one, boys," he said.

"Yeah," Scutter said, "let's have a good one." Even from where I stood it was unnerving.

The preliminaries done, Hiller led Meinecke back to the corner and pushed him down into the chair to wait for the bell.

"Get him loose," he said to me, gesturing impatiently. "Can't you see he's tight?" I proceeded to massage Kurt's neck. It was like kneading banjo strings.

"Okay," said Norman fiercely to Meinecke, "you know what to do. We've been over this like a thousand times. Scutter's a street fighter. How does a street fighter go?"

"He does a couple of dekes and then takes a run at you," said Meinecke reciting from memory. "He tries to knock you off your feet."

"And you go?" coaxed Hiller.

Meinecke didn't reply. He was staring across the ring where Scutter was cutting up, kicking out his bare feet right, left, right, left, as if he was booting somebody's knackers off. His supporters were falling all over themselves laughing.

"Are you fucking listening to me or not?" demanded Hiller.

Kurt looked up at him, bewildered.

"You go how?" repeated Norman. "How?"

"I cover up," said Kurt.

"That's right. Elbows in tight to the ribs, chin down on the wishbone, gloves up high like Floyd Patterson," said Hiller, illustrating. "Be a bomb shelter. No way that dink can hurt you. And don't hit back," Norman emphasized. "Not until I say. You hit back – what happens?"

"I open up the defence."

"Right. And peckerhead there puts your lights out. So remember our number one rule is – no hitting!"

The bell rang. Kurt stood like a zombie. "And don't forget – laugh at him. Cool Hand Luke the fucker," was Norman's last bit of advice.

It happened just the way Hiller said it would. Cocky Scutter grinning, feinting, pecking at Meinecke's gloves, skipping on his bare feet. Then the kamikaze rush. Meinecke ducking low to meet it. A storm of wild blows raining down on his back, his shoulders, uppercuts smacking into the forearms protecting his face, a punch skidding off the crown of his tipped skull. And then the 15-second flurry was spent and Scutter was left panting, momentarily winded.

Meinecke slowly straightened up, gingerly flexing his arms and revealing splotches of fiery red on his back and shoulders where he had been hit. There was an expression on his face I'd never seen before, a sort of puzzled exasperation, annoyance.

Norman was screaming his lungs out. "Defense! Defense!" A brief moment of hesitation, or regret, and then Kurt obediently lifted his gloves high and settled warily into the Floyd Patterson peekaboo crouch that Hiller had been coaching him in during the past week. For the remainder of the round he grimly and obediently followed Hiller's fight plan, stayed a punching bag. As first Scutter was wary and cautiously circled Meinecke, flicking out jabs which bounced off Kurt's forehead and bee-stung his ears. But realizing he had nothing to fear, Scutter went to work, throwing short, vicious hooks in behind the elbows (not quite kidney punches but close) which Kurt kept stubbornly pinned to his ribs the way Hiller had taught him. Every blow he absorbed screwed Meinecke's mouth a little more crooked, drew his eyes into tighter slits. He was paying a price.

Kurt's performance was not going down well with the crowd. Their mood was changing, the chant of "Master! Master!" died away as disappointment seized them. Someone yelled "Fight!" and someone else, "Chickenshit!" When Dooey clanged on the pie plate to end the round, Kurt Meinecke's return to the corner was greeted, here and there, with boos.

Norman was all over him as soon as his ass dropped on the chair. "Goddamn it," he hissed, "you aren't Cool Handing him. Laugh at the fucker! Tease him! Tell him he hits like a homo! You're forgetting what I said. What'd I say? 'Ninety percent of boxing is mental.' You're overlooking the mental. Laugh at him!"

"You can laugh at him," said Kurt, probing his rib cage with the thumb of his glove. "You got no idea how hard he hits."

Norman slapped the glove away. "Stop that!" he said. "He's watching you." It was true. Scutter was pointing in our direction and making smirking asides to his brother.

"Look at him," Kurt said, brooding. "Acts as if I'm nothing. Think he's so smart."

Dooey beat the pie plate. Norman caught Meinecke by the hairs on the nape of his neck as he was rising. "Remember," he said, tugging them for emphasis, "Cool Hand Luke him. And no hitting back! I'm warning you, Meinecke, no hitting!"

For the next three rounds Kurt did exactly as he was told. There was plenty of hitting and none of it was done by him. When Scutter did his ham-handed Ali imitations, dancing circles around Meinecke, inviting attack, parading and flaunting his jaw within easy range of the Master of Disaster who inexplicably declined to strike, this incited the bloodthirsty mob into more taunts and jeers, the cue for Scutter to stop dead in his tracks and pepper Meinecke with a storm of punches.

Each time Kurt came back to the corner, he added another injury to the catalogue, a mouse swelling under the left eye, a cut inside the mouth that kept him drooling pink saliva into the plastic bucket, a raw lace scrape on the side of the neck, knots and eggs popping up all over his head.

It was the humiliation that worked the change in him. He began to beg, really beg Hiller to let him hit back. Kurt had always been so mild, nice was maybe the word for him, that I would never have guessed he had the stuff in him to hate. But the look on his face told me he'd found it, or, rather, Hiller had found it for him. He was like one of those neglected dogs tied in a backyard which you know has taken one kick too many and wants to sink its teeth into somebody. Kurt wanted a bite, too, but Hiller wouldn't give it to him. He kept telling him to do what he was told, stick to the plan, and Meinecke kept asking when, when, when do I get to hit him?

By the end of the seventh round Meinecke was in bad shape, blood leaking out of both nostrils, an eye swollen shut, a split lip. I put my mouth to his ear and said, "Get it over, Kurt. Next time he hits you – drop. Fuck this noise."

"I got to get my chance. All of them laughing at me. It isn't that I don't *want* to hit him. If Norman would just let me hit him. When Norman says – then look out." He was staring across the ring at Scutter.

Norman shoved me roughly to one side. "How many fucking times I got to say it!" he shouted at Meinecke. "You're supposed to be lipping him and you stand there like a goddamn dummy! Yap at him! Tell him he's a pussy! Do something!"

"I can't. I get mixed up. It's the noise. I can't remember what I'm supposed to say," Meinecke said, on the verge of tears. "Just let me hit him, Norman."

"You got to earn the right to hit him," said Hiller. "I want you to be professional. You think I invested all this time in you so's you can go out there and make me look like a loser? You get him mad, really mad, I'll let you hit him. For Christ's sakes we got a plan here." He paused. "Be a fucking man, Meinecke."

Meinecke went out and took another battering. He stood there with his gloves up, elbows clamped down hard on his ribs, chin ducked into his chest, and took his beating. Wobbling and staggering, he took it. He was flinching now before he was even hit, out of fear of being hit. But he didn't try to run from it. And when the bell rang and Scutter turned to stalk back to his corner he tried more. There he stood with his arms hanging helplessly at his sides, his mouth working. I knew what he was doing. He was trying to take hold of those things that Hiller wanted him to say and fling them after Scutter, but his rage and his shame were obstacles to his finding them. Or perhaps he didn't have mean, dirty taunts in him, only blind, suffocating rage. He stuttered, he stammered. "Yyy-ou," he said. "Yyy-ou..." But it was useless, hopeless. The crowd was whooping and caterwauling. "Pardon me?" they shouted. "Come again?" "Take a seat, harelip!"

Defeated, he blundered back to the rest of The Magnificent Seven in conference in his corner. Norman was not sympathetic. "I couldn't believe my ears," he said. "Who holds your fucking hand when you cross the street, Meinecke?" Kurt did not say anything. He dropped on the chair and covered his face with the gloves. I could only guess what was going on behind them. The sight of Meinecke sitting there with his face covered was quieting the hall.

Norman exploited the hush for his own purposes. "Hey," I heard him shout across the ring to Scutter. "Meinecke says for you to pull all the stops out. Either that or get a dress. He says you're a pussy puncher, Scutter! And he eats pussy!"

Scutter squinted, the mask of acne darkened. "Yeah?" he shouted back. "Yeah?"

"Fucking right." Hiller poked Meinecke. "Do I speak the truth, or do I speak the truth? Is that pussy over there, or is that pussy over there?" Meinecke slowly raised his face from his gloves. He scanned the hall with glazed eyes. "Pussy," he said in a quiet, muffled voice.

Hiller cupped his hand behind his ear. "What's that? I'm not getting that."

"Pussy," Meinecke said, loudly this time. "Definitely pussy."

"You heard it from the horse's mouth," shouted Hiller. "Go home and put a rag on, Scutter. Get ready to bleed."

"That flabby fuck is dead," Scutter said. "Right where he sits he's dead."

But Hiller wasn't listening. Already he was squatting down directly before Meinecke, hands on his fighter's knees, looking up into his face, speaking urgently. "Listen, he's mad. We got him mad. The bell goes, he's going to take a run at you. Just like round one. Take four steps into the ring and then wait. Wait for him. He's coming on, he's coming on hard, and you cold-cock him. Same as hitting the heavy bag. Same punch. He's bowling in, he doesn't expect nothing, and you stiff him. Understand?"

"You mean hit him?" Kurt asked. He didn't seem to understand he was finally getting the green light.

"Not *hit* him," said Norman. "*Kill* the fucker."

Meinecke thudded his gloves together. He'd got it.

I was holding my breath. I let it out when Dooey clanged the pie plate. Scutter was coming in, hard. Kurt stopped, braced himself per instructions, swung. Swung like he'd done a thousand times at the heavy bag, one of those economical, sweet punches with the hip and the shoulder behind it and something added to the physics of it – pure hate. All that and Scutter collided right in front of my eyes. I heard a sound like knuckles cracking, saw a head snapping back, the whites of eyes flashing as they rolled in their sockets, heels skittering, and down he went, head bouncing off the floor with a leaden clunk.

You could have heard a pin drop. Scutter rolled over, got his hands and knees under him. Dark red drops of blood splashed onto the floor from his nose, swept back and forth in a fine spray when he shook his head, trying to clear it.

"Count! Count, fuck face!" Norman screamed at Broward. He did. The first two numbers into a stunned silence; the next two into the kind of hysterical uproar occasioned by the death of one god and the birth of another. At five, Scutter began to creep about on all fours like some old blind dog trying to find the scent home. He crawled over to Broward's legs, clutched one, and shakily started to pull himself up.

Scutter was reeling, one arm clasped around Broward's waist, when Meinecke stepped in and chopped two hard, desperate blows into his temple, sending him crashing. It didn't quite stop there either. The Master of Disaster, sobbing uncontrollably, kept pounding Scutter where he lay on the floor until Broward, Hiller, and me managed to drag him off.

For months afterward Hiller told and retold the story of how he had engineered the greatest upset in boxing history since Cassius Clay whipped Sonny Liston.

"I trained him perfect," he'd say. "I brought him along just so. As soon as I seen him hit the heavy bag, well, there was no question but he could hit. The problem was making him *want* to hit. Fucking guy was too nice for his own good. So I took the mental approach because if he seen the damage he could do hitting somebody – he wouldn't want to hit people any more. That's where Hop Jump came in. Somebody to dance the night away with because no way, Jose, was Hop Jump going to let himself get hit.

"Scutter I was worried about. For him I designed the Cool Hand Luke defence. After a couple of rounds of that, Scutter figured he didn't have nothing to worry about. And Meinecke – the pounding he was taking – that had to get to him, that had to piss him off. And everybody laughing at him, that twisted him, and me sitting on him, not letting him hit, that twisted him more. Psychology. He had to blow. I loaded him, I cocked him, I pulled the trigger."

Kurt was never the same guy after the fight. Deke, Hop Jump, Murph, everybody in Hiller's gang began to notice that he was avoiding them. He avoided me too. No more long conversations late at night after the pool room closed down, walking those empty streets and talking about how, just around the corner, things were going to fall into place for us. When we ran into each other, we nodded, said a few words about nothing, and then edged away from each other like people who share a secret they would sooner forget.

There were other changes. His hair grew longer. He quit the football team, didn't bother to go out for wrestling. He began to hang around with strange types, two or three assholes who had published poems in the yearbook about Vietnam and babies crying in Watts. Deke said he had heard that Meinecke was taking acoustic guitar lessons. Hiller said, "Fuck him. You can drag a person up to your level but if they don't make an effort they'll sink back to where they naturally belong." Meinecke and his new friends cut a lot of classes and spent afternoons at the house of a girl whose mother worked, listening to records, smoking grass. Finally, with only three months of school to go before graduation, Kurt dropped out.

The last that was seen of Kurt Meinecke he was standing at the edge of the highway at five o'clock on a Sunday morning with his thumb stuck out. When those that had spotted him passed that way again a few hours later, he was gone.

JORDAN WHEELER

THE SEVENTH WAVE

The sky was wet. Jerry Ducharme stared through the screen window of his pup tent and watched it fall. Raindrops splashed his nose. He could hear footsteps and talking as people walked past, but the bushes and trees hid them. They gabbed merrily as the rain fell. Jerry shook his head. He pulled lint from his navel and scratched his belly, then a stone fell on the tent. Another one hit the car. Suddenly people began running and shouting, their feet splashing through puddles. Jerry looked up. Hail.

Lynn Lake struggled with the zipper of the pup tent, her body wet with the Pacific Ocean and the coastal rain.

"Damn it Jerry, I can't get this thing open," she muttered. Jerry sat up and undid the thing. She burst in spraying water across the tent. A drop landed in his navel. Lynn fell to the floor and cuddled up to him like young kittens do, burying herself in his warm skin. Jerry pulled the sleeping bag over her shivering body. The hail stopped and it rained again. Then the rain stopped. Jerry stifled laughter.

"It's not funny," she told him, touching her tender skull. "It hurt." He couldn't hold back. Laughter burst out and hit her in the face. She buried her fist in his stomach. Jerry felt his face burn red as the jolt filled his body. He couldn't breathe. He rolled over and pulled his knees up to his chest.

"I'm sorry, did I hurt you?" Lynn asked. Jerry groaned, waiting for his breath to come back. Lynn kissed him slow and soft beneath his ear. "I'll kiss it better," she whispered. Jerry felt the air fill his lungs. Gingerly he rolled onto his back. Lynn slid down and kissed him on the belly, then she stopped and stared at a hair. Jerry stared at the ceiling. She plucked the hair and he flinched.

"Look," she said. "It's grey." Jerry grabbed it and held it up to his eyes. She passed him his glasses. Sure enough, the hair was white.

"I'll be damned," he mused.

"I think it's distinguishing," she told him. "A sign of wisdom."

"A sign of age."

"You're not that old."

There was something in the way she said "that." He was old, but not "that" old. Old like a '65 Chevy, but not a Model T. Old like a raisin not yet mouldy. Old like a turn-of-the-century barn before it falls. Old. "Don't worry, you should see how grey my dad is."

Jerry sighed. "Isn't it time for lunch?"

Canada is known for a lot of things, but not its surfing. There's Waikiki, Uluwatu, Kuta, but in Canada, the best known surfing spot is the West Edmonton Mall. Then there's a spot three hours west of Vancouver – Long Beach. Twelve miles of sand stretching to the open sea. At one time you could camp and drive on the beach. Then the government took over, made it a national park, and called it Pacific Rim. But at Long Beach there's surf. Not a Waikiki surf, or an Uluwatu surf, but surf. Pacific Rim surf.

Jerry had never surfed. He was an undergraduate from Brandon attending UBC. He met Lynn there. "Lynn Lake," he mused, thinking of the Manitoba town. "I have relatives there." So they talked. Then they started going out. Lynn's friend,

Georgina, had a boyfriend, Mr. Muscles, who surfed. When the July long weekend happened, Lynn and Georgina decided the four of them should do something. Mr. Muscles suggested surfing and the first thing that came to Jerry's mind was the mall. He had never heard of Long Beach.

"Look at the waves," Lynn gushed. Jerry did. They'd been there 10 minutes and he was already tired of sucking in his gut. She watched Georgina and Mr. Muscles, Mike, through a pair of binoculars. Jerry sipped from his beer. He was on his fifth when the sun broke. Mike and Georgina bounded up the beach. Lynn passed him a wet suit. Jerry looked at her, confused.

"You said you'd surf if the sun broke," she told him. She reached for the boards. Jerry looked up and cursed the sun. The sun smiled. Mike moved in and assumed authority. Jerry was a novice, so he should try bodysurfing first.

"Whose body do I surf on?" Jerry asked. They laughed and he decided to keep his mouth shut. He donned the wet suit and followed Mike toward the water watching the waves break toward shore. From a distance they looked safe enough, almost pretty. His feet hit the water and he leapt into the air. Ice.

"The bodysuit will keep you warm," Mike assured him. At waist level Jerry forgot what warm was. Maybe when his first layer of skin numbed u he'd be all right. Small waves hit him. Jerry was surprised at their force. He turned and faced the beach where Lynn stood with a Nikon camera. A large wave knocked him off his feet. The salt stung his eyes. He stood up and followed Mike with a waddle induced by numbness and five beers.

They started to swim. The waves were relentless. Jerry felt like a hunk of driftwood. "How much further?" he yelled. Mike pointed to where the waves were breaking.

"Past there," he said. Jerry started getting nervous. He was in the Pacific, a mass of water 16 times the size of Canada. He might wash ashore in Okinawa. Give me mosquitoes, he thought, bull-flies, something to swipe at. The sea foamed and swallowed. Salt and sand grazed his teeth. He surfaced and there was calm.

"They come in groups of seven," Mike told him.

Like dwarfs, Jerry thought, or elevens and Big Gulps. Sea gulls flew overhead. Ocean buzzards. A new group of seven began. Mike and Jerry bobbed and swayed like discarded pop bottles at the sea's mercy. If there were messages in the bottles, Jerry's would read five beers too many.

"Get ready," Mike yelled. Jerry copied Mike and began swimming toward shore. The water level dropped and Mike accelerated. Jerry followed. From behind, a wave caught them. Jerry felt his body rise as Mike slid down the wave's face. The wave curled with Jerry in it, tons of water crushing in on itself. It drove him face first into the sand, then twisted and fluttered him about. Ten seconds later, the sea released him. Jerry tried to stand, but his head hit the bottom. He flipped and shot up into the sun gasping for breath. His forehead was scraped from his hairline to his nose. Mike swam over.

"Some fun, eh? What happened to your forehead?"

"A shark bit me," Jerry said heading for shore, his forehead stinging with salt.

There was a lineup at the outdoor shower. Surfers and their boards stood like totems. At the front of the line, Jerry was beneath the shower. Water splashed at his scrape as Lynn plucked out sand with tweezers. A herd of giggling kids surrounded them, some threw stones at Jerry's feet.

"Must we do this here?" he asked. Lynn squinted and plucked.

"There's no running water at our campsite. How did you maim yourself like this?"

"It was a shark."

Lynn pulled back. "All done." Jerry turned and walked into the closest bush. He came out beside a Winnebago. A middle-aged couple from Burbank were playing crib. Jerry waved and walked through to the next campsite. A surfboard rammed into him. Another muscle-bound kid peered from behind.

"Sorry," the kid said, toddling off. Jerry produced a smile.

"Are you lost or something?" Jerry turned. A woman his age was sitting in a lawn chair.

"I was taking a shortcut."

"What happened to your forehead?"

Jerry saw some instinctual, motherly concern. "Shark," he said. The woman laughed.

"Would you like a beer?"

"Sure. I noticed your boyfriend there. I'm going out with a younger woman myself." He read the licence plate on her Hyundai. Idaho. The woman returned with two Coors.

"He's my son," she said, crooning. "But thanks for the compliment." Jerry nodded, then accepted the beer.

"You seem depressed," Lynn said as they sat by the fire pit. Jerry was looking up at Orion. Orion flickered back.

"You want to go golfing tomorrow?"

"That was your first try," she said, trying to soothe him. "I thought you did well."

"It was that damn shark." He breathed in the night air and let his belly hang, trying not to listen to Mike and Georgina doing naughty things in their tent. Lynn didn't seem to notice.

"You deserve another try. Once you get it, you won't believe how much fun it can be," Lynn said. "Mike says it might help if you were stoned."

"Mushrooms," Mike called from the tent, evidently finished. "I did it in Bali. You can eat them in the restaurants there. It puts you in the perfect state of mind for letting go and feeling the rhythm of the waves."

"That so," Jerry said.

"Yeah, so come on old man, give it another try."

Jerry looked at Lynn. "Anything to save our relationship." Lynn giggled and cuddled up to him. Jerry cuddled back.

With dawn came rain that lasted until they awoke and beyond. Muscles Mike was glum. Jerry whistled as he prepared breakfast. "Isn't that a Simon and Garfunkel tune?" Georgina asked. "My mom has all their records."

"Mott The Hoople," said Jerry. "We're out of Perrier, I'm going to the store."

Jerry trotted for three-quarters of a mile and stopped short of the Pacific Rim Groceries' parking lot. He wasn't sure if he could make it over the speed bumps. He bought a pack of smokes, a case of Perrier, and returned the Deep Woods OFF he bought on their way in. "I'm from Brandon," he shrugged. "It's a habit." The grocer smiled. He was a young kid. Probably from UBC, too, Jerry mused.

"What happened to your forehead?" the kid asked.

"Shark," said Jerry. The kid smiled knowingly.

"If you get in trouble, then the trick is to tuck and duck under."

"Tuck and duck," Jerry repeated. The kid nodded.

The sun broke and they ate mushroom omelettes without eggs. "I don't feel a thing," Jerry confessed to Lynn as they passed beneath the needly limbs of a cedar on their way to the beach. Lynn shrugged.

"Sometimes you don't get a reaction," she said.

He peered through sea drop crystals, vaguely aware that his feet were no longer planted, then rolled lazily onto his back exposing his navel to the sky. If only our eyes were on the tops of our heads, he thought, watching the small clouds. The sea lapped at his ears. His toes touched the air and he was filled with a lightness of being. He rotated his head like a panoramic camera. The trees were upside down, but it seemed plausible. No telling why the ocean didn't fall.

"Wave!" Mike shouted.

Mushrooms, Jerry thought. He turned and treaded before an eight-foot wave, noticing how curiously huge the curl looked. Intrigued and trusting, he watched the tons of water wash toward him. Mike was swimming frantically toward shore. Give it up, Muscles, Jerry thought, it's going to catch you. Still the wave rose. The wind of the water. Then a hurricane of wet heaved and stomped on Jerry. People on the beach gasped.

It was soft as kisses went, Jerry thought, but somehow clinical. He opened his eyes and saw Mike and a crowd of people over him. "Are you all right?" Mike asked.

"Yeah," Jerry sighed. "I felt the rhythm of the wave." He got up and walked back to the ocean, the crowd yammering in his wake. "Tuck and duck," he repeated to himself. The words imprinted in the corners of his skull (mushroom murals were everywhere else), and he tucked and ducked all afternoon between lectures on the Native perspective of the "Native problem." "We're not the problem, you guys are," he expounded. Mike wanted to escape, but they were in the ocean.

"I mastered the tuck and duck," Jerry told Lynn that night as they lay on the grass staring at the moon.

"Did you ever think of the moon in terms of gender?" Jerry wondered if she had eaten another omelette. "The moon is woman. You know, the lunar cycle, our menstruation. The sun is man, commanding, garish."

"But I like the moon."

"Of course you like the moon, you're the sun."

Jerry shook his head. "Mushrooms are dangerous, especially when bodysurfing," he said and headed to bed.

Like a miracle, the sunshine persisted. Jerry and Lynn walked to the store the following morning for more eggs and beef jerky, and met up with the woman from Idaho and her surfing son.

"No more sharks?" she asked.

"Just jellyfish," Jerry answered.

The surfer snickered. They walked to the store as a group. Then in pairs on the way back. Lynn with the surfer and Jerry with Idaho. "I'm divorced and my kid's twenty. I've got all this time on my hands," she said. Jerry watched her feet.

"I'm getting my Master's."

"What's it like?" she asked, looking at Lynn. "She's awfully young."

"Like watching Bambi."

Camp Idaho came first. Jerry watched her go fondly, then turned to see Lynn watching Idaho's son go fondly. Lynn and Jerry walked back toward their camp arm in arm, then gradually separated. When they walked into lot 69, Mike and

Georgina were frying oysters. Jerry dumped the eggs on the skillet. Mike added mushrooms.

"I was thinking about what you said yesterday."

"About what?" Jerry queried.

"Indians."

"Mmmm."

"Don't you think all the ethnic groups should be treated equal?"

"We're not ethnic, we're aboriginal. Are we going surfing?"

"Try a raw oyster first," Georgina said. Jerry tried it, then threw up. He saw a melancholy expression on Lynn's face. They left for the beach and her melancholy persisted. Jerry searched within himself and found some of his own.

There was wind – ocean wind – moist, fresh, and fast. It pushed back his hair like it did to the trees, their branches reaching inland. The sea stood before him, waiting. Jerry felt enticed, but intimidated. The sea was big. He could get swallowed and wash up years later in Hiroshima among the crabs and sea urchins. The Souris River never had waves like this.

As Georgina and Mike frolicked in the driftwood, Lynn leaned against Jerry as he stood contemplating the Pacific. "You would have rather stayed in Vancouver, huh?"

Jerry watched the gulls fly against the wind, others dove for fish. Then his eyes dropped to the sand where flies picked at dried kelp.

"It's a beautiful place," he said.

"Are you gonna try again? I'll go with you."

Jerry sighed, letting out his tummy a bit too much. Mike and Georgina joined them, and they walked into the surf. The waves were still huge. Jerry tucked and ducked as the others rode, but by noon, he attempted his first ride. He missed, but felt its breaking point.

"Let's go in for lunch," Lynn yelled. Jerry shook his head.

"I'm getting the hang of it, I think." Lynn turned and went for port. Jerry turned to the sea. Come on, he thought, where's that big one. He bobbed and peered over the smaller waves looking for the larger ones. When they came, he was invariably out of position. He nearly caught a five-footer, but it stuck him in the sand, reopening the gash on his forehead.

He could feel his toes going numb, despite the rubber suit. The little waves peppered his face with salt, but he watched for the big ones. A new cycle began. Wave one was little. Jerry counted. Wave two, wave three. Wave four was big, Jerry tucked and ducked, then swam out to meet wave number five. It was huge. Jerry felt the rush of water being pulled into the wave, giving it its volume. "Christ," he muttered, then tucked and ducked. The fringe of the wave's swirl caught him as he surfaced, but he escaped and swam to meet wave number six. Surfers on the beach took note. They cursed themselves for taking lunch. Number six came, and it was mammoth. Jerry wondered if he'd miscounted, this was the largest wave he'd seen since they arrived. He tried looking over it, but couldn't. It rose and he swallowed, then tucked and ducked. He felt the power of the wave rush past, but he was disappointed in his retreat. If there was a seventh, he would ride it.

Jerry surfaced and looked west. Twenty yards before him was a ten-foot wall of water closing in fast. The surfers on the beach guffawed and spat. They watched as Jerry turned to ride.

Jerry swam, his arms and legs flailing. Water receded beneath him and he was swallowed up by the growing wave. Jerry swam harder. The water started to rise. The wave hadn't yet curled, but it had steepened. He looked up and behind. The wave was almost on top of him. He felt his body being picked up and propelled. He was now at the wave's mercy. It swung him up its face. Jerry nearly panicked. This wave wouldn't scrape his head – it would crush it. He saw the curl out of the corner of his eye and waited for it to crush him as his arms and legs picked up tempo. The wave curled to his right. Jerry turned to his left and the wave dropped him a couple of feet down its face. He stuck out his right hand to steer himself left and quit kicking. The wave grabbed him, and he rode.

It lasted all of 10 seconds, but it was an exhilarating 10 seconds. Jerry frolicked in the white water like a pig in mud howling at the daylight moon. Tourists clapped. He waded from the Pacific in triumph. "Hey mister," a kid yelled. "What happened to your forehead?"

"Bodysurfing," Jerry gushed.

Further up the beach he found Lynn sitting with Mike, Georgina, and the surfer kid from Idaho.

"Great ride," Mike congratulated. "Want an oyster?" Jerry shook his head.

"We've leaving after lunch," Lynn said. "Dave is coming with us." Jerry looked at the surfer kid.

"It's a drag travelling with your mom," the kid drawled.

Jerry smirked. "I bet."

They took down Mike and Georgina's tent first. Mike scrambled to gather the used condoms. Dave the surfer was gone, packing his stuff. "Mike has four tickets to REM," Lynn said, as they packed their clothes in the pup tent. "They're at the Coliseum tonight."

"Who?"

"REM."

Jerry nodded, wondering who in the hell they were. His *Rolling Stone* subscription ran out years ago. They separated their sleeping bags. Lynn rolled hers up as Jerry packed his unread Beatrice Culleton novel. He'd wanted to read it over the weekend. He rolled up his green, down-filled sleeping bag slowly. It grew like the seventh wave. Jerry stopped and sat. Lynn was tying hers up when she noticed. "What is it?" she asked.

Jerry looked at his toes, then at her. "I think I'm gonna stay."

They were silent, motionless. The words became clear. "The waves got to you, huh?" She smiled. Jerry laughed.

"I think it's best," he said. She nodded. "No hard feelings?" She shook her head, then hugged him.

Running footsteps stomped into camp. "Okay dudes, I'm packed." It was Dave the surfer kid.

There was plenty of leftover beer and food. Mike and Georgina offered to leave them. "If you get bored, visit my mom. She could use the company," Dave the surfer kid told him.

"Just hope she finds you when she gets back to Van."

"Yeah," the kid laughed. They piled into the car leaving Lynn and Jerry to say goodbye. They stood silent, then it started to rain. Lynn waved with her fingers and got into the car. Jerry crawled into the pup tent and curled up with his novel, waiting for the rain to end. He could hear the waves crush the beach.

A little later, he was sitting with Karen, Mrs. Idaho, sipping his politically correct beer in her large tent. The rain hadn't stopped. "I've been on the same path for 20 years. I want something different now," she was saying.

Jerry sniffed the ocean breeze as it spilled through the screen windows. "I want a house by the ocean."

NOTES ON THE AUTHORS

BLAISE, CLARK (b. 1940). Novelist, short story writer, and editor, born in Fargo, North Dakota. Blaise's fiction includes the novels *Lunar Attractions* (1979), *Lusts* (1983), and *If I Were Me* (1997), as well as dozens of short stories collected in four volumes: *Southern Stories* (2001), *Pittsburgh Stories* (2001), *Montreal Stories* (2003), and *World Body* (2006). In 2003 he was awarded an exceptional achievement award by the American Academy of Arts and Letters. After spending his childhood moving around the United States where his Canadian parents were living and working, Blaise settled in Montreal, Québec, and later San Francisco, California, where he now lives.

BOWERING, GEORGE (b. 1935). Poet, critic, novelist, and editor, born in Penticton, British Columbia. Bowering won the 1969 Governor General's Literary Award for Poetry for *The Gangs of Kosmos* and the 1980 Governor General's Award for Fiction for his novel *Burning Water*. He has published over 40 books including the collection of short stories *The Rain Barrel* (1994); the historical work *Egoists and Autocrats: The Prime Ministers of Canada* (1999); the volumes of poetry, *Kerrisdale Elegies* (1984), *Urban Snow* (1992), *Changing on the Fly* (2004, short-listed for the Griffin Prize); the memoir *The Moustache: Memoirs of Greg Curnoe* (1993); and the novel *Shoot!* (1994). Bowering is Professor Emeritus at Simon Fraser University, where he taught for thirty years. In 2002, Bowering was appointed the first Canadian Poet Laureate, a position he held until 2004. He lives in Vancouver, British Columbia.

BRAND, DIONNE (b. 1953). Born in Guayguayare, Trinidad, Brand moved to Toronto in 1970. She has published several volumes of poetry, including *Land to Light On* which won the Governor General's Award in 1997, *Thirsty* (2002, shortlisted for the Griffin Poetry Prize), and *Inventory* (2005). Brand's fiction includes the short story collection *San Souci and Other Stories* (1989), and the novels *At the Full and Change of the Moon* (1999), and *What We All Long For* (2004). Her non-fiction publications include *No Burden to Carry* (1991), *Bread Out of Stone* (1994), and *A Map to the Door of No Return* (2001). She currently lives in Toronto and teaches at the University of Guelph.

CALLAGHAN, BARRY (b. 1937). Born in Toronto, the son of Morley Callaghan, he became an English professor at York University and also founded the journal *Exile* and the publishing house Exile Editions. Callaghan is a poet, novelist, journalist and translator; he has been awarded more than a dozen National Magazine Awards, the Pushcart Prize, and the inaugural W.O. Mitchell Award in 1998; his books include *The Hogg Poems and Drawings* (1978), *The Black Queen Stories* (1983), the memoir *Barrelhouse Kings* (1998), two volumes of collected non-fiction, *Raise You Five* (2005) and *Raise You Ten* (2006), the short story collection *Between Trains* (2007), and the novel *Beside Still Waters* (2009).

CALLAGHAN, MORLEY (1903-1990). Novelist and short story writer, born in Toronto. Callaghan studied law at Osgoode Hall and was called to the bar, but never practiced law. His novels include *Such Is My Beloved* (1934), *More Joy in Heaven* (1937), and *The Loved and the Lost* which won the Governor General's Award in 1951. A well-known short story writer, Callaghan published numerous collections such as *Now That April's Here* (1936) and *Morley Callaghan's Stories* (1959), the children's story *Luke Baldwin's Vow* (1948), and *That Summer in Paris* (1963), a memoir about his youthful literary adventures abroad. He was made a Companion of the Order of Canada in 1982.

CARRIER, ROCH (b. 1937). Novelist, poet, playwright, essayist, born in Sainte-Justine, Québec. Carrier's novel *La Guerre, Yes Sir!* (1968) made his reputation in Québec and abroad. Other publications include *Floralie, où es-tu?* (1969), *Il est par là le soleil* (1970), *De l'Amour dans la feraille* (1984), and *Heartbreaks Along the Road* (1987). In 1992, Carrier's *Prayers of a Very Wise Child* (*Prières d'un enfant très très sage*) won the Stephen Leacock Memorial Medal for Humour. His most famous short story is "Le chandail de hockey" ("The Hockey Sweater"), published in 1979. In 1991 he was made an Officer of the Order of Canada, and from 1997-2004 Carrier was the National Librarian of Canada. He makes his home in Québec.

COHEN, MATT (1942-1999). Born in Montreal and raised in Kingston, Ontario, Cohen published 20 works of fiction in his lifetime. They include *Korsoniloff* (1969), *The Disinherited* (1974), *Flowers of Darkness* (1981), *Emotional Arithmetic* (1990), *The Bookseller* (1993), and *Last Seen* (1996). His final novel, *Elizabeth and After* won the 1999 Governor General's Award for Fiction. Cohen also published several collections of short stories, poetry, books for young adults, and children's books (under the name Teddy Jam). His last work was the memoir *Typing: A Life in 26 Keys.* The Matt Cohen Prize – In Celebration of a Writing Life is awarded annually by the Writer's Trust of Canada.

DAVIDSON, CRAIG (b. 1976). Novelist and short story writer, born in Toronto. In 2005, Davidson published his first short story collection, *Rust and Bone.* His novel, *The Fighter,* was published in 2007. Davidson currently lives in Iowa City.

FAWCETT, BRIAN (b. 1944). Writer, poet, born in Prince George, British Columbia. Fawcett's fiction includes *My Career With the Leafs and Other Stories* (1982), *Cambodia: A Book for People Who Find Television Too Slow* (1986), and *Gender Wars: A Novel and Some Conversation About Sex and Gender* (1994). His poetry includes *Friends* (1971), *Permanent Relationships* (1975), and *Aggressive Transport* (1982). He is also a non-fiction writer whose book, *Virtual Clearcut: Or, the Way Things Are in My Hometown,* won the 2003 Pearson Prize for Canadian non-fiction. Fawcett currently makes his home in Toronto.

GOVIER, KATHERINE (b. 1948). Born in Edmonton, Govier writes fiction and non-fiction; she has been a visiting lecturer in Canadian and British universities, and now lives in Toronto. She has published eight novels and three collections of short fiction, including *Random Descent* (1979), *Going Through the Motions* (1982), *Fables of Brunswick Avenue* (1985), *Angel Walk* (1996), *The Truth Teller* (2000), *Creation* (2002), and *Three Views of Crystal Water* (2005). She received the Marion Engel Award in 1997.

GRIFFITHS, LINDA (b. 1956). Writer, playwright, born in Montreal, Québec. Griffiths' many dramatic works include the plays *Maggie and Pierre* (1981), *Jessica* (1987), *Brother André's Heart* (1992), *The Darling Family* (1992), *The Duchess* (1998), *Alien Creature* (2000), and *Age of Arousal* (2007). In 1989 she published the non-fiction book, *The Book of Jessica: A Theatrical Transformation.* She is the winner of numerous awards, including five Dora Mavor Moore awards, and a Gemini Award. Griffiths currently works and lives in Toronto.

HEIGHTON, STEVEN (b. 1961). Poet, writer, born in Toronto. His works of poetry include *Stalin's Carnival* (1989, Gerald Lampert Award winner), *Foreign Ghosts* (1989), *The Ecstasy of Skeptics* (1994, Governor General's Award finalist), and *The Address Book* (2004). He is also the author of two books of short stories, *Flight Paths of the Emperor* (1992) and *On Earth As It Is* (1995), as well as several works of fiction, including *The Shadow Boxer* (2000), and *Afterlands* (2005). Heighton currently makes his home in Kingston, Ontario.

JARMAN, MARK (b. 1955). Novelist, poet, short story writer, born in Edmonton, Alberta. He is the author of the novel *Salvage King Ya!* (1997), the poetry collection, *Killing the Swan* (1986), and four short story collections: *New Orleans is Sinking* (1998), *Dancing Nightly in the Tavern* (1984), *19 Knives* (2000), and *My White Planet* (2008). In 2002 he published a travel book entitled *Ireland's Eye*. Jarman currently lives in Fredericton, where he teaches creative writing at the Universty of New Brunswick.

KINSELLA, W.P. (b. 1935). Short story writer, poet, novelist, playwright, born at Edmonton, Alberta. Kinsella has published twenty-one books of fiction, including *Dance Me Outside* (1977), *The Fencepost Chronicles* (1987), and *The Iowa Baseball Confederacy* (1985). Three of his works – including *Shoeless Joe* (1982), which became the movie *Field of Dreams* – have been made into major motion pictures. His most recent collection of short stories, *Japanese Baseball and Other Stories,* was published in 2000. He edited *Diamonds Forever: Reflections from the Field, the Dugout & the Bleachers* (1997) and co-wrote the Japanese nonfiction book *Ichiro Dreams: Ichiro Suzuki and the Seattle Mariners* (2002). Kinsella currently lives in White Rock, British Columbia and is a Member of the Order of Canada and of the Order of British Columbia.

LEACOCK, STEPHEN (1869-1944). Born in Swanmore, England, Leacock settled in Ontario in 1876 with his family, and later taught in the Department of Economics and Political Science at McGill University in Montreal. His collections of humorous stories, in over thirty volumes, include *Literary Lapses* (1910), *Nonsense Novels* (1911), *Sunshine Sketches of a Little Town* (1912), *Arcadian Adventures of the Idle Rich* (1914), *Frenzied Fiction* (1918), and *Winsome Winnie* (1920), and earned him substantial literary fame. The Stephen Leacock Museum, his old family home, located in Orillia, Ontario, is open year-round.

MILLIKEN, BARRY (b. 1944). Writer and artist born in Windsor, Ontario, and raised on the Kettle & Stony Point First Nation reserve on the shore of Lake Huron. At age seventeen, Milliken left the reservation to attend art school and eventually to work in Toronto. After travelling abroad, Milliken returned to Canada in 1971 to pursue a career in both commercial and fine art, and writing. In 2001, Milliken returned to live and work in his home community which has resulted in the production of two volumes of stories written in collaboration with Elders and Veterans of that First Nation. He continues to live and work in his home community.

MONTGOMERY, L.M. (1874-1942). Born in Clifton, (now New London), Prince Edward Island, she moved to Ontario after her marriage, and is one of Canada's most famous authors. Her first novel, *Anne of Green Gables* (1908), gained her international recognition; she produced many sequels, including *Anne of Avonlea* (1909), *Anne of the Island* (1915), and *Anne of Windy Poplars* (1936). In addition, she published several short story collections and a series featuring *Emily of New Moon* (1923), among other works.

MOODIE, SUSANNA (1803-1885). Born in Bungay, England, Moodie's writings on settler life have made her a legendary figure in Canada. In 1932 Moodie and her husband emigrated to Canada largely for financial reasons. She published *Roughing It in the Bush* (1952), *Life in the Clearings* (1853), *Flora Lyndsay* (1854), as well as numerous poems, articles, and other fictional and autobiographical works. Mrs. Moodie lived in or near Belleville, Ontario, until the death of her husband in 1869, from which time she lived chiefly in Toronto until her own death.

MOORE, LISA (b. 1964). Short story writer, novelist, born in St. John's, Newfoundland. Her first collection of short stories, *Degrees of Nakedness*, was published in 1995, followed by *Open* (2002, Giller Prize finalist). Her two novels are *Alligator* (2005) and *February* (2009). Moore teaches creative writing workshops in cities across Canada, including St. John's, Newfoundland, where she still lives.

PIGEON, MARGUERITE (b. 1971). Writer of fiction and poetry, born in Blind River, Ontario. Her short stories have appeared in a variety of journals, including *Grain* and *Taddle Creek*. She is currently completing her first novel, *Mil Sueños*, and her poetry collection, *Inventory*, will appear in spring 2009 with Anvil Press. She currently lives in Vancouver.

RICHLER, MORDECAI (1931-2001). Born in Montreal, the setting of his most famous novels such as *The Apprenticeship of Duddy Kravitz* (1959), *St. Urbain's Horseman* (1971), and *Solomon Gursky Was Here* (1989). Richler lived abroad from 1954 to 1972, mostly in London but also, briefly, in Paris. He was awarded the Governor General's Award for *Cocksure* and *Hunting Tigers Under Glass* in 1969, and for *St. Urbain's Horseman* in 1972. His novel, *Barney's Version* won the Giller Prize in 1997. He is also the author of children's books, including *Jacob Two-Two Meets the Hooded Fang* (1975) and *Jacob Two-Two and the Dinosaur* (1987), screenplays, and over three hundred journalistic pieces. In 2001 he was made a Companion of the Order of Canada.

SCHOEMPERLEN, DIANE (b. 1954). Novelist, short story writer, teacher and editor, born in Thunder Bay, Ontario. She is the author of several books of short stories, including *Frogs and Other Stories* (1986), *Hockey Night in Canada* (1987), *The Man of My Dreams* (1990), *Forms of Devotion* (1998, Governor General's Award winner), and *Red Plaid Shirt: Stories New and Collected*. Her novels include *Lady of the Lost and Found* (2002) and *At a Loss for Words: A Post-Romantic Novel* (2008). She is also author of the non-fiction work *Names of the Dead: An Elegy to Victims of September 11* (2004). Schoemperlen currently makes her home in Kingston, Ontario.

THAUBERGER, RUDY (b. 1961). Thauberger is a short story writer, playwright and screenwriter, born in Saskatoon, Saskatchewan. He has published numerous short stories and articles, including the short story "Goalie," which has been anthologized over twenty times. Thauberger wrote the screenplay for the feature film, *The Rhino Brothers*, and is the co-writer of the feature film, *Rover*. He currently lives in British Columbia, and is on faculty at the Vancouver Film School.

UPPAL, PRISCILA (b. 1974). Poet and novelist, born in Ottawa, Ontario. Uppal has published several collections of poetry, including *How to Draw Blood From a Stone* (1998), *Confessions of a Fertility Expert* (1999), *Pretending to Die* (2001), *Live Coverage* (2003), *Holocaust Dream* (2005), and *Ontological Necessities* (2006, shortlisted for the

Griffin Poetry Prize). She has also published the novels *The Divine Economy of Salvation* (2002) and *To Whom It May Concern* (2009), as well as the work of criticism *We Are What We Mourn: The Contemporary English-Canadian Elegy*. Works as editor include *Red Silk: South-Asian Canadian Women's Poetry*, and *The Exile Book of Poetry in Translation: 20 Canadian Poets Take On the World*. Uppal lives in Toronto where she is a professor of English at York University.

VANDERHAEGHE, GUY (b. 1951). Writer, novelist, playwright, born in Esterhazy, Saskatchewan. Vanderhaeghe won the Governor General's Award in 1982 for his first book, *Man Descending*, and in 1996, for *The Englishman's Boy*. Other publications include *My Present Age* (1984), *The Trouble with Heroes and Other Stories* (1983), *Homesick* (1989), *Things As They Are?* (1992), and *The Last Crossing* (2002). Vanderhaeghe lives in Saskatoon, and since 1993 he has served as a visiting professor of English at St. Thomas More College at the University of Saskatchewan.

WHEELER, JORDAN (b. 1964). Born in Victoria, British Columbia, Wheeler is the author of a collection of three novellas called *Brothers in Arms* (1989), as well as two children's books, *Just a Walk* (1998) and *Chuck in the City* (2002). He also works in film, video, and popular theatre. Wheeler currently lives in Winnipeg, Manitoba, where he teaches scriptwriting.

PERMISSIONS

CLARKE BLAISE "The Sociology of Love," from *World Body,* reprinted by permission of the author and The Porcupine's Quill Inc. GEORGE BOWERING "October 1, 1961," reprinted by permission of the author. DIONNE BRAND "I Used to Like the Dallas Cowboys," reprinted by permission of the author. BARRY CALLAGHAN "The Cohen in Cowan," reprinted by permission of the author. MORLEY CALLAGHAN "The Chiseler," reprinted by permission of the Morley Callaghan estate. ROCH CARRIER "The Hockey Sweater," from *The Hockey Sweater and Other stories* copyright 1979 Roch Carrier; translated by Sheila Fischman; reprinted with permission from the author and House of Anansi Press. MATT COHEN "Vogel," reprinted by permission of Strickland Ltd., copyright Strickland Ltd., 2009. CRAIG DAVIDSON "The Rifleman," from *Rust and Bone,* copyright Craig Davidson, 2005; reprinted by permission of the author and Penguin Group (Canada), a Division of Pearson Canada Inc. BRIAN FAWCETT "My Career With the Leafs" from *My Career with the Leafs and Other Stories,* copyright 1982 Brian Fawcett; reprinted by permission of the author and Talon Books. KATHERINE GOVIER "Eternal Snow," reprinted by permission of the author. LINDA GRIFFITHS "A Game of Inches," reprinted by permission of the author. STEVEN HEIGHTON "A Right Like Yours," reprinted by permission of the author. MARK JARMAN "The Scout's Lament," from *19 Knives,* copyright 2000 Mark Jarman; reprinted by permission of the author and House of Anansi Press. W.P. KINSELLA "Diehard," reprinted by permission of the author. BARRY MILLIKEN "Run," reprinted by permission of the author. LISA MOORE "The Stylist," from *Open,* copyright 2002 Lisa Moore; reprinted by permission of House of Anansi Press. MARGUERITE PIGEON "Endurance," reprinted by permission of the author. MORDECAI RICHLER "Playing Ball on Hampstead Heath," reprinted by permission of the Mordecai Richler estate. DIANE SCHOEMPERLEN "Hockey Night in Canada," reprinted by permission of the author. RUDY THAUBERGER "Goalie," reprinted by permission of the author. PRISCILA UPPAL "Vertigo," reprinted by permission of the author. GUY VANDERHAEGHE "The Master of Disaster," from *Things As They Are?,* copyright 1992 Guy Vanderhaeghe; published by McClelland & Stewart Ltd (Canada) and Grove Atlantic (U.S.); reprinted by permission of the publishers. JORDAN WHEELER "The Seventh Wave," reprinted by permission of the author.

All attempts were made to obtain permission from all copyright holders whose material is included in this book, but in some cases this has not proved possible at the time of going to press. The publisher therefore wishes to thank these copyright holders who are included without acknowledgement, and would be pleased to rectify any errors or omissions in future editions.

Recycled
Supporting responsible use
of forest resources
www.fsc.org Cert no. SGS-COC-2624
© 1996 Forest Stewardship Council

FSC

100%